W9-BLK-223

Ann M. Martin

The BABY-SITTERS CLUB

Mary Anne Saves the Day

A GRAPHIC NOVEL BY
RAINA TELGEMEIER

graphix

AN IMPRINT OF

SCHOLASTIC

Text copyright © 2007 by Ann M. Martin.
Art copyright © 2007 by Raina Telgemeier.

All rights reserved. Published by Graphix, an imprint of Scholastic Inc., *Publishers since 1920*. SCHOLASTIC, GRAPHIX, THE BABY-SITTERS CLUB, and associated logos are trademarks and/or registered trademarks of Scholastic Inc.

No part of this publication may be reproduced, stored in a retrieval system, or transmitted in any form or by any means, electronic, mechanical, photocopying, recording, or otherwise, without written permission of the publisher. For information regarding permission, write to Scholastic Inc., Attention: Permissions Department, 557 Broadway, New York, NY 10012.

Library of Congress Cataloging-In-Publication Data
Telgemeier, Raina.
Mary Anne saves the day : a graphic novel / by Raina Telgemeier;
p. cm. – (Baby-sitters Club)

Based on: Mary Anne saves the day / Ann M. Martin

ISBN-13: 978-0-439-88516-4
ISBN-10: 0-439-88516-7

1. Graphic novels. II. Martin, Ann M., 1955– Mary Anne saves the day. III. Title.

PN6727.T294M37 2007
741.5973–dc22
2007061727

17 16 15   14 15 16 17

First edition, September 2007
Lettering by John Green
Edited by David Levithan
Book design by Kristina Albertson
Creative Director: David Saylor
Printed in China   38

This book is for Beth McKeever Perkins,
my old baby-sitting buddy.
With Love
(and years of memories).
A. M. M.

Thanks to Marion Vitus, Alisa Harris, Alison Wilgus, Zack
Giallongo, Seve Flack, Hope Larson, KC Witherell, and John
Green. And of course, thanks to my husband, Dave
Roman, for always encouraging me to do my best.
R. T.

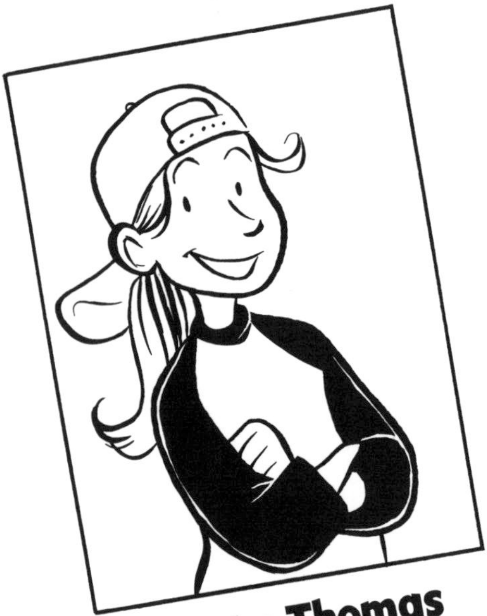

Kristy Thomas
President

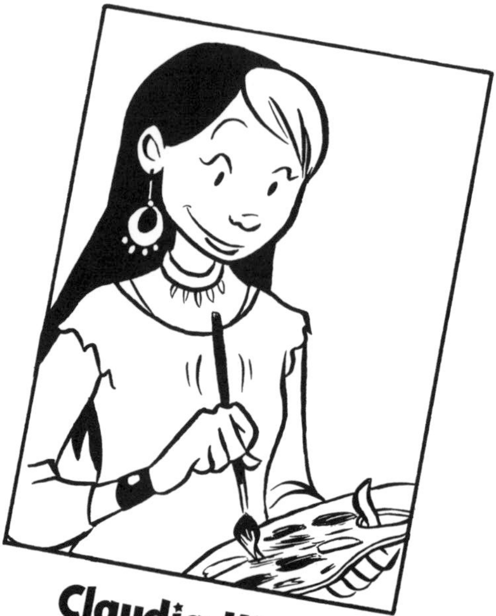

Claudia Kishi
Vice-President

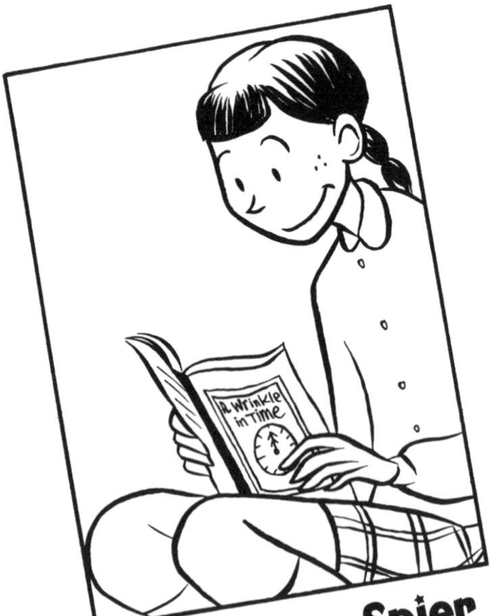
A Wrinkle in Time

Mary Anne Spier
Secretary

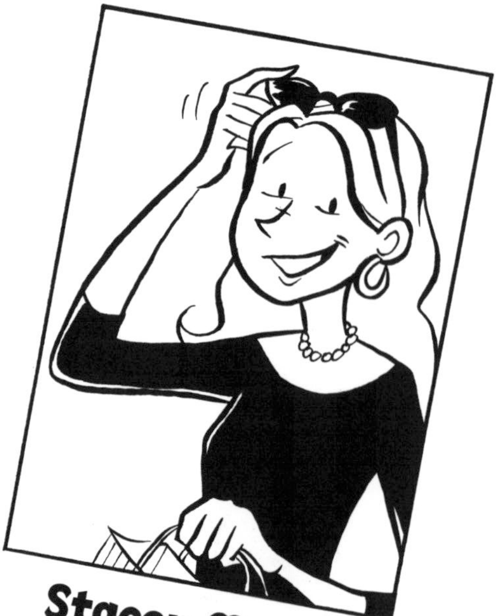

Stacey McGill
Treasurer

Chapter 1

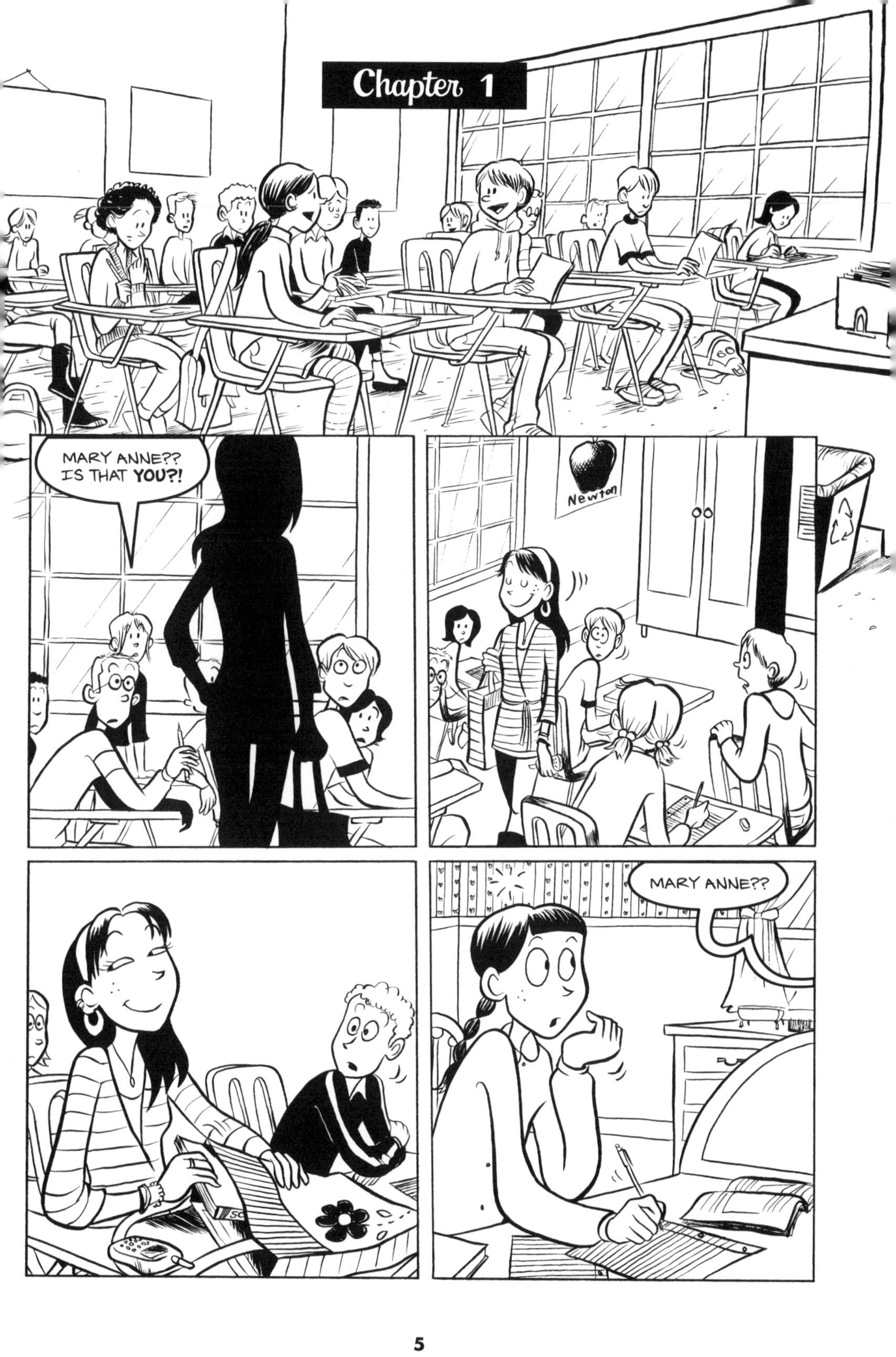
MARY ANNE?? IS THAT YOU?!
Newton
MARY ANNE??

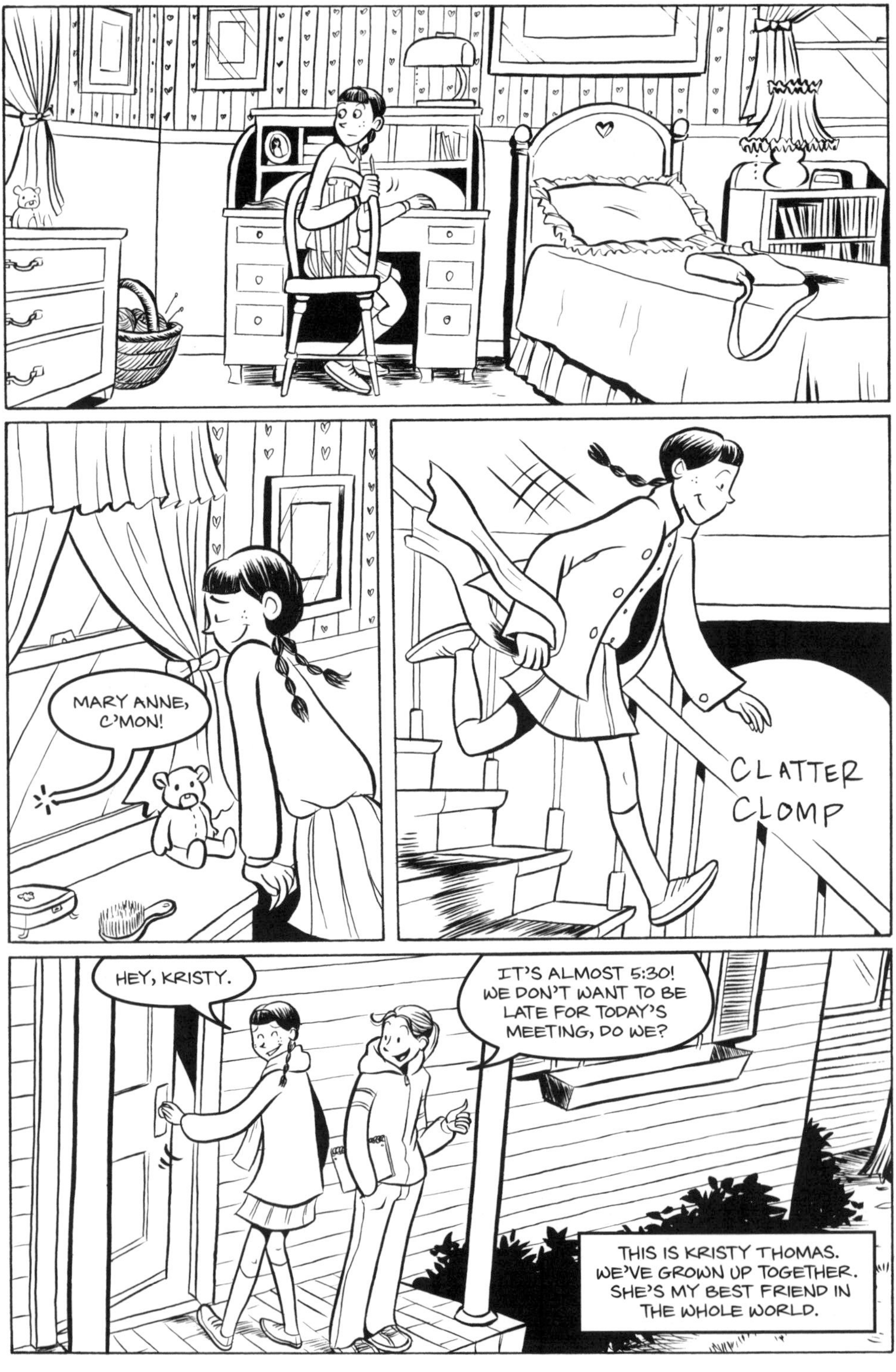
MARY ANNE,
C'MON!
CLATTER
CLOMP
HEY, KRISTY.
IT'S ALMOST 5:30! WE DON'T WANT TO BE LATE FOR TODAY'S MEETING, DO WE?
THIS IS KRISTY THOMAS. WE'VE GROWN UP TOGETHER. SHE'S MY BEST FRIEND IN THE WHOLE WORLD.

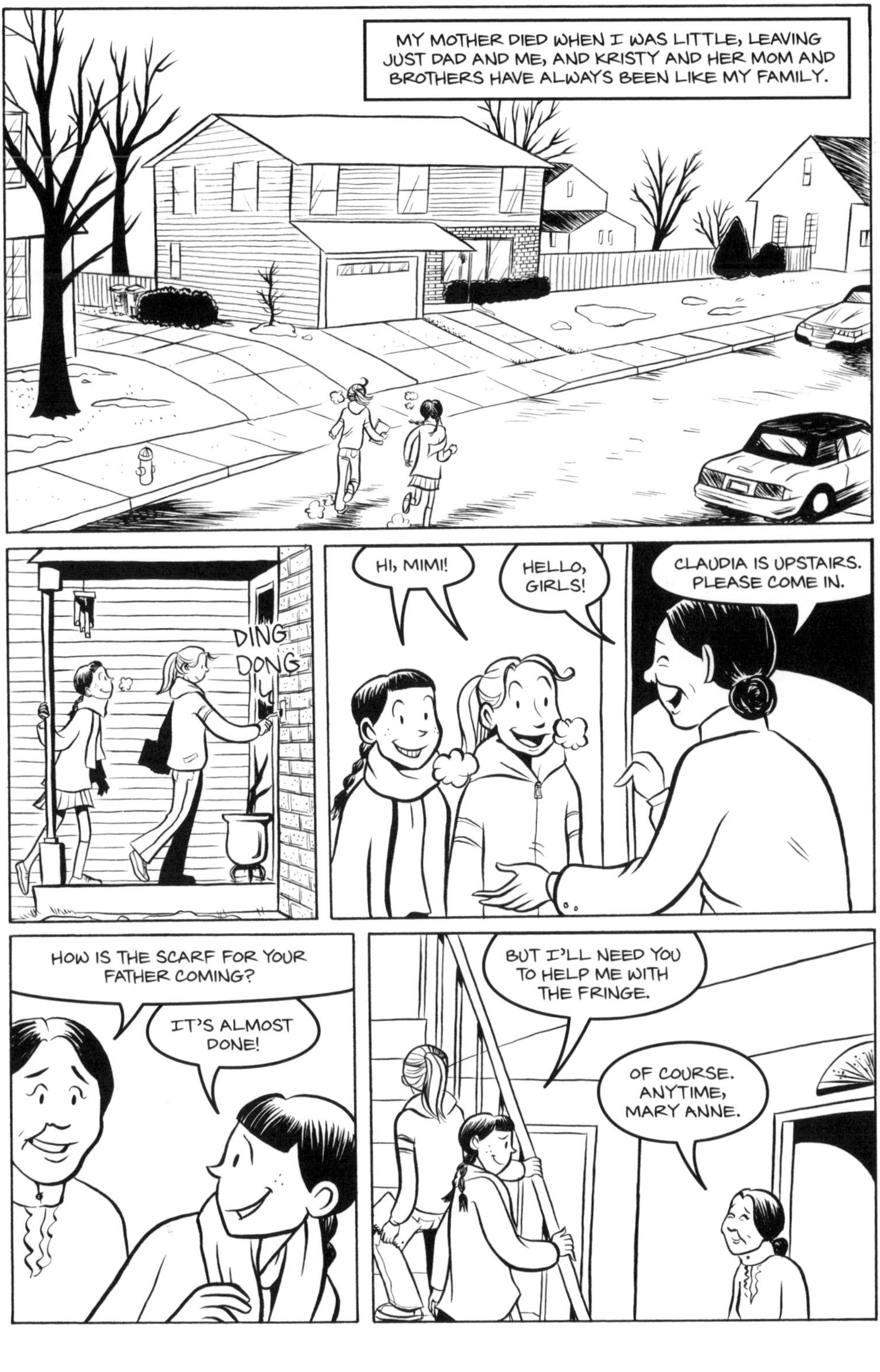
MY MOTHER DIED WHEN I WAS LITTLE, LEAVING JUST DAD AND ME, AND KRISTY AND HER MOM AND BROTHERS HAVE ALWAYS BEEN LIKE MY FAMILY.
DING DONG
HI, MIMI!
HELLO, GIRLS!
CLAUDIA IS UPSTAIRS. PLEASE COME IN.
HOW IS THE SCARF FOR YOUR FATHER COMING?
IT'S ALMOST DONE!
BUT I'LL NEED YOU TO HELP ME WITH THE FRINGE.
OF COURSE. ANYTIME, MARY ANNE.

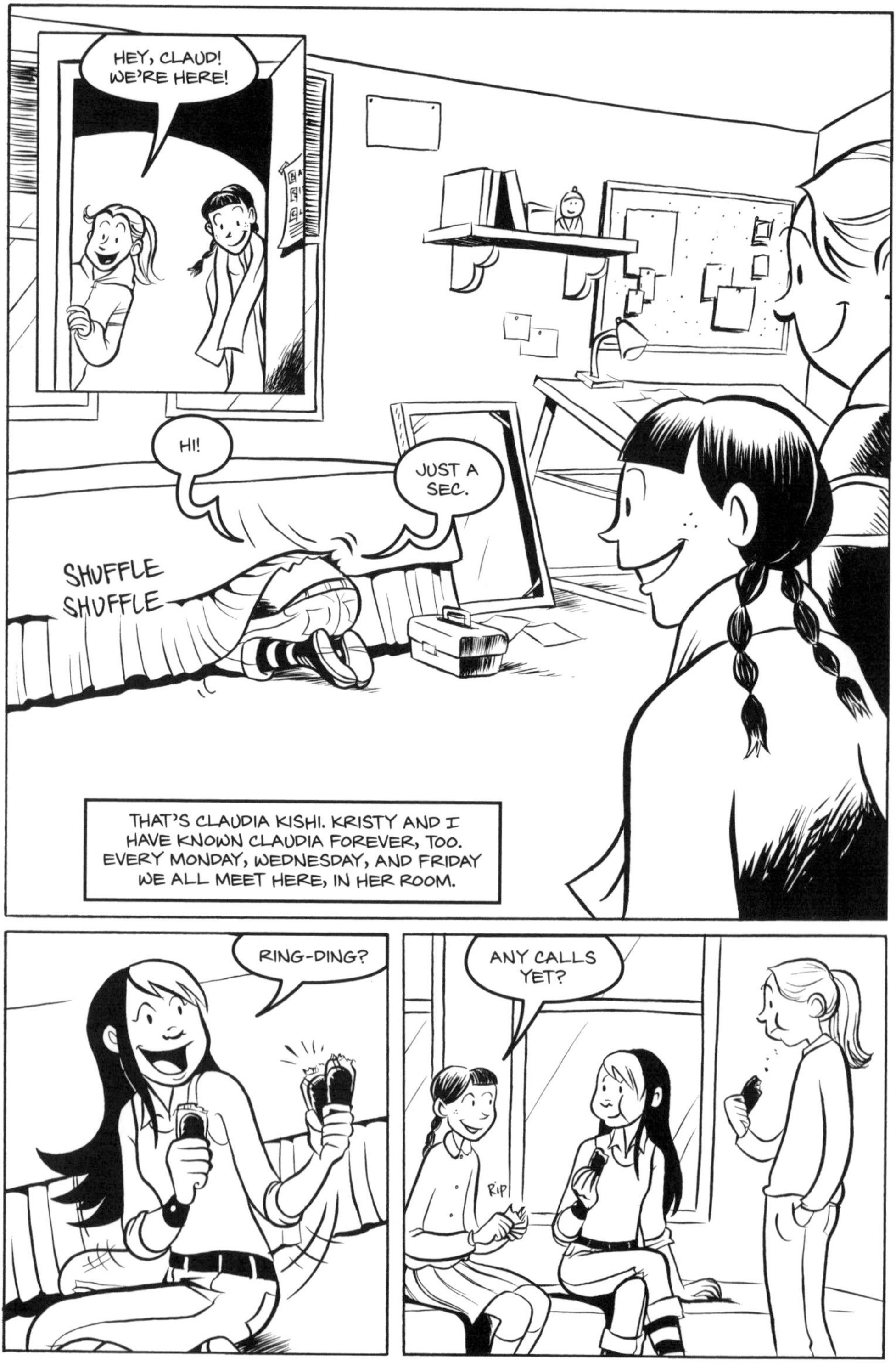

HEY, CLAUD! WE'RE HERE!
HI!
JUST A SEC.
SHUFFLE SHUFFLE
THAT'S CLAUDIA KISHI. KRISTY AND I HAVE KNOWN CLAUDIA FOREVER, TOO. EVERY MONDAY, WEDNESDAY, AND FRIDAY WE ALL MEET HERE, IN HER ROOM.
RING-DING?
ANY CALLS YET?
RIP

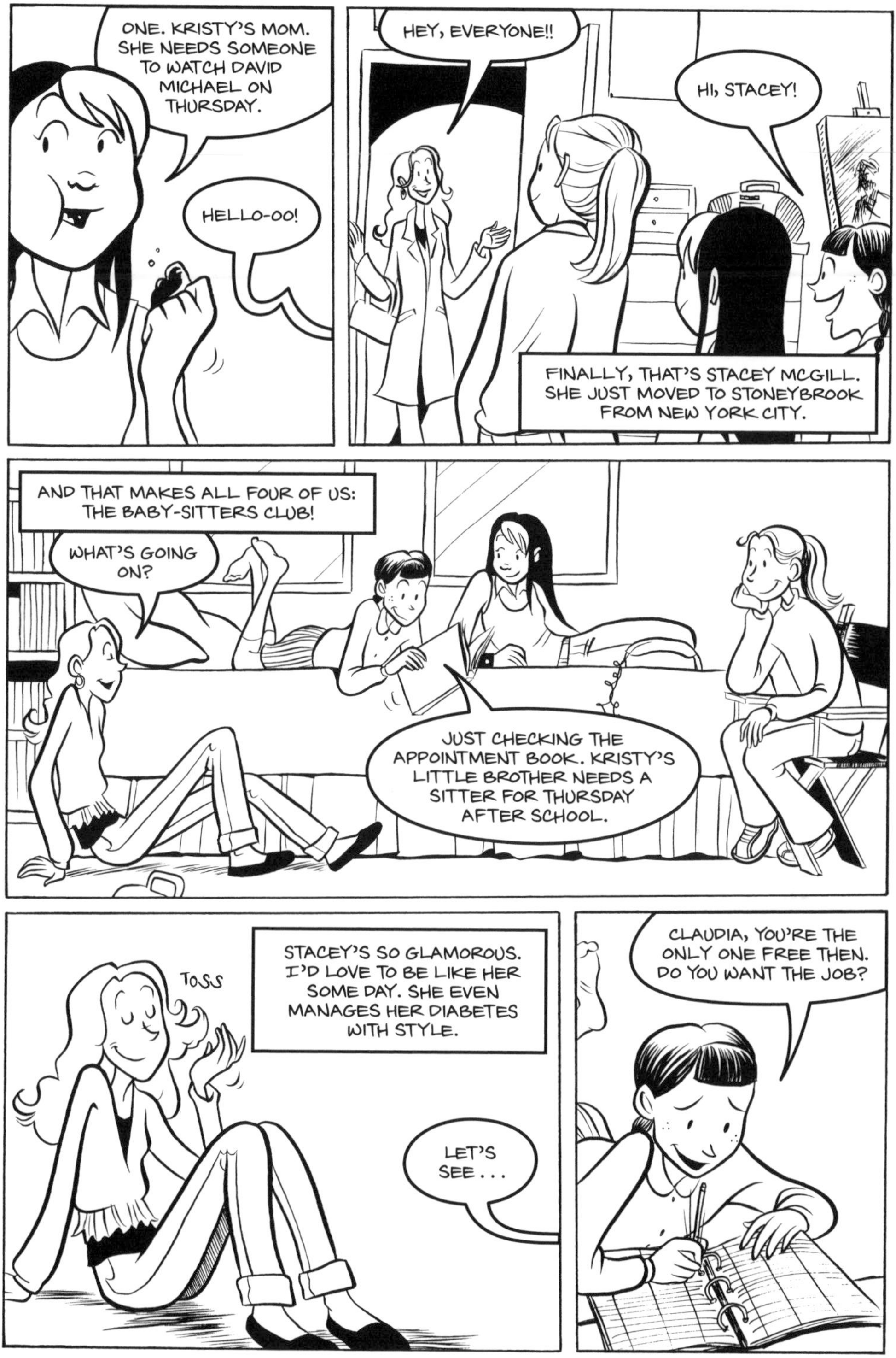
ONE. KRISTY'S MOM. SHE NEEDS SOMEONE TO WATCH DAVID MICHAEL ON THURSDAY.
HELLO-OO!
HEY, EVERYONE!!
HI, STACEY!
FINALLY, THAT'S STACEY MCGILL. SHE JUST MOVED TO STONEYBROOK FROM NEW YORK CITY.
AND THAT MAKES ALL FOUR OF US: THE BABY-SITTERS CLUB!
WHAT'S GOING ON?
JUST CHECKING THE APPOINTMENT BOOK. KRISTY'S LITTLE BROTHER NEEDS A SITTER FOR THURSDAY AFTER SCHOOL.
TOSS
STACEY'S SO GLAMOROUS. I'D LOVE TO BE LIKE HER SOME DAY. SHE EVEN MANAGES HER DIABETES WITH STYLE.
LET'S SEE . . .
CLAUDIA, YOU'RE THE ONLY ONE FREE THEN. DO YOU WANT THE JOB?

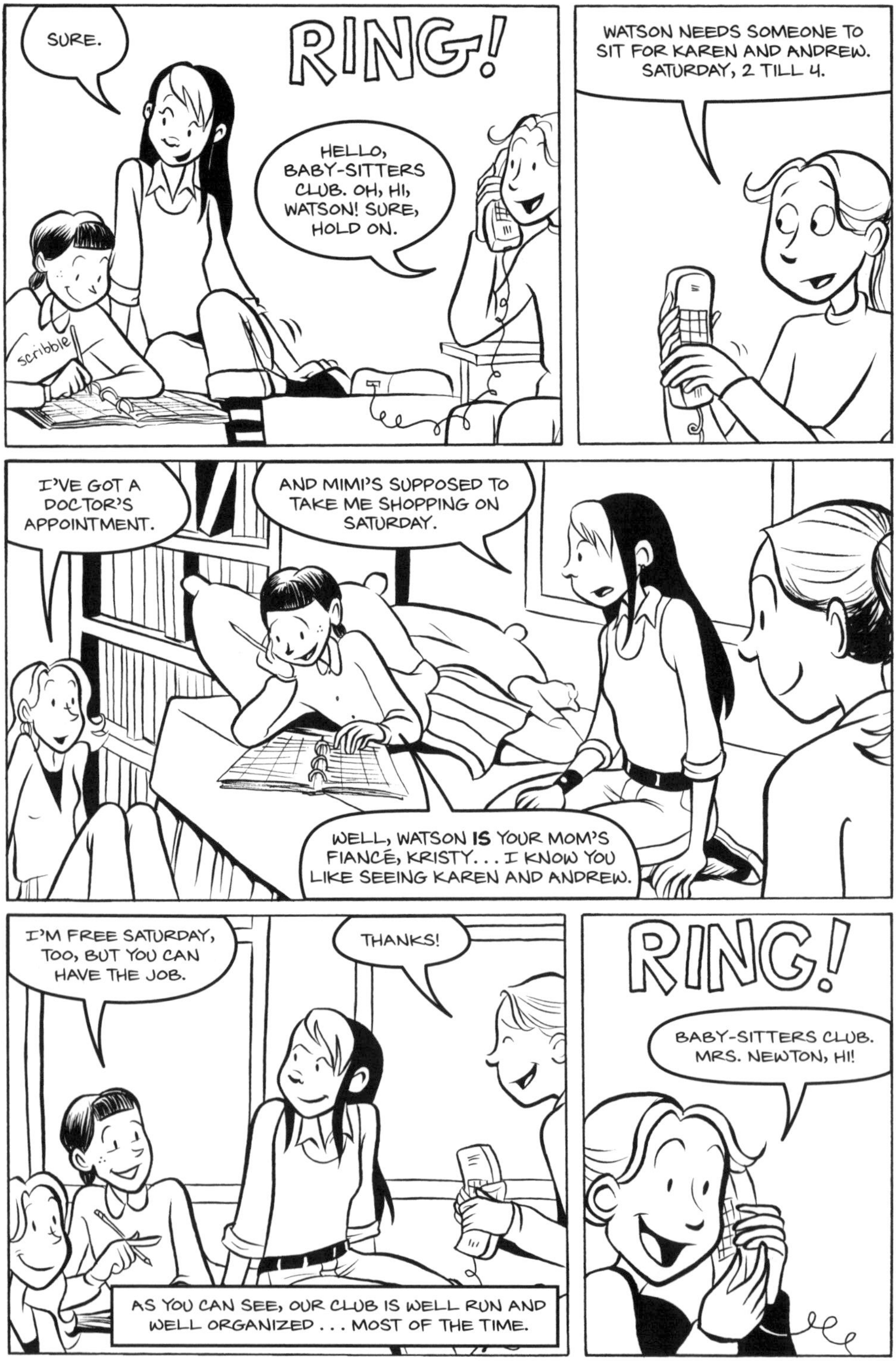
SURE.
RING!
HELLO, BABY-SITTERS CLUB. OH, HI, WATSON! SURE, HOLD ON.
scribble
WATSON NEEDS SOMEONE TO SIT FOR KAREN AND ANDREW. SATURDAY, 2 TILL 4.
I'VE GOT A DOCTOR'S APPOINTMENT.
AND MIMI'S SUPPOSED TO TAKE ME SHOPPING ON SATURDAY.
WELL, WATSON **IS** YOUR MOM'S FIANCÉ, KRISTY . . . I KNOW YOU LIKE SEEING KAREN AND ANDREW.
I'M FREE SATURDAY, TOO, BUT YOU CAN HAVE THE JOB.
THANKS!
AS YOU CAN SEE, OUR CLUB IS WELL RUN AND WELL ORGANIZED . . . MOST OF THE TIME.
RING!
BABY-SITTERS CLUB. MRS. NEWTON, HI!

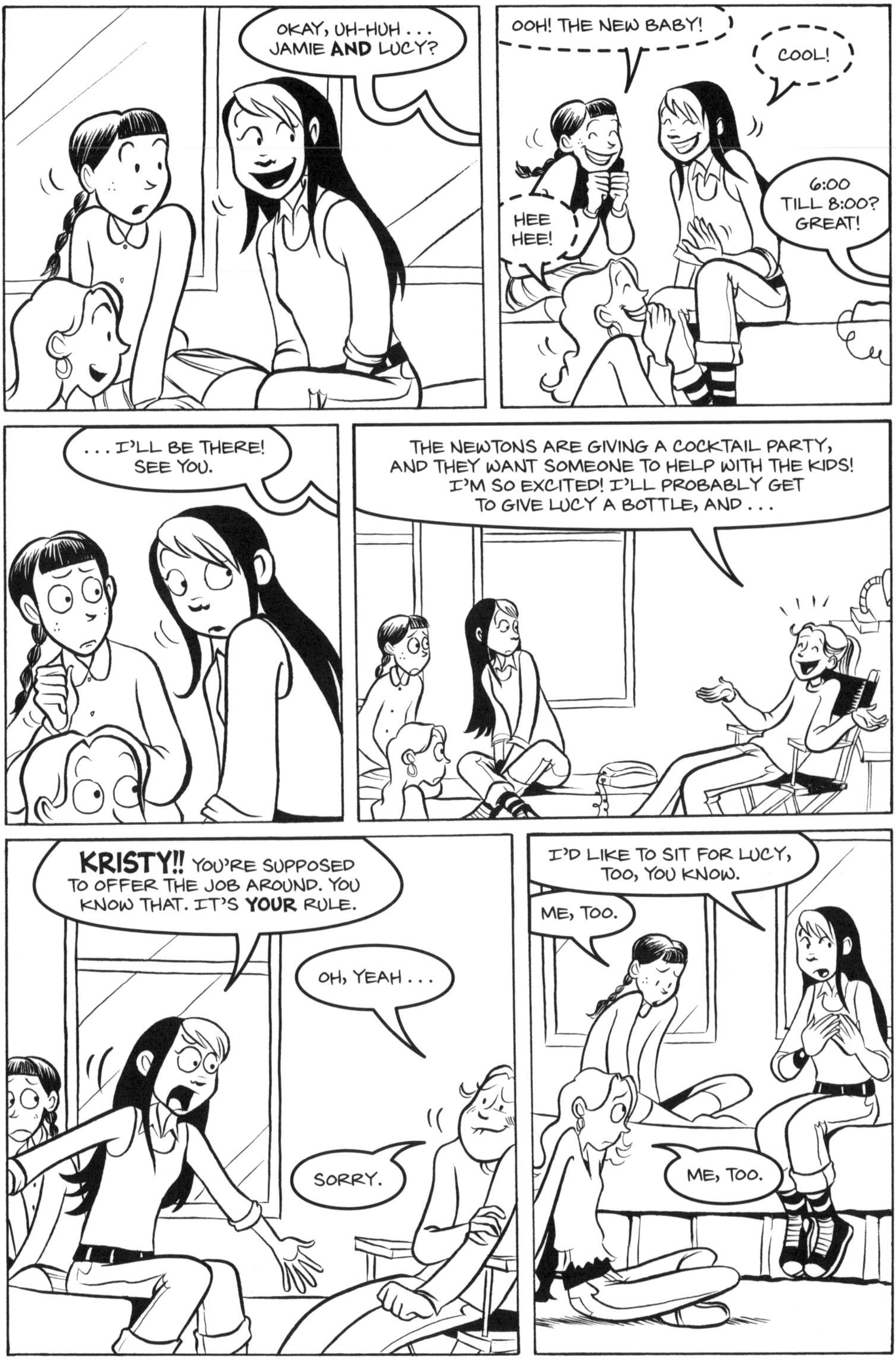
OKAY, UH-HUH . . . JAMIE **AND** LUCY?
OOH! THE NEW BABY!
COOL!
6:00 TILL 8:00? GREAT!
HEE HEE!
. . . I'LL BE THERE! SEE YOU.
THE NEWTONS ARE GIVING A COCKTAIL PARTY, AND THEY WANT SOMEONE TO HELP WITH THE KIDS! I'M SO EXCITED! I'LL PROBABLY GET TO GIVE LUCY A BOTTLE, AND . . .
KRISTY!! YOU'RE SUPPOSED TO OFFER THE JOB AROUND. YOU KNOW THAT. IT'S **YOUR** RULE.
OH, YEAH . . .
SORRY.
I'D LIKE TO SIT FOR LUCY, TOO, YOU KNOW.
ME, TOO.
ME, TOO.

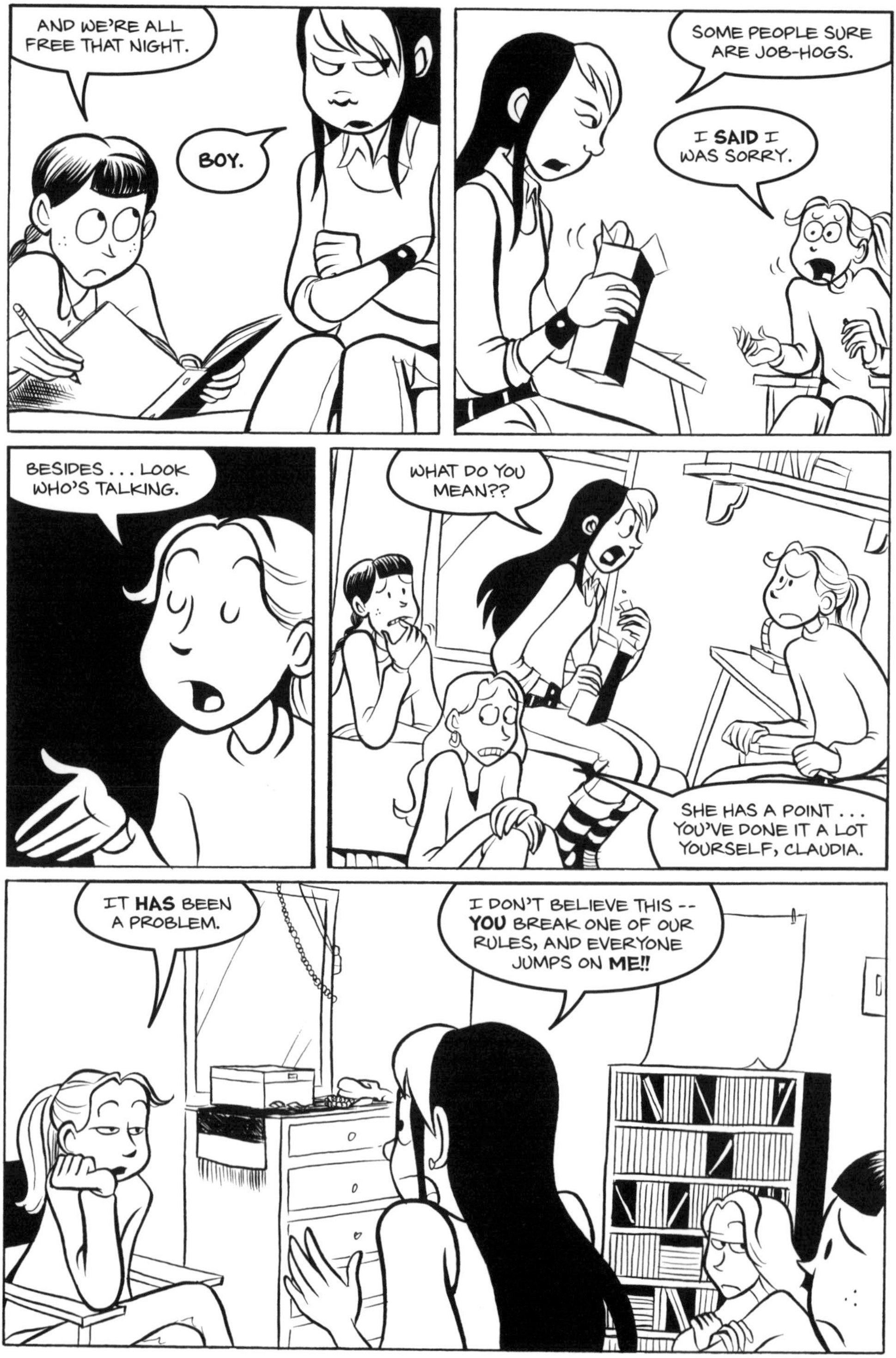
AND WE'RE ALL FREE THAT NIGHT.
BOY.
SOME PEOPLE SURE ARE JOB-HOGS.
I SAID I WAS SORRY.
BESIDES . . . LOOK WHO'S TALKING.
WHAT DO YOU MEAN??
SHE HAS A POINT . . . YOU'VE DONE IT A LOT YOURSELF, CLAUDIA.
IT HAS BEEN A PROBLEM.
I DON'T BELIEVE THIS -- YOU BREAK ONE OF OUR RULES, AND EVERYONE JUMPS ON ME!!

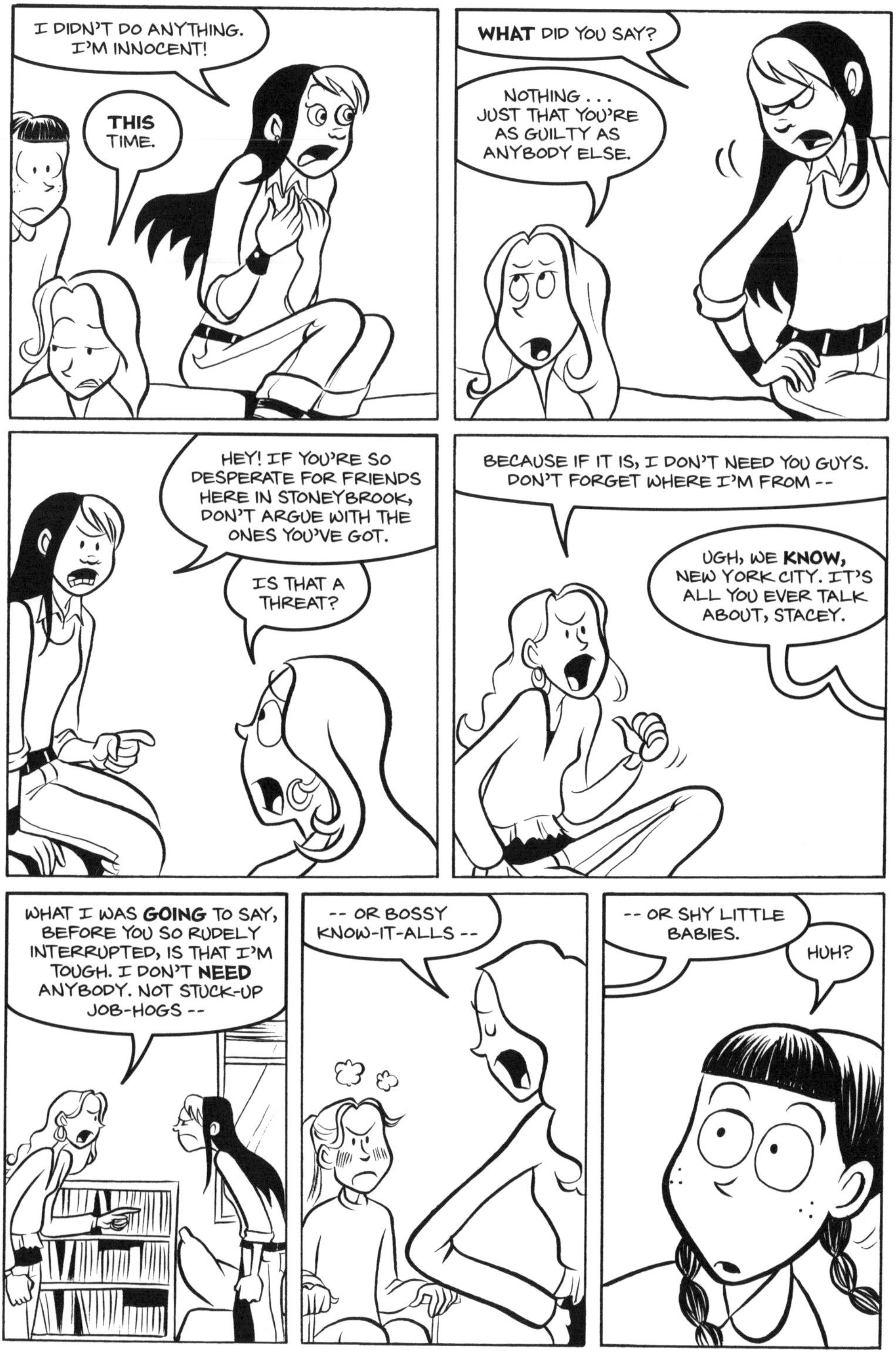
I DIDN'T DO ANYTHING. I'M INNOCENT!
THIS TIME.
WHAT DID YOU SAY?
NOTHING . . . JUST THAT YOU'RE AS GUILTY AS ANYBODY ELSE.
HEY! IF YOU'RE SO DESPERATE FOR FRIENDS HERE IN STONEYBROOK, DON'T ARGUE WITH THE ONES YOU'VE GOT.
IS THAT A THREAT?
BECAUSE IF IT IS, I DON'T NEED YOU GUYS. DON'T FORGET WHERE I'M FROM --
UGH, WE KNOW, NEW YORK CITY. IT'S ALL YOU EVER TALK ABOUT, STACEY.
WHAT I WAS GOING TO SAY, BEFORE YOU SO RUDELY INTERRUPTED, IS THAT I'M TOUGH. I DON'T NEED ANYBODY. NOT STUCK-UP JOB-HOGS --
-- OR BOSSY KNOW-IT-ALLS --
-- OR SHY LITTLE BABIES.
HUH?

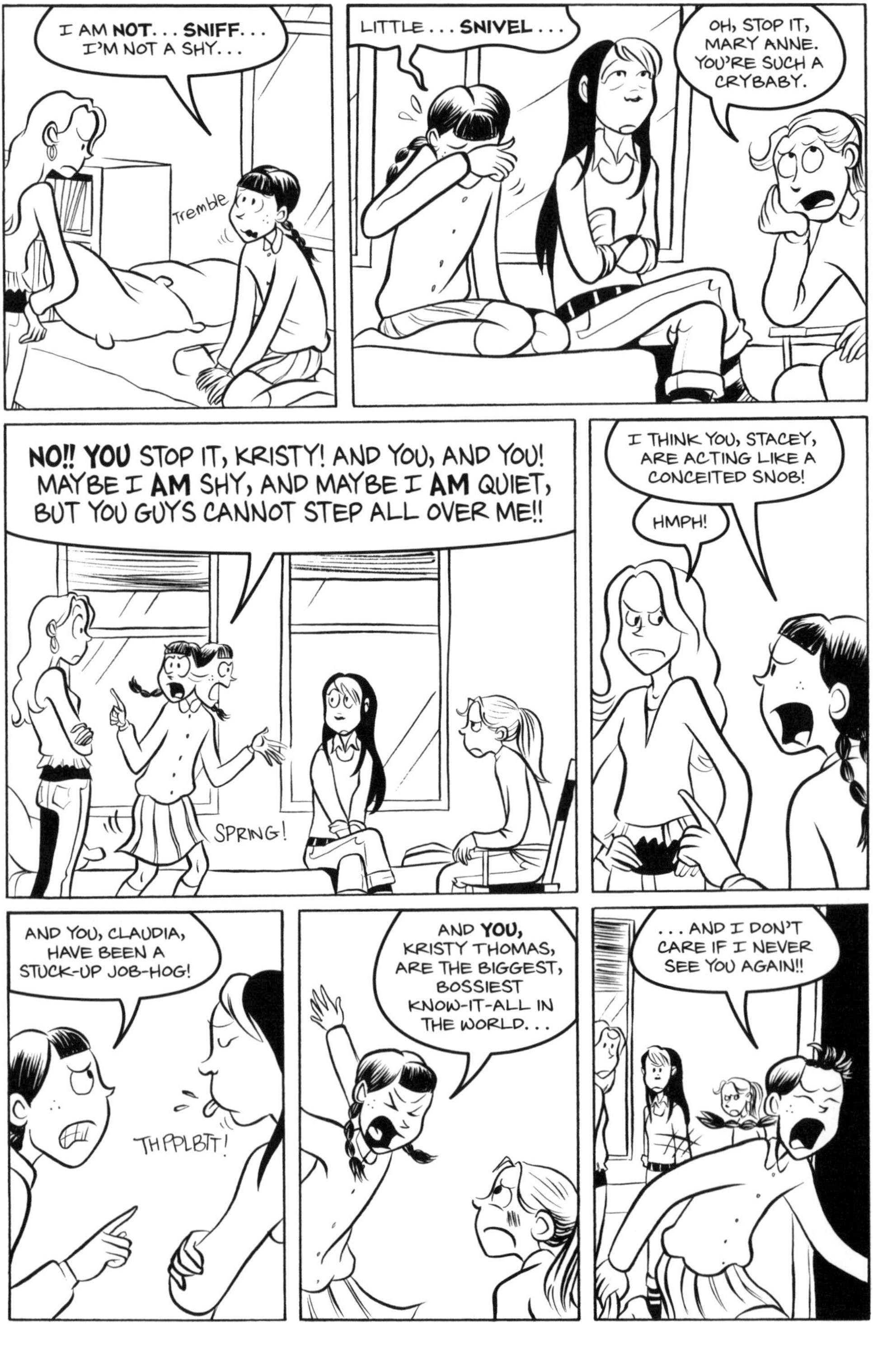
I AM NOT. . . SNIFF. . . I'M NOT A SHY. . .
Tremble
LITTLE . . . SNIVEL . . .
OH, STOP IT, MARY ANNE. YOU'RE SUCH A CRYBABY.
NO!! YOU STOP IT, KRISTY! AND YOU, AND YOU! MAYBE I AM SHY, AND MAYBE I AM QUIET, BUT YOU GUYS CANNOT STEP ALL OVER ME!!
SPRING!
I THINK YOU, STACEY, ARE ACTING LIKE A CONCEITED SNOB!
HMPH!
AND YOU, CLAUDIA, HAVE BEEN A STUCK-UP JOB-HOG!
THPPLBTT!
AND YOU, KRISTY THOMAS, ARE THE BIGGEST, BOSSIEST KNOW-IT-ALL IN THE WORLD. . .
. . . AND I DON'T CARE IF I NEVER SEE YOU AGAIN!!

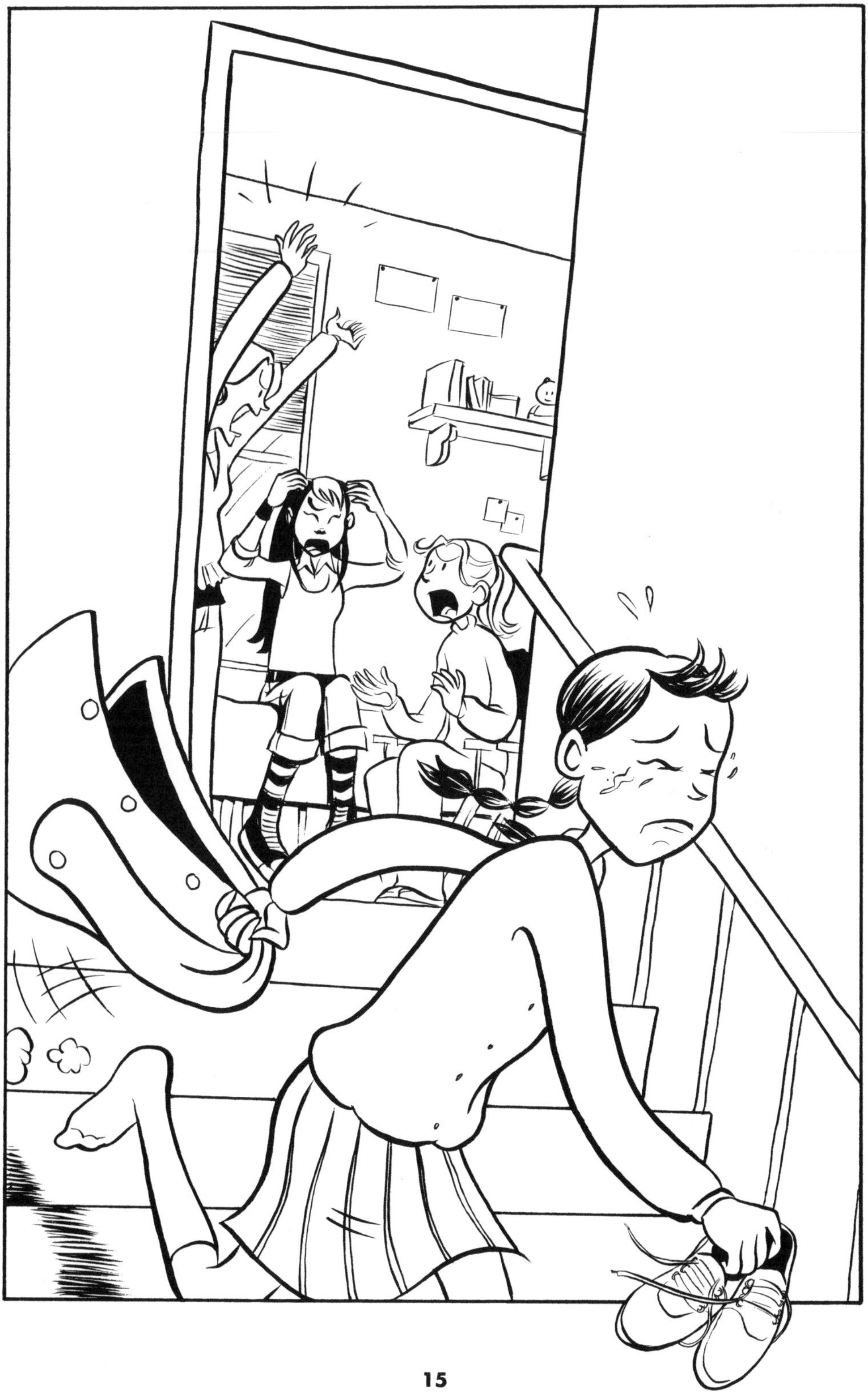

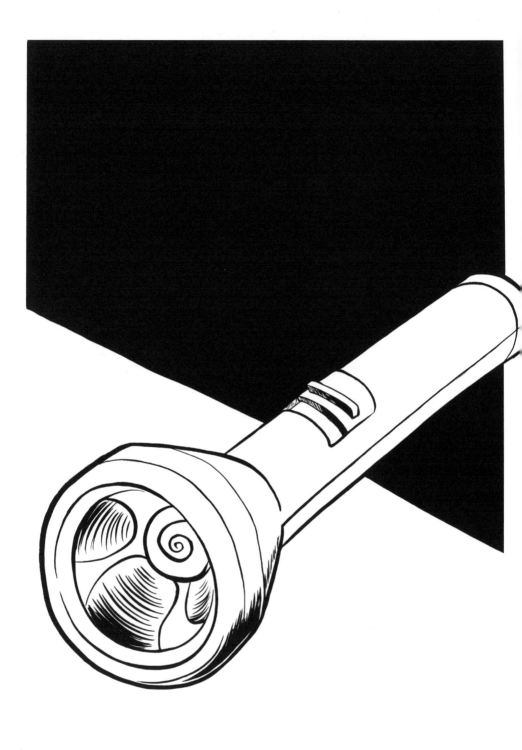

Chapter 2

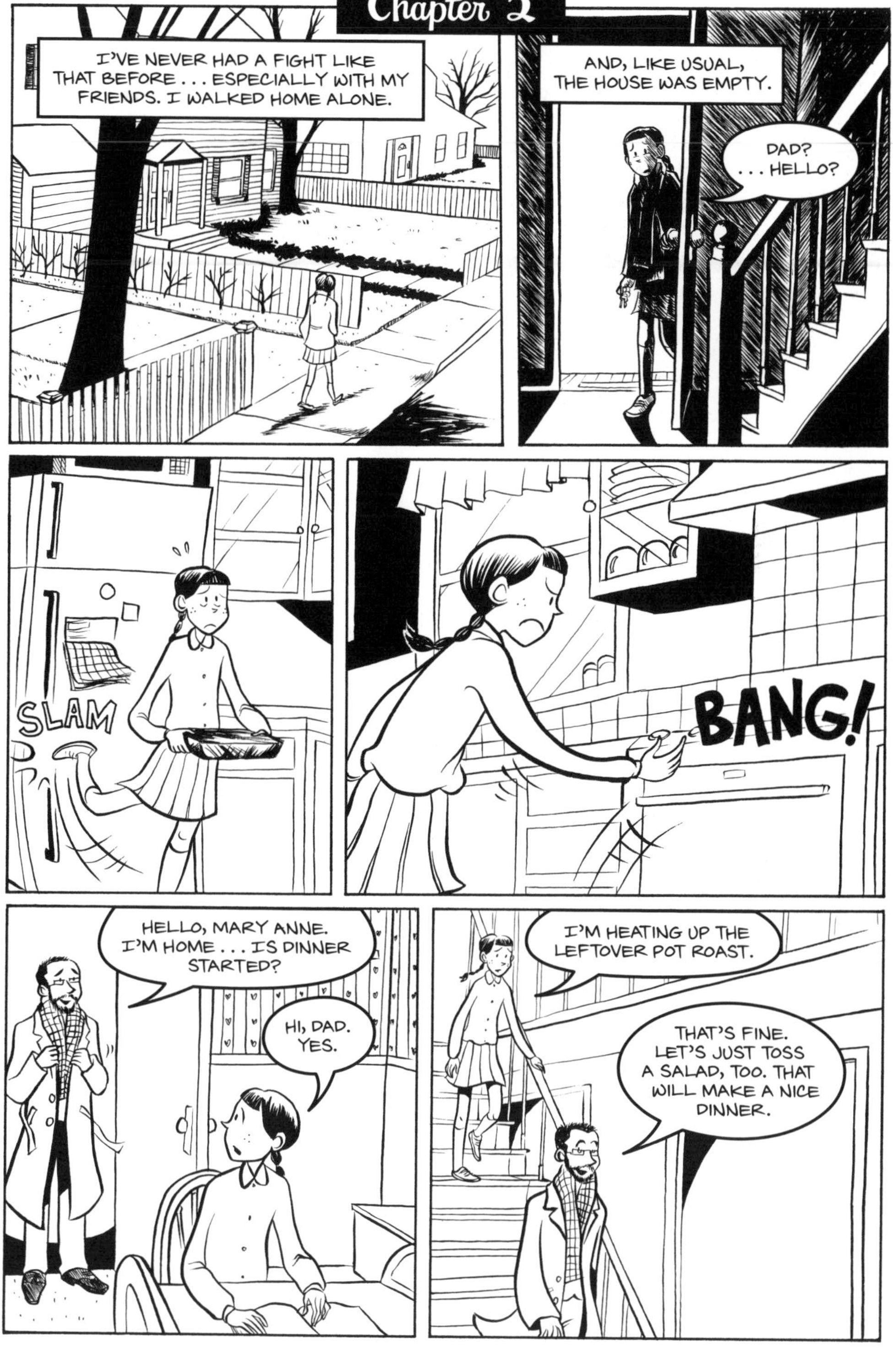
I'VE NEVER HAD A FIGHT LIKE THAT BEFORE . . . ESPECIALLY WITH MY FRIENDS. I WALKED HOME ALONE.
AND, LIKE USUAL, THE HOUSE WAS EMPTY.
DAD? . . . HELLO?
SLAM
BANG!
HELLO, MARY ANNE. I'M HOME . . . IS DINNER STARTED?
HI, DAD. YES.
I'M HEATING UP THE LEFTOVER POT ROAST.
THAT'S FINE. LET'S JUST TOSS A SALAD, TOO. THAT WILL MAKE A NICE DINNER.

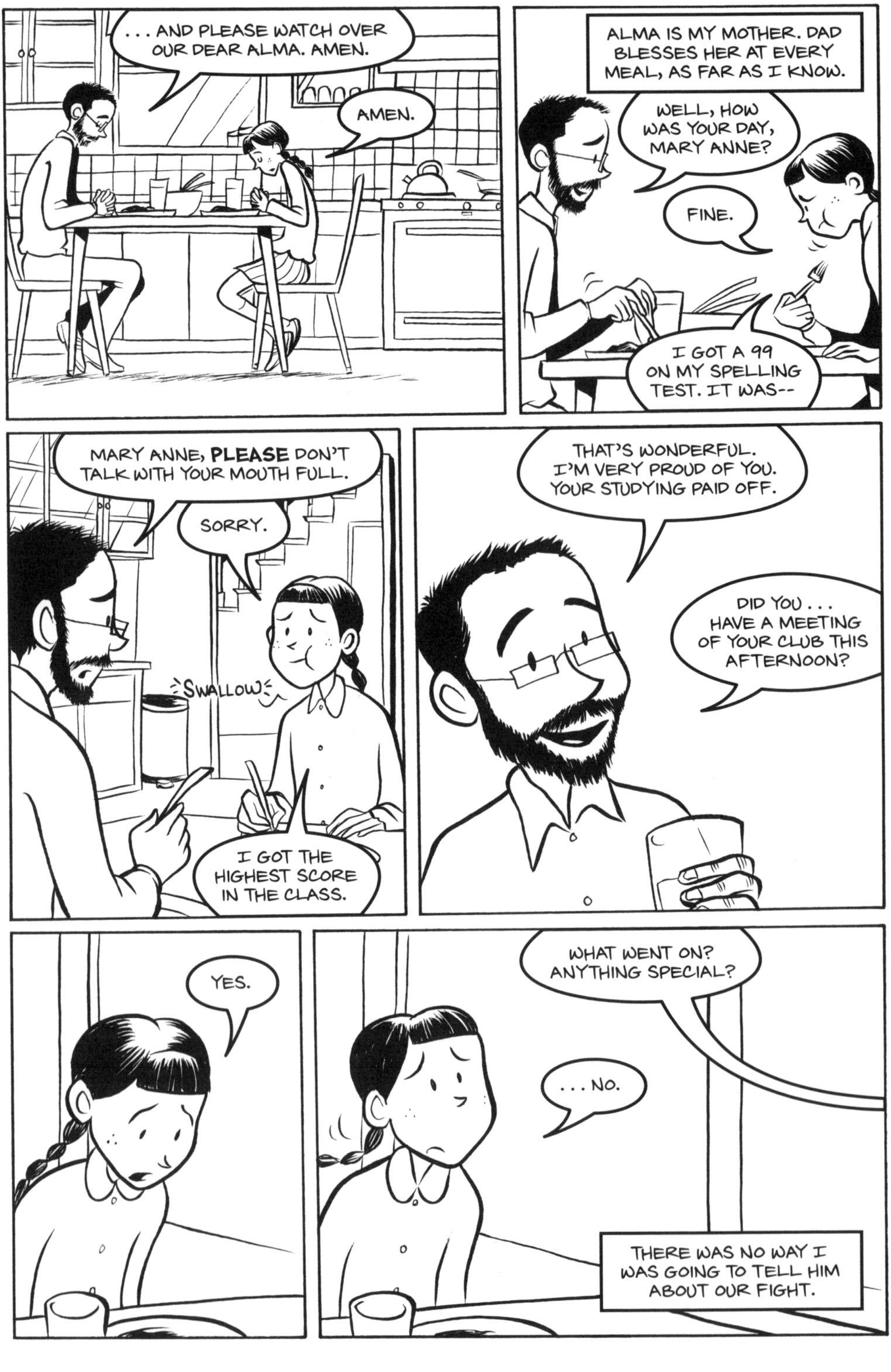
. . . AND PLEASE WATCH OVER OUR DEAR ALMA. AMEN.
AMEN.
ALMA IS MY MOTHER. DAD BLESSES HER AT EVERY MEAL, AS FAR AS I KNOW.
WELL, HOW WAS YOUR DAY, MARY ANNE?
FINE.
I GOT A 99 ON MY SPELLING TEST. IT WAS--
MARY ANNE, **PLEASE** DON'T TALK WITH YOUR MOUTH FULL.
SORRY.
SWALLOW
I GOT THE HIGHEST SCORE IN THE CLASS.
THAT'S WONDERFUL. I'M VERY PROUD OF YOU. YOUR STUDYING PAID OFF.
DID YOU . . . HAVE A MEETING OF YOUR CLUB THIS AFTERNOON?
YES.
WHAT WENT ON? ANYTHING SPECIAL?
. . . NO.
THERE WAS NO WAY I WAS GOING TO TELL HIM ABOUT OUR FIGHT.

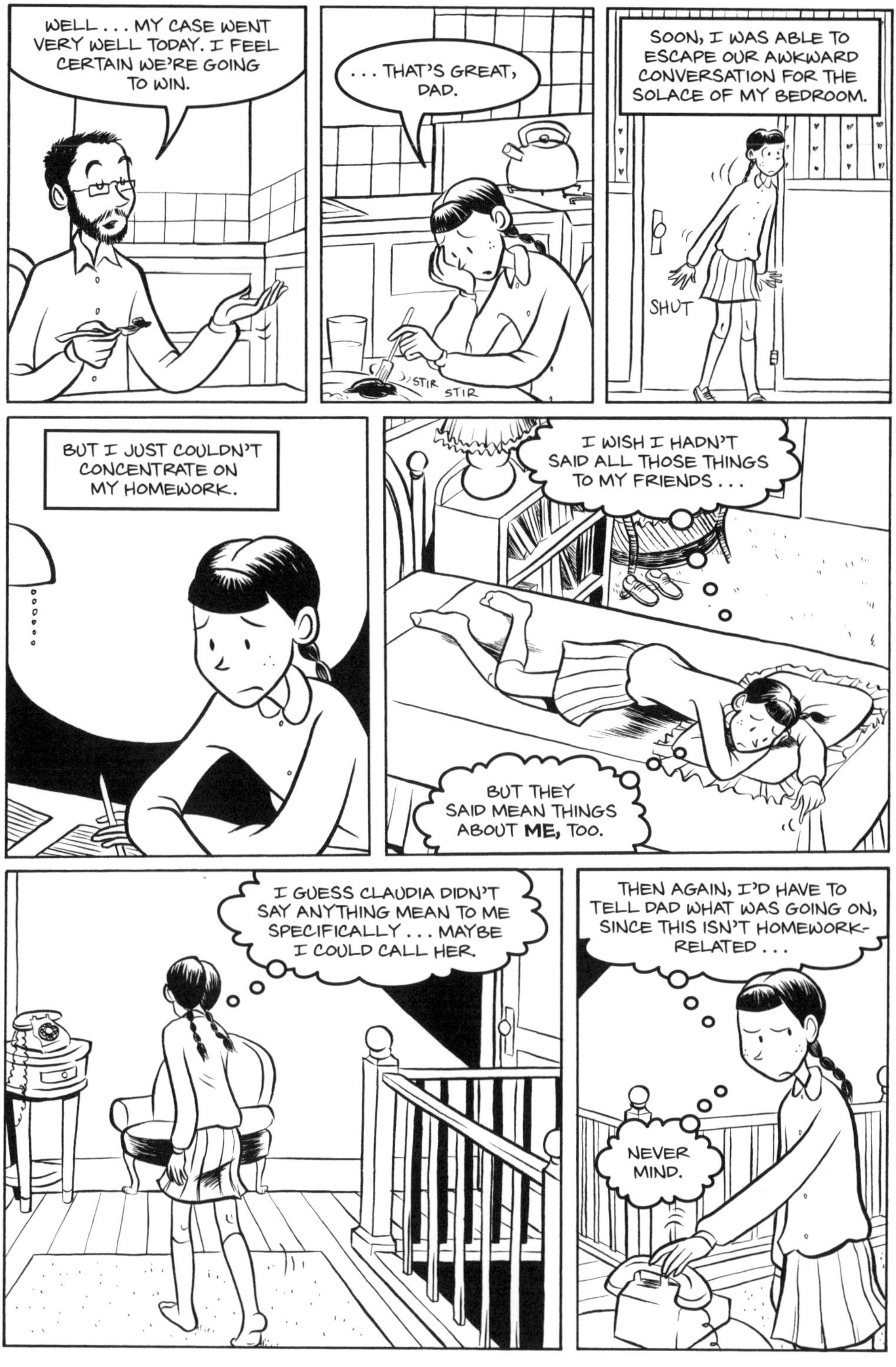
WELL . . . MY CASE WENT VERY WELL TODAY. I FEEL CERTAIN WE'RE GOING TO WIN.
. . . THAT'S GREAT, DAD.
STIR STIR
SOON, I WAS ABLE TO ESCAPE OUR AWKWARD CONVERSATION FOR THE SOLACE OF MY BEDROOM.
SHUT
BUT I JUST COULDN'T CONCENTRATE ON MY HOMEWORK.
I WISH I HADN'T SAID ALL THOSE THINGS TO MY FRIENDS . . .
BUT THEY SAID MEAN THINGS ABOUT **ME**, TOO.
I GUESS CLAUDIA DIDN'T SAY ANYTHING MEAN TO ME SPECIFICALLY . . . MAYBE I COULD CALL HER.
THEN AGAIN, I'D HAVE TO TELL DAD WHAT WAS GOING ON, SINCE THIS ISN'T HOMEWORK-RELATED . . .
NEVER MIND.

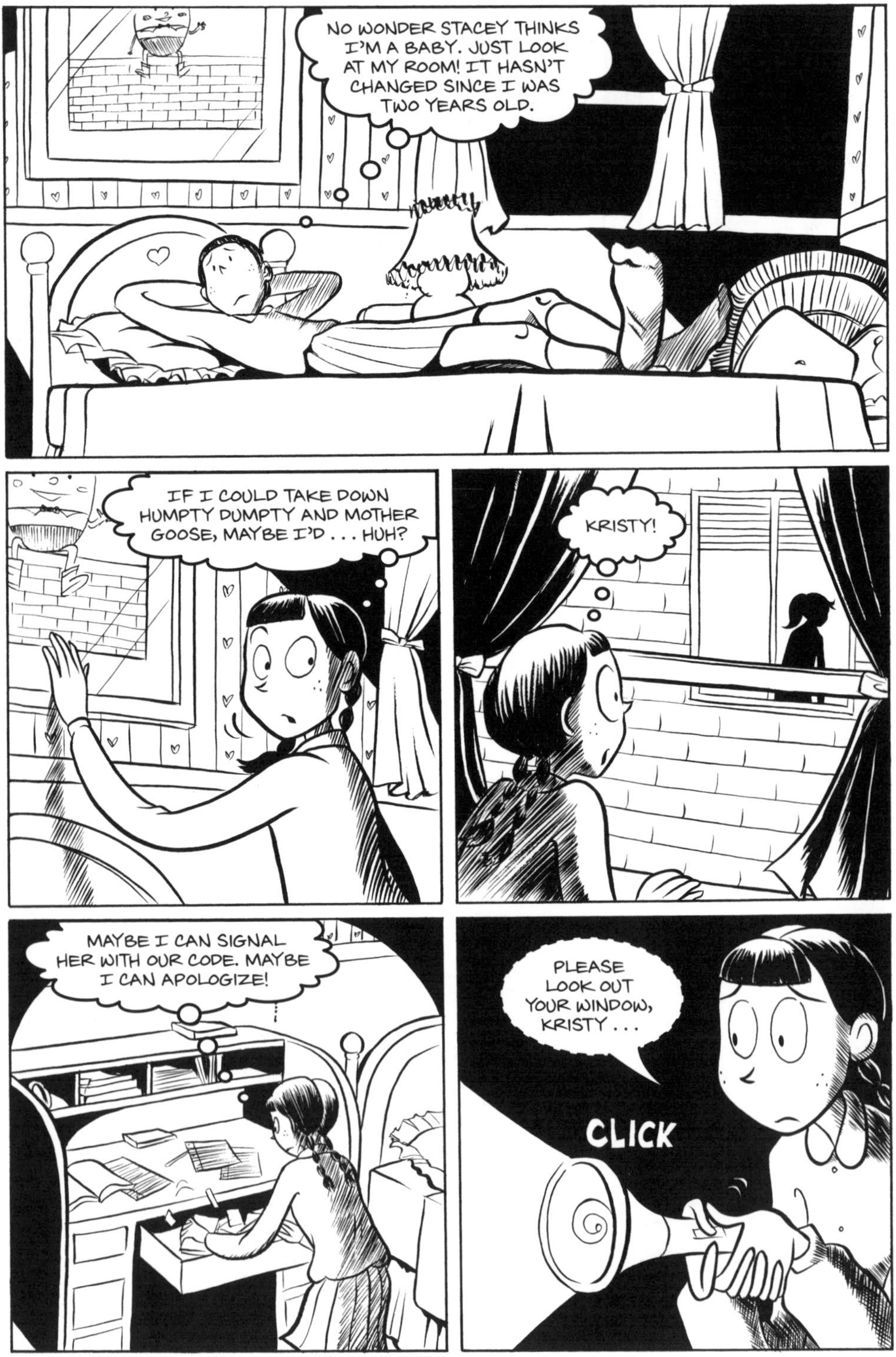
NO WONDER STACEY THINKS I'M A BABY. JUST LOOK AT MY ROOM! IT HASN'T CHANGED SINCE I WAS TWO YEARS OLD.
IF I COULD TAKE DOWN HUMPTY DUMPTY AND MOTHER GOOSE, MAYBE I'D . . . HUH?
KRISTY!
MAYBE I CAN SIGNAL HER WITH OUR CODE. MAYBE I CAN APOLOGIZE!
PLEASE LOOK OUT YOUR WINDOW, KRISTY . . .
CLICK

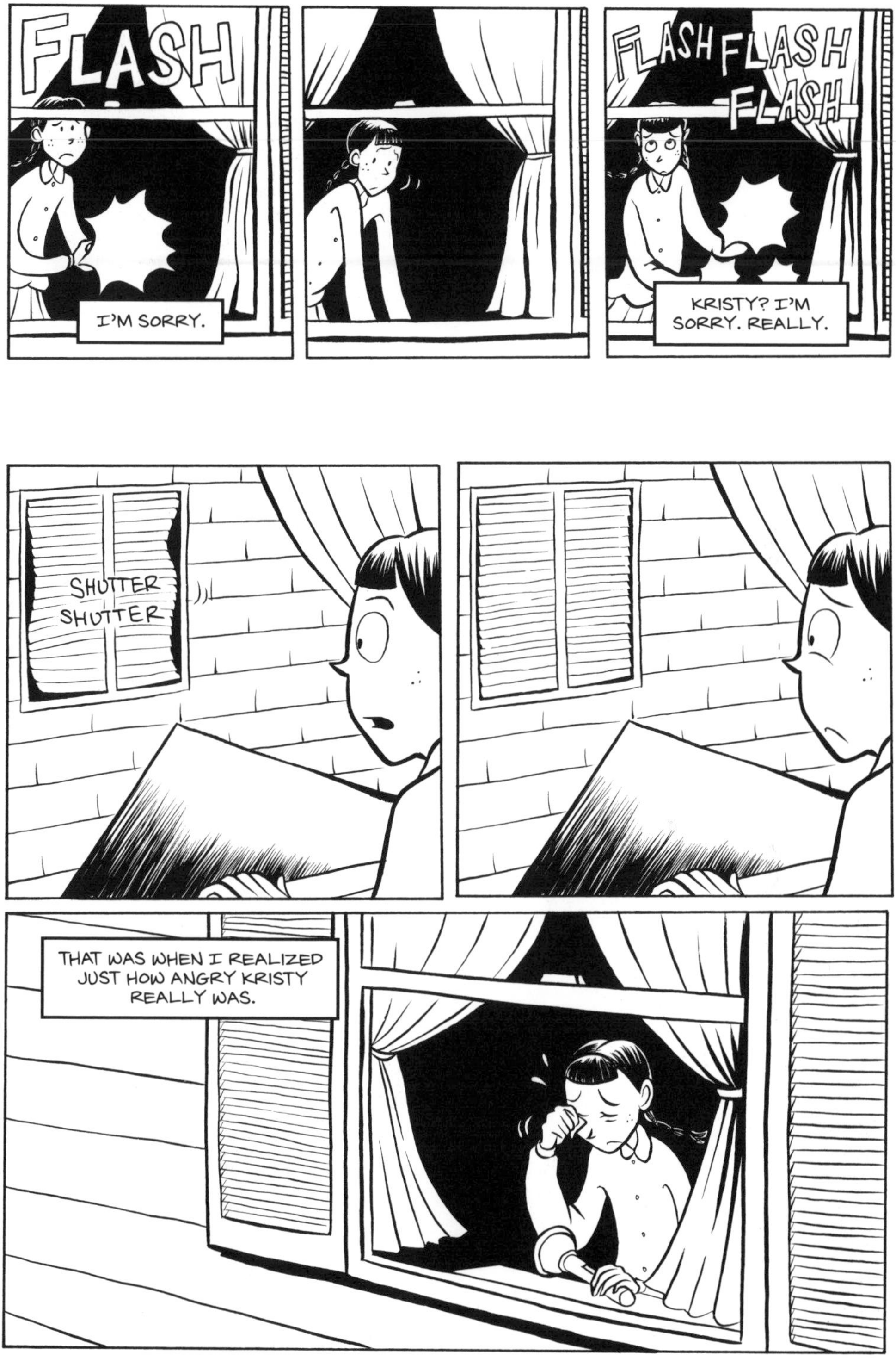
FLASH
I'M SORRY.
FLASH FLASH
FLASH
KRISTY? I'M SORRY. REALLY.
SHUTTER
SHUTTER
THAT WAS WHEN I REALIZED JUST HOW ANGRY KRISTY REALLY WAS.

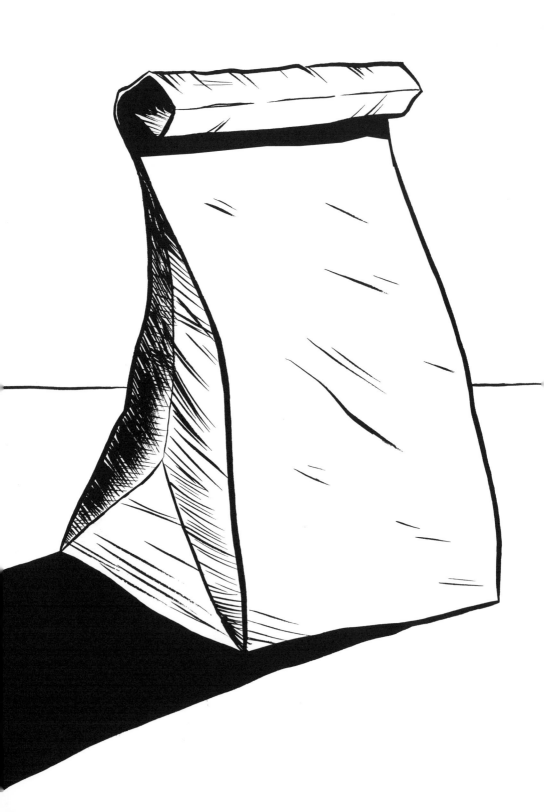

Chapter 3

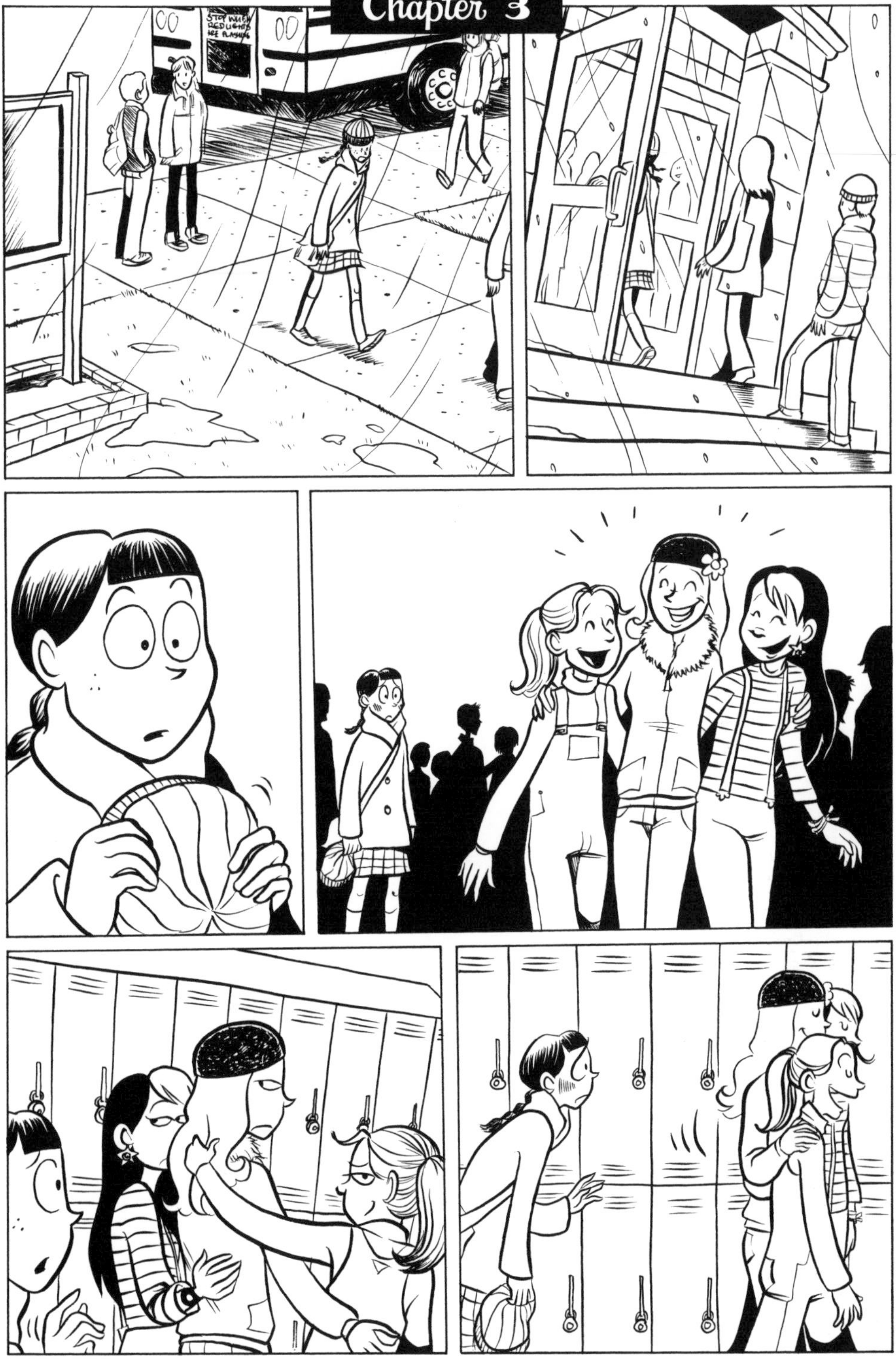
STOP WHEN RED LIGHTS ARE FLASHING

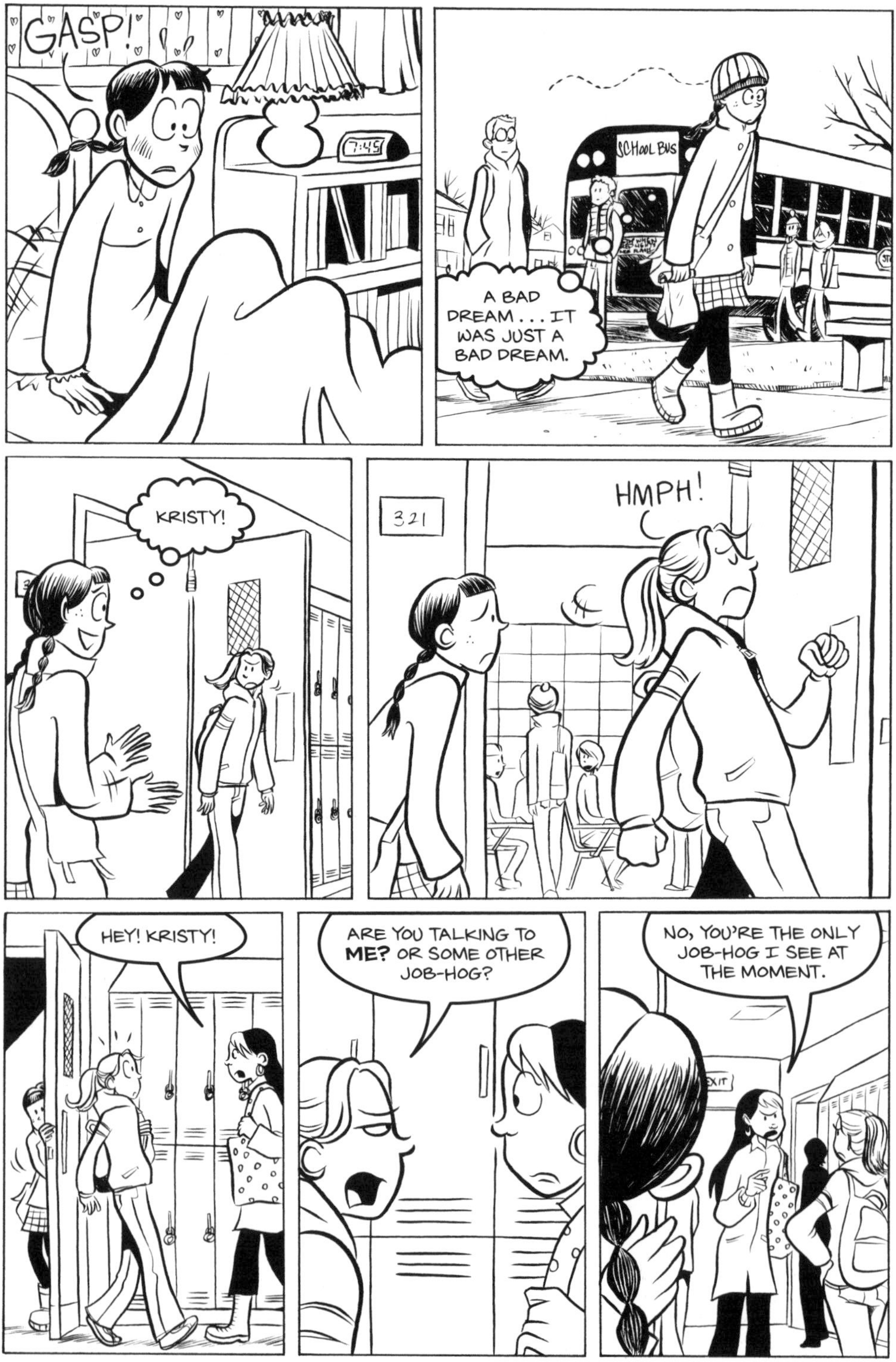
GASP!
A BAD DREAM . . . IT WAS JUST A BAD DREAM.
SCHOOL BUS
KRISTY!
321
HMPH!
HEY! KRISTY!
ARE YOU TALKING TO **ME?** OR SOME OTHER JOB-HOG?
NO, YOU'RE THE ONLY JOB-HOG I SEE AT THE MOMENT.
EXIT

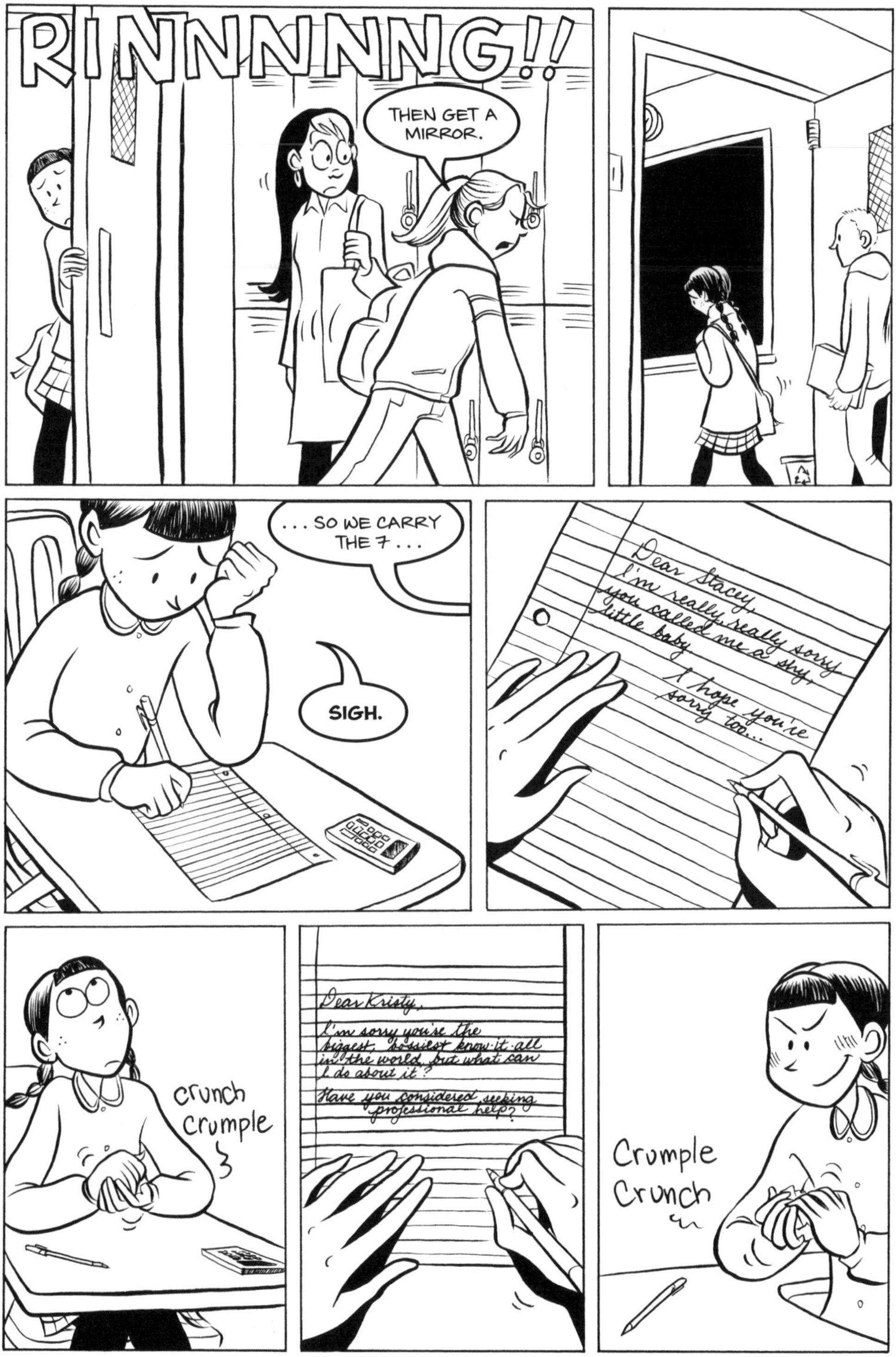
RINNNNNG!!
THEN GET A MIRROR.
. . . SO WE CARRY THE 7 . . .
SIGH.
Dear Stacey,
I'm really, really sorry you called me a shy, little baby.
I hope you're sorry too...
crunch crumple
Dear Kristy,
I'm sorry you're the biggest, bossiest know-it-all in the world, but what can I do about it?
Have you considered seeking professional help?
Crumple Crunch

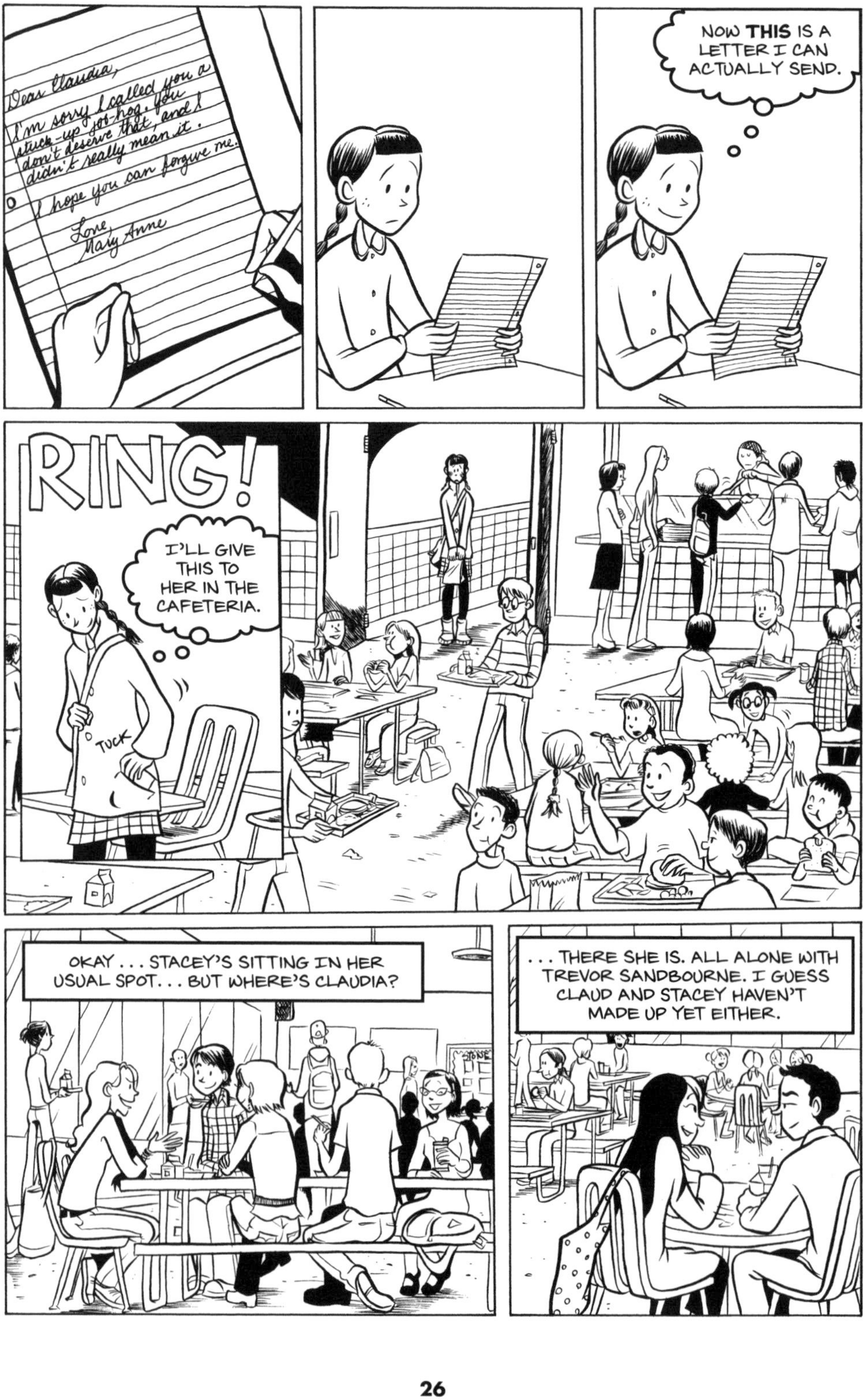
Dear Claudia,
I'm sorry I called you a stuck-up job-hog. You don't deserve that, and I didn't really mean it.
I hope you can forgive me.
Love, Mary Anne
NOW THIS IS A LETTER I CAN ACTUALLY SEND.
RING!
I'LL GIVE THIS TO HER IN THE CAFETERIA.
TUCK
OKAY . . . STACEY'S SITTING IN HER USUAL SPOT. . . BUT WHERE'S CLAUDIA?
. . . THERE SHE IS. ALL ALONE WITH TREVOR SANDBOURNE. I GUESS CLAUD AND STACEY HAVEN'T MADE UP YET EITHER.

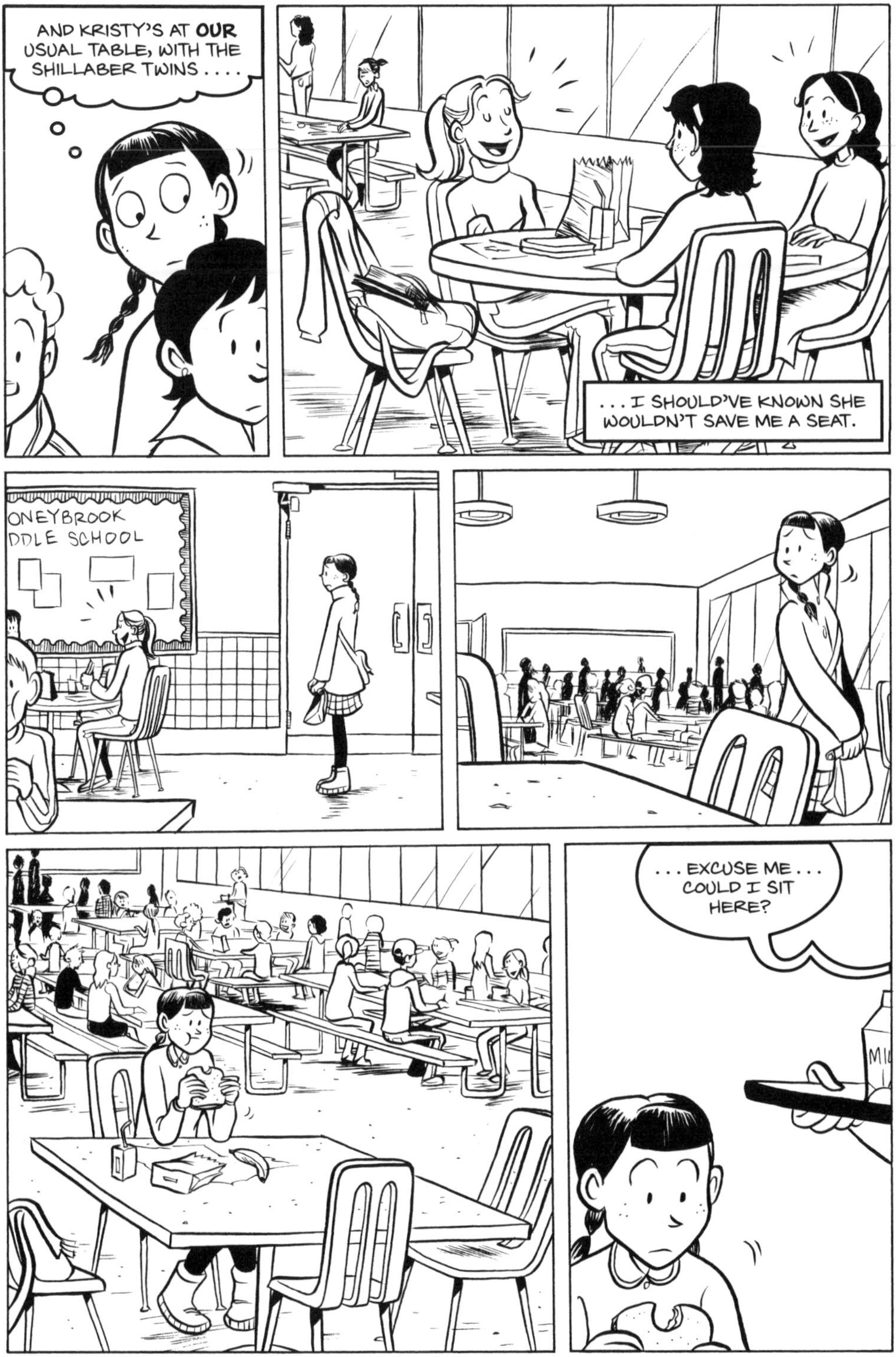
AND KRISTY'S AT **OUR** USUAL TABLE, WITH THE SHILLABER TWINS . . . .
. . . I SHOULD'VE KNOWN SHE WOULDN'T SAVE ME A SEAT.
ONEYBROOK
DDLE SCHOOL
. . . EXCUSE ME . . . COULD I SIT HERE?

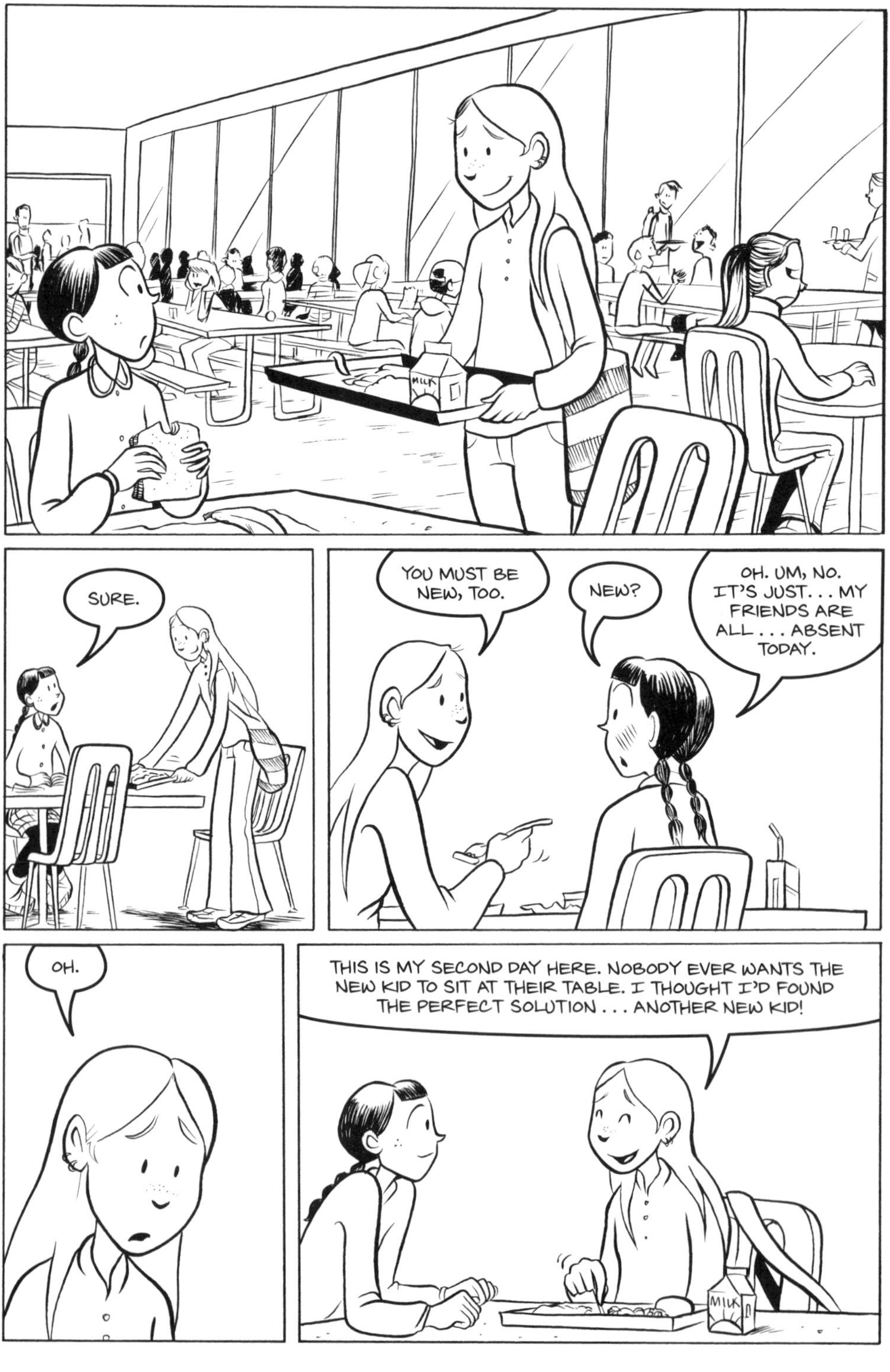
SURE.
YOU MUST BE NEW, TOO.
NEW?
OH. UM, NO. IT'S JUST. . . MY FRIENDS ARE ALL . . . ABSENT TODAY.
OH.
THIS IS MY SECOND DAY HERE. NOBODY EVER WANTS THE NEW KID TO SIT AT THEIR TABLE. I THOUGHT I'D FOUND THE PERFECT SOLUTION . . . ANOTHER NEW KID!

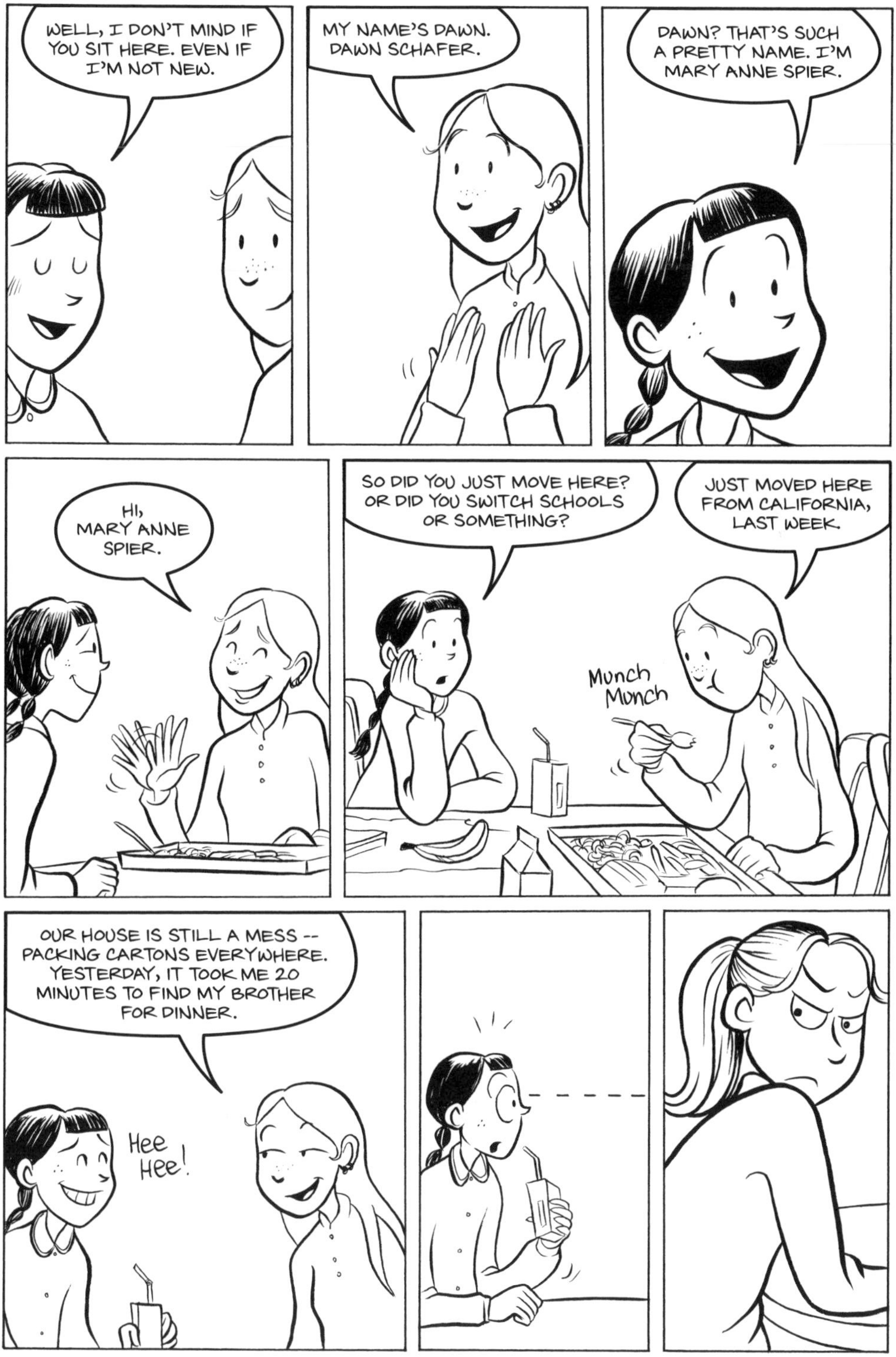
WELL, I DON'T MIND IF YOU SIT HERE. EVEN IF I'M NOT NEW.
MY NAME'S DAWN. DAWN SCHAFER.
DAWN? THAT'S SUCH A PRETTY NAME. I'M MARY ANNE SPIER.
HI, MARY ANNE SPIER.
SO DID YOU JUST MOVE HERE? OR DID YOU SWITCH SCHOOLS OR SOMETHING?
JUST MOVED HERE FROM CALIFORNIA, LAST WEEK.
Munch Munch
OUR HOUSE IS STILL A MESS -- PACKING CARTONS EVERYWHERE. YESTERDAY, IT TOOK ME 20 MINUTES TO FIND MY BROTHER FOR DINNER.
Hee Hee!

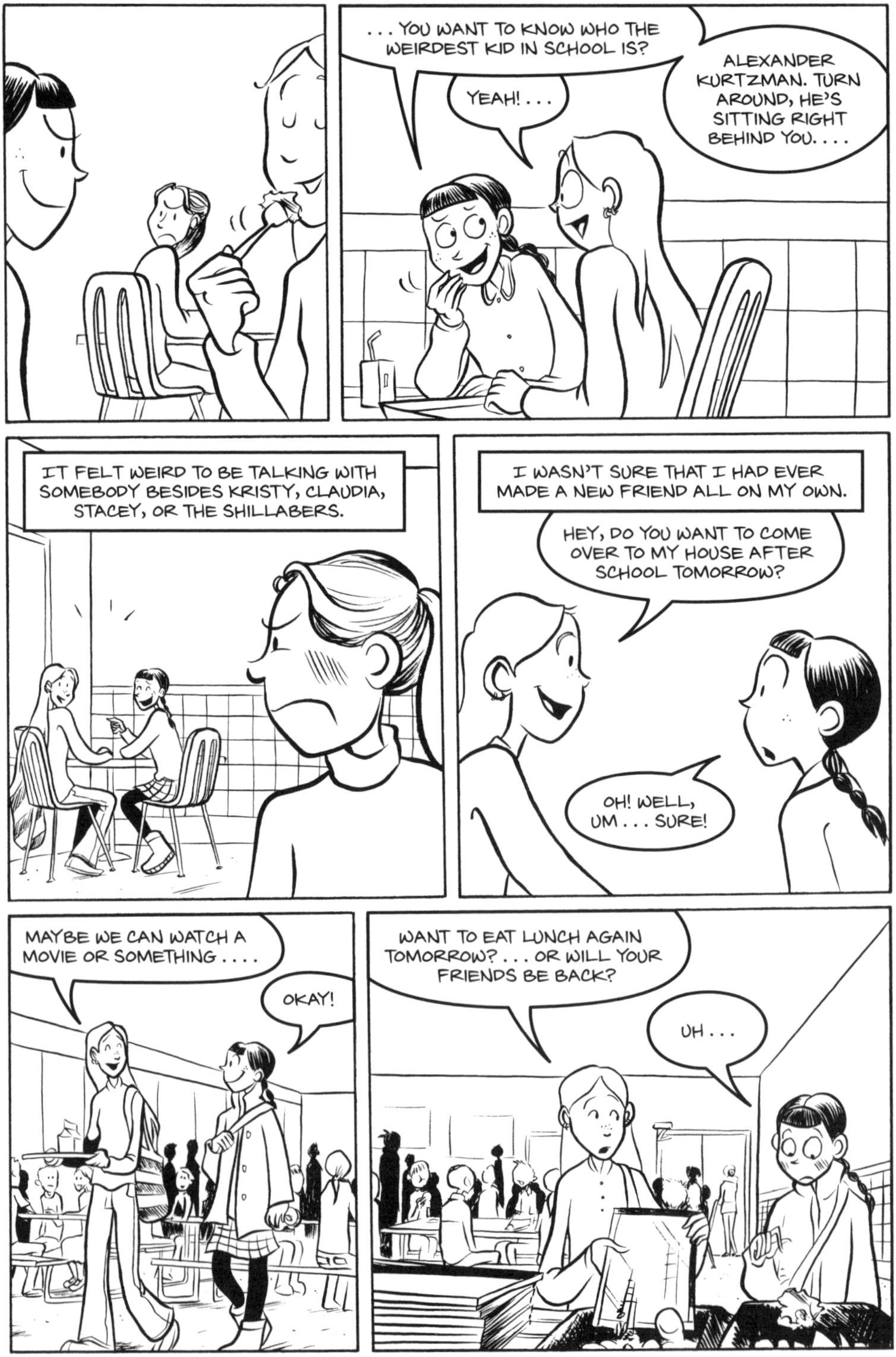

. . . YOU WANT TO KNOW WHO THE WEIRDEST KID IN SCHOOL IS?
YEAH! . . .
ALEXANDER KURTZMAN. TURN AROUND, HE'S SITTING RIGHT BEHIND YOU. . . .
IT FELT WEIRD TO BE TALKING WITH SOMEBODY BESIDES KRISTY, CLAUDIA, STACEY, OR THE SHILLABERS.
I WASN'T SURE THAT I HAD EVER MADE A NEW FRIEND ALL ON MY OWN.
HEY, DO YOU WANT TO COME OVER TO MY HOUSE AFTER SCHOOL TOMORROW?
OH! WELL, UM . . . SURE!
MAYBE WE CAN WATCH A MOVIE OR SOMETHING . . . .
OKAY!
WANT TO EAT LUNCH AGAIN TOMORROW? . . . OR WILL YOUR FRIENDS BE BACK?
UH . . .

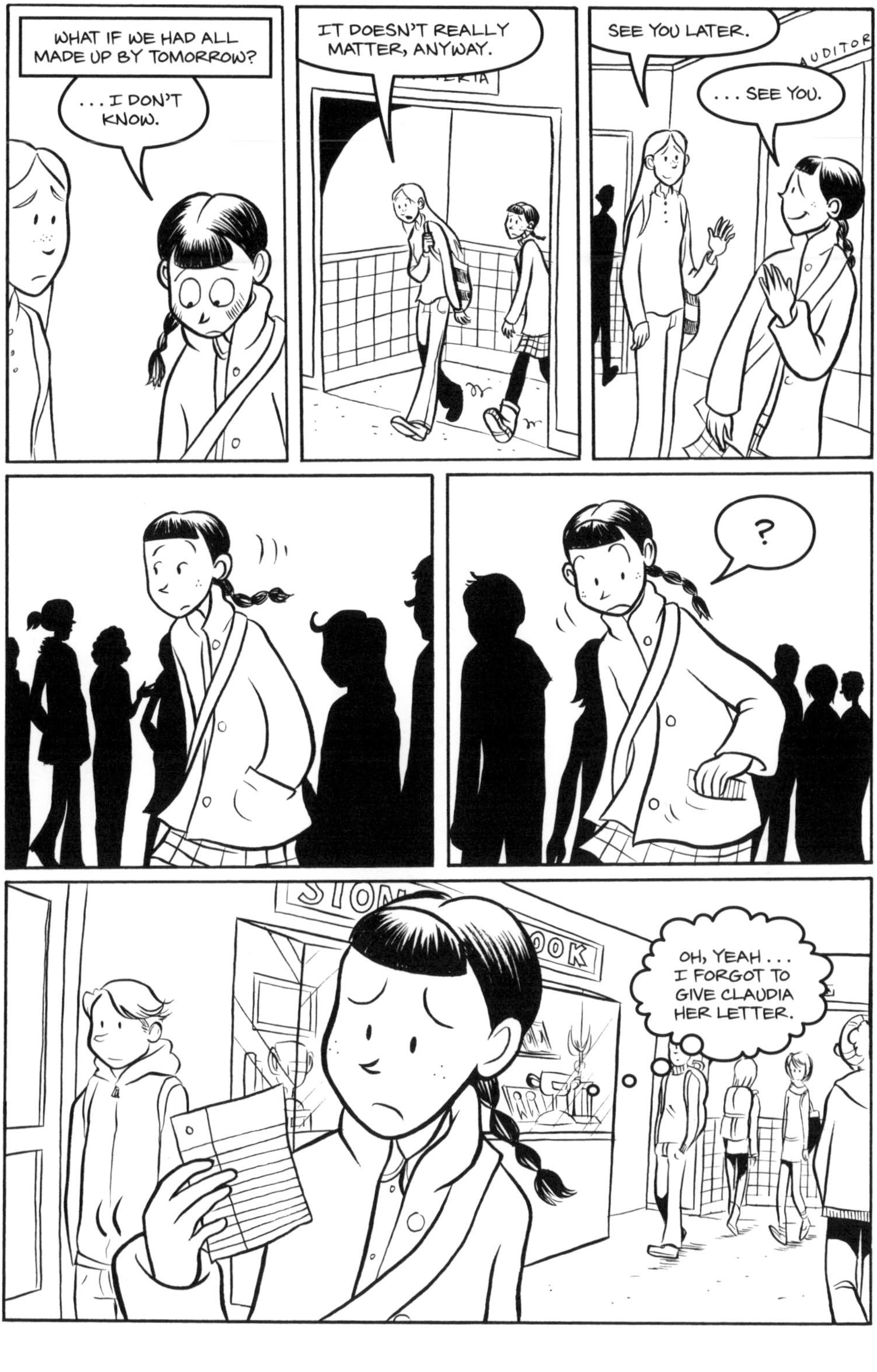
WHAT IF WE HAD ALL MADE UP BY TOMORROW?
. . . I DON'T KNOW.
IT DOESN'T REALLY MATTER, ANYWAY.
SEE YOU LATER.
AUDITOR
. . . SEE YOU.
?
OH, YEAH . . . I FORGOT TO GIVE CLAUDIA HER LETTER.

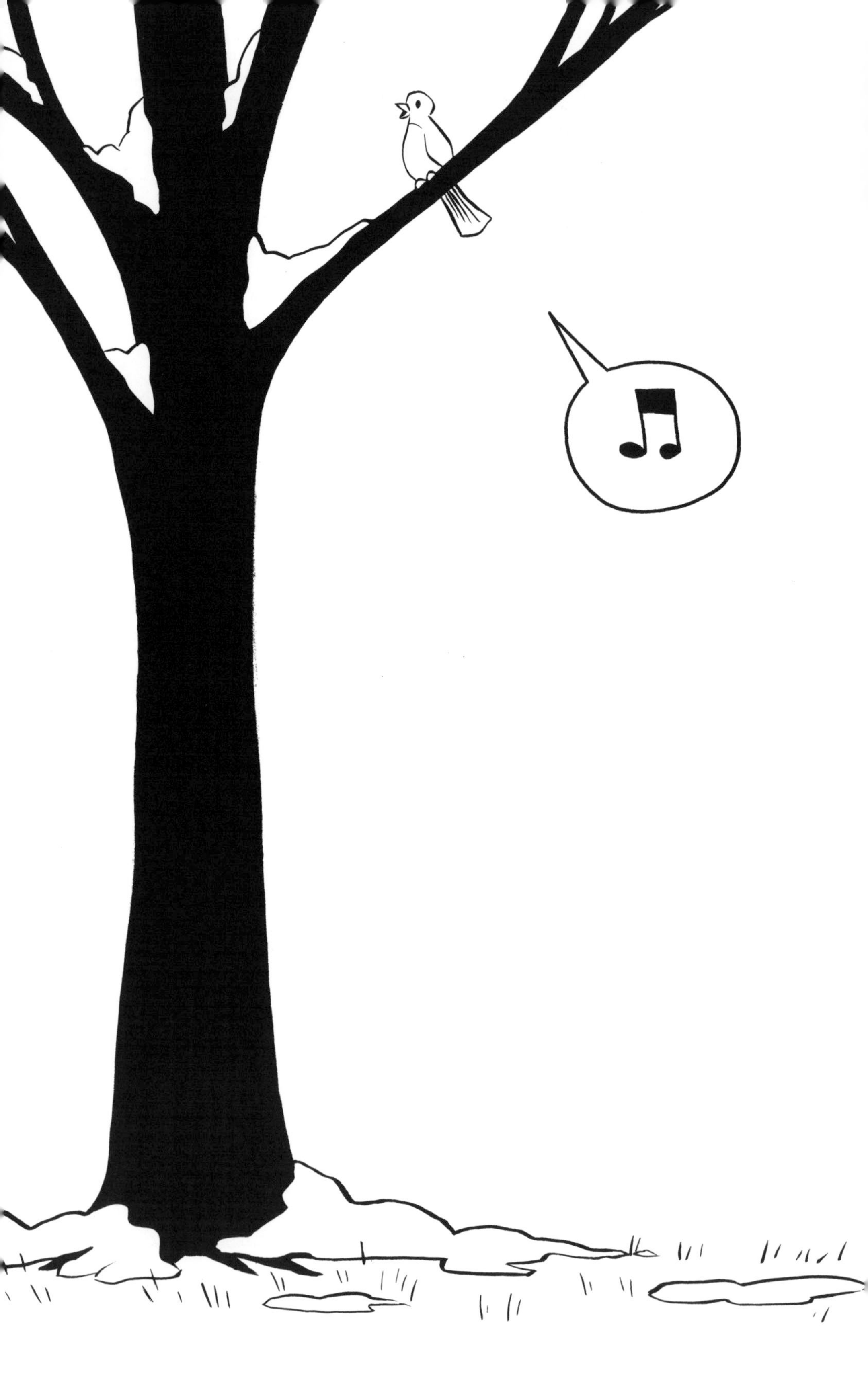

Chapter 4

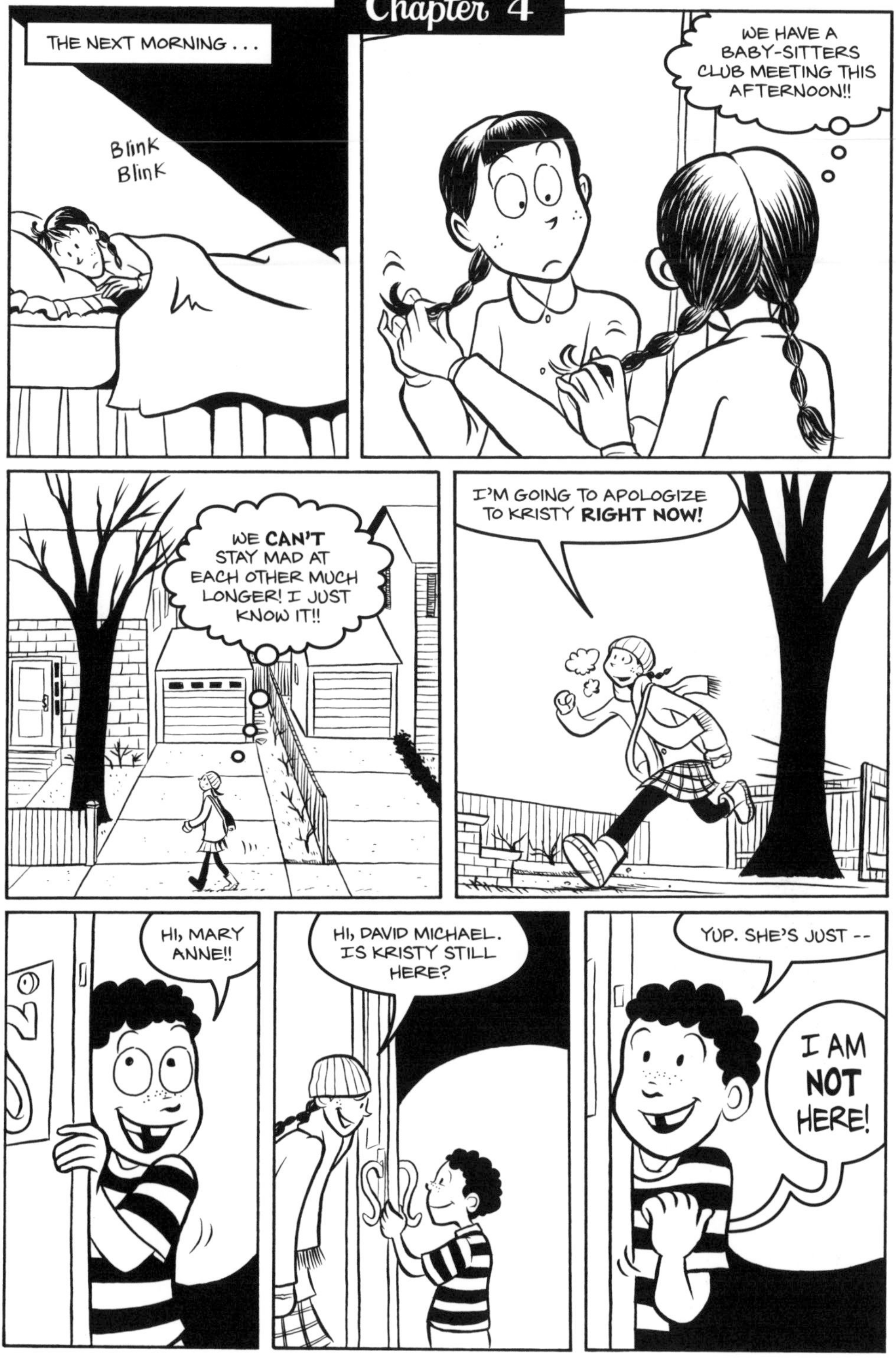
THE NEXT MORNING . . .
Blink
Blink
WE HAVE A BABY-SITTERS CLUB MEETING THIS AFTERNOON!!
WE **CAN'T** STAY MAD AT EACH OTHER MUCH LONGER! I JUST KNOW IT!!
I'M GOING TO APOLOGIZE TO KRISTY **RIGHT NOW!**
HI, MARY ANNE!!
HI, DAVID MICHAEL. IS KRISTY STILL HERE?
YUP. SHE'S JUST --
I AM **NOT** HERE!

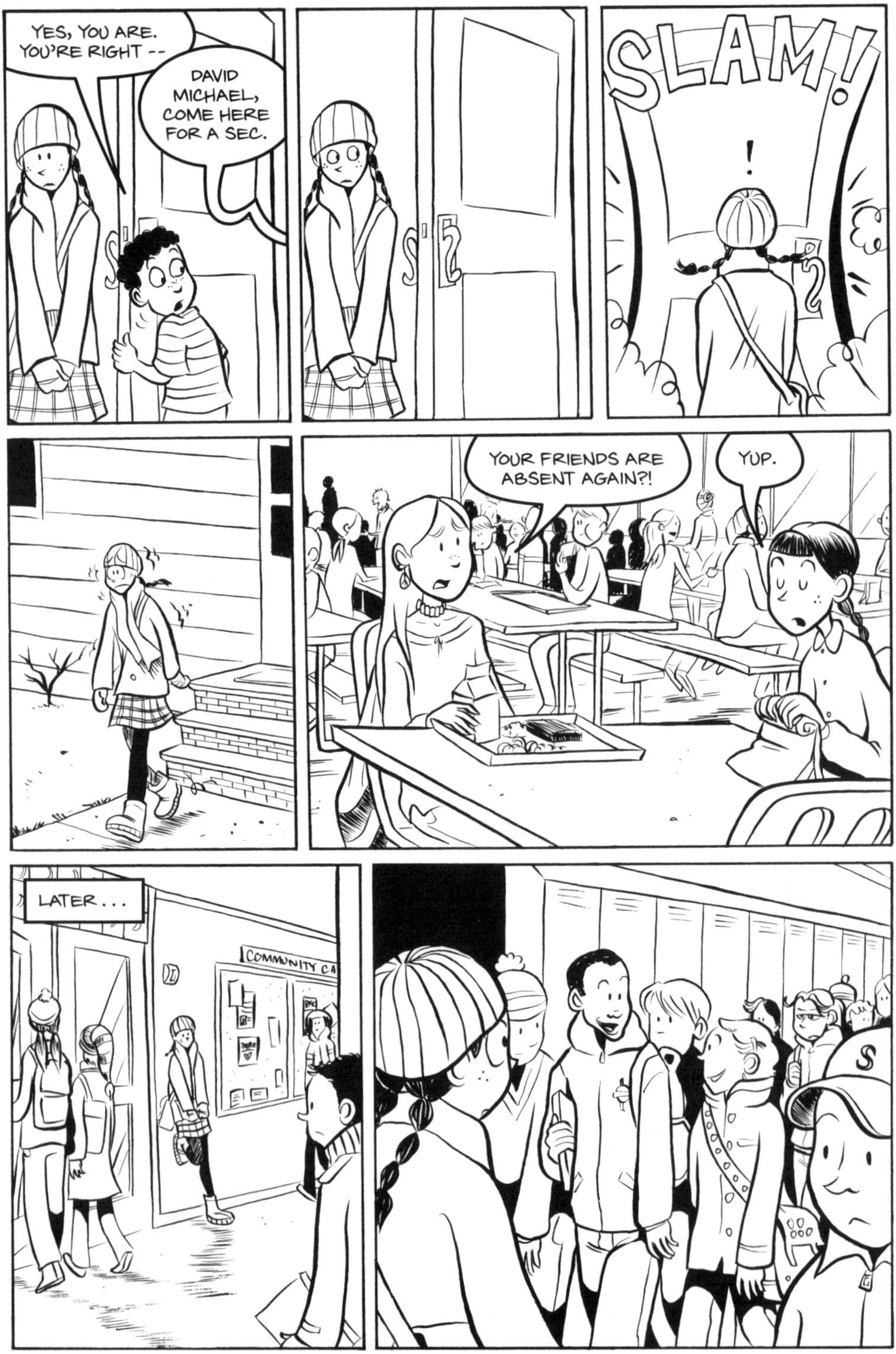
YES, YOU ARE. YOU'RE RIGHT --
DAVID MICHAEL, COME HERE FOR A SEC.
SLAM!
!
YOUR FRIENDS ARE ABSENT AGAIN?!
YUP.
LATER...
COMMUNITY CA

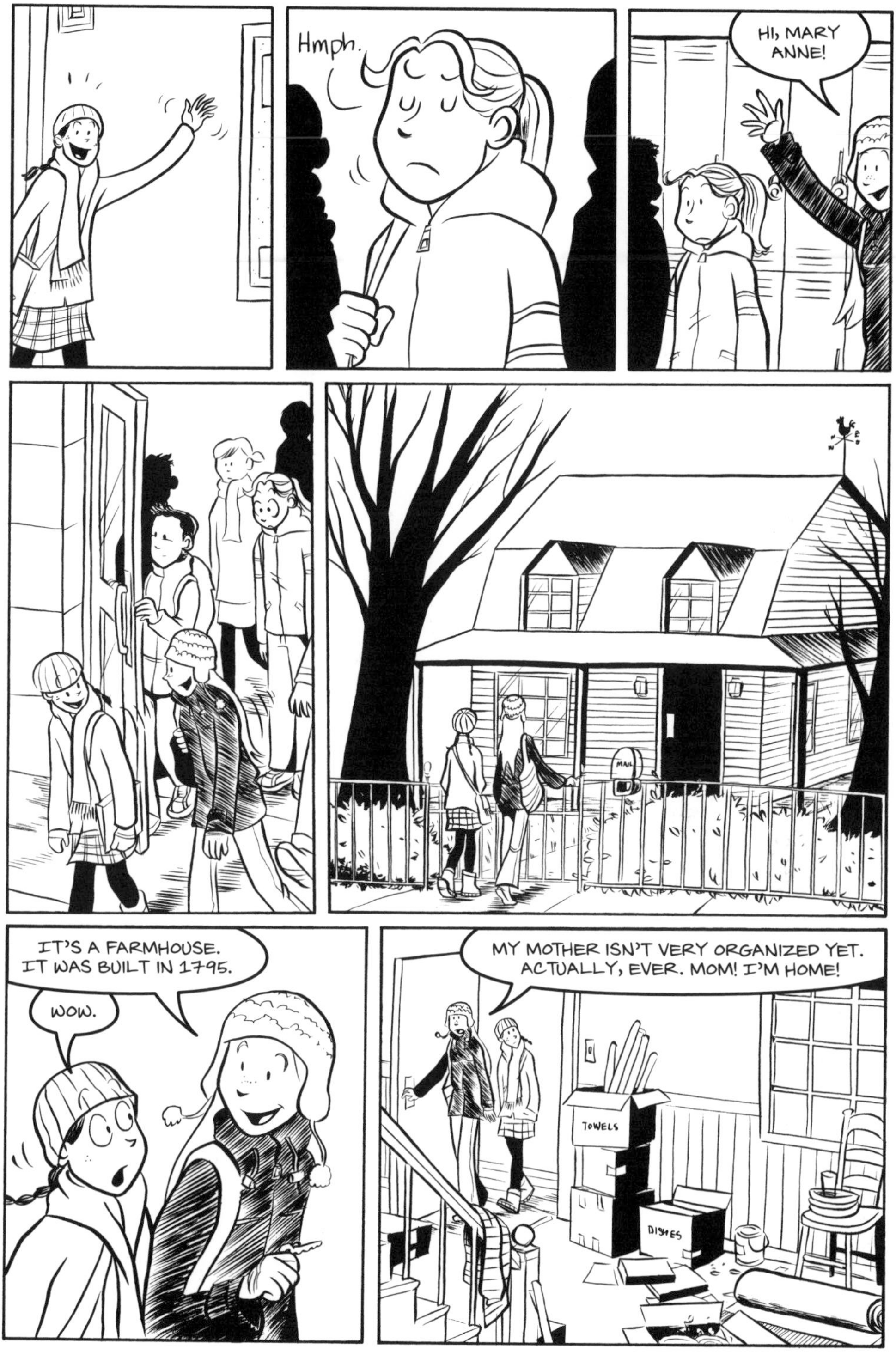
Hmph.
HI, MARY ANNE!
MAIL
IT'S A FARMHOUSE. IT WAS BUILT IN 1795.
WOW.
MY MOTHER ISN'T VERY ORGANIZED YET. ACTUALLY, EVER. MOM! I'M HOME!
TOWELS
DISHES

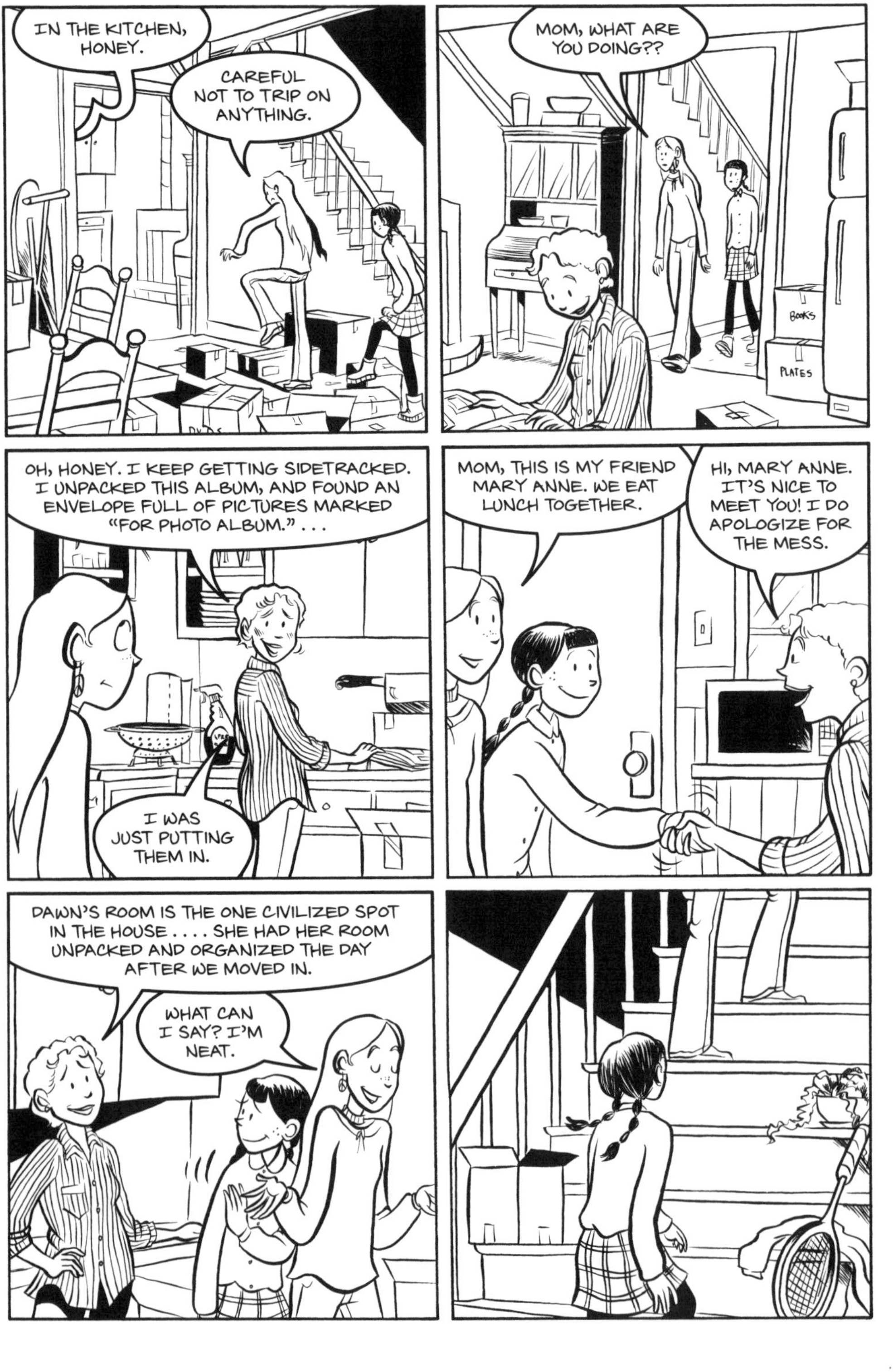
IN THE KITCHEN, HONEY.
CAREFUL NOT TO TRIP ON ANYTHING.
MOM, WHAT ARE YOU DOING??
OH, HONEY. I KEEP GETTING SIDETRACKED. I UNPACKED THIS ALBUM, AND FOUND AN ENVELOPE FULL OF PICTURES MARKED "FOR PHOTO ALBUM." . . .
I WAS JUST PUTTING THEM IN.
MOM, THIS IS MY FRIEND MARY ANNE. WE EAT LUNCH TOGETHER.
HI, MARY ANNE. IT'S NICE TO MEET YOU! I DO APOLOGIZE FOR THE MESS.
DAWN'S ROOM IS THE ONE CIVILIZED SPOT IN THE HOUSE . . . . SHE HAD HER ROOM UNPACKED AND ORGANIZED THE DAY AFTER WE MOVED IN.
WHAT CAN I SAY? I'M NEAT.
BOOKS
PLATES

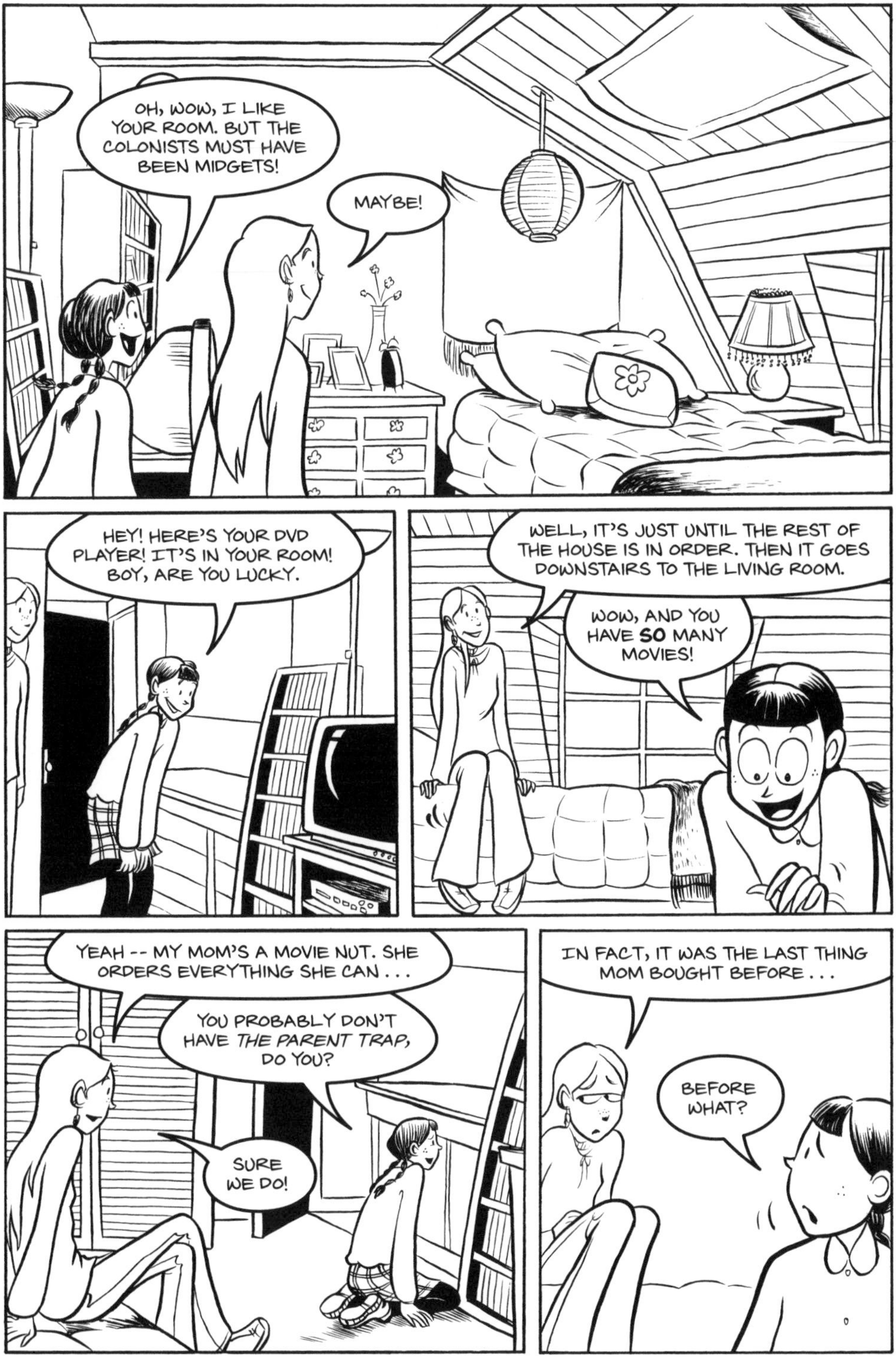
OH, WOW, I LIKE YOUR ROOM. BUT THE COLONISTS MUST HAVE BEEN MIDGETS!
MAYBE!
HEY! HERE'S YOUR DVD PLAYER! IT'S IN YOUR ROOM! BOY, ARE YOU LUCKY.
WELL, IT'S JUST UNTIL THE REST OF THE HOUSE IS IN ORDER. THEN IT GOES DOWNSTAIRS TO THE LIVING ROOM.
WOW, AND YOU HAVE **SO** MANY MOVIES!
YEAH -- MY MOM'S A MOVIE NUT. SHE ORDERS EVERYTHING SHE CAN . . .
YOU PROBABLY DON'T HAVE *THE PARENT TRAP*, DO YOU?
SURE WE DO!
IN FACT, IT WAS THE LAST THING MOM BOUGHT BEFORE . . .
BEFORE WHAT?

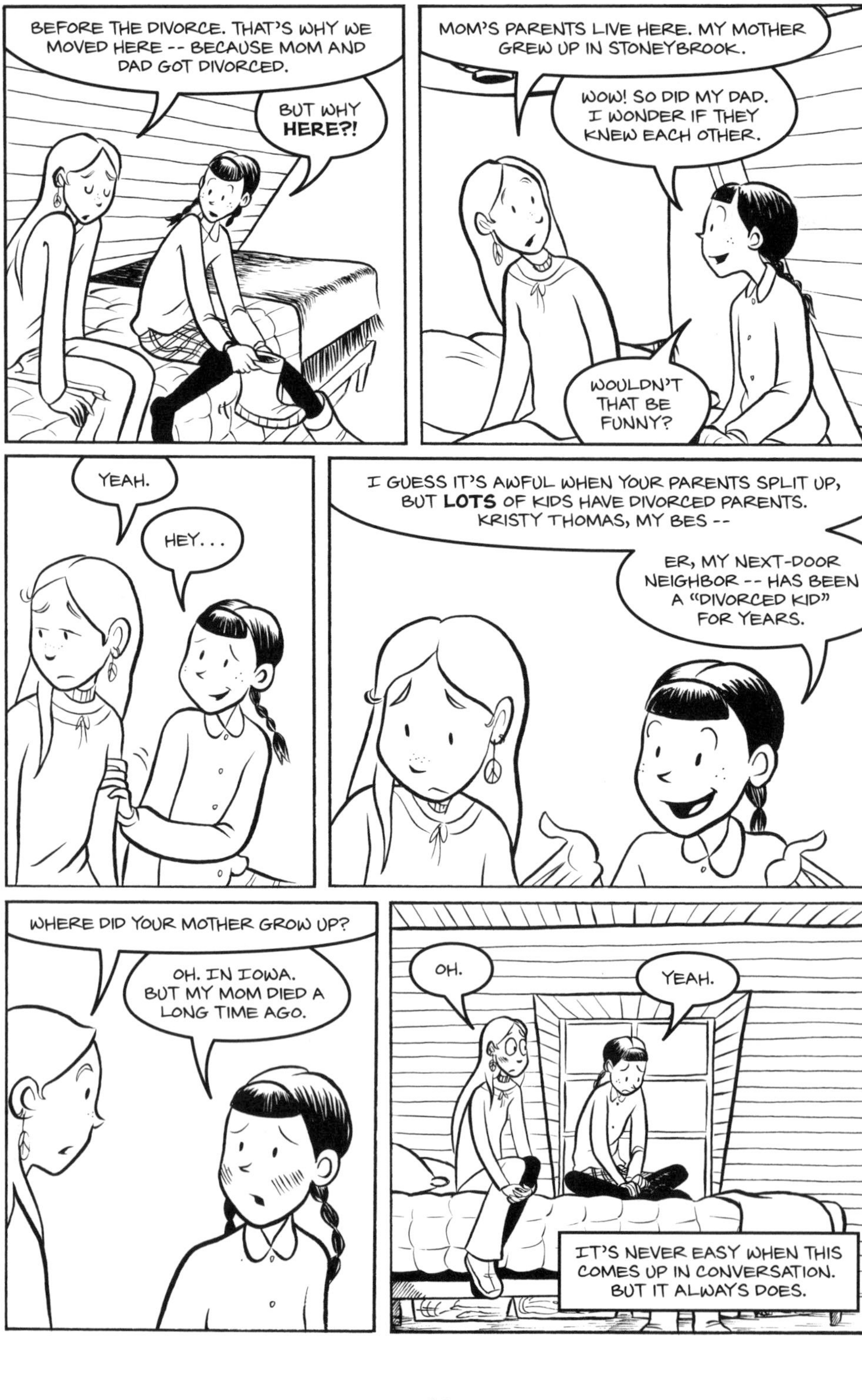
BEFORE THE DIVORCE. THAT'S WHY WE MOVED HERE -- BECAUSE MOM AND DAD GOT DIVORCED.
BUT WHY **HERE?!**
MOM'S PARENTS LIVE HERE. MY MOTHER GREW UP IN STONEYBROOK.
WOW! SO DID MY DAD. I WONDER IF THEY KNEW EACH OTHER.
WOULDN'T THAT BE FUNNY?
YEAH.
HEY...
I GUESS IT'S AWFUL WHEN YOUR PARENTS SPLIT UP, BUT **LOTS** OF KIDS HAVE DIVORCED PARENTS. KRISTY THOMAS, MY BES --
ER, MY NEXT-DOOR NEIGHBOR -- HAS BEEN A "DIVORCED KID" FOR YEARS.
WHERE DID YOUR MOTHER GROW UP?
OH. IN IOWA. BUT MY MOM DIED A LONG TIME AGO.
OH.
YEAH.
IT'S NEVER EASY WHEN THIS COMES UP IN CONVERSATION. BUT IT ALWAYS DOES.

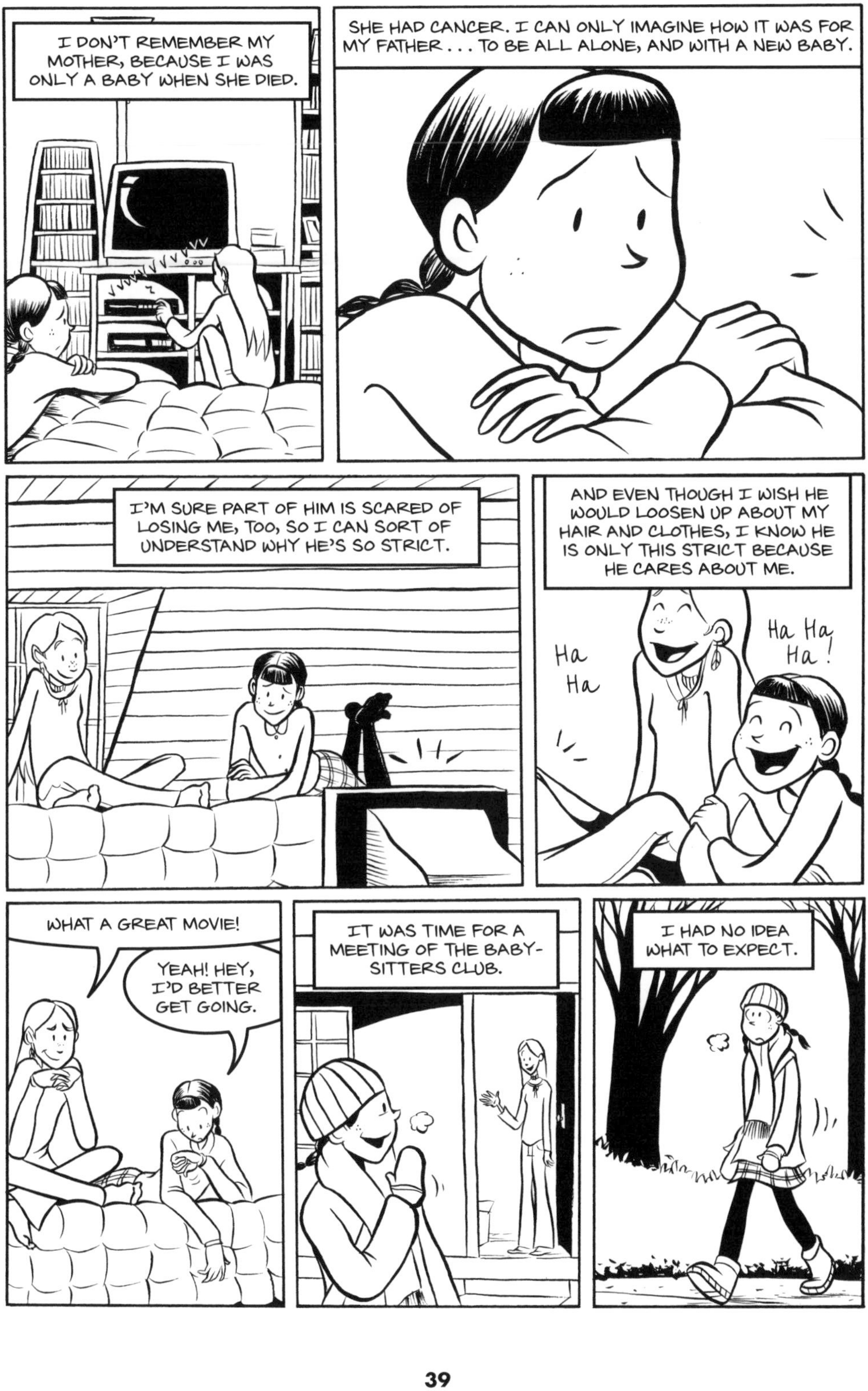
I DON'T REMEMBER MY MOTHER, BECAUSE I WAS ONLY A BABY WHEN SHE DIED.
SHE HAD CANCER. I CAN ONLY IMAGINE HOW IT WAS FOR MY FATHER . . . TO BE ALL ALONE, AND WITH A NEW BABY.
I'M SURE PART OF HIM IS SCARED OF LOSING ME, TOO, SO I CAN SORT OF UNDERSTAND WHY HE'S SO STRICT.
AND EVEN THOUGH I WISH HE WOULD LOOSEN UP ABOUT MY HAIR AND CLOTHES, I KNOW HE IS ONLY THIS STRICT BECAUSE HE CARES ABOUT ME.
Ha Ha
Ha Ha Ha!
WHAT A GREAT MOVIE!
YEAH! HEY, I'D BETTER GET GOING.
IT WAS TIME FOR A MEETING OF THE BABY-SITTERS CLUB.
I HAD NO IDEA WHAT TO EXPECT.

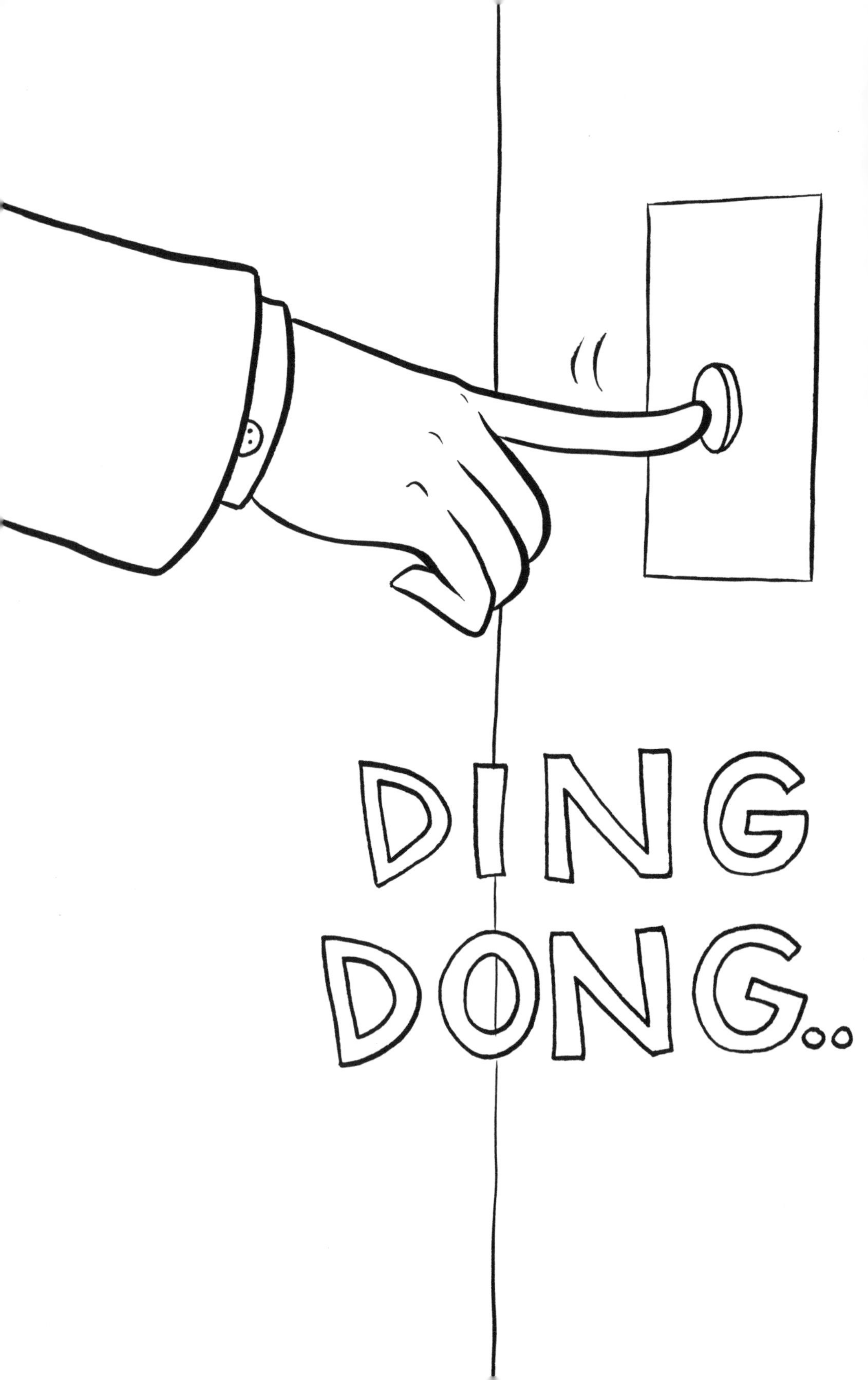
DING DONG..

Chapter 5

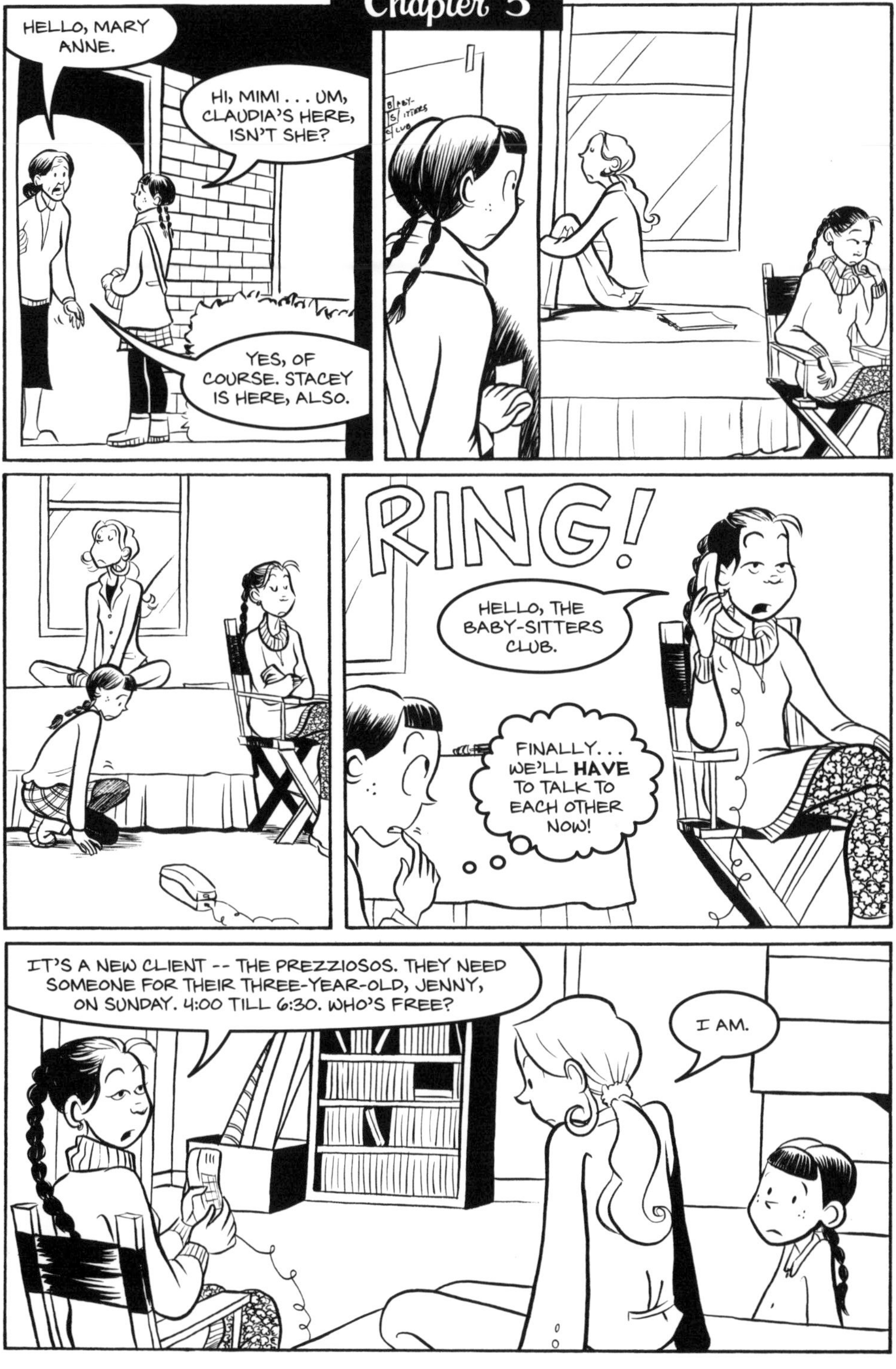
HELLO, MARY ANNE.
HI, MIMI . . . UM, CLAUDIA'S HERE, ISN'T SHE?
YES, OF COURSE. STACEY IS HERE, ALSO.
BABY-SITTERS CLUB
RING!
HELLO, THE BABY-SITTERS CLUB.
FINALLY . . . WE'LL HAVE TO TALK TO EACH OTHER NOW!
IT'S A NEW CLIENT -- THE PREZZIOSOS. THEY NEED SOMEONE FOR THEIR THREE-YEAR-OLD, JENNY, ON SUNDAY. 4:00 TILL 6:30. WHO'S FREE?
I AM.

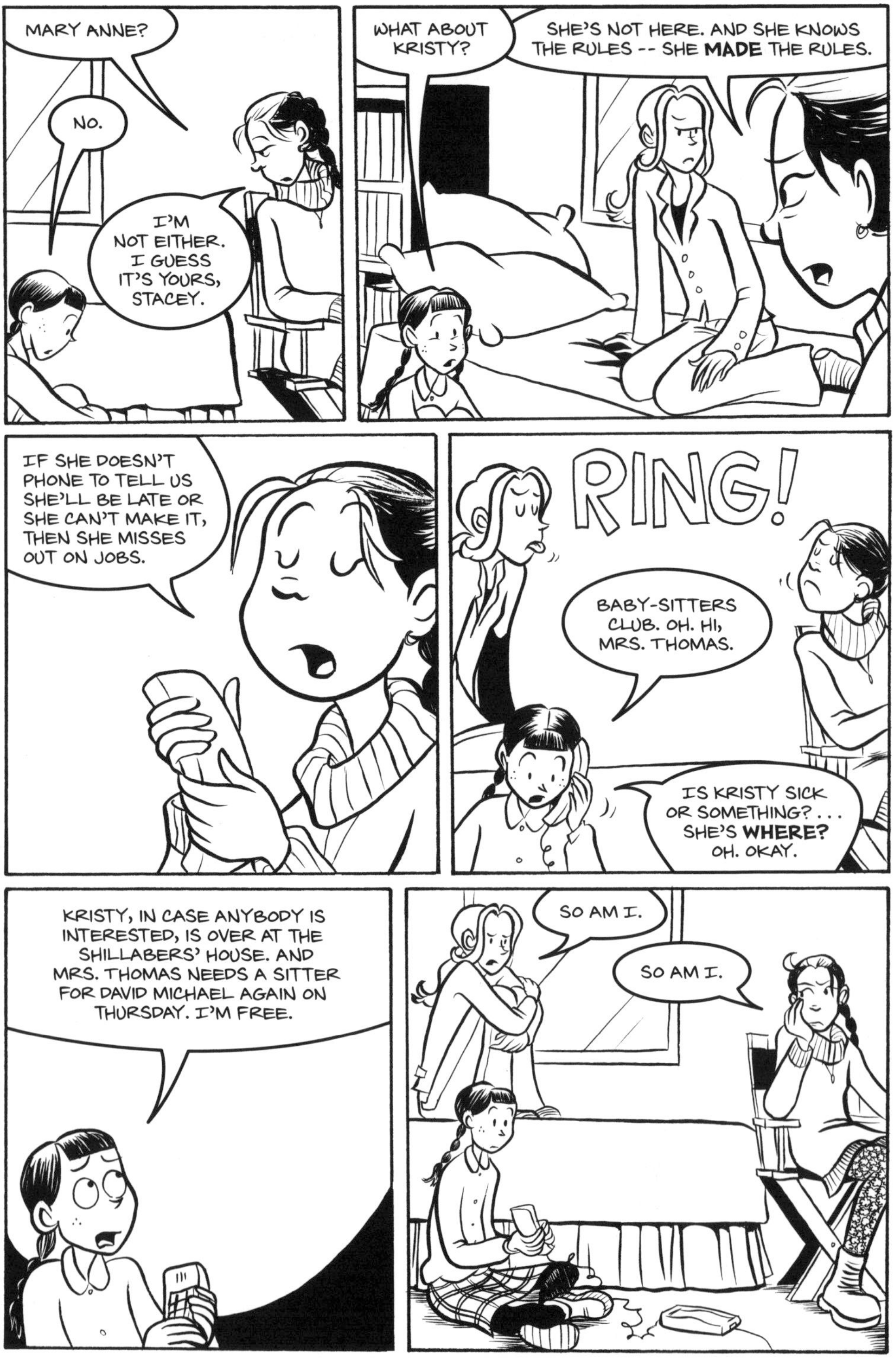
MARY ANNE?
NO.
I'M NOT EITHER. I GUESS IT'S YOURS, STACEY.
WHAT ABOUT KRISTY?
SHE'S NOT HERE. AND SHE KNOWS THE RULES -- SHE **MADE** THE RULES.
IF SHE DOESN'T PHONE TO TELL US SHE'LL BE LATE OR SHE CAN'T MAKE IT, THEN SHE MISSES OUT ON JOBS.
RING!
BABY-SITTERS CLUB. OH. HI, MRS. THOMAS.
IS KRISTY SICK OR SOMETHING? . . . SHE'S **WHERE?** OH. OKAY.
KRISTY, IN CASE ANYBODY IS INTERESTED, IS OVER AT THE SHILLABERS' HOUSE. AND MRS. THOMAS NEEDS A SITTER FOR DAVID MICHAEL AGAIN ON THURSDAY. I'M FREE.
SO AM I.
SO AM I.

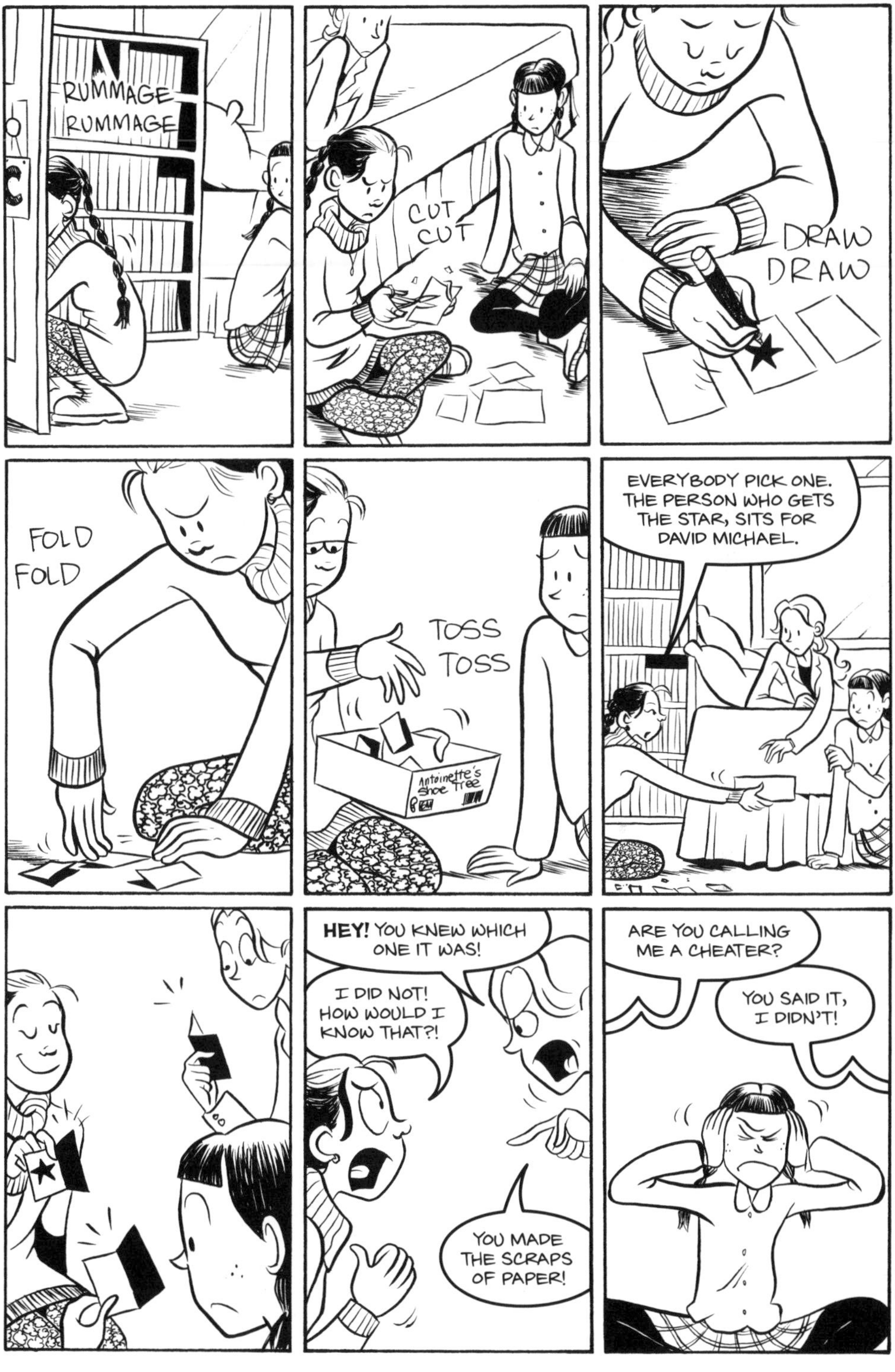
RUMMAGE
RUMMAGE
CUT
CUT
DRAW
DRAW
FOLD
FOLD
TOSS
TOSS
Antoinette's Shoe Tree
EVERYBODY PICK ONE. THE PERSON WHO GETS THE STAR, SITS FOR DAVID MICHAEL.
HEY! YOU KNEW WHICH ONE IT WAS!
I DID NOT! HOW WOULD I KNOW THAT?!
YOU MADE THE SCRAPS OF PAPER!
ARE YOU CALLING ME A CHEATER?
YOU SAID IT, I DIDN'T!

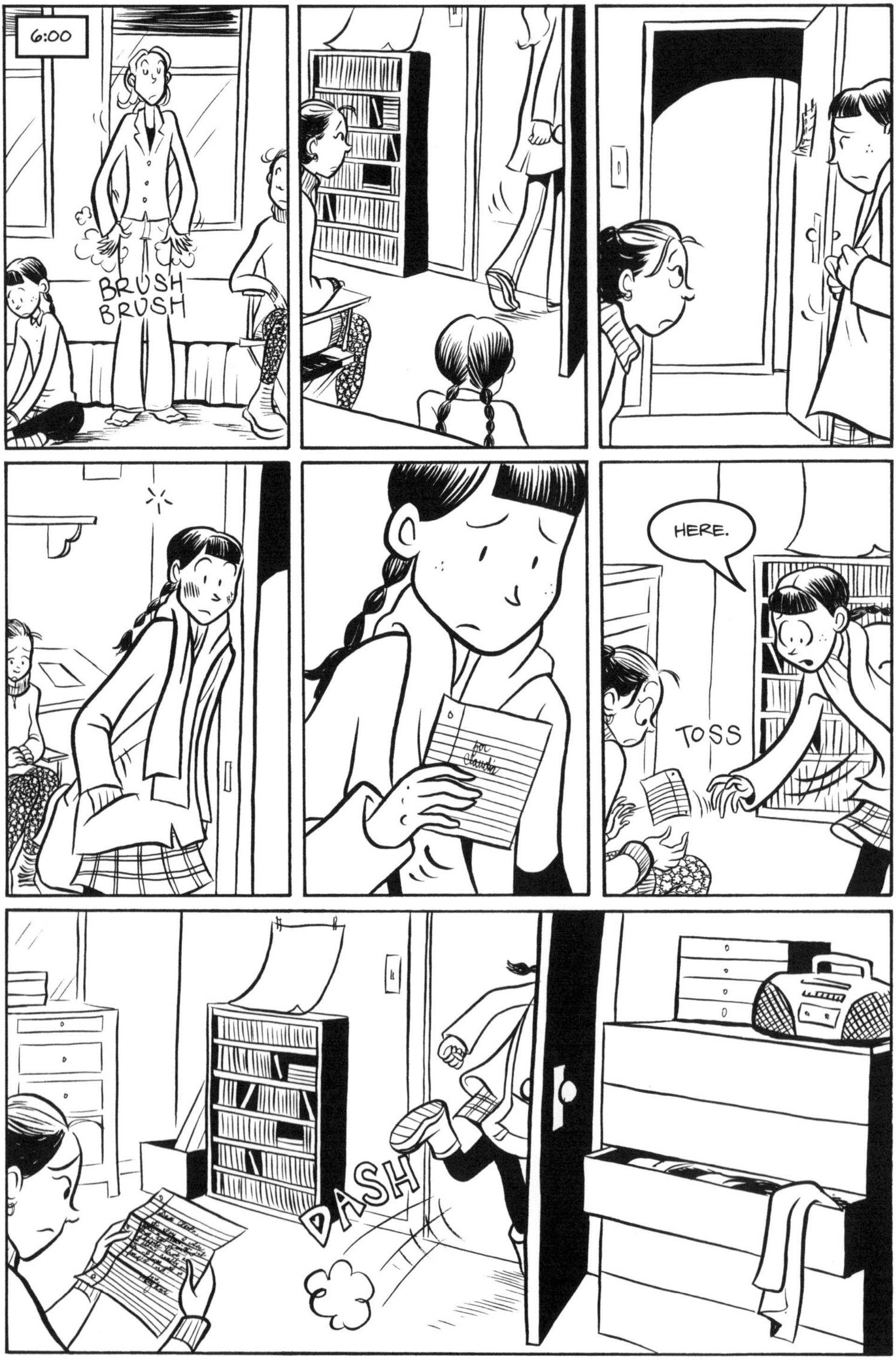
6:00
BRUSH BRUSH
HERE.
TOSS
DASH

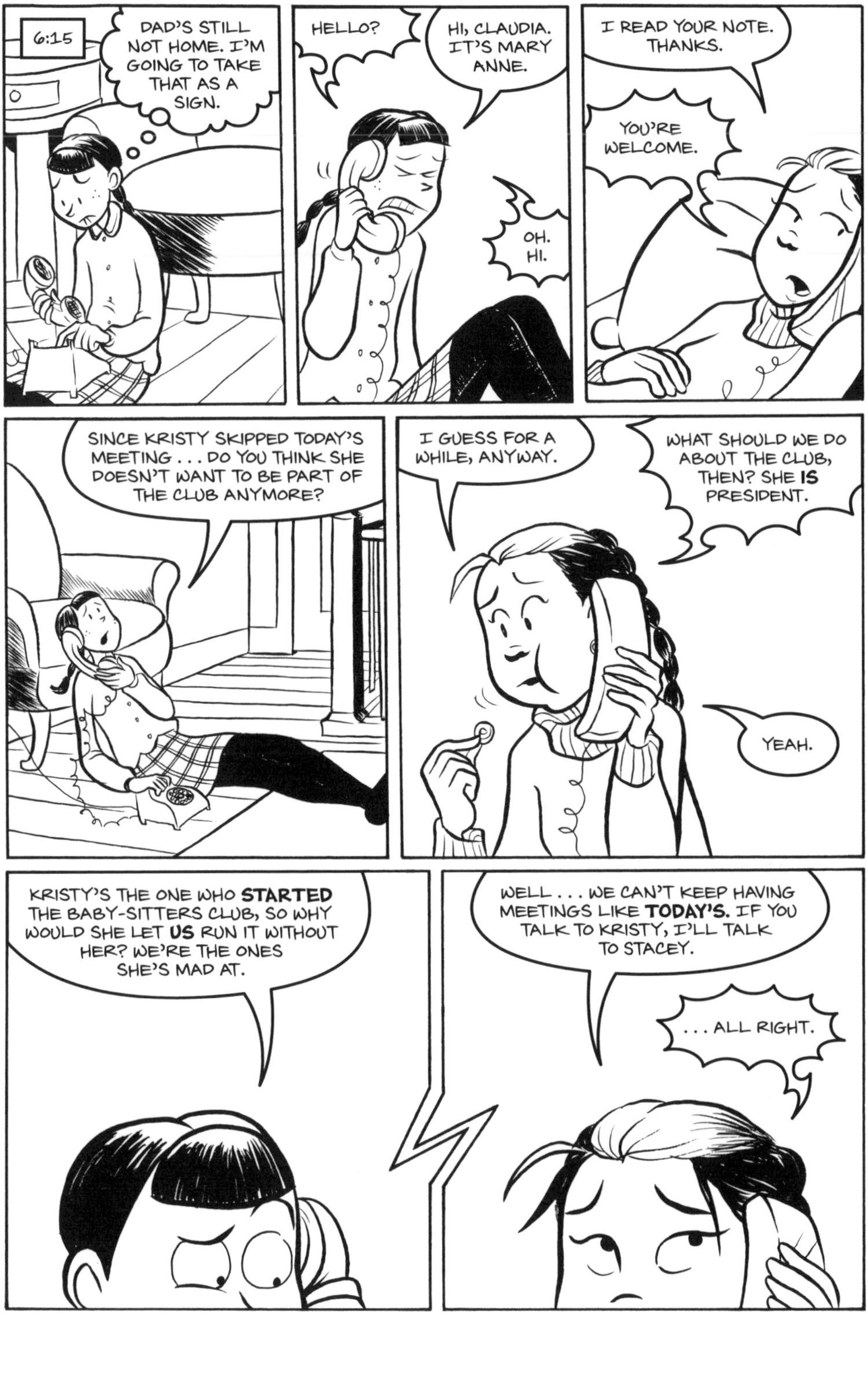
6:15
DAD'S STILL NOT HOME. I'M GOING TO TAKE THAT AS A SIGN.
HELLO?
HI, CLAUDIA. IT'S MARY ANNE.
OH. HI.
I READ YOUR NOTE. THANKS.
YOU'RE WELCOME.
SINCE KRISTY SKIPPED TODAY'S MEETING . . . DO YOU THINK SHE DOESN'T WANT TO BE PART OF THE CLUB ANYMORE?
I GUESS FOR A WHILE, ANYWAY.
WHAT SHOULD WE DO ABOUT THE CLUB, THEN? SHE **IS** PRESIDENT.
YEAH.
KRISTY'S THE ONE WHO **STARTED** THE BABY-SITTERS CLUB, SO WHY WOULD SHE LET **US** RUN IT WITHOUT HER? WE'RE THE ONES SHE'S MAD AT.
WELL . . . WE CAN'T KEEP HAVING MEETINGS LIKE **TODAY'S.** IF YOU TALK TO KRISTY, I'LL TALK TO STACEY.
. . . ALL RIGHT.

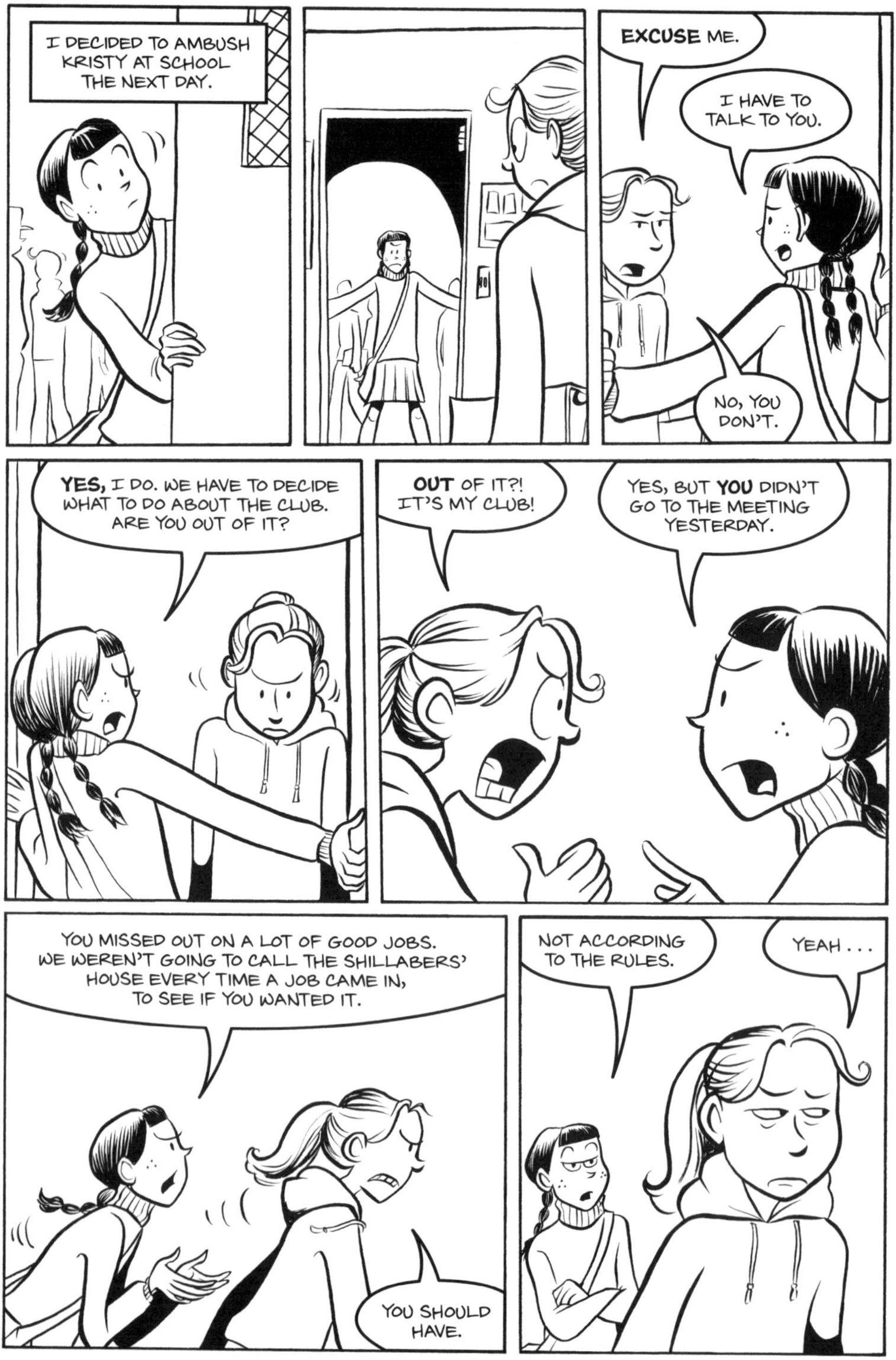
I DECIDED TO AMBUSH KRISTY AT SCHOOL THE NEXT DAY.
EXCUSE ME.
I HAVE TO TALK TO YOU.
NO, YOU DON'T.
YES, I DO. WE HAVE TO DECIDE WHAT TO DO ABOUT THE CLUB. ARE YOU OUT OF IT?
OUT OF IT?! IT'S MY CLUB!
YES, BUT YOU DIDN'T GO TO THE MEETING YESTERDAY.
YOU MISSED OUT ON A LOT OF GOOD JOBS. WE WEREN'T GOING TO CALL THE SHILLABERS' HOUSE EVERY TIME A JOB CAME IN, TO SEE IF YOU WANTED IT.
YOU SHOULD HAVE.
NOT ACCORDING TO THE RULES.
YEAH . . .

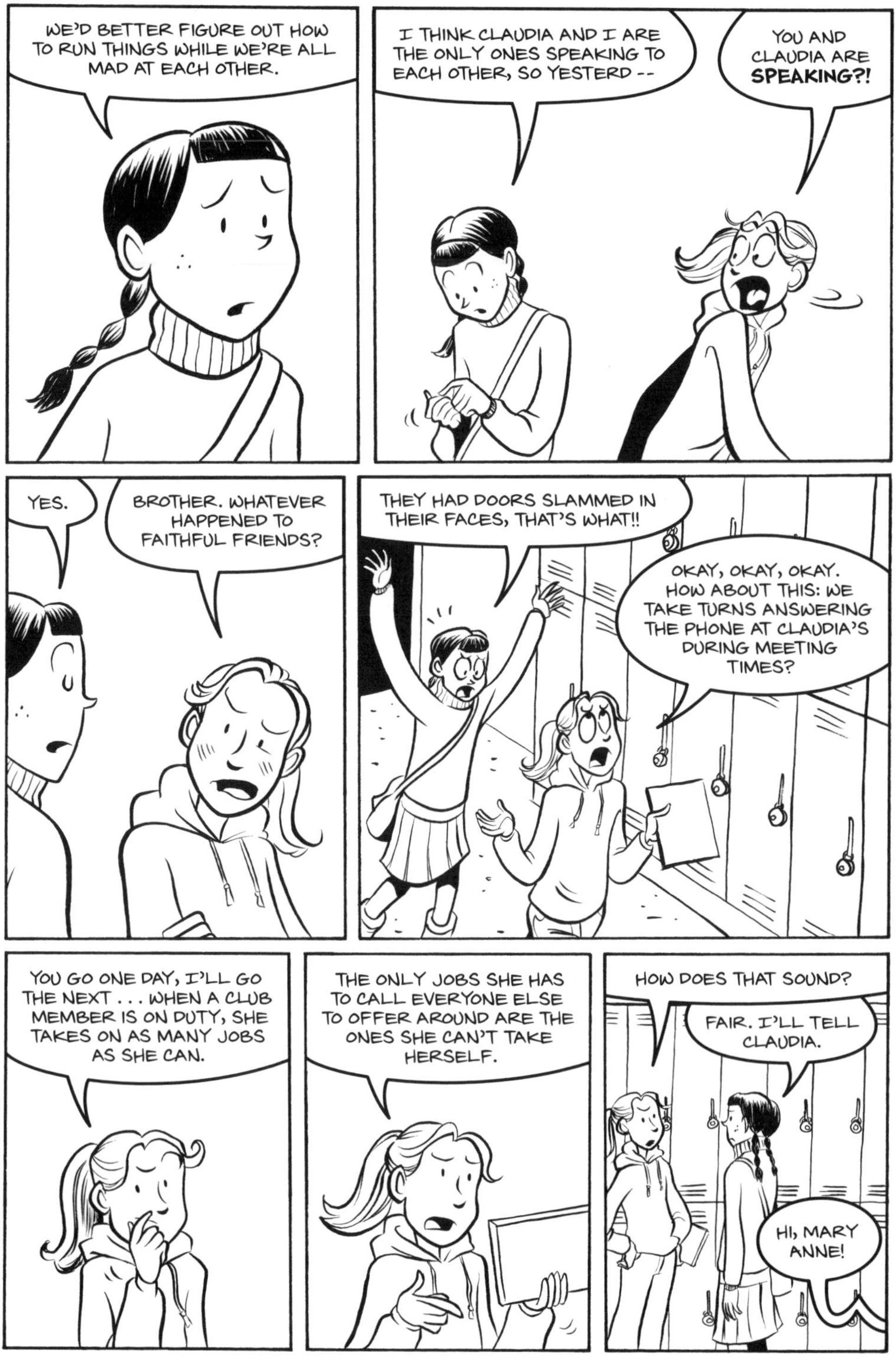
WE'D BETTER FIGURE OUT HOW TO RUN THINGS WHILE WE'RE ALL MAD AT EACH OTHER.
I THINK CLAUDIA AND I ARE THE ONLY ONES SPEAKING TO EACH OTHER, SO YESTERD --
YOU AND CLAUDIA ARE **SPEAKING?!**
YES.
BROTHER. WHATEVER HAPPENED TO FAITHFUL FRIENDS?
THEY HAD DOORS SLAMMED IN THEIR FACES, THAT'S WHAT!!
OKAY, OKAY, OKAY. HOW ABOUT THIS: WE TAKE TURNS ANSWERING THE PHONE AT CLAUDIA'S DURING MEETING TIMES?
YOU GO ONE DAY, I'LL GO THE NEXT . . . WHEN A CLUB MEMBER IS ON DUTY, SHE TAKES ON AS MANY JOBS AS SHE CAN.
THE ONLY JOBS SHE HAS TO CALL EVERYONE ELSE TO OFFER AROUND ARE THE ONES SHE CAN'T TAKE HERSELF.
HOW DOES THAT SOUND?
FAIR. I'LL TELL CLAUDIA.
HI, MARY ANNE!

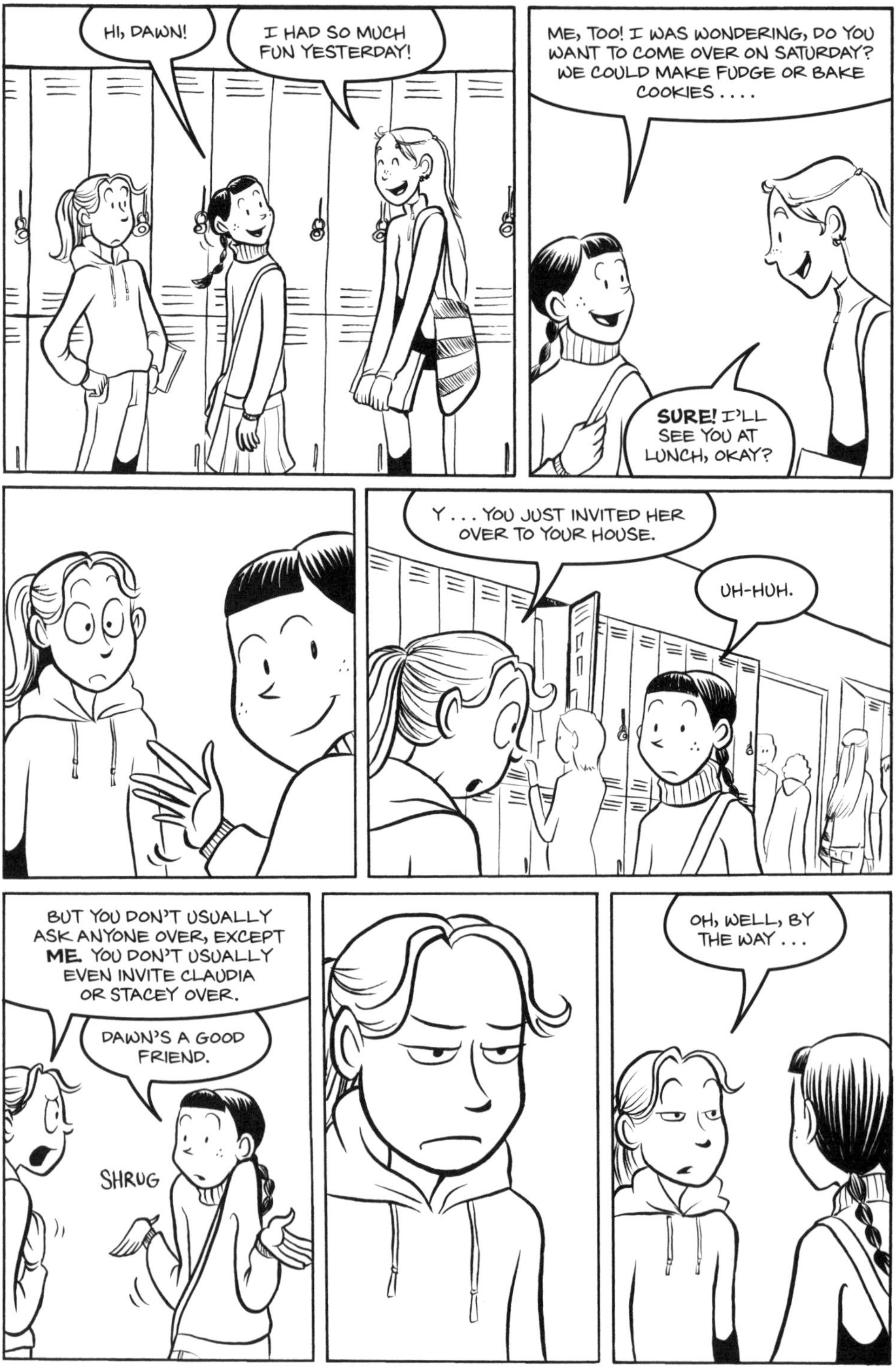
HI, DAWN!
I HAD SO MUCH FUN YESTERDAY!
ME, TOO! I WAS WONDERING, DO YOU WANT TO COME OVER ON SATURDAY? WE COULD MAKE FUDGE OR BAKE COOKIES . . . .
SURE! I'LL SEE YOU AT LUNCH, OKAY?
Y . . . YOU JUST INVITED HER OVER TO YOUR HOUSE.
UH-HUH.
BUT YOU DON'T USUALLY ASK ANYONE OVER, EXCEPT ME. YOU DON'T USUALLY EVEN INVITE CLAUDIA OR STACEY OVER.
DAWN'S A GOOD FRIEND.
SHRUG
OH, WELL, BY THE WAY . . .

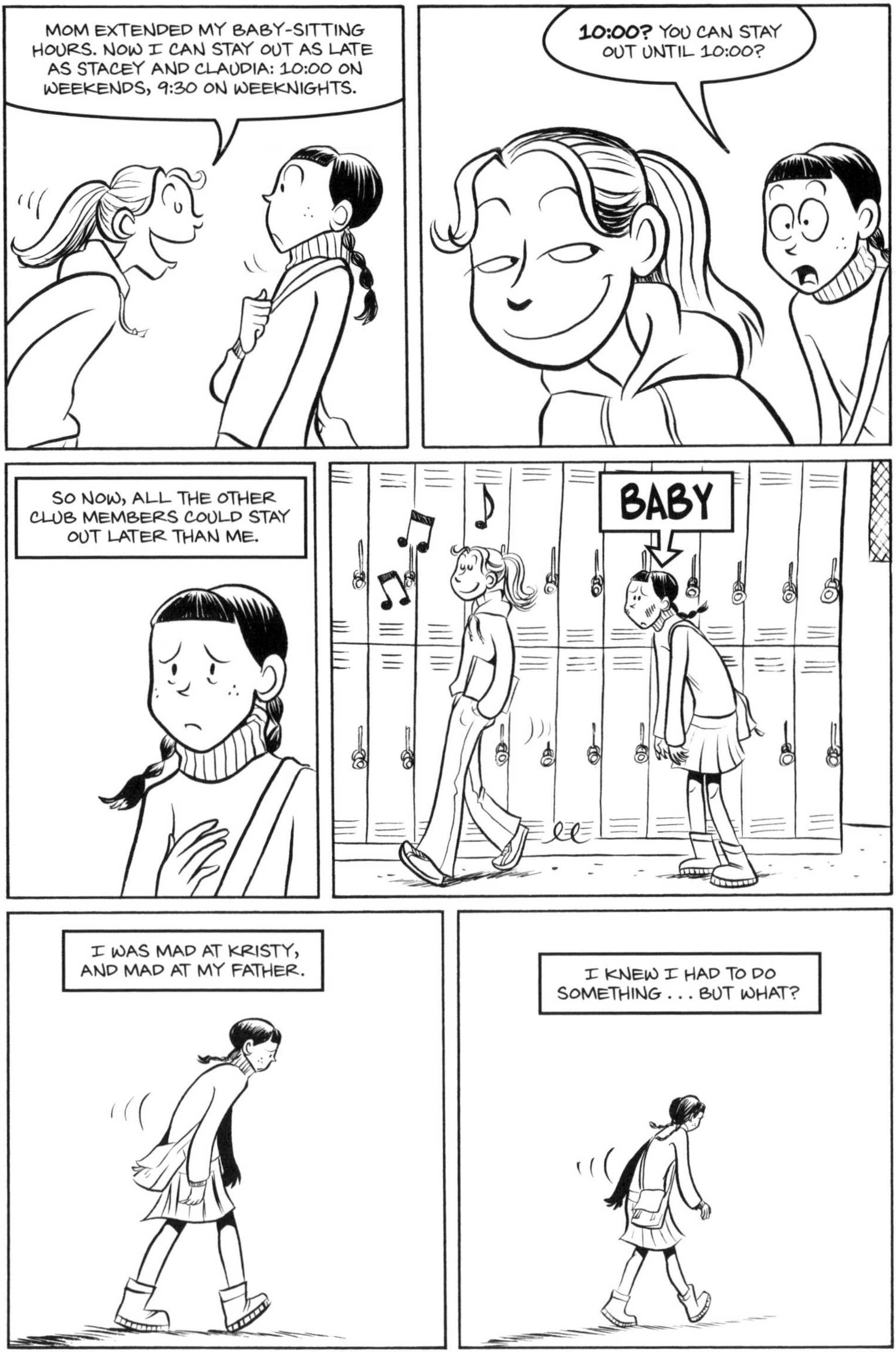
MOM EXTENDED MY BABY-SITTING HOURS. NOW I CAN STAY OUT AS LATE AS STACEY AND CLAUDIA: 10:00 ON WEEKENDS, 9:30 ON WEEKNIGHTS.
10:00? YOU CAN STAY OUT UNTIL 10:00?
SO NOW, ALL THE OTHER CLUB MEMBERS COULD STAY OUT LATER THAN ME.
BABY
I WAS MAD AT KRISTY, AND MAD AT MY FATHER.
I KNEW I HAD TO DO SOMETHING . . . BUT WHAT?

Sunday, January 11

This afternoon, I sat for Jenny Prezzioso. Jenny is three.
She's the Pikes' neighbor, so I had met her a few times before
today. She and her parents both look very prim and proper
but Mrs. Prezzioso is the only one who acts that way. She
looks like she just stepped out of the pages of a magazine.
And she dresses Jenny as if every day were Easter Sunday:
frilly dresses, lacy socks, and ribbons in her hair. Mrs. P probably
thinks "jeans" is a dirty word.

Mr. P, on the other hand, looks like he'd rather be dozing
in front of the TV in sweats, a T-shirt, and mismatched socks.
And Jenny tries hard, but she just isn't what her mother wants
her to be...

Stacey

Chapter 6

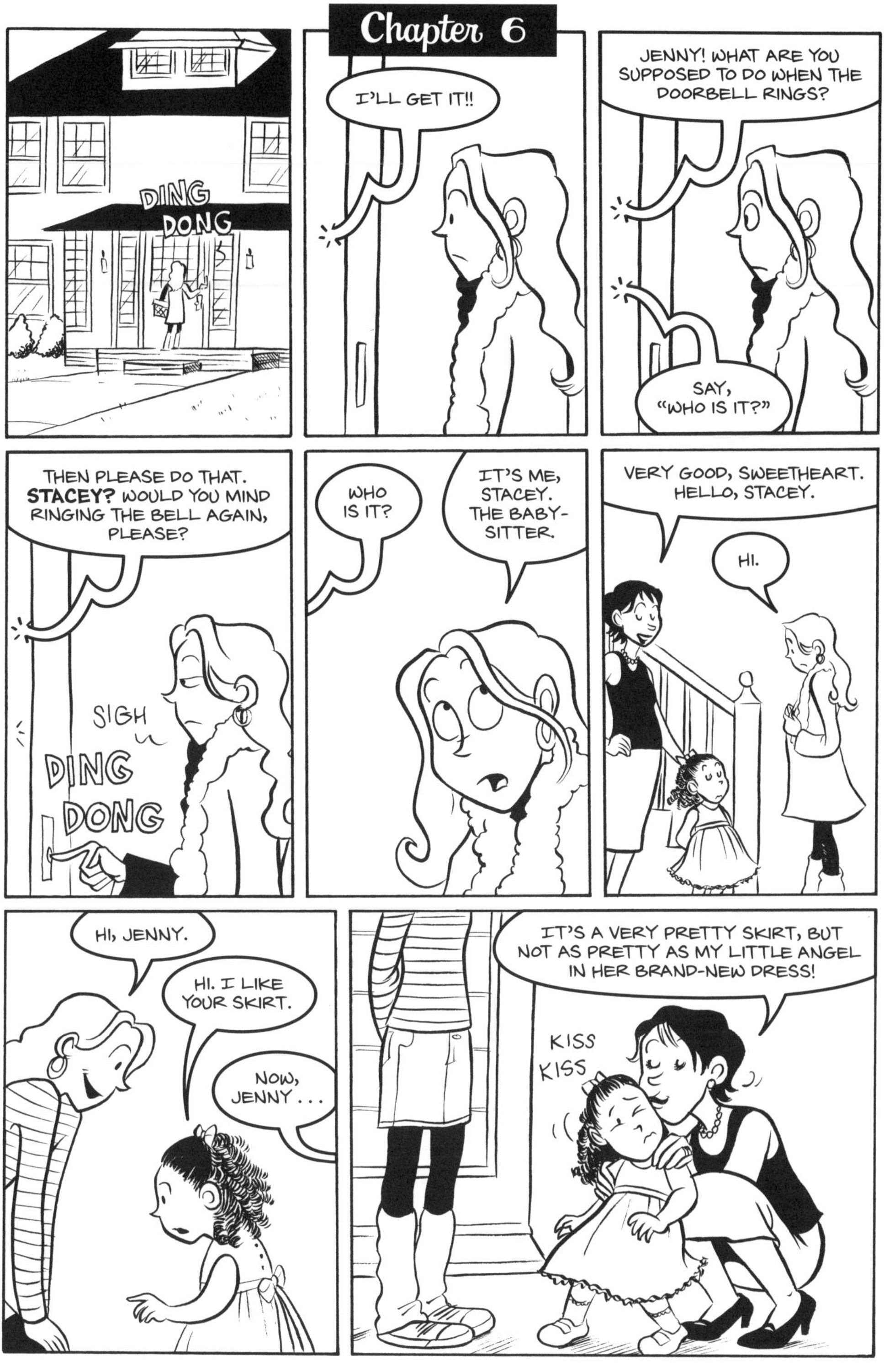

DING DONG
I'LL GET IT!!
JENNY! WHAT ARE YOU SUPPOSED TO DO WHEN THE DOORBELL RINGS?
SAY, "WHO IS IT?"
THEN PLEASE DO THAT. STACEY? WOULD YOU MIND RINGING THE BELL AGAIN, PLEASE?
SIGH
DING DONG
WHO IS IT?
IT'S ME, STACEY. THE BABY-SITTER.
VERY GOOD, SWEETHEART. HELLO, STACEY.
HI.
HI, JENNY.
HI. I LIKE YOUR SKIRT.
NOW, JENNY . . .
IT'S A VERY PRETTY SKIRT, BUT NOT AS PRETTY AS MY LITTLE ANGEL IN HER BRAND-NEW DRESS!
KISS KISS

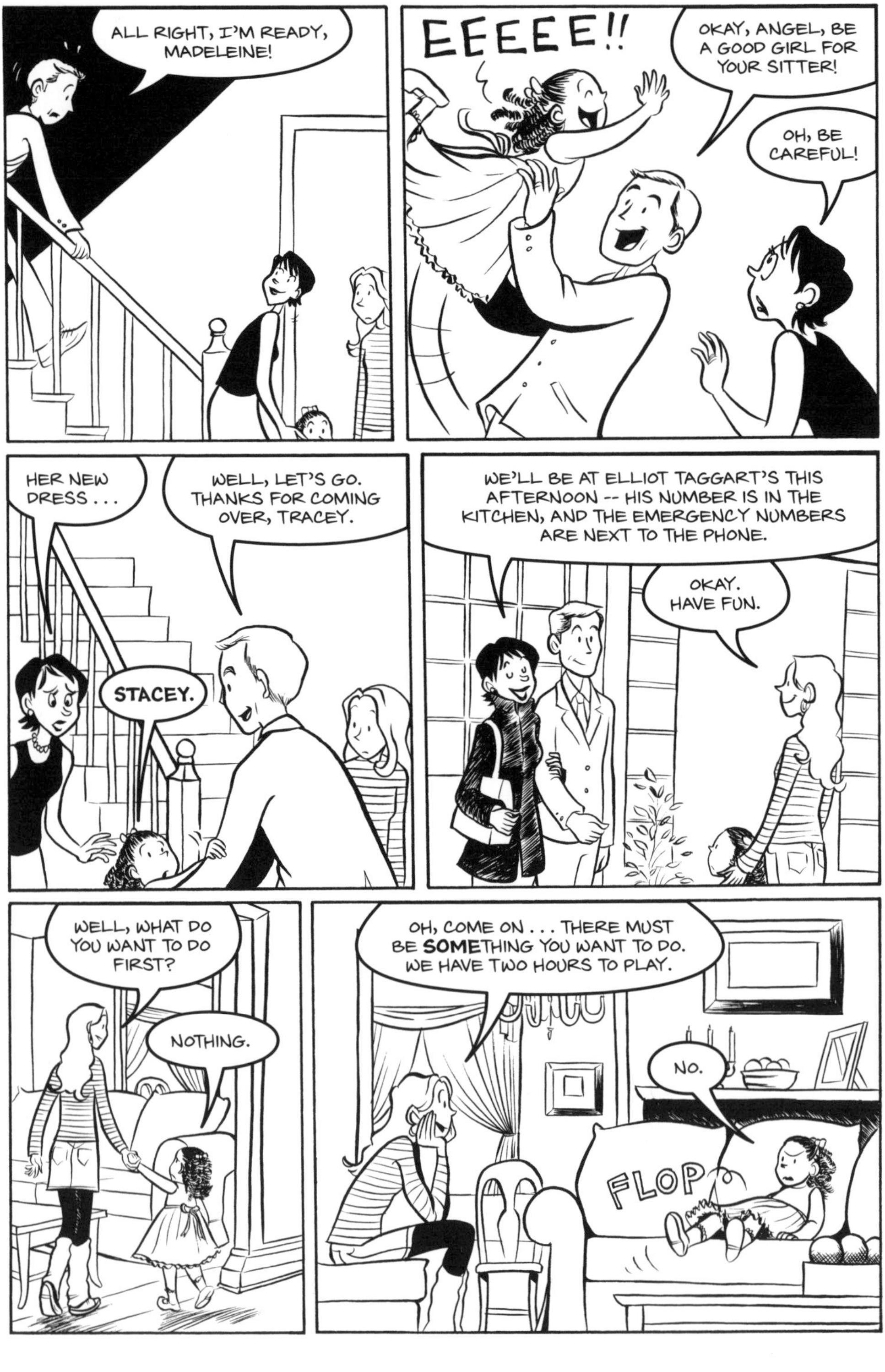
ALL RIGHT, I'M READY, MADELEINE!
EEEEE!!
OKAY, ANGEL, BE A GOOD GIRL FOR YOUR SITTER!
OH, BE CAREFUL!
HER NEW DRESS . . .
WELL, LET'S GO. THANKS FOR COMING OVER, TRACEY.
STACEY.
WE'LL BE AT ELLIOT TAGGART'S THIS AFTERNOON -- HIS NUMBER IS IN THE KITCHEN, AND THE EMERGENCY NUMBERS ARE NEXT TO THE PHONE.
OKAY. HAVE FUN.
WELL, WHAT DO YOU WANT TO DO FIRST?
NOTHING.
OH, COME ON . . . THERE MUST BE **SOME**THING YOU WANT TO DO. WE HAVE TWO HOURS TO PLAY.
NO.
FLOP

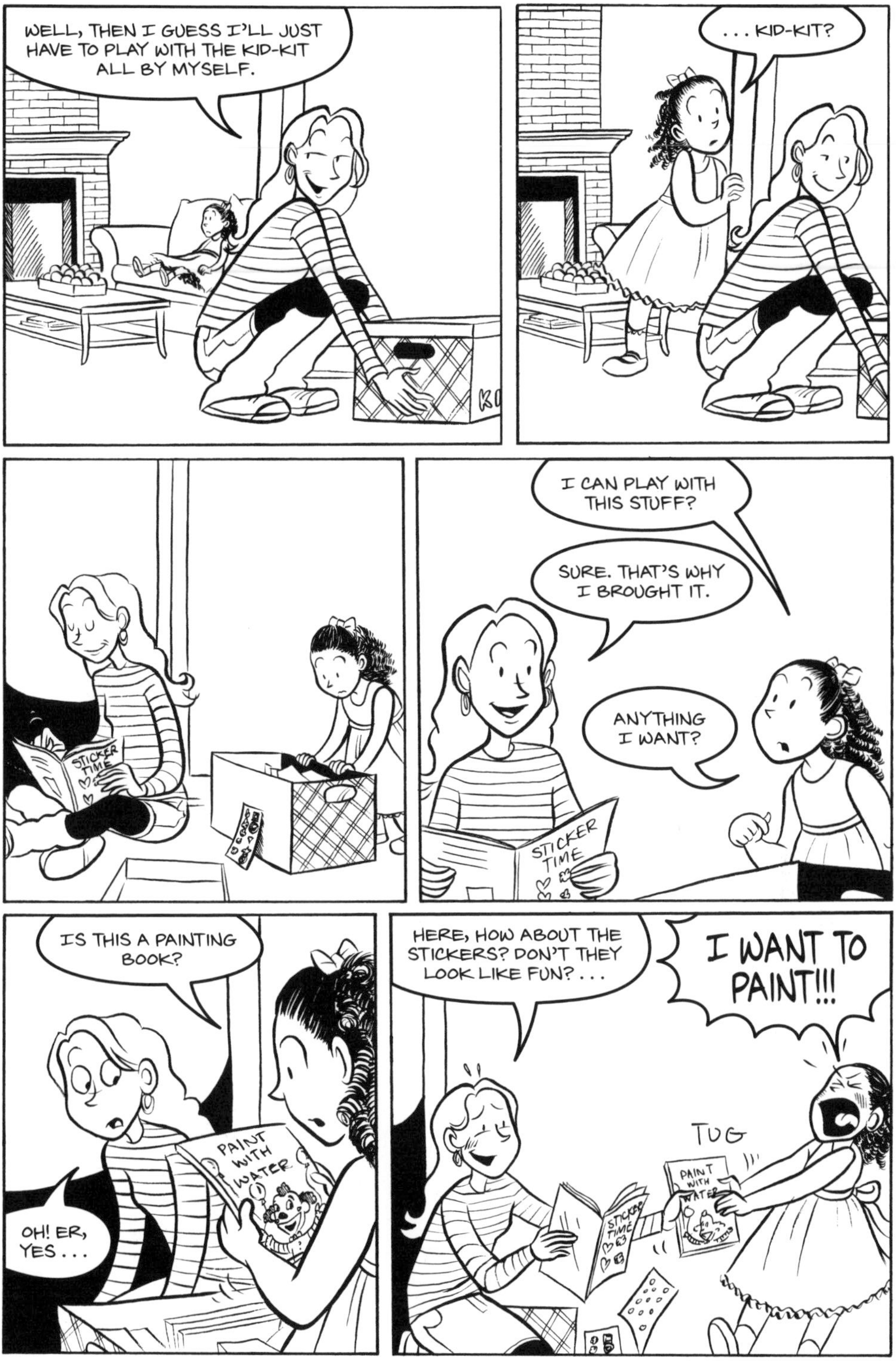
WELL, THEN I GUESS I'LL JUST HAVE TO PLAY WITH THE KID-KIT ALL BY MYSELF.
. . . KID-KIT?
STICKER TIME
I CAN PLAY WITH THIS STUFF?
SURE. THAT'S WHY I BROUGHT IT.
ANYTHING I WANT?
STICKER TIME
IS THIS A PAINTING BOOK?
PAINT WITH WATER
OH! ER, YES . . .
HERE, HOW ABOUT THE STICKERS? DON'T THEY LOOK LIKE FUN? . . .
I WANT TO PAINT!!!
TUG
STICKER TIME
PAINT WITH WATER

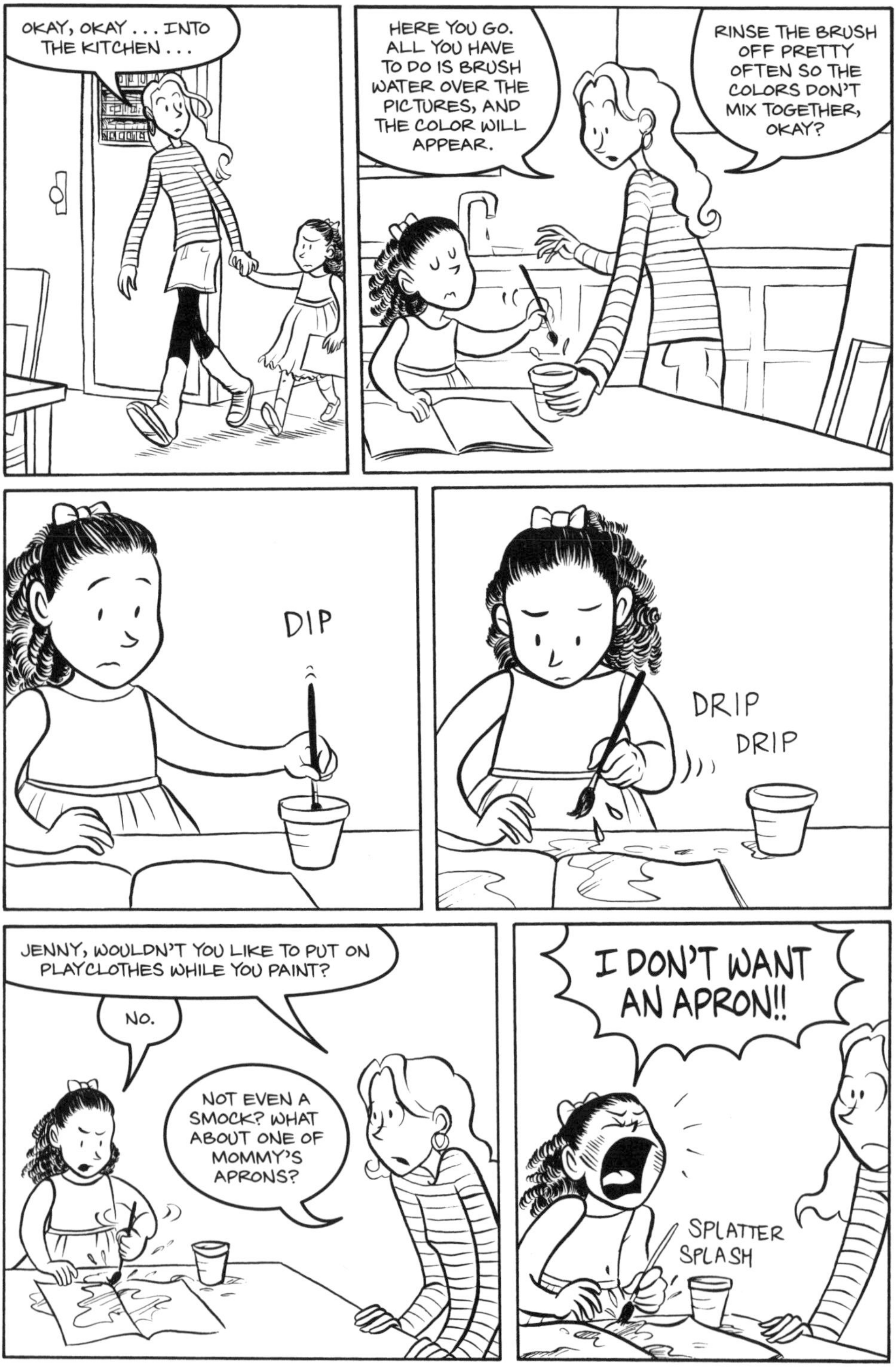
OKAY, OKAY . . . INTO THE KITCHEN . . .
HERE YOU GO. ALL YOU HAVE TO DO IS BRUSH WATER OVER THE PICTURES, AND THE COLOR WILL APPEAR.
RINSE THE BRUSH OFF PRETTY OFTEN SO THE COLORS DON'T MIX TOGETHER, OKAY?
DIP
DRIP
DRIP
JENNY, WOULDN'T YOU LIKE TO PUT ON PLAYCLOTHES WHILE YOU PAINT?
NO.
NOT EVEN A SMOCK? WHAT ABOUT ONE OF MOMMY'S APRONS?
I DON'T WANT AN APRON!!
SPLATTER
SPLASH

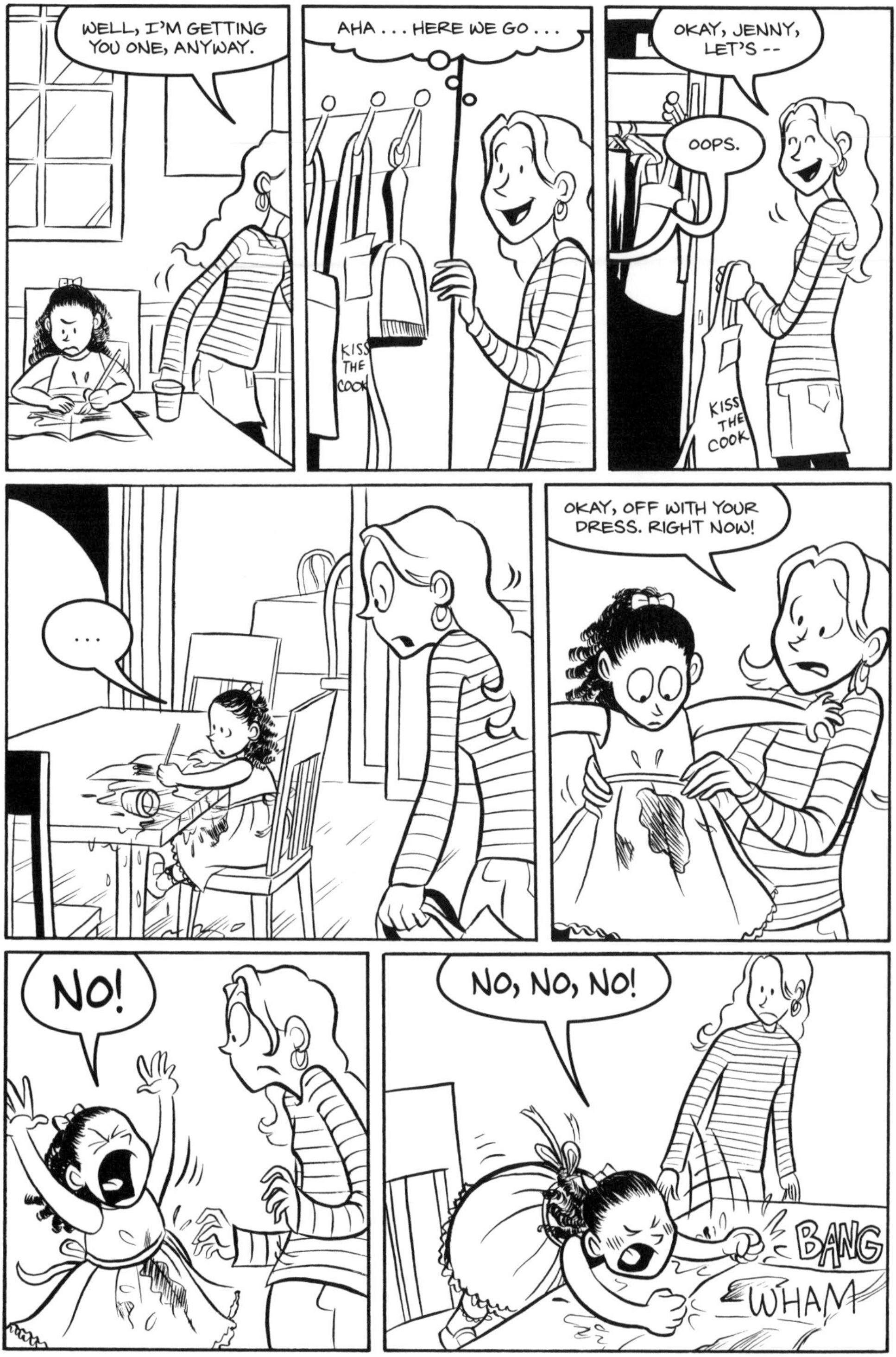
WELL, I'M GETTING YOU ONE, ANYWAY.
AHA . . . HERE WE GO . . .
KISS THE COOK
OKAY, JENNY, LET'S --
OOPS.
KISS THE COOK
. . .
OKAY, OFF WITH YOUR DRESS. RIGHT NOW!
NO!
NO, NO, NO!
BANG
WHAM

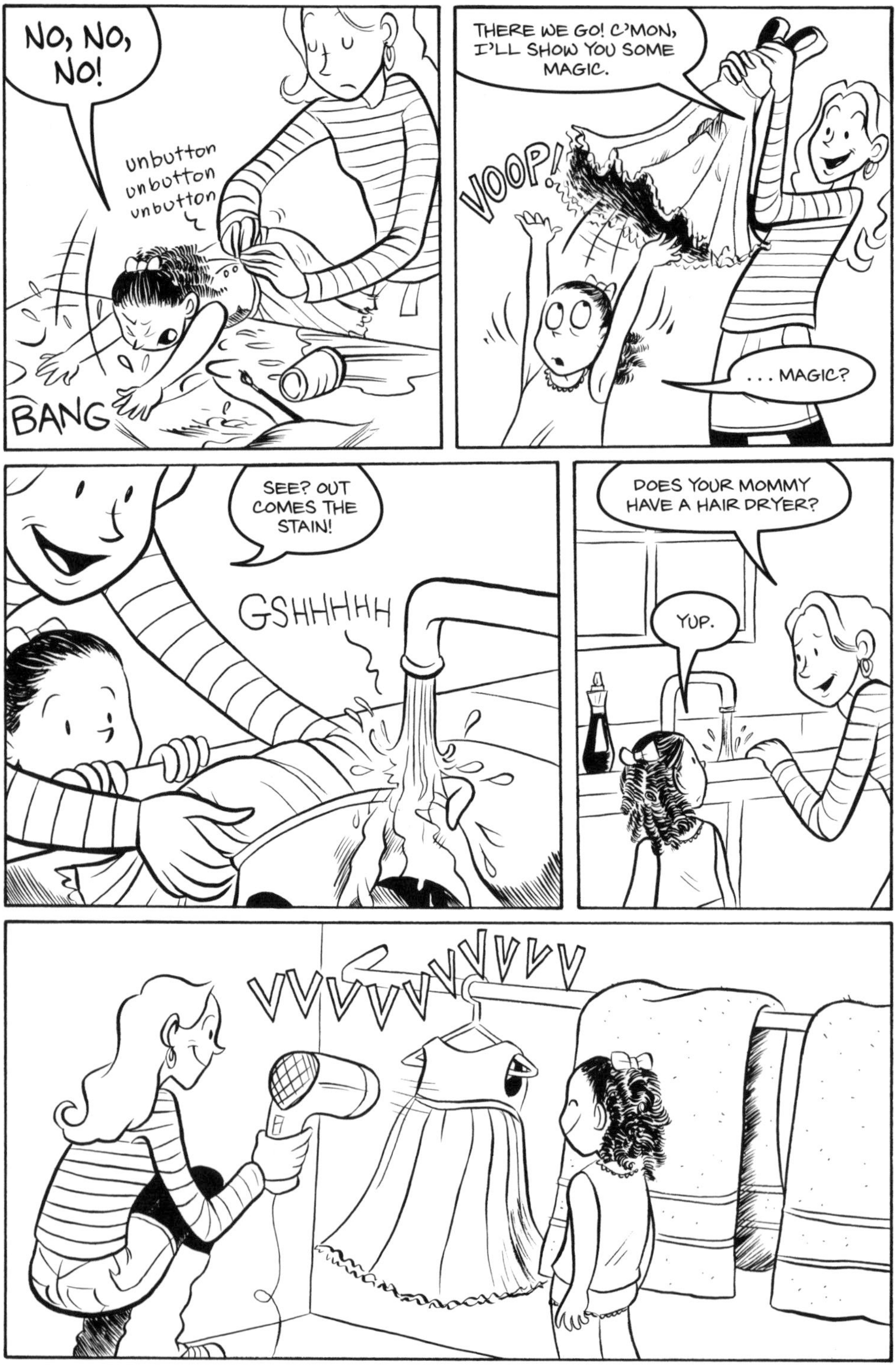
NO, NO, NO!
unbutton unbutton unbutton
BANG
THERE WE GO! C'MON, I'LL SHOW YOU SOME MAGIC.
VOOP!
. . . MAGIC?
SEE? OUT COMES THE STAIN!
GSHHHHH
DOES YOUR MOMMY HAVE A HAIR DRYER?
YUP.
VVVVVVVVVVV

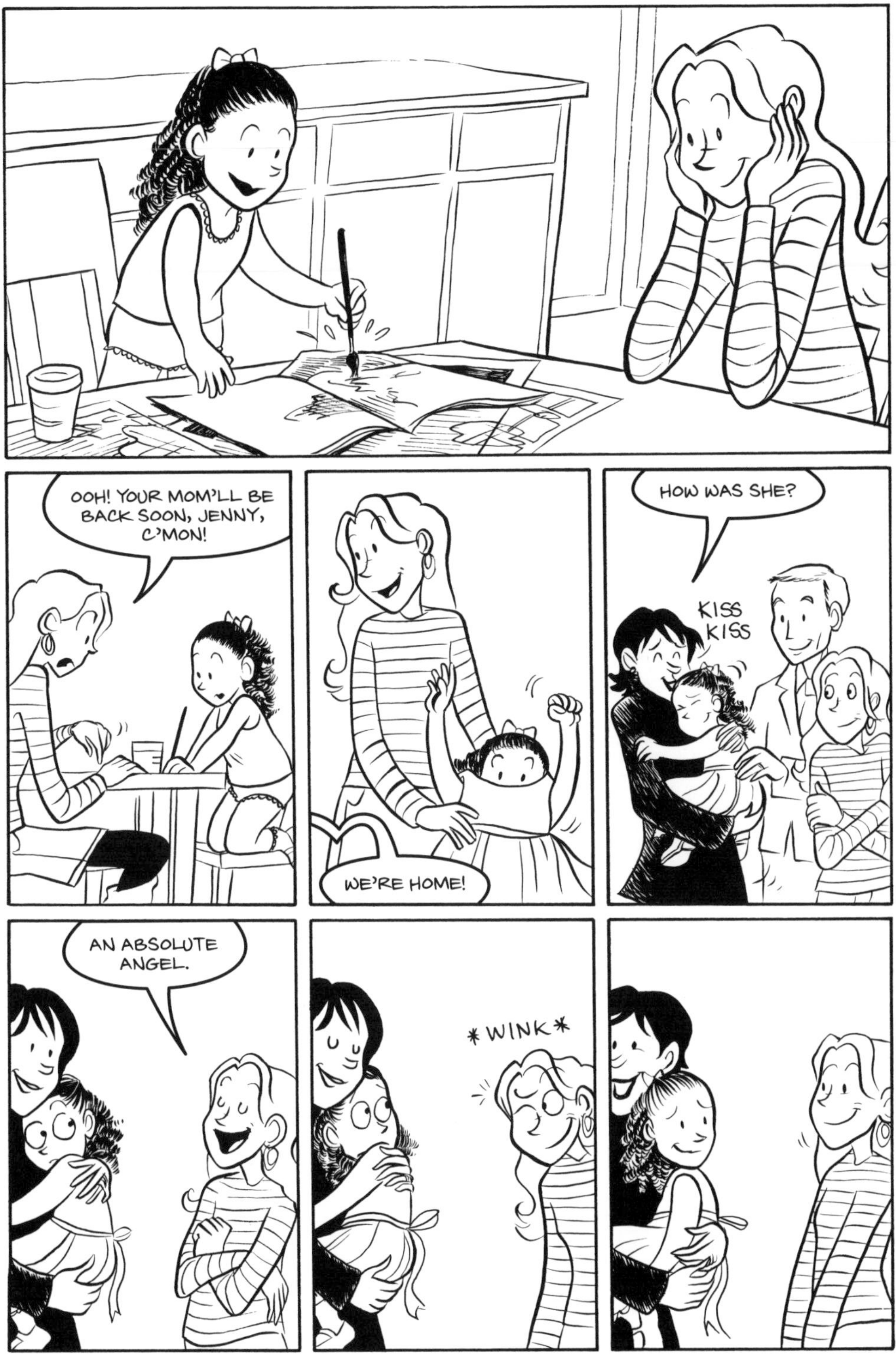
OOH! YOUR MOM'LL BE BACK SOON, JENNY, C'MON!
WE'RE HOME!
HOW WAS SHE?
KISS KISS
AN ABSOLUTE ANGEL.
WINK

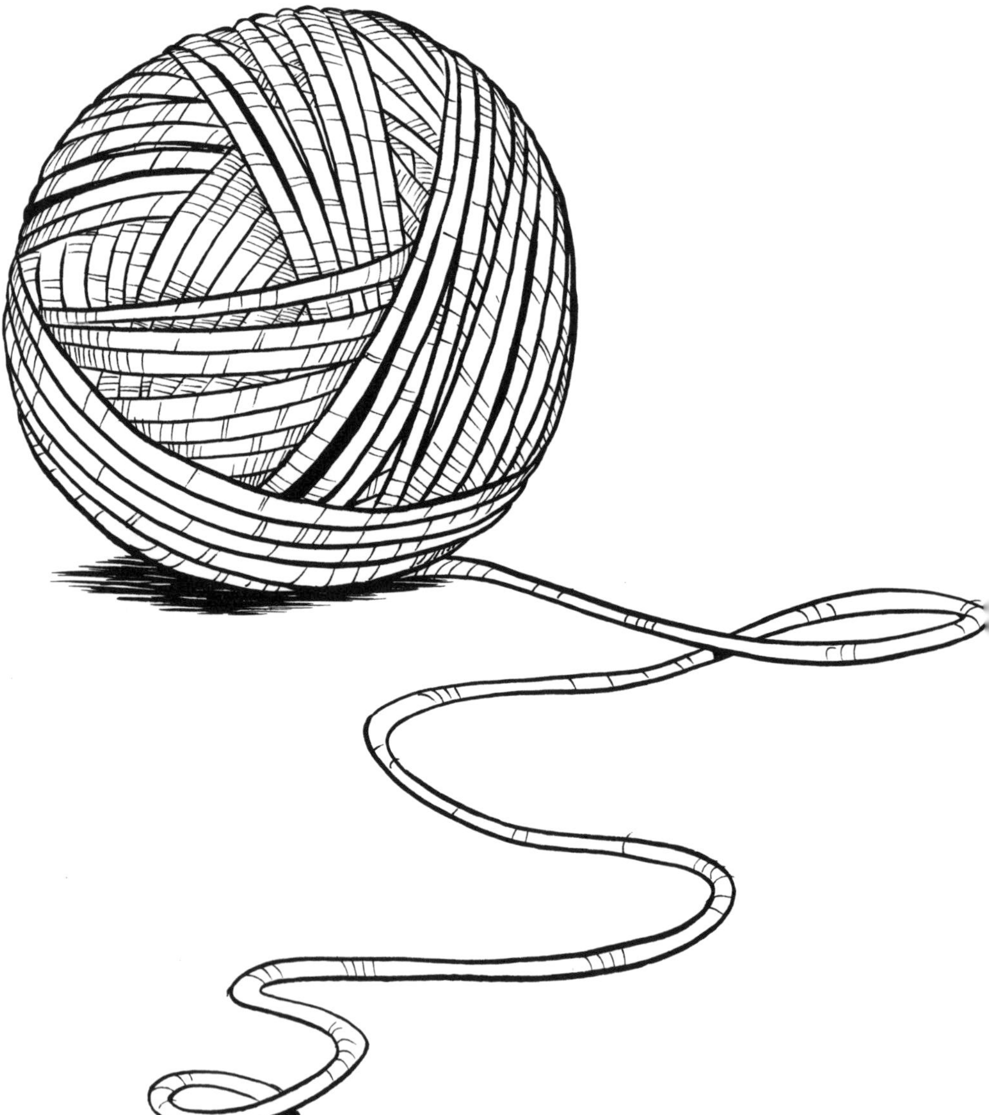

Chapter 7

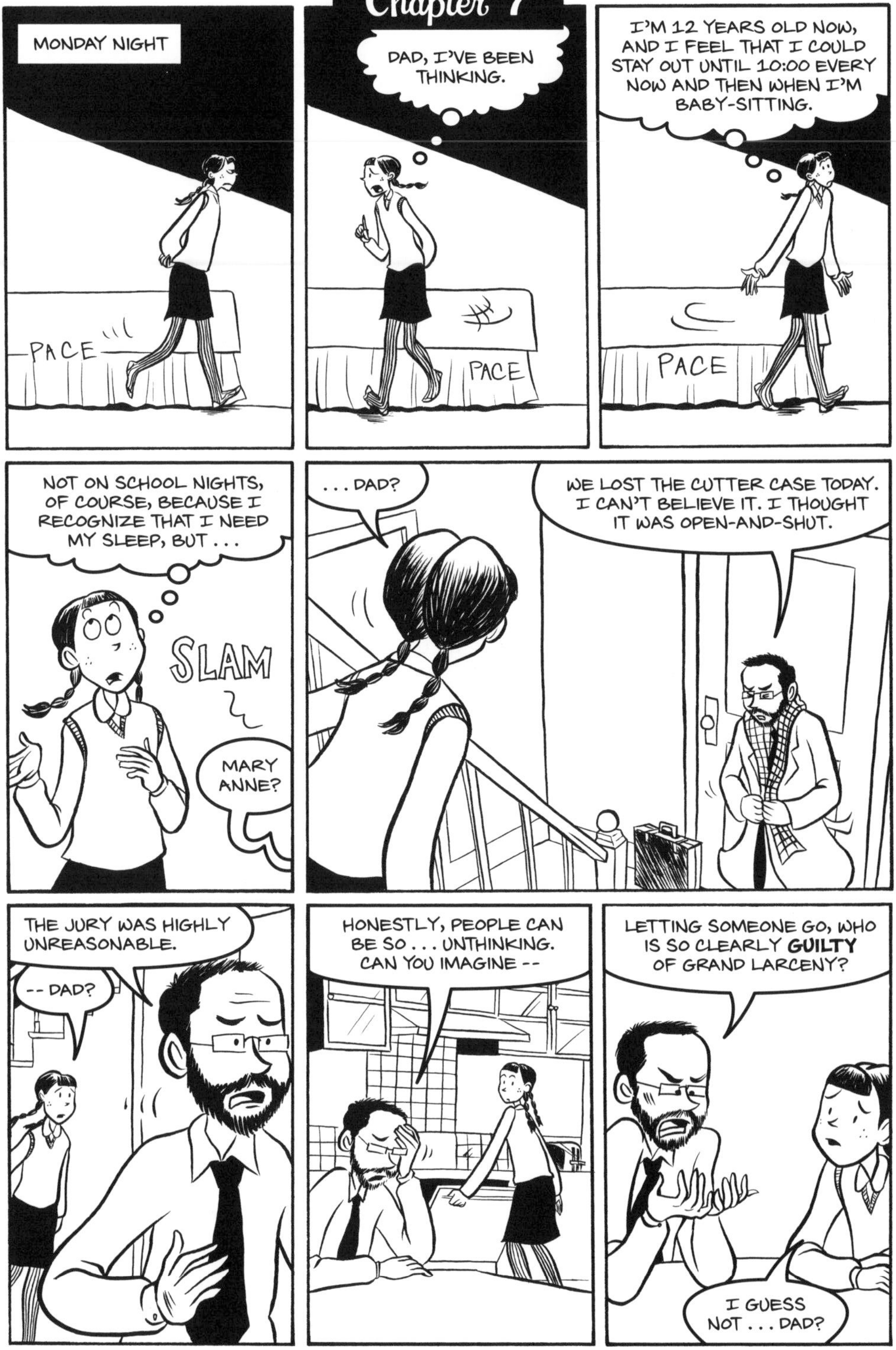
MONDAY NIGHT
DAD, I'VE BEEN THINKING.
PACE
PACE
I'M 12 YEARS OLD NOW, AND I FEEL THAT I COULD STAY OUT UNTIL 10:00 EVERY NOW AND THEN WHEN I'M BABY-SITTING.
PACE
NOT ON SCHOOL NIGHTS, OF COURSE, BECAUSE I RECOGNIZE THAT I NEED MY SLEEP, BUT . . .
SLAM
MARY ANNE?
. . . DAD?
WE LOST THE CUTTER CASE TODAY. I CAN'T BELIEVE IT. I THOUGHT IT WAS OPEN-AND-SHUT.
THE JURY WAS HIGHLY UNREASONABLE.
-- DAD?
HONESTLY, PEOPLE CAN BE SO . . . UNTHINKING. CAN YOU IMAGINE --
LETTING SOMEONE GO, WHO IS SO CLEARLY **GUILTY** OF GRAND LARCENY?
I GUESS NOT . . . DAD?

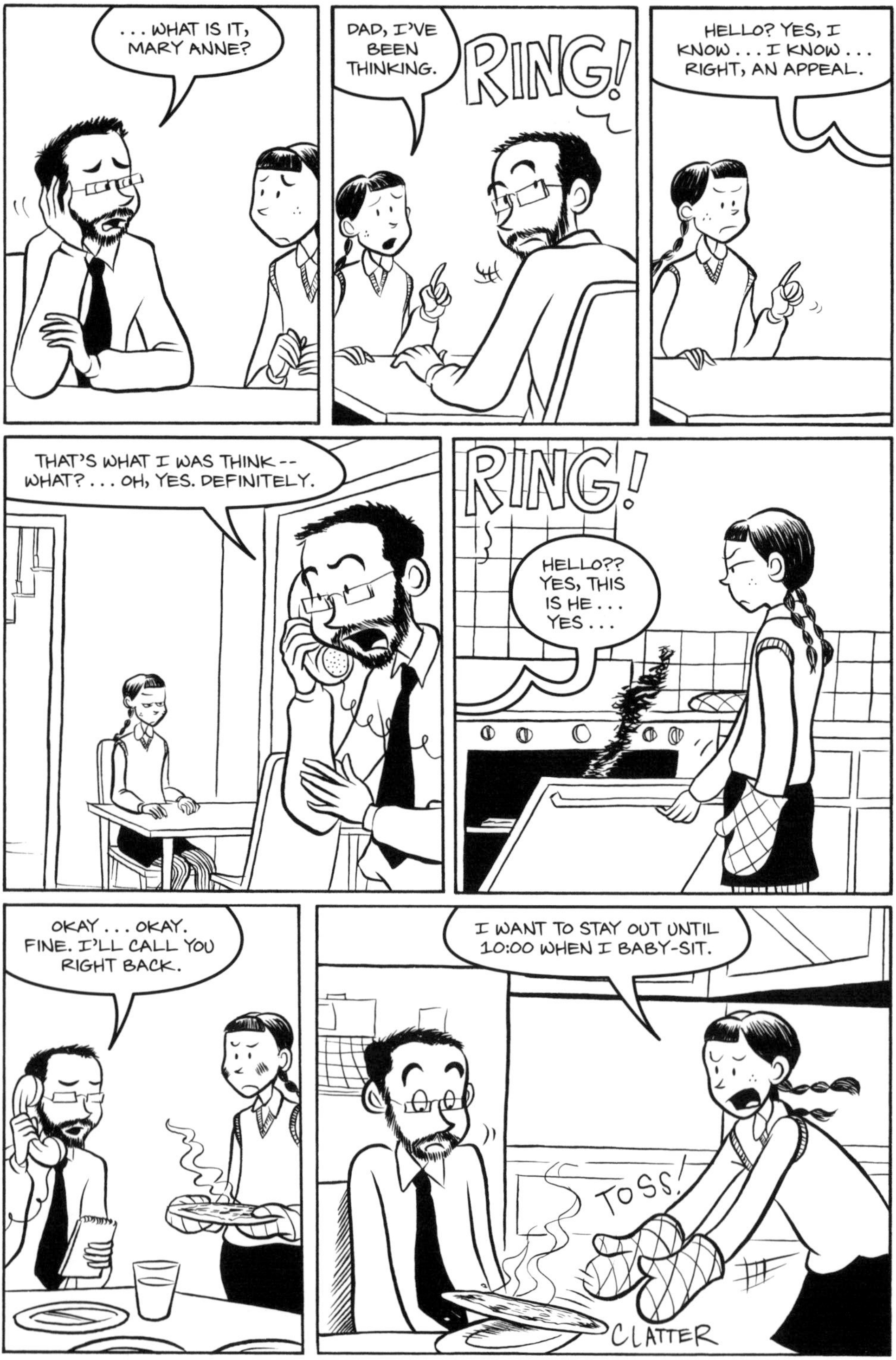
. . . WHAT IS IT, MARY ANNE?
DAD, I'VE BEEN THINKING.
RING!
HELLO? YES, I KNOW . . . I KNOW . . . RIGHT, AN APPEAL.
THAT'S WHAT I WAS THINK-- --WHAT? . . . OH, YES. DEFINITELY.
RING!
HELLO?? YES, THIS IS HE . . . YES . . .
OKAY . . . OKAY. FINE. I'LL CALL YOU RIGHT BACK.
I WANT TO STAY OUT UNTIL 10:00 WHEN I BABY-SIT.
TOSS!
CLATTER

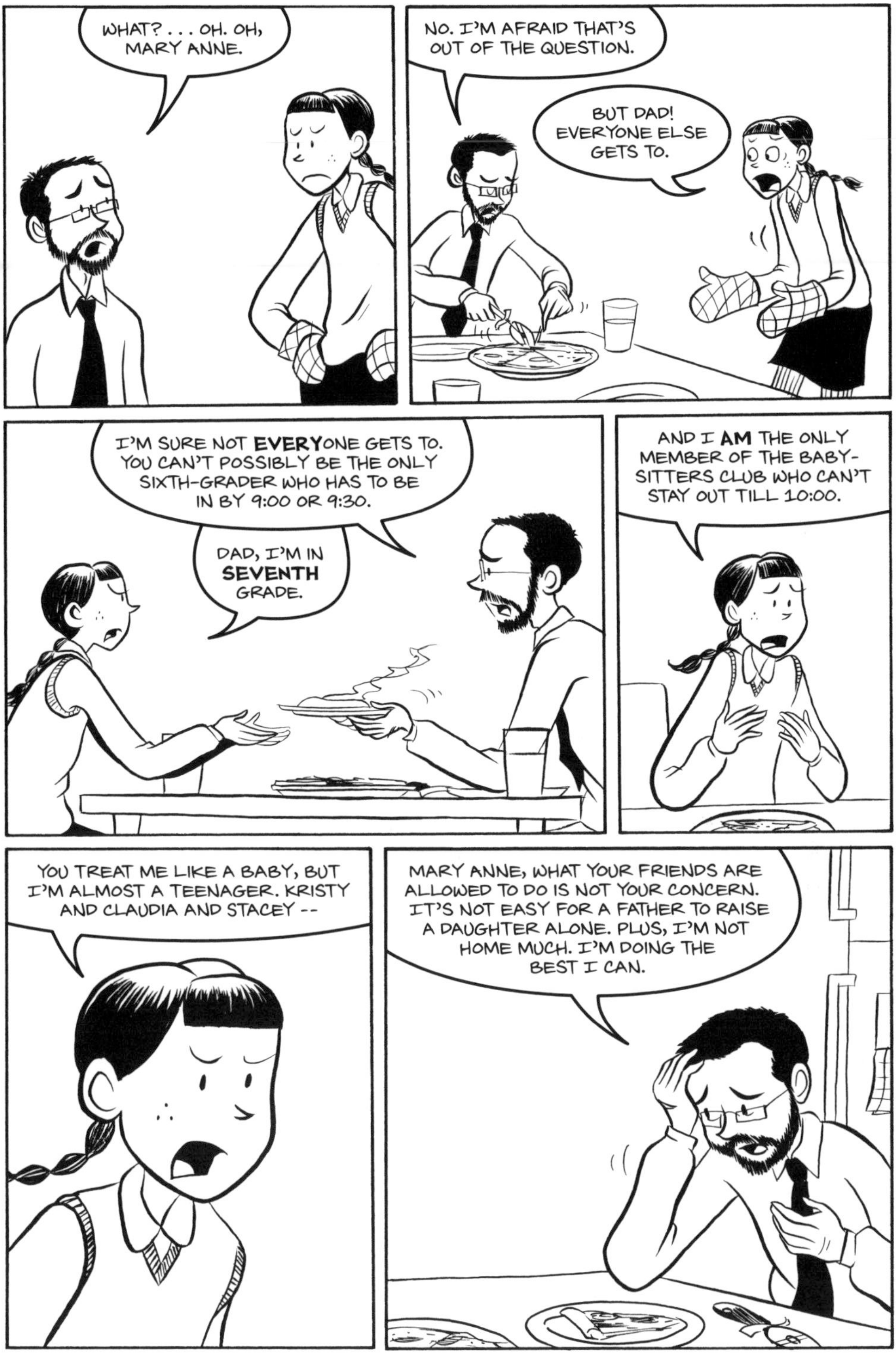
WHAT? . . . OH. OH, MARY ANNE.
NO. I'M AFRAID THAT'S OUT OF THE QUESTION.
BUT DAD! EVERYONE ELSE GETS TO.
I'M SURE NOT **EVERY**ONE GETS TO. YOU CAN'T POSSIBLY BE THE ONLY SIXTH-GRADER WHO HAS TO BE IN BY 9:00 OR 9:30.
DAD, I'M IN **SEVENTH** GRADE.
AND I **AM** THE ONLY MEMBER OF THE BABY-SITTERS CLUB WHO CAN'T STAY OUT TILL 10:00.
YOU TREAT ME LIKE A BABY, BUT I'M ALMOST A TEENAGER. KRISTY AND CLAUDIA AND STACEY --
MARY ANNE, WHAT YOUR FRIENDS ARE ALLOWED TO DO IS NOT YOUR CONCERN. IT'S NOT EASY FOR A FATHER TO RAISE A DAUGHTER ALONE. PLUS, I'M NOT HOME MUCH. I'M DOING THE BEST I CAN.

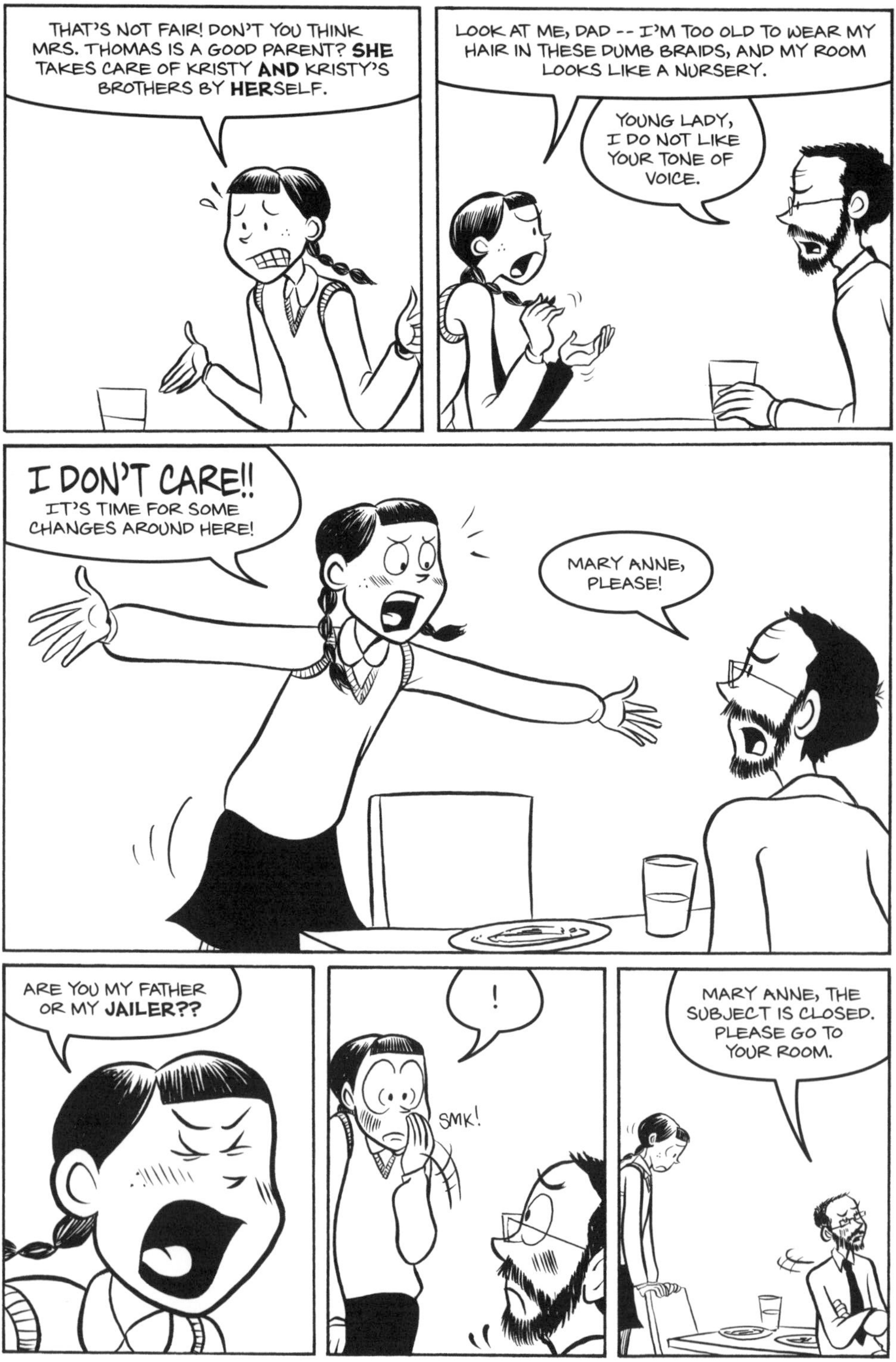
THAT'S NOT FAIR! DON'T YOU THINK MRS. THOMAS IS A GOOD PARENT? **SHE** TAKES CARE OF KRISTY **AND** KRISTY'S BROTHERS BY **HER**SELF.
LOOK AT ME, DAD -- I'M TOO OLD TO WEAR MY HAIR IN THESE DUMB BRAIDS, AND MY ROOM LOOKS LIKE A NURSERY.
YOUNG LADY, I DO NOT LIKE YOUR TONE OF VOICE.
I DON'T CARE!! IT'S TIME FOR SOME CHANGES AROUND HERE!
MARY ANNE, PLEASE!
ARE YOU MY FATHER OR MY **JAILER??**
!
SMK!
MARY ANNE, THE SUBJECT IS CLOSED. PLEASE GO TO YOUR ROOM.

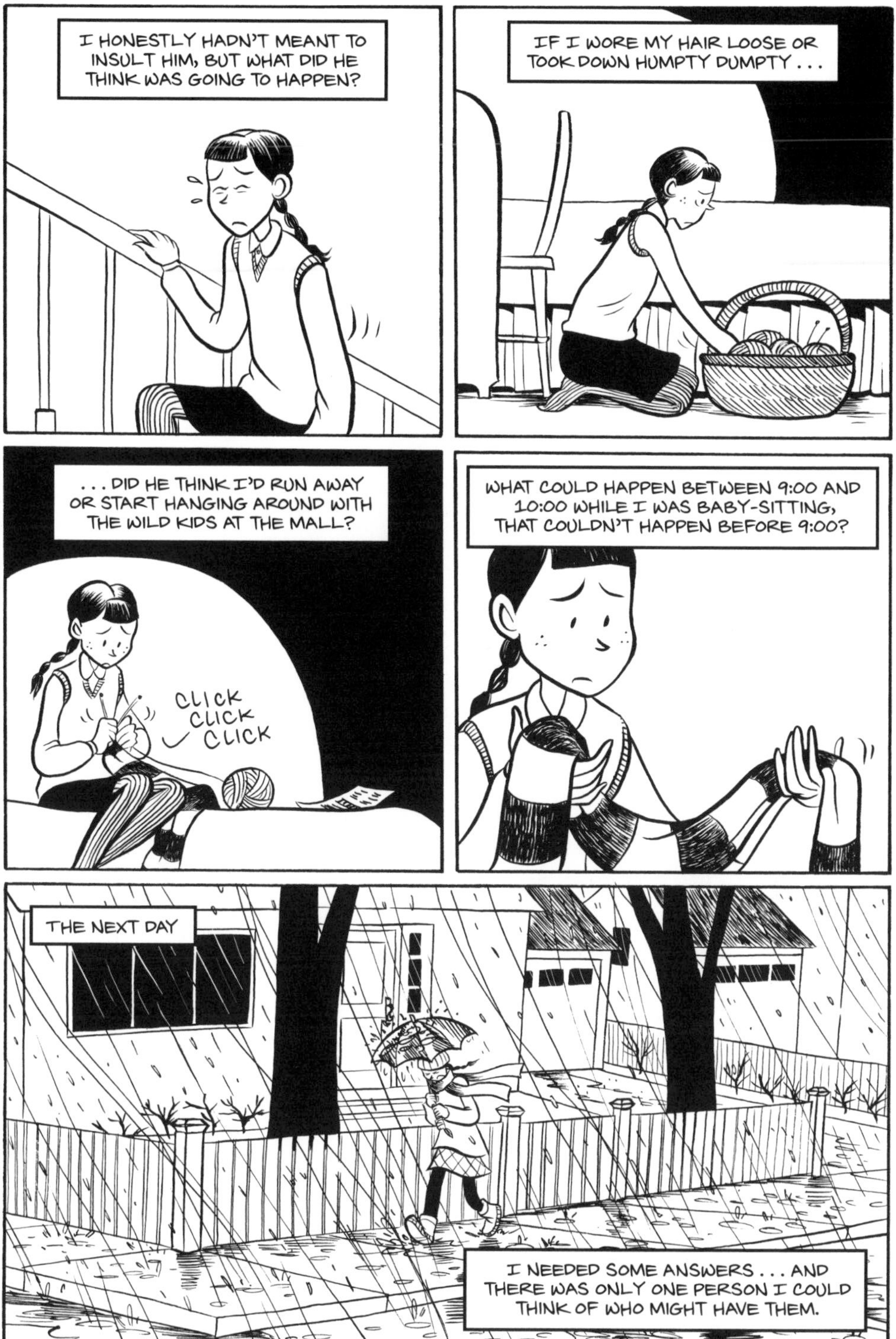
I HONESTLY HADN'T MEANT TO INSULT HIM, BUT WHAT DID HE THINK WAS GOING TO HAPPEN?
IF I WORE MY HAIR LOOSE OR TOOK DOWN HUMPTY DUMPTY . . .
. . . DID HE THINK I'D RUN AWAY OR START HANGING AROUND WITH THE WILD KIDS AT THE MALL?
CLICK CLICK CLICK
WHAT COULD HAPPEN BETWEEN 9:00 AND 10:00 WHILE I WAS BABY-SITTING, THAT COULDN'T HAPPEN BEFORE 9:00?
THE NEXT DAY
I NEEDED SOME ANSWERS . . . AND THERE WAS ONLY ONE PERSON I COULD THINK OF WHO MIGHT HAVE THEM.

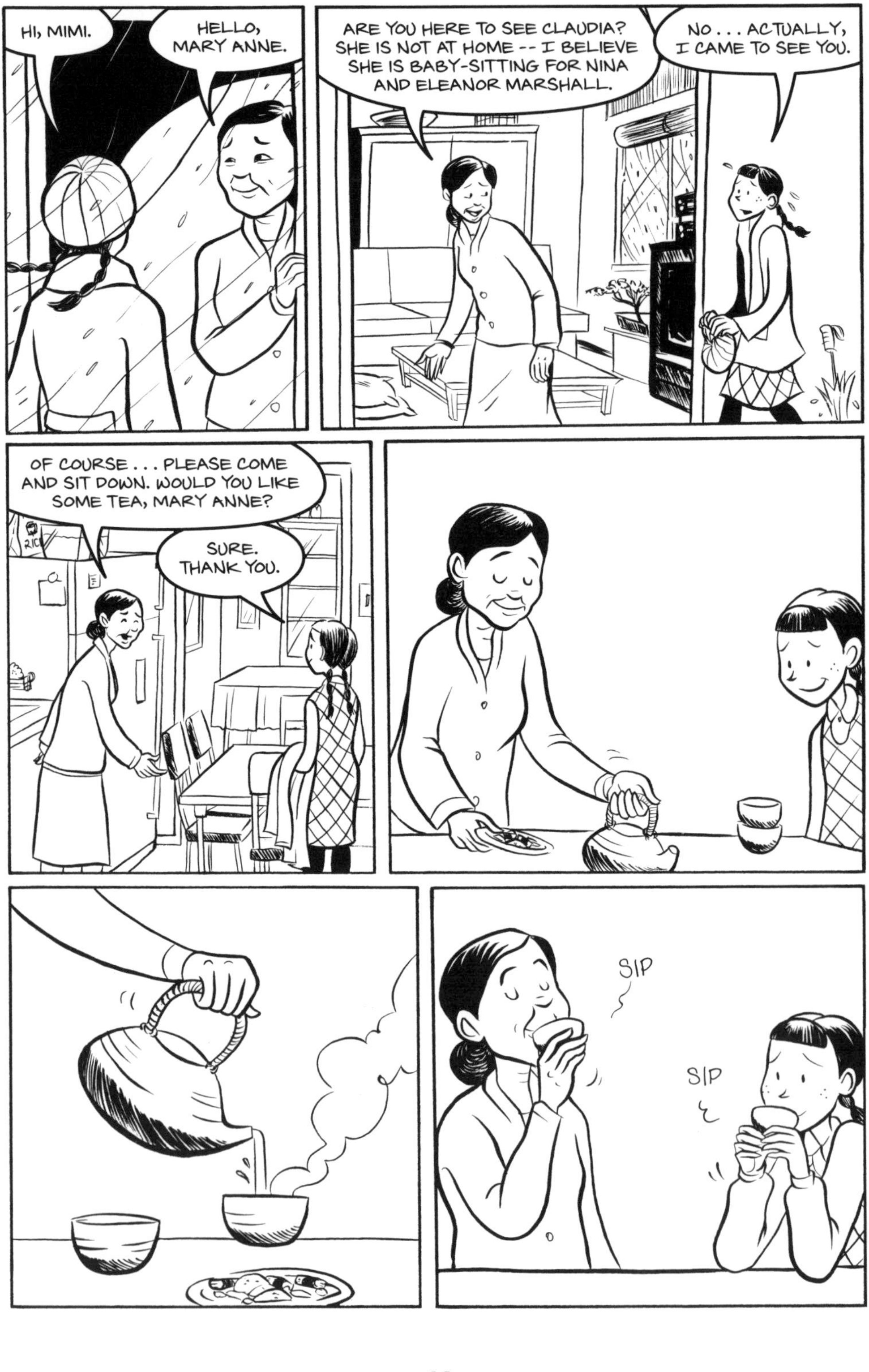
HI, MIMI.
HELLO, MARY ANNE.
ARE YOU HERE TO SEE CLAUDIA? SHE IS NOT AT HOME -- I BELIEVE SHE IS BABY-SITTING FOR NINA AND ELEANOR MARSHALL.
NO . . . ACTUALLY, I CAME TO SEE YOU.
OF COURSE . . . PLEASE COME AND SIT DOWN. WOULD YOU LIKE SOME TEA, MARY ANNE?
SURE. THANK YOU.
SIP
SIP

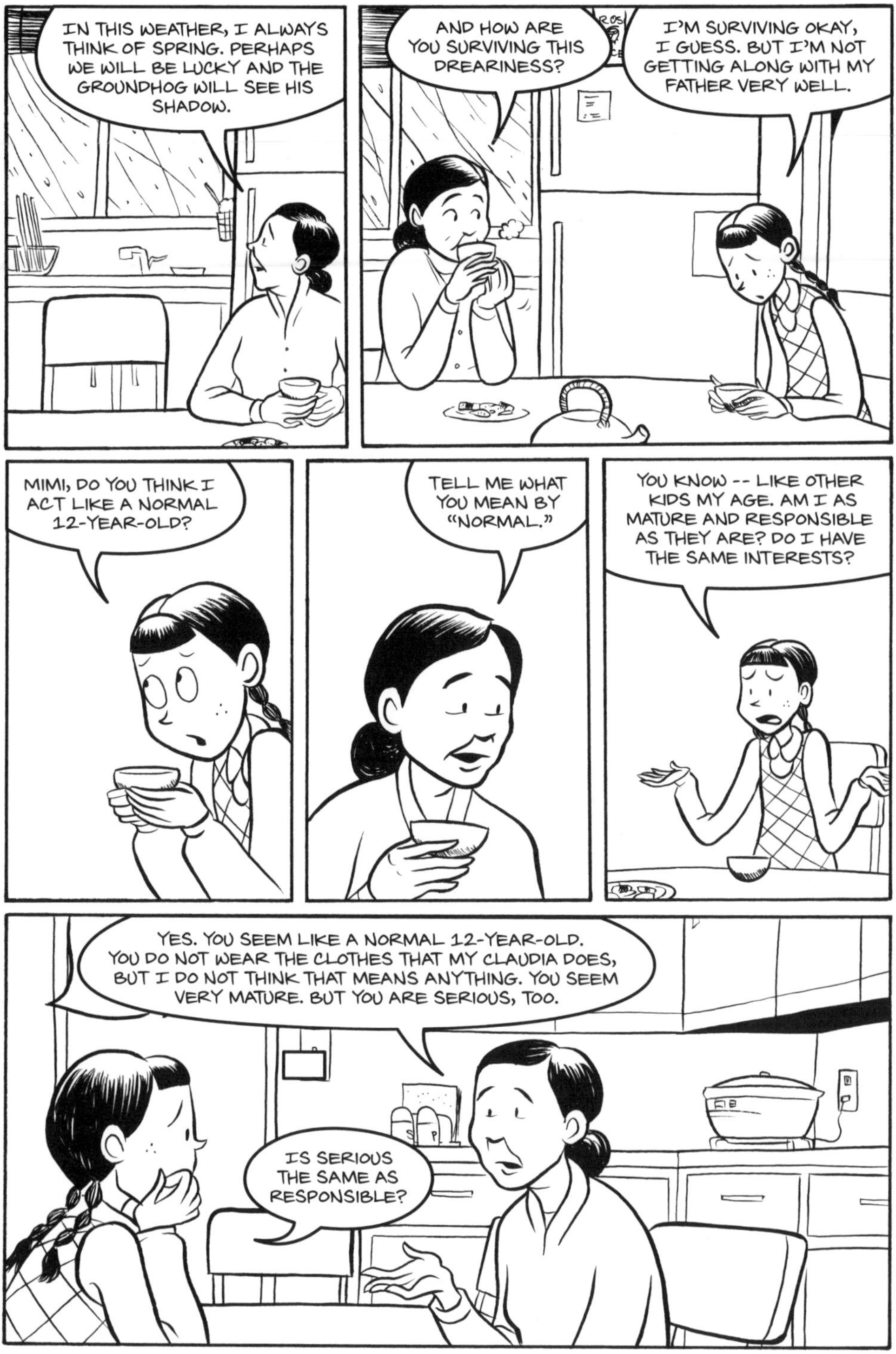
IN THIS WEATHER, I ALWAYS THINK OF SPRING. PERHAPS WE WILL BE LUCKY AND THE GROUNDHOG WILL SEE HIS SHADOW.
AND HOW ARE YOU SURVIVING THIS DREARINESS?
I'M SURVIVING OKAY, I GUESS. BUT I'M NOT GETTING ALONG WITH MY FATHER VERY WELL.
MIMI, DO YOU THINK I ACT LIKE A NORMAL 12-YEAR-OLD?
TELL ME WHAT YOU MEAN BY "NORMAL."
YOU KNOW -- LIKE OTHER KIDS MY AGE. AM I AS MATURE AND RESPONSIBLE AS THEY ARE? DO I HAVE THE SAME INTERESTS?
YES. YOU SEEM LIKE A NORMAL 12-YEAR-OLD. YOU DO NOT WEAR THE CLOTHES THAT MY CLAUDIA DOES, BUT I DO NOT THINK THAT MEANS ANYTHING. YOU SEEM VERY MATURE. BUT YOU ARE SERIOUS, TOO.
IS SERIOUS THE SAME AS RESPONSIBLE?

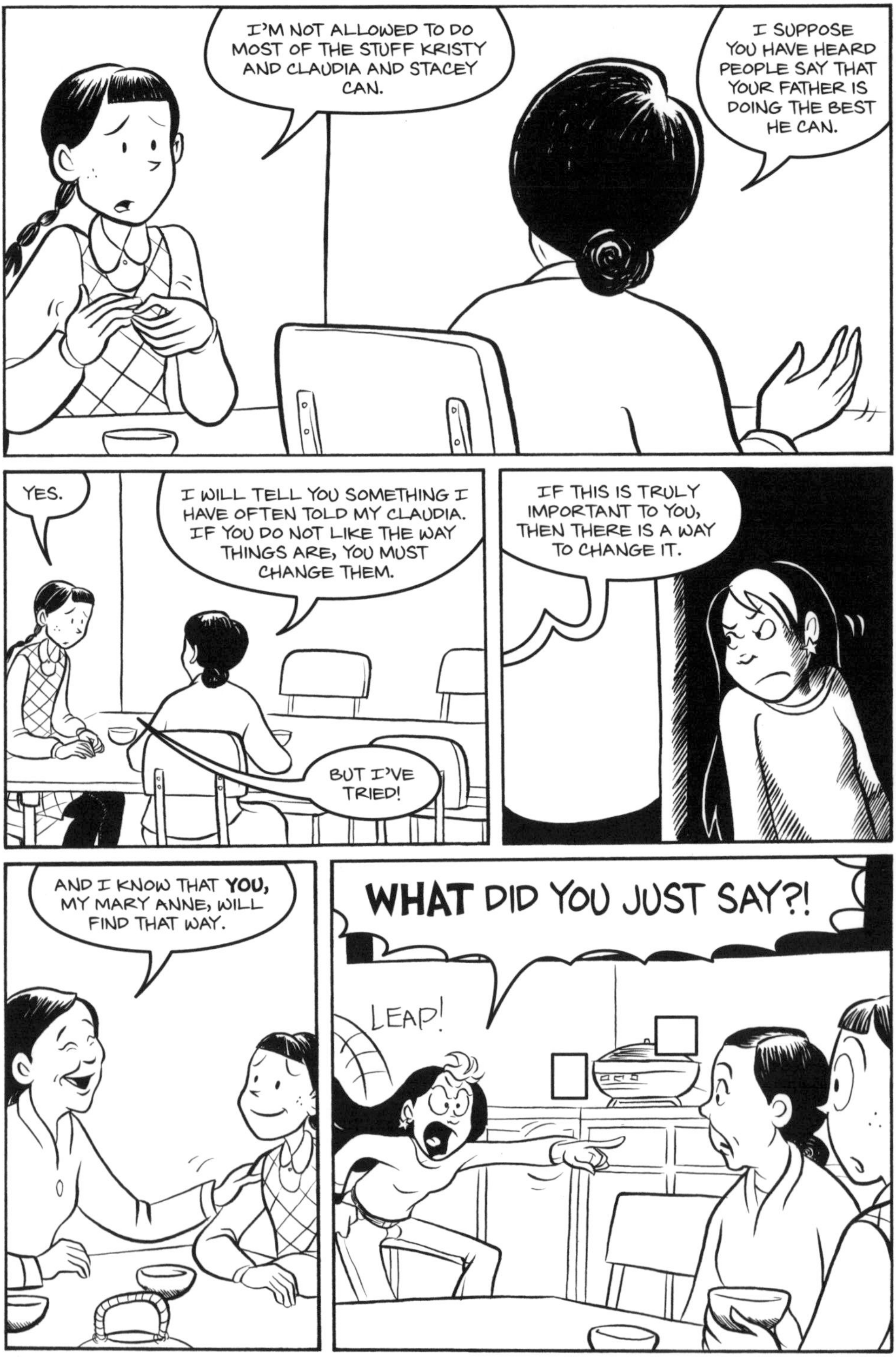
I'M NOT ALLOWED TO DO MOST OF THE STUFF KRISTY AND CLAUDIA AND STACEY CAN.
I SUPPOSE YOU HAVE HEARD PEOPLE SAY THAT YOUR FATHER IS DOING THE BEST HE CAN.
YES.
I WILL TELL YOU SOMETHING I HAVE OFTEN TOLD MY CLAUDIA. IF YOU DO NOT LIKE THE WAY THINGS ARE, YOU MUST CHANGE THEM.
BUT I'VE TRIED!
IF THIS IS TRULY IMPORTANT TO YOU, THEN THERE IS A WAY TO CHANGE IT.
AND I KNOW THAT **YOU**, MY MARY ANNE, WILL FIND THAT WAY.
WHAT DID YOU JUST SAY?!
LEAP!

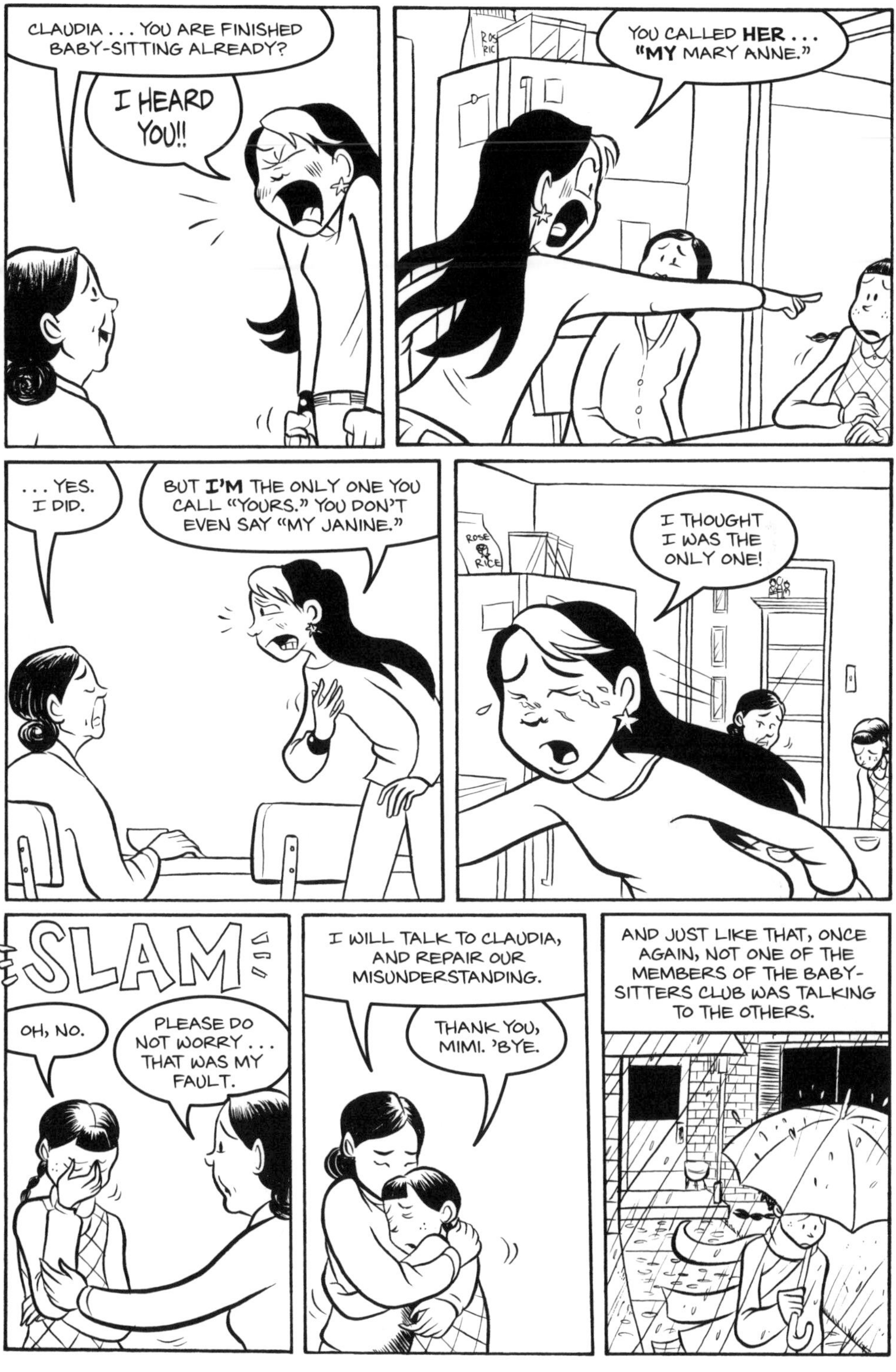
CLAUDIA . . . YOU ARE FINISHED BABY-SITTING ALREADY?
I HEARD YOU!!
YOU CALLED **HER** . . . **"MY** MARY ANNE."
. . . YES. I DID.
BUT **I'M** THE ONLY ONE YOU CALL "YOURS." YOU DON'T EVEN SAY "MY JANINE."
I THOUGHT I WAS THE ONLY ONE!
SLAM
OH, NO.
PLEASE DO NOT WORRY . . . THAT WAS MY FAULT.
I WILL TALK TO CLAUDIA, AND REPAIR OUR MISUNDERSTANDING.
THANK YOU, MIMI. 'BYE.
AND JUST LIKE THAT, ONCE AGAIN, NOT ONE OF THE MEMBERS OF THE BABY-SITTERS CLUB WAS TALKING TO THE OTHERS.

Teusday, January 20

I am so made! I know this
notebook is for writing our siting jobs
so we can keep track of club problems.
Well, this is not a sitting job, but
I have a club probleme. Her name
is Mary Ame Spier or as she is
otherwise known MY MARY ANNE.
Where does Mary Anne get off being
so chummy with Mimi? It isn't
fair. It's one thing for Mimi to
help her with her ~~niting~~ knitting
but today they were sharing tea
in the special cups and Mimi
called her My Mary Ame.
NO FAIR. So there.
                        * Claudia *

Chapter 8

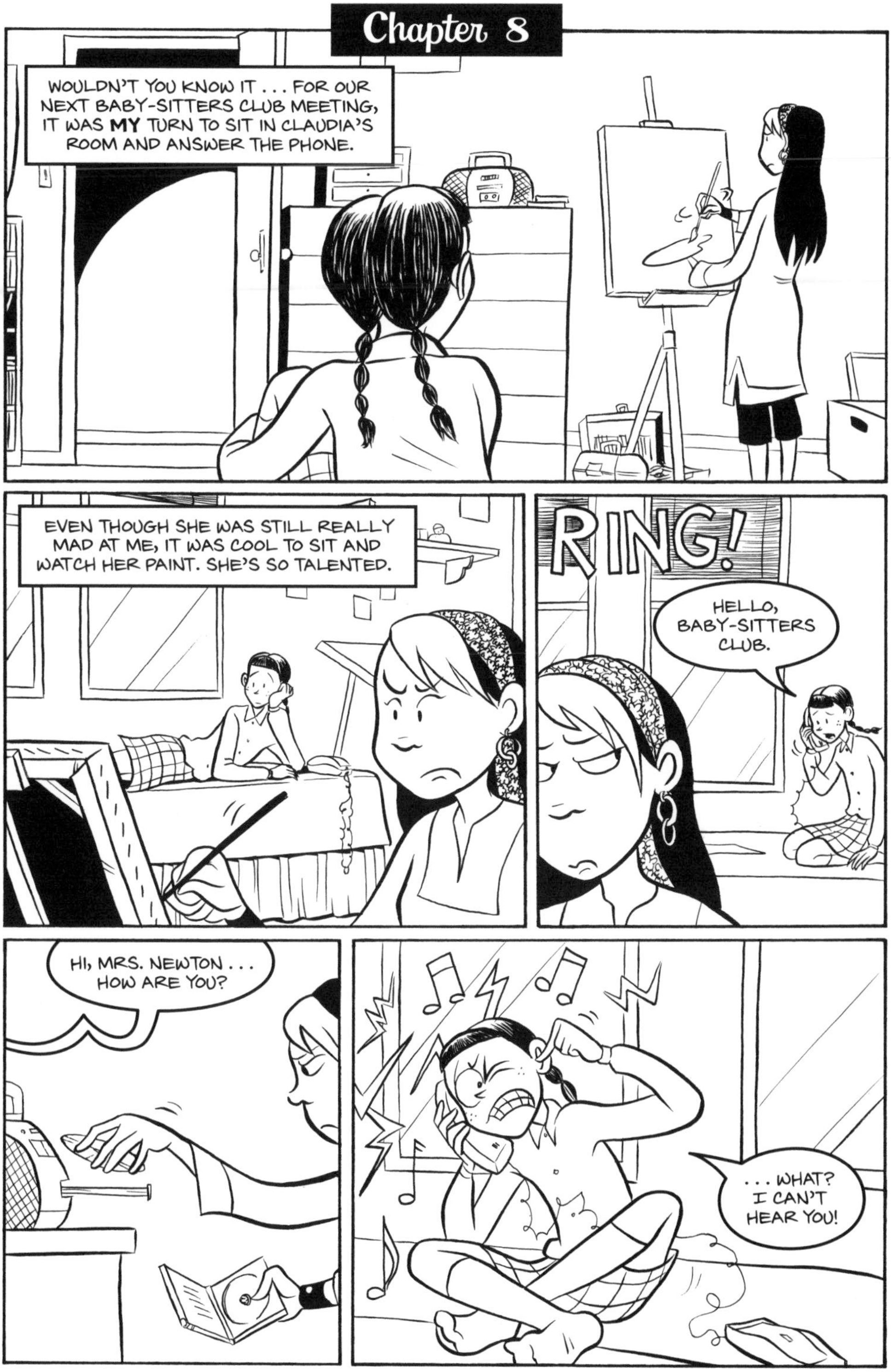

WOULDN'T YOU KNOW IT . . . FOR OUR NEXT BABY-SITTERS CLUB MEETING, IT WAS **MY** TURN TO SIT IN CLAUDIA'S ROOM AND ANSWER THE PHONE.
EVEN THOUGH SHE WAS STILL REALLY MAD AT ME, IT WAS COOL TO SIT AND WATCH HER PAINT. SHE'S SO TALENTED.
RING!
HELLO, BABY-SITTERS CLUB.
HI, MRS. NEWTON . . . HOW ARE YOU?
. . . WHAT? I CAN'T HEAR YOU!

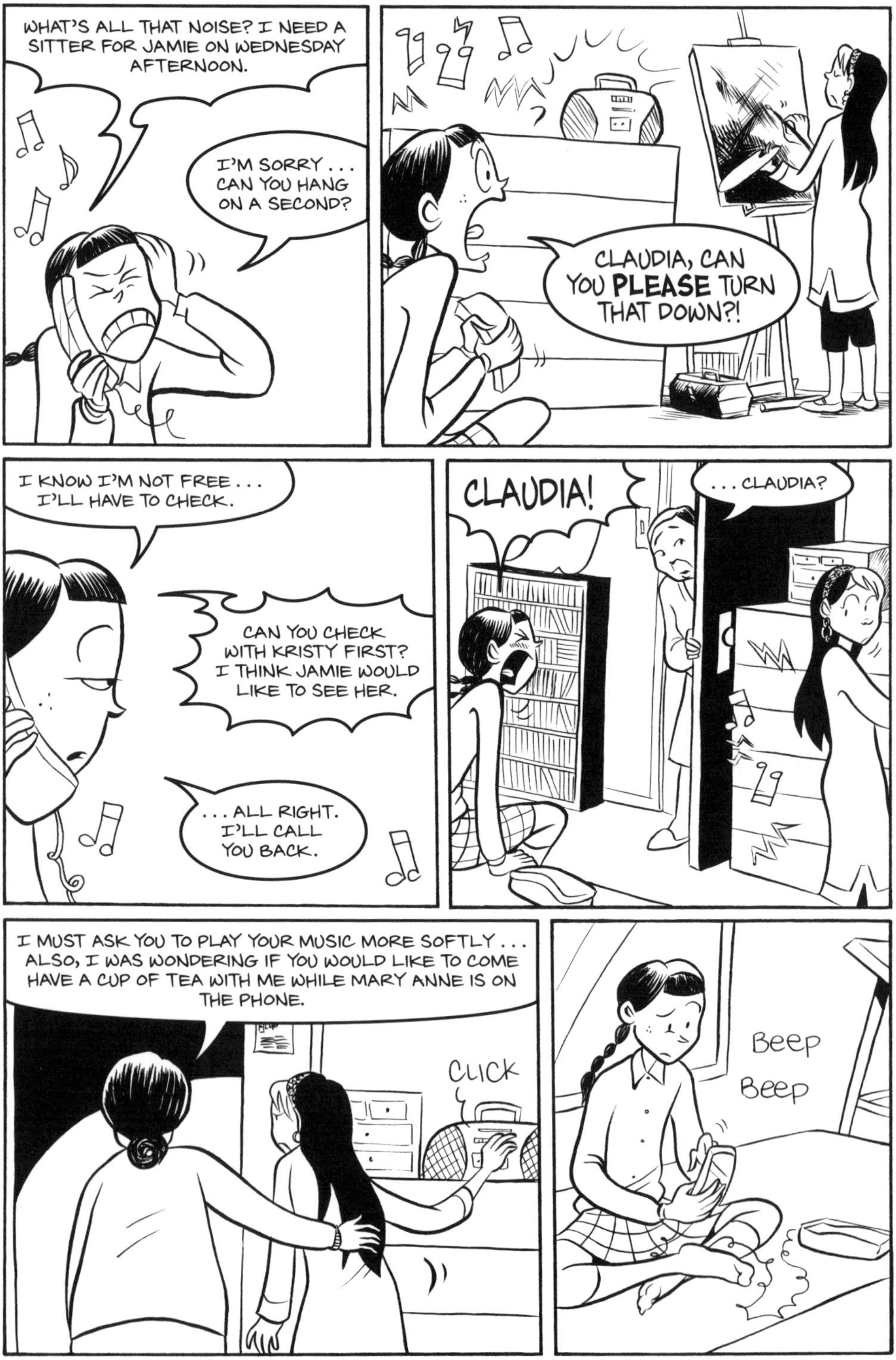
WHAT'S ALL THAT NOISE? I NEED A SITTER FOR JAMIE ON WEDNESDAY AFTERNOON.
I'M SORRY . . . CAN YOU HANG ON A SECOND?
CLAUDIA, CAN YOU **PLEASE** TURN THAT DOWN?!
I KNOW I'M NOT FREE . . . I'LL HAVE TO CHECK.
CAN YOU CHECK WITH KRISTY FIRST? I THINK JAMIE WOULD LIKE TO SEE HER.
. . . ALL RIGHT. I'LL CALL YOU BACK.
CLAUDIA!
. . . CLAUDIA?
I MUST ASK YOU TO PLAY YOUR MUSIC MORE SOFTLY . . . ALSO, I WAS WONDERING IF YOU WOULD LIKE TO COME HAVE A CUP OF TEA WITH ME WHILE MARY ANNE IS ON THE PHONE.
CLICK
Beep
Beep

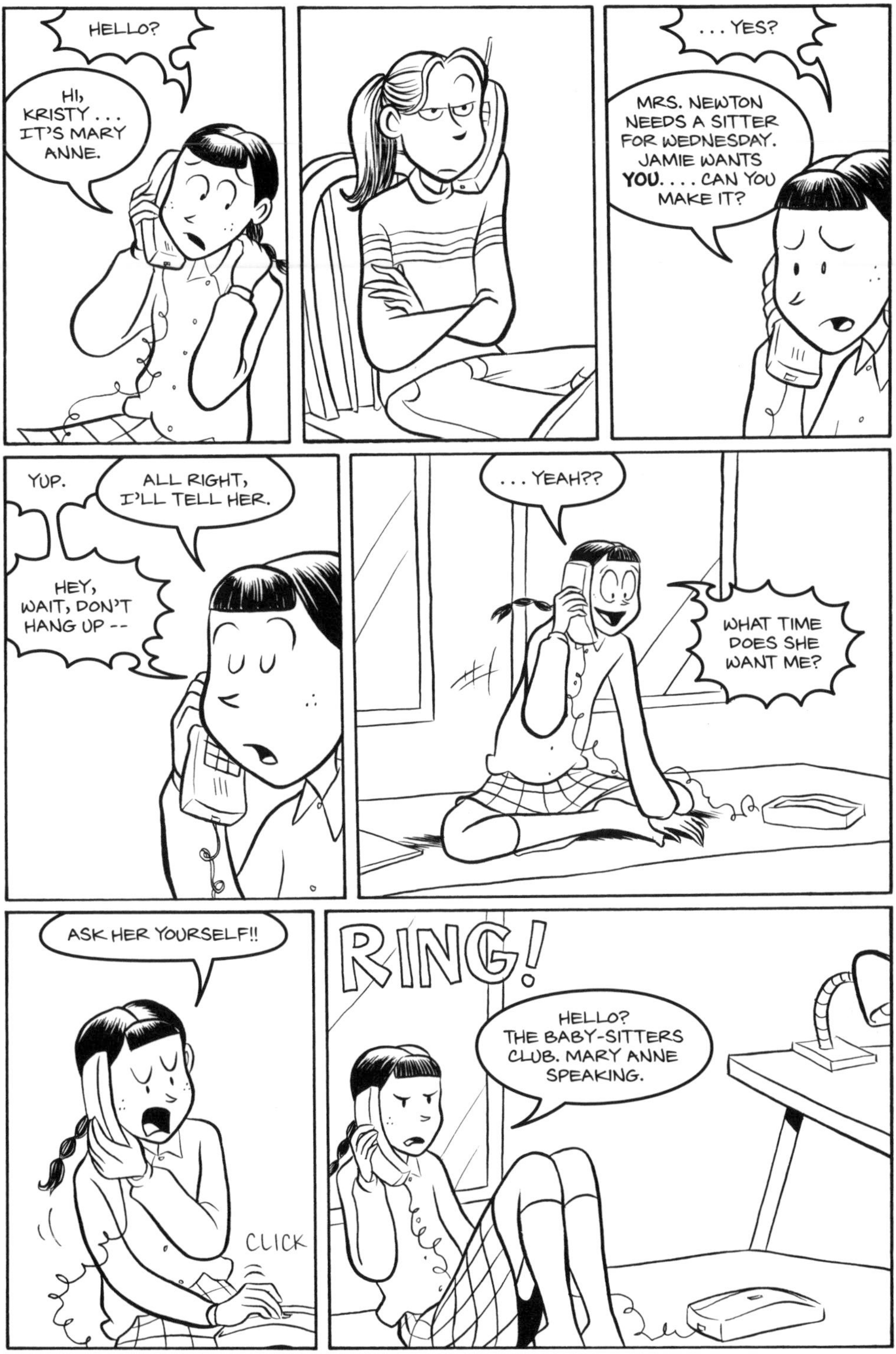
HELLO?
HI, KRISTY . . . IT'S MARY ANNE.
. . . YES?
MRS. NEWTON NEEDS A SITTER FOR WEDNESDAY. JAMIE WANTS **YOU**. . . . CAN YOU MAKE IT?
YUP.
ALL RIGHT, I'LL TELL HER.
HEY, WAIT, DON'T HANG UP --
. . . YEAH??
WHAT TIME DOES SHE WANT ME?
ASK HER YOURSELF!!
CLICK
RING!
HELLO? THE BABY-SITTERS CLUB. MARY ANNE SPEAKING.

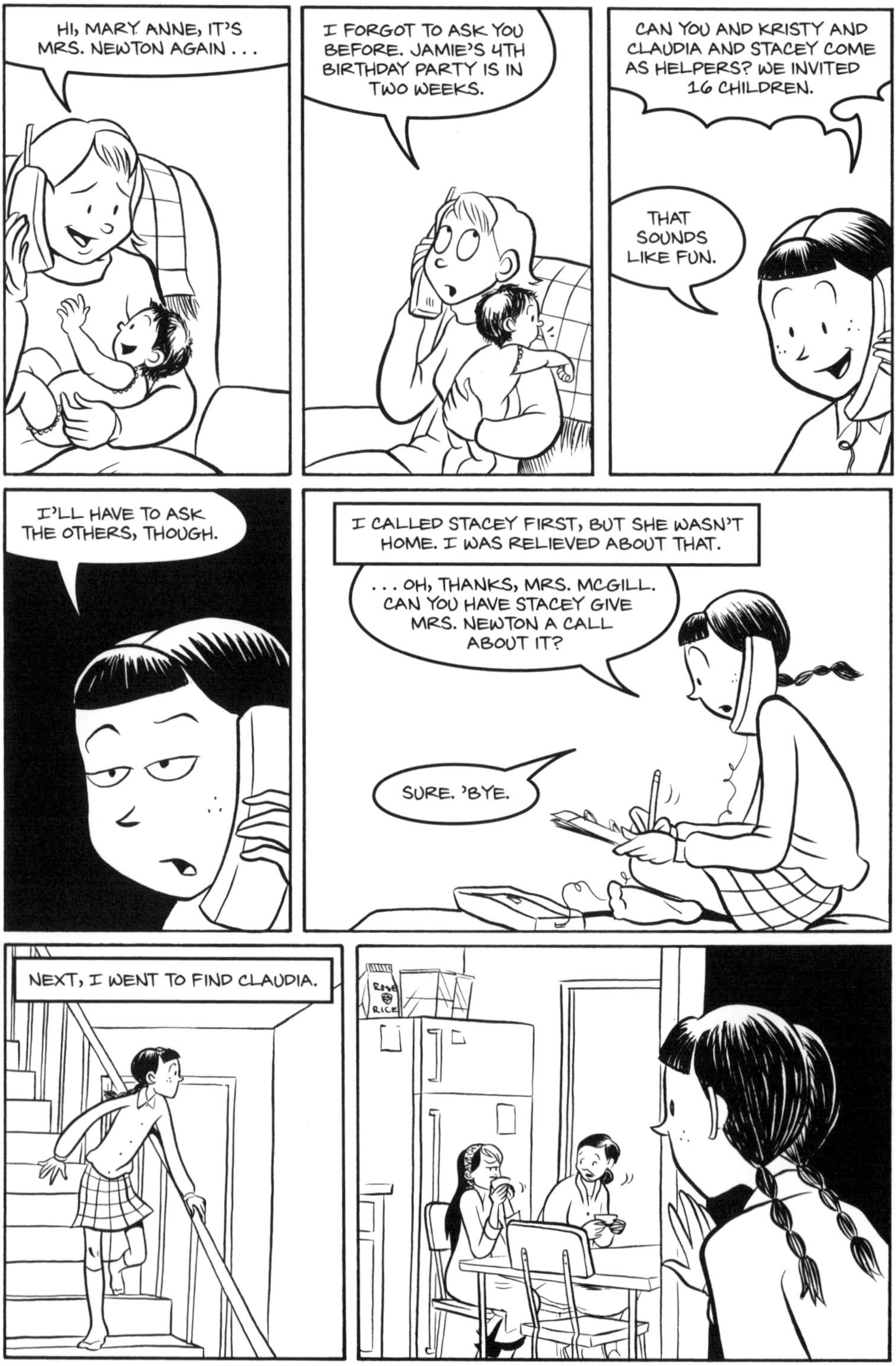
HI, MARY ANNE, IT'S MRS. NEWTON AGAIN . . .
I FORGOT TO ASK YOU BEFORE. JAMIE'S 4TH BIRTHDAY PARTY IS IN TWO WEEKS.
CAN YOU AND KRISTY AND CLAUDIA AND STACEY COME AS HELPERS? WE INVITED 16 CHILDREN.
THAT SOUNDS LIKE FUN.
I'LL HAVE TO ASK THE OTHERS, THOUGH.
I CALLED STACEY FIRST, BUT SHE WASN'T HOME. I WAS RELIEVED ABOUT THAT.
. . . OH, THANKS, MRS. MCGILL. CAN YOU HAVE STACEY GIVE MRS. NEWTON A CALL ABOUT IT?
SURE. 'BYE.
NEXT, I WENT TO FIND CLAUDIA.
ROSE RICE

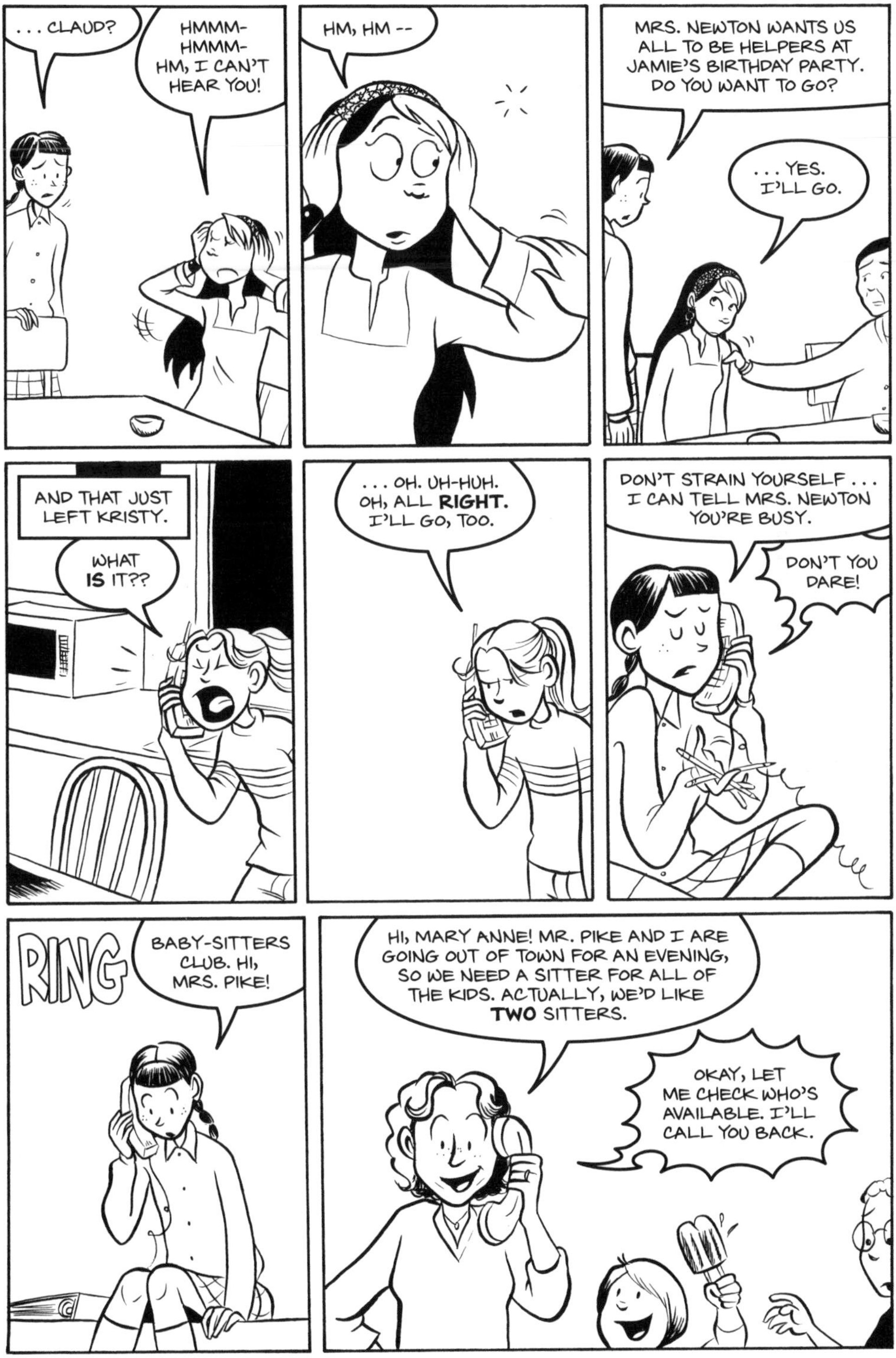

. . . CLAUD?
HMMM-HMMM-HM, I CAN'T HEAR YOU!
HM, HM --
MRS. NEWTON WANTS US ALL TO BE HELPERS AT JAMIE'S BIRTHDAY PARTY. DO YOU WANT TO GO?
. . . YES. I'LL GO.
AND THAT JUST LEFT KRISTY.
WHAT **IS** IT??
. . . OH. UH-HUH. OH, ALL **RIGHT.** I'LL GO, TOO.
DON'T STRAIN YOURSELF . . . I CAN TELL MRS. NEWTON YOU'RE BUSY.
DON'T YOU DARE!
RING
BABY-SITTERS CLUB. HI, MRS. PIKE!
HI, MARY ANNE! MR. PIKE AND I ARE GOING OUT OF TOWN FOR AN EVENING, SO WE NEED A SITTER FOR ALL OF THE KIDS. ACTUALLY, WE'D LIKE **TWO** SITTERS.
OKAY, LET ME CHECK WHO'S AVAILABLE. I'LL CALL YOU BACK.

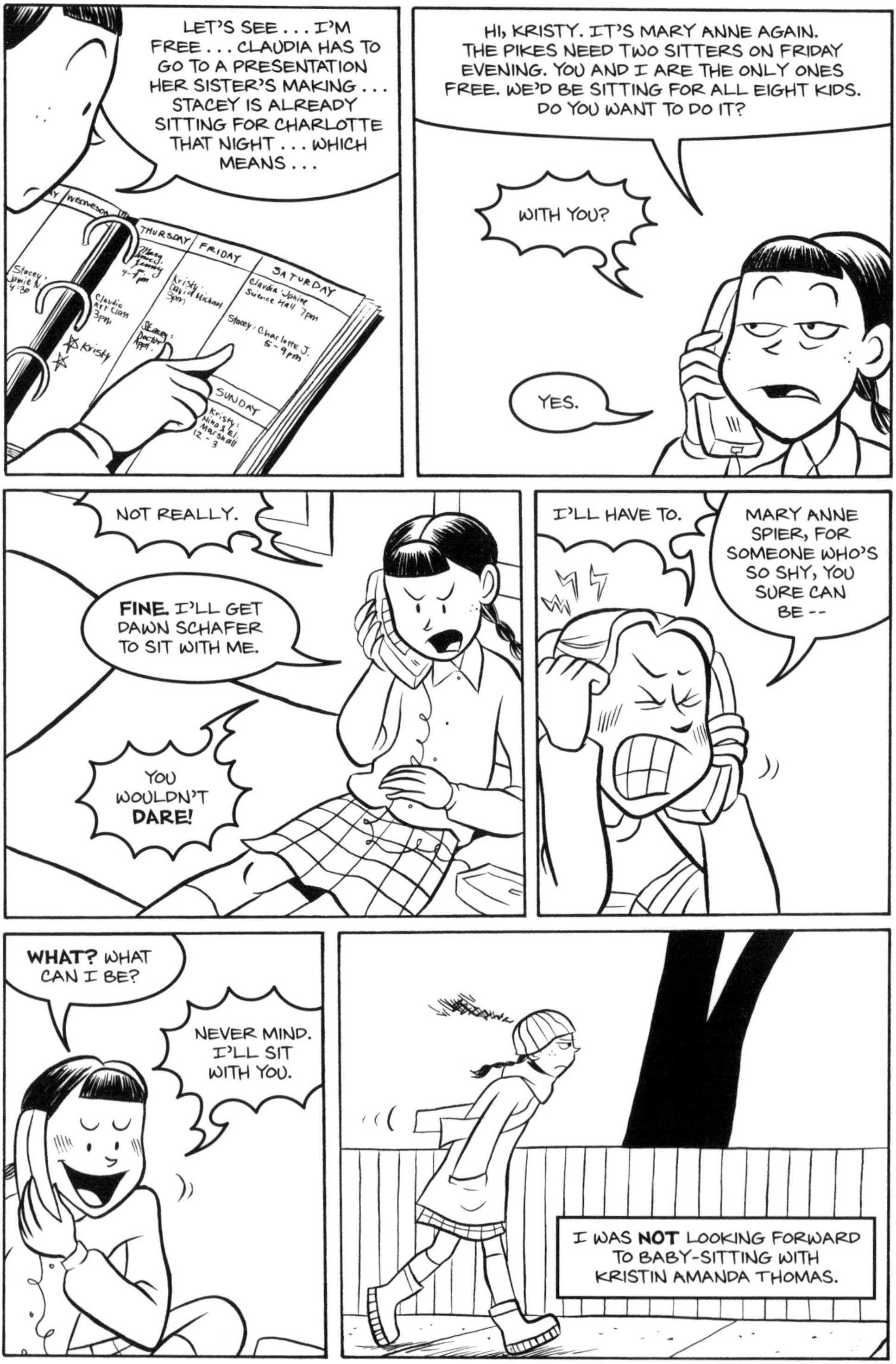
LET'S SEE . . . I'M FREE . . . CLAUDIA HAS TO GO TO A PRESENTATION HER SISTER'S MAKING . . . STACEY IS ALREADY SITTING FOR CHARLOTTE THAT NIGHT . . . WHICH MEANS . . .
HI, KRISTY. IT'S MARY ANNE AGAIN. THE PIKES NEED TWO SITTERS ON FRIDAY EVENING. YOU AND I ARE THE ONLY ONES FREE. WE'D BE SITTING FOR ALL EIGHT KIDS. DO YOU WANT TO DO IT?
WITH YOU?
YES.
NOT REALLY.
FINE. I'LL GET DAWN SCHAFER TO SIT WITH ME.
YOU WOULDN'T **DARE!**
I'LL HAVE TO.
MARY ANNE SPIER, FOR SOMEONE WHO'S SO SHY, YOU SURE CAN BE --
WHAT? WHAT CAN I BE?
NEVER MIND. I'LL SIT WITH YOU.
I WAS **NOT** LOOKING FORWARD TO BABY-SITTING WITH KRISTIN AMANDA THOMAS.

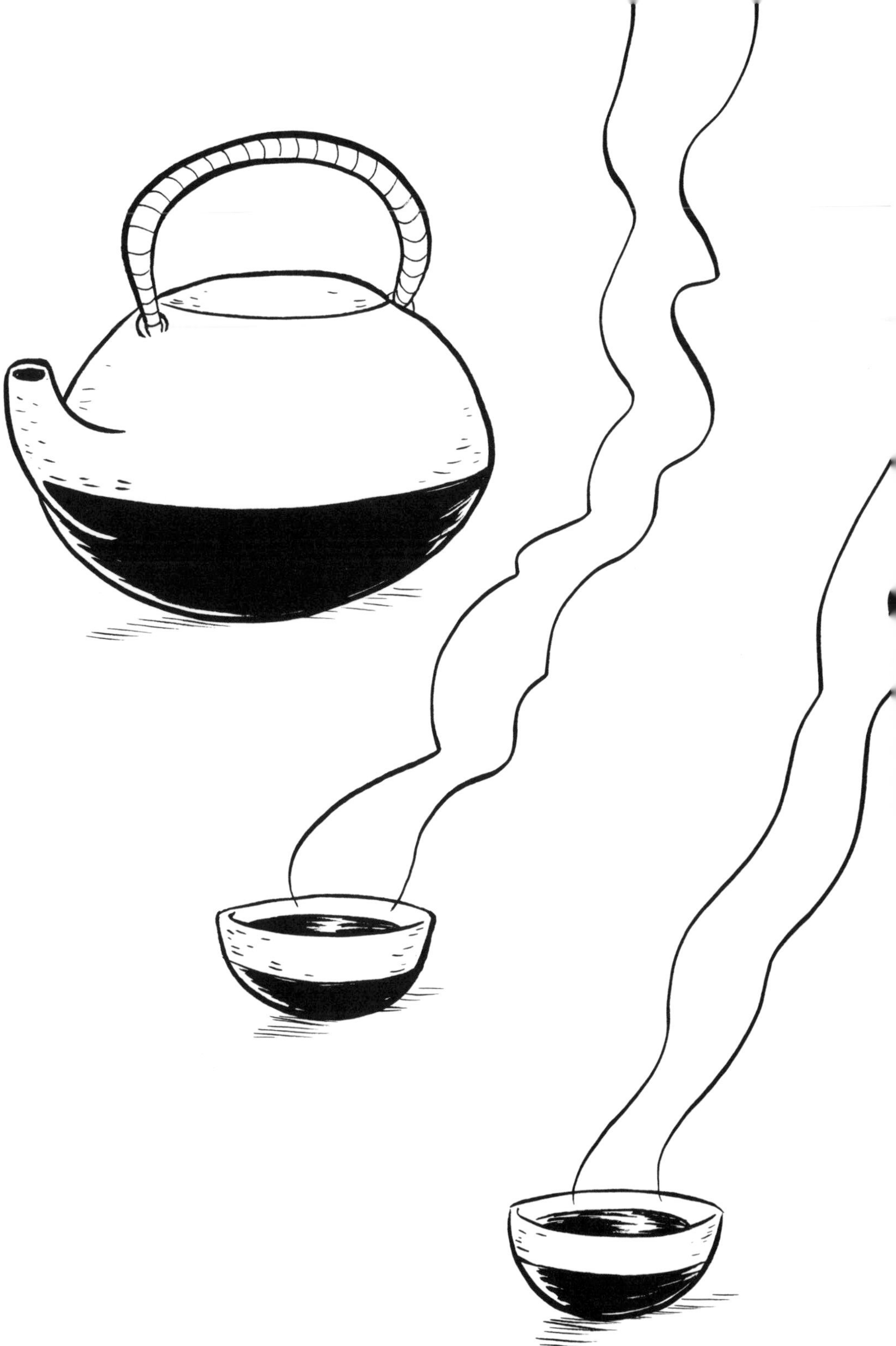

Saturday, January 31

Yesterday, Mary Anne and I baby-sat for the Pikes. I'm really surprised that we were able to pull it off. Hereby let it be known that it is possible:

① For two people to baby-sit for eight kids without losing their sanity (the sitters' & the kids), and

② for the baby-sitters to accomplish this without ever speaking to each other.

There should be a Baby-sitters' Hall of Fame where experiences like ours could be recorded and preserved for all to read about. To do what we did takes a lot of imagination.

... And a really good fight, I guess.

Kristy

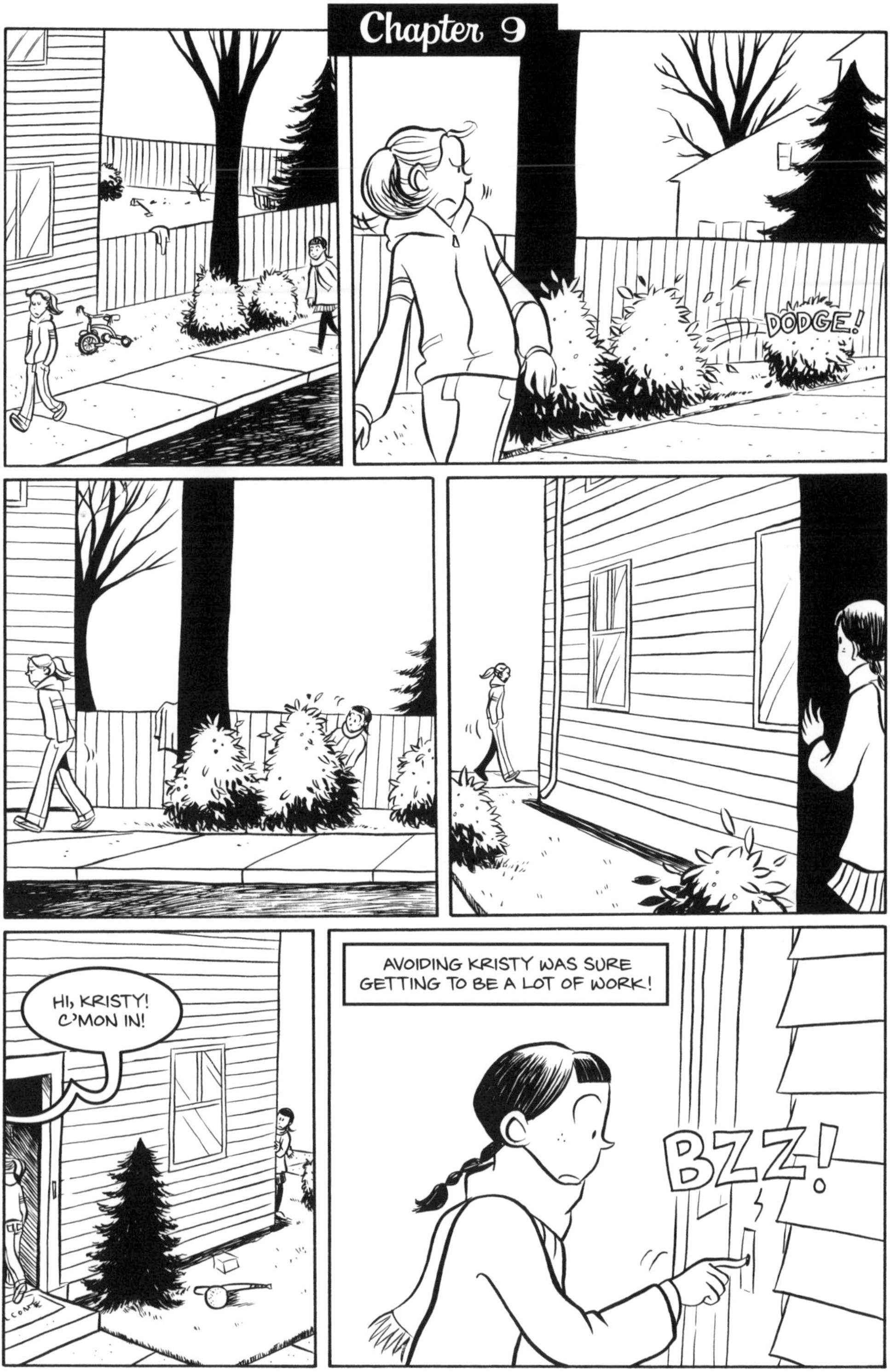
Chapter 9
DODGE!
HI, KRISTY! C'MON IN!
AVOIDING KRISTY WAS SURE GETTING TO BE A LOT OF WORK!
BZZ!

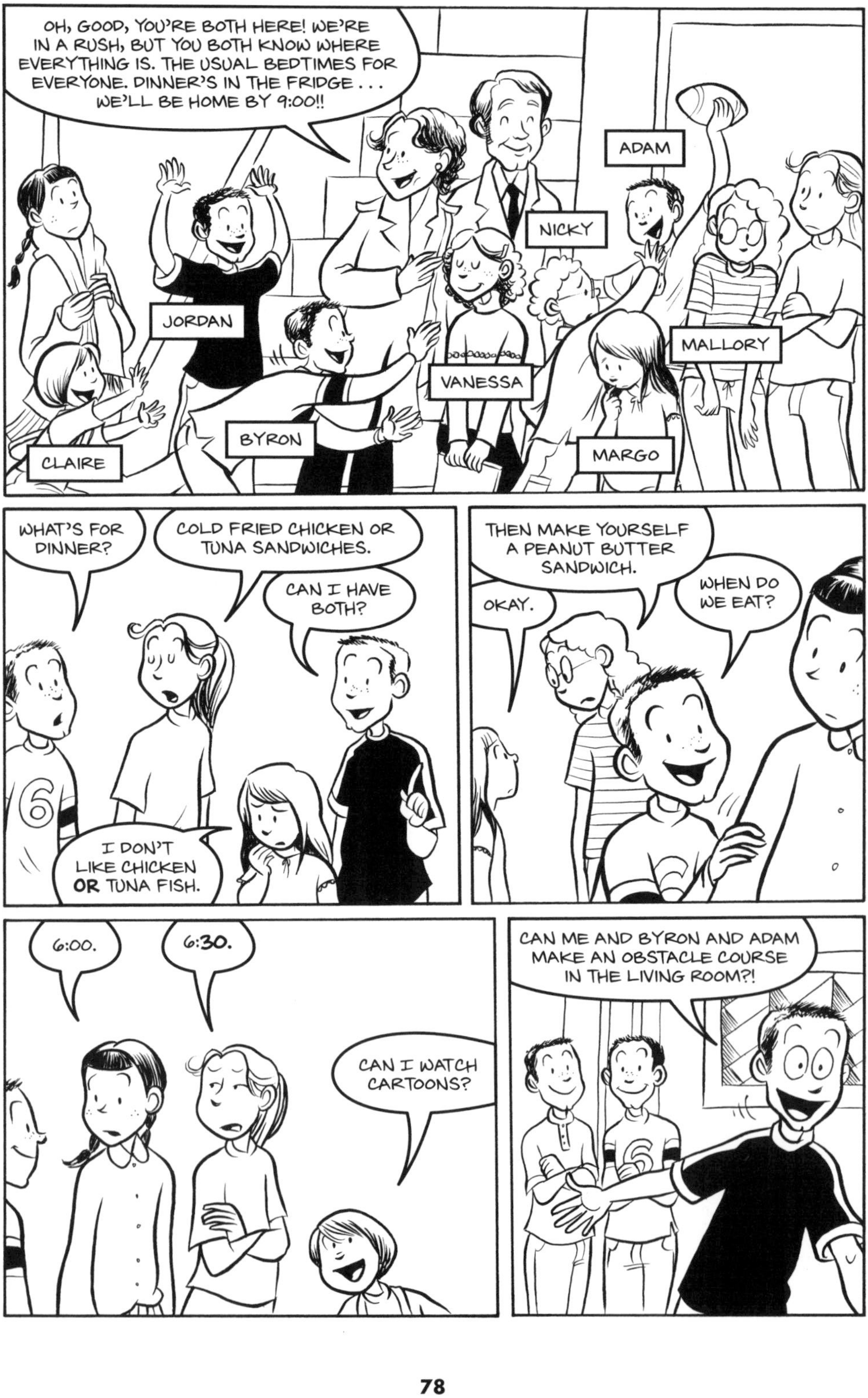
OH, GOOD, YOU'RE BOTH HERE! WE'RE IN A RUSH, BUT YOU BOTH KNOW WHERE EVERYTHING IS. THE USUAL BEDTIMES FOR EVERYONE. DINNER'S IN THE FRIDGE . . . WE'LL BE HOME BY 9:00!!
ADAM
NICKY
JORDAN
MALLORY
VANESSA
BYRON
MARGO
CLAIRE
WHAT'S FOR DINNER?
COLD FRIED CHICKEN OR TUNA SANDWICHES.
CAN I HAVE BOTH?
I DON'T LIKE CHICKEN **OR** TUNA FISH.
THEN MAKE YOURSELF A PEANUT BUTTER SANDWICH.
OKAY.
WHEN DO WE EAT?
6:00.
6:**30.**
CAN I WATCH CARTOONS?
CAN ME AND BYRON AND ADAM MAKE AN OBSTACLE COURSE IN THE LIVING ROOM?!

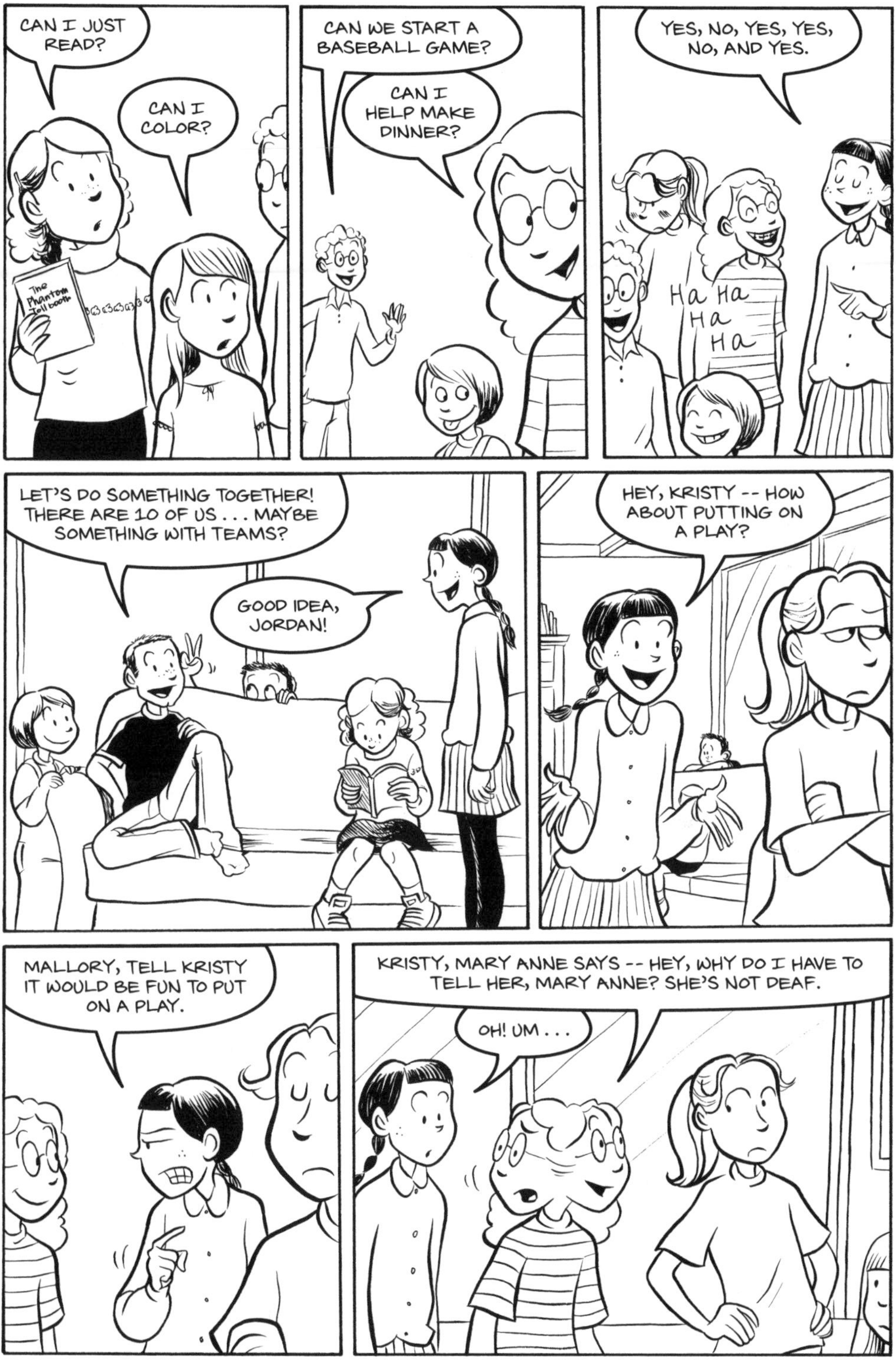
CAN I JUST READ?
CAN I COLOR?
The Phantom Tollbooth
CAN WE START A BASEBALL GAME?
CAN I HELP MAKE DINNER?
YES, NO, YES, YES, NO, AND YES.
Ha Ha Ha Ha
LET'S DO SOMETHING TOGETHER! THERE ARE 10 OF US . . . MAYBE SOMETHING WITH TEAMS?
GOOD IDEA, JORDAN!
HEY, KRISTY -- HOW ABOUT PUTTING ON A PLAY?
MALLORY, TELL KRISTY IT WOULD BE FUN TO PUT ON A PLAY.
KRISTY, MARY ANNE SAYS -- HEY, WHY DO I HAVE TO TELL HER, MARY ANNE? SHE'S NOT DEAF.
OH! UM . . .

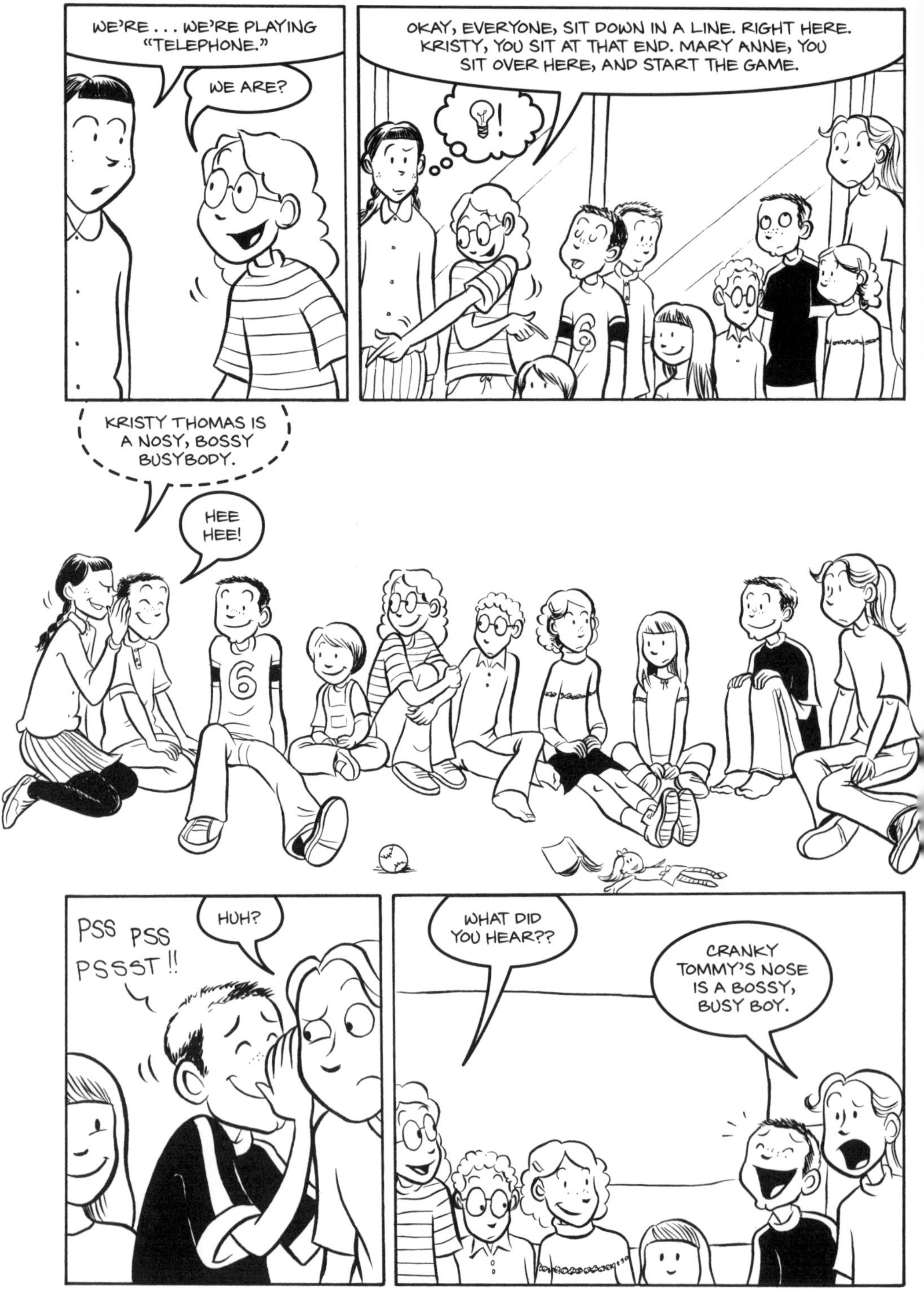
WE'RE . . . WE'RE PLAYING "TELEPHONE."
WE ARE?
OKAY, EVERYONE, SIT DOWN IN A LINE. RIGHT HERE. KRISTY, YOU SIT AT THAT END. MARY ANNE, YOU SIT OVER HERE, AND START THE GAME.
KRISTY THOMAS IS A NOSY, BOSSY BUSYBODY.
HEE HEE!
PSS PSS PSSST !!
HUH?
WHAT DID YOU HEAR??
CRANKY TOMMY'S NOSE IS A BOSSY, BUSY BOY.

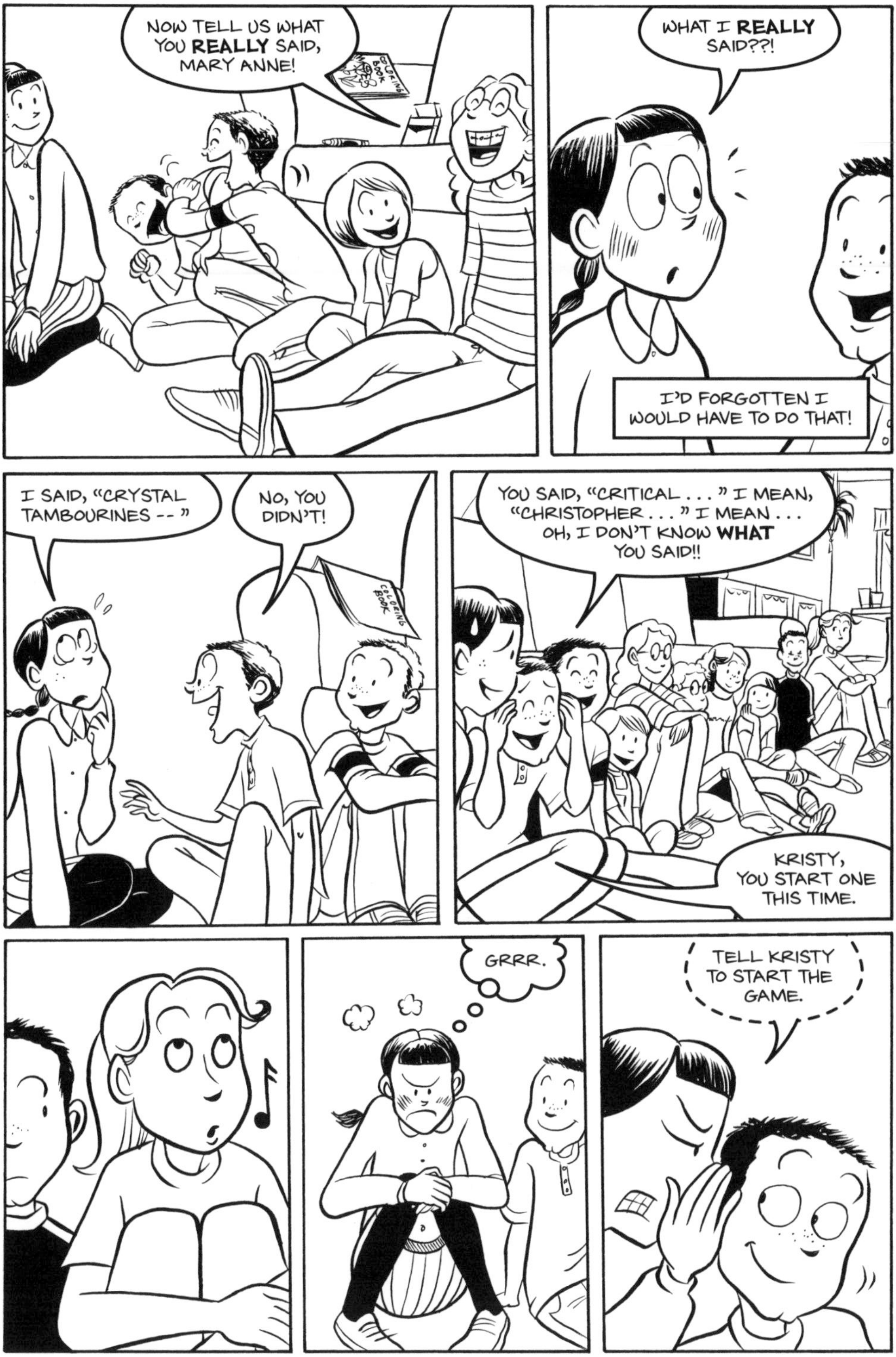
NOW TELL US WHAT YOU **REALLY** SAID, MARY ANNE!
COLORING BOOK
WHAT I **REALLY** SAID??!
I'D FORGOTTEN I WOULD HAVE TO DO THAT!
I SAID, "CRYSTAL TAMBOURINES -- "
NO, YOU DIDN'T!
COLORING BOOK
YOU SAID, "CRITICAL . . ." I MEAN, "CHRISTOPHER . . ." I MEAN . . . OH, I DON'T KNOW **WHAT** YOU SAID!!
KRISTY, YOU START ONE THIS TIME.
GRRR.
TELL KRISTY TO START THE GAME.

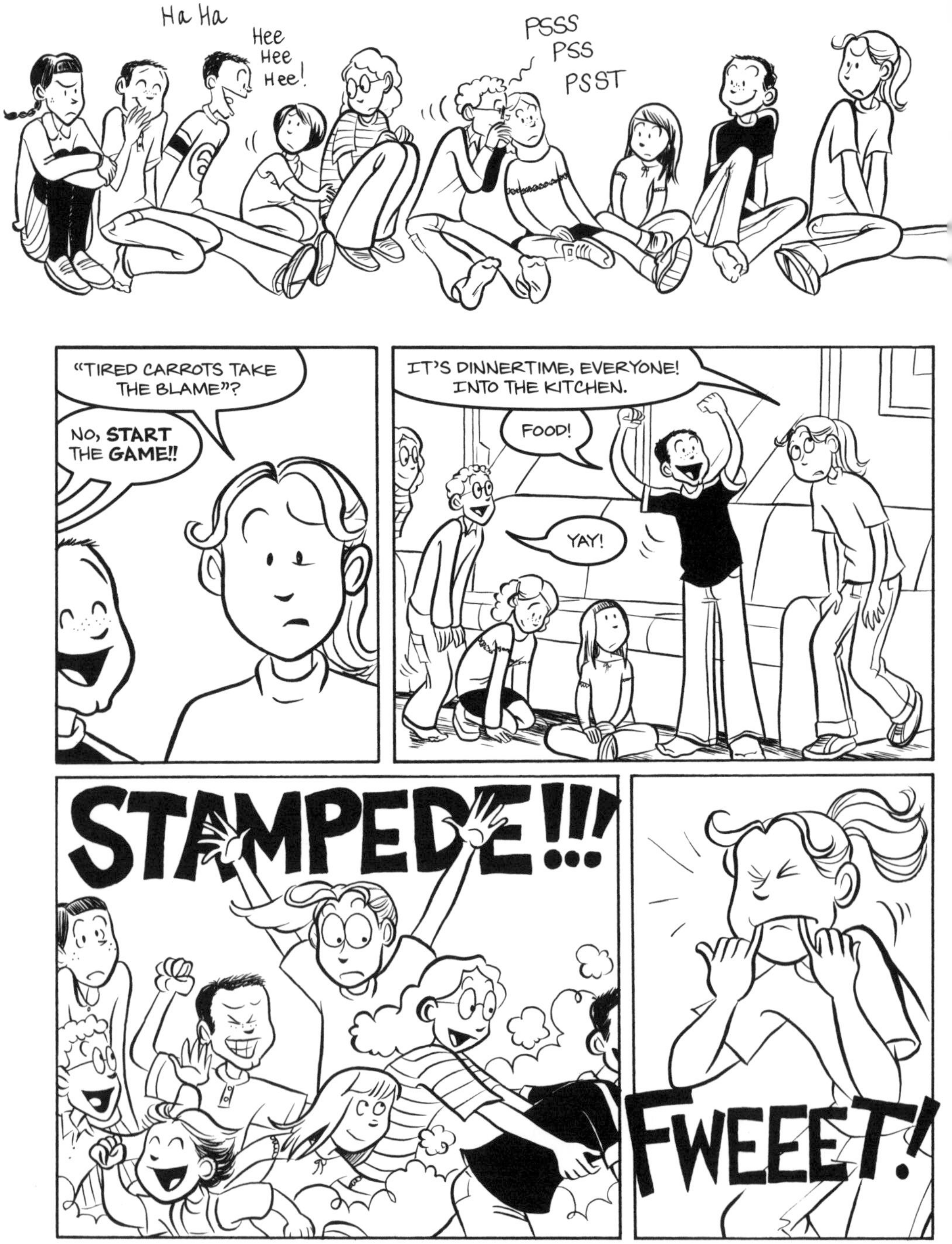
Ha Ha
Hee Hee Hee!
PSSS PSS PSST
"TIRED CARROTS TAKE THE BLAME"?
NO, **START** THE **GAME**!!
IT'S DINNERTIME, EVERYONE! INTO THE KITCHEN.
FOOD!
YAY!
STAMPEDE!!!
FWEEET!

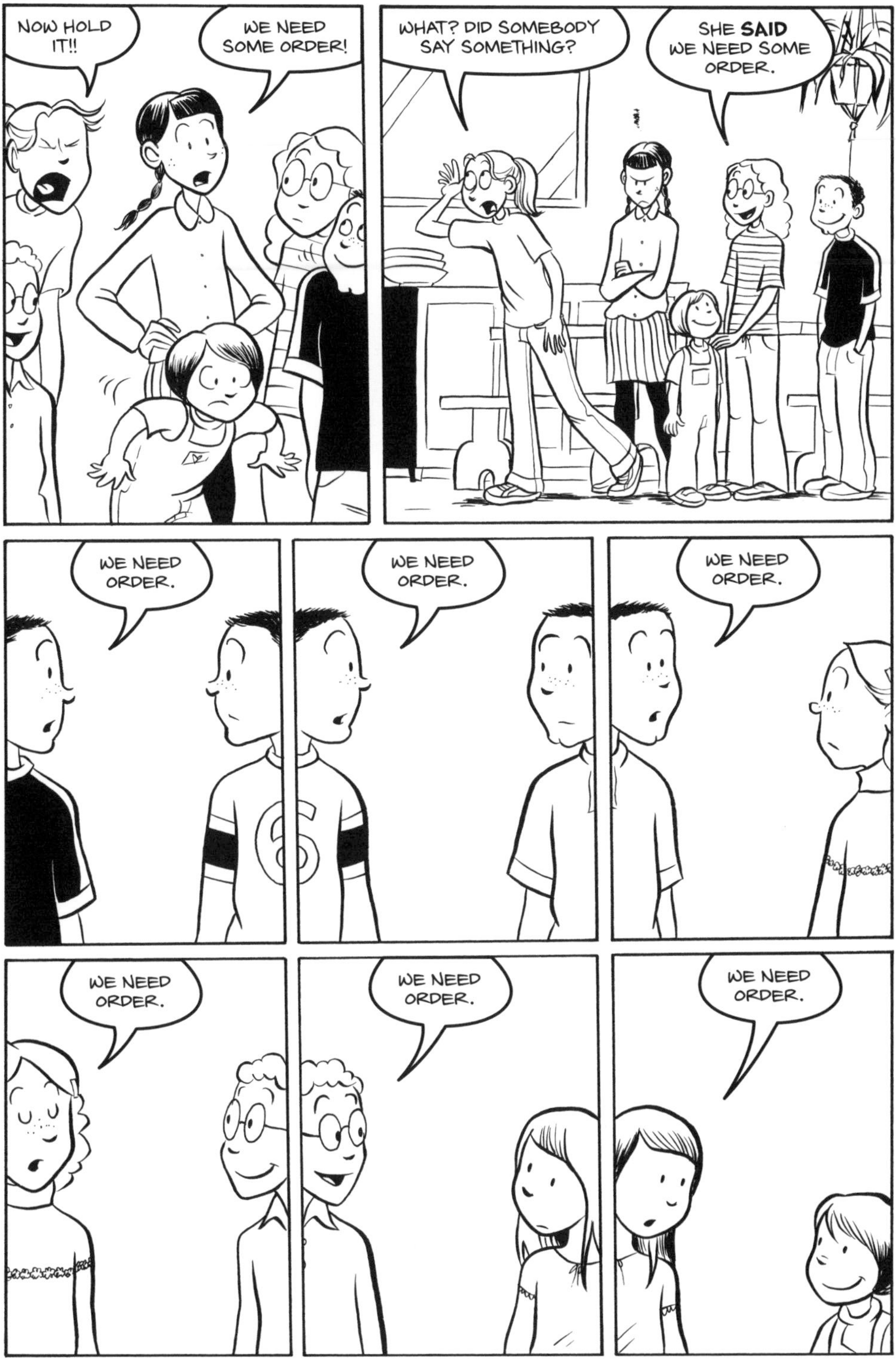
NOW HOLD IT!!
WE NEED SOME ORDER!
WHAT? DID SOMEBODY SAY SOMETHING?
SHE **SAID** WE NEED SOME ORDER.
WE NEED ORDER.
WE NEED ORDER.
WE NEED ORDER.
WE NEED ORDER.
WE NEED ORDER.
WE NEED ORDER.

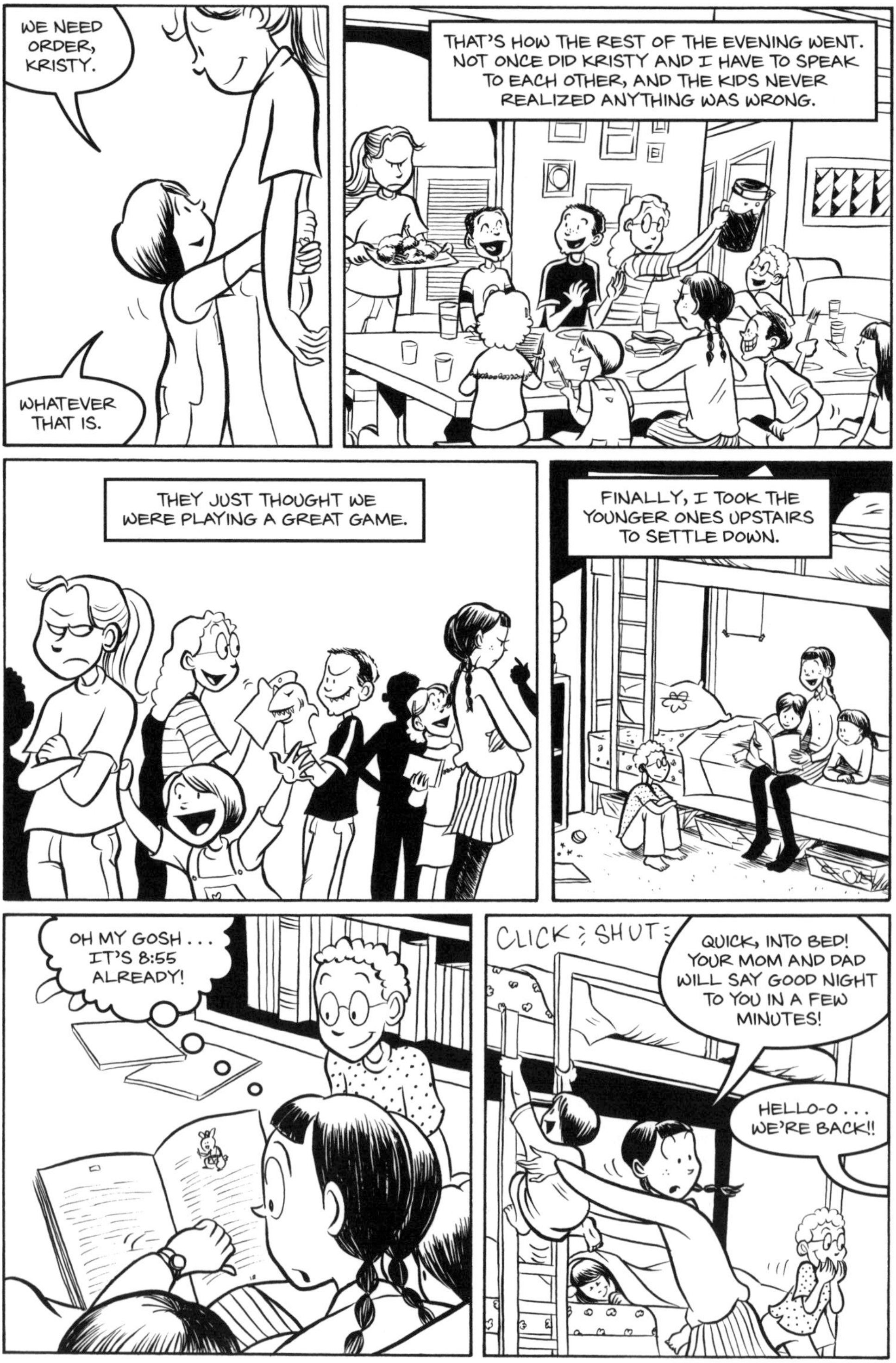
WE NEED ORDER, KRISTY.
WHATEVER THAT IS.
THAT'S HOW THE REST OF THE EVENING WENT. NOT ONCE DID KRISTY AND I HAVE TO SPEAK TO EACH OTHER, AND THE KIDS NEVER REALIZED ANYTHING WAS WRONG.
THEY JUST THOUGHT WE WERE PLAYING A GREAT GAME.
FINALLY, I TOOK THE YOUNGER ONES UPSTAIRS TO SETTLE DOWN.
OH MY GOSH . . . IT'S 8:55 ALREADY!
CLICK
SHUT
QUICK, INTO BED! YOUR MOM AND DAD WILL SAY GOOD NIGHT TO YOU IN A FEW MINUTES!
HELLO-O . . . WE'RE BACK!!

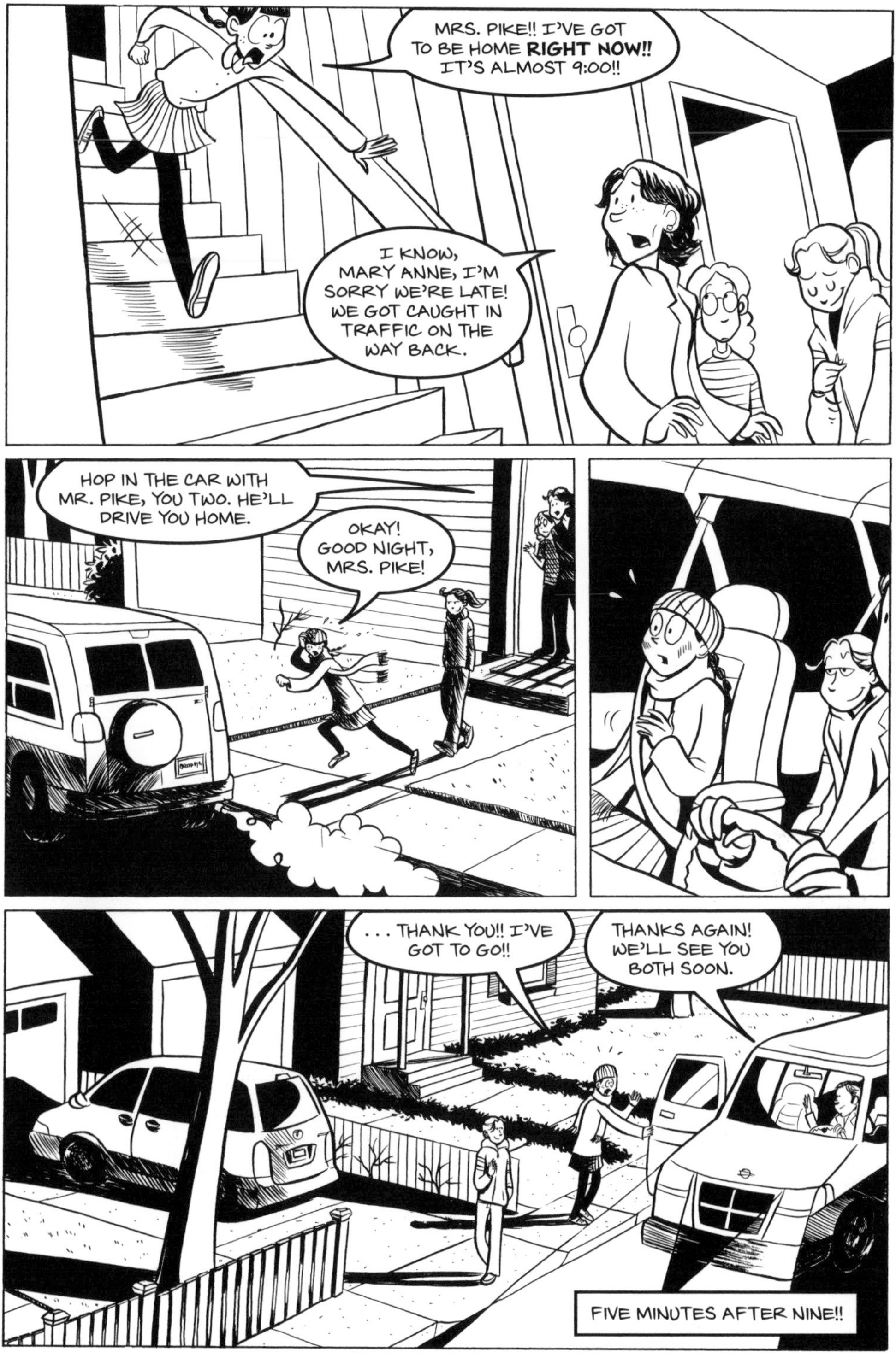
MRS. PIKE!! I'VE GOT TO BE HOME **RIGHT NOW!!** IT'S ALMOST 9:00!!
I KNOW, MARY ANNE, I'M SORRY WE'RE LATE! WE GOT CAUGHT IN TRAFFIC ON THE WAY BACK.
HOP IN THE CAR WITH MR. PIKE, YOU TWO. HE'LL DRIVE YOU HOME.
OKAY! GOOD NIGHT, MRS. PIKE!
. . . THANK YOU!! I'VE GOT TO GO!!
THANKS AGAIN! WE'LL SEE YOU BOTH SOON.
FIVE MINUTES AFTER NINE!!

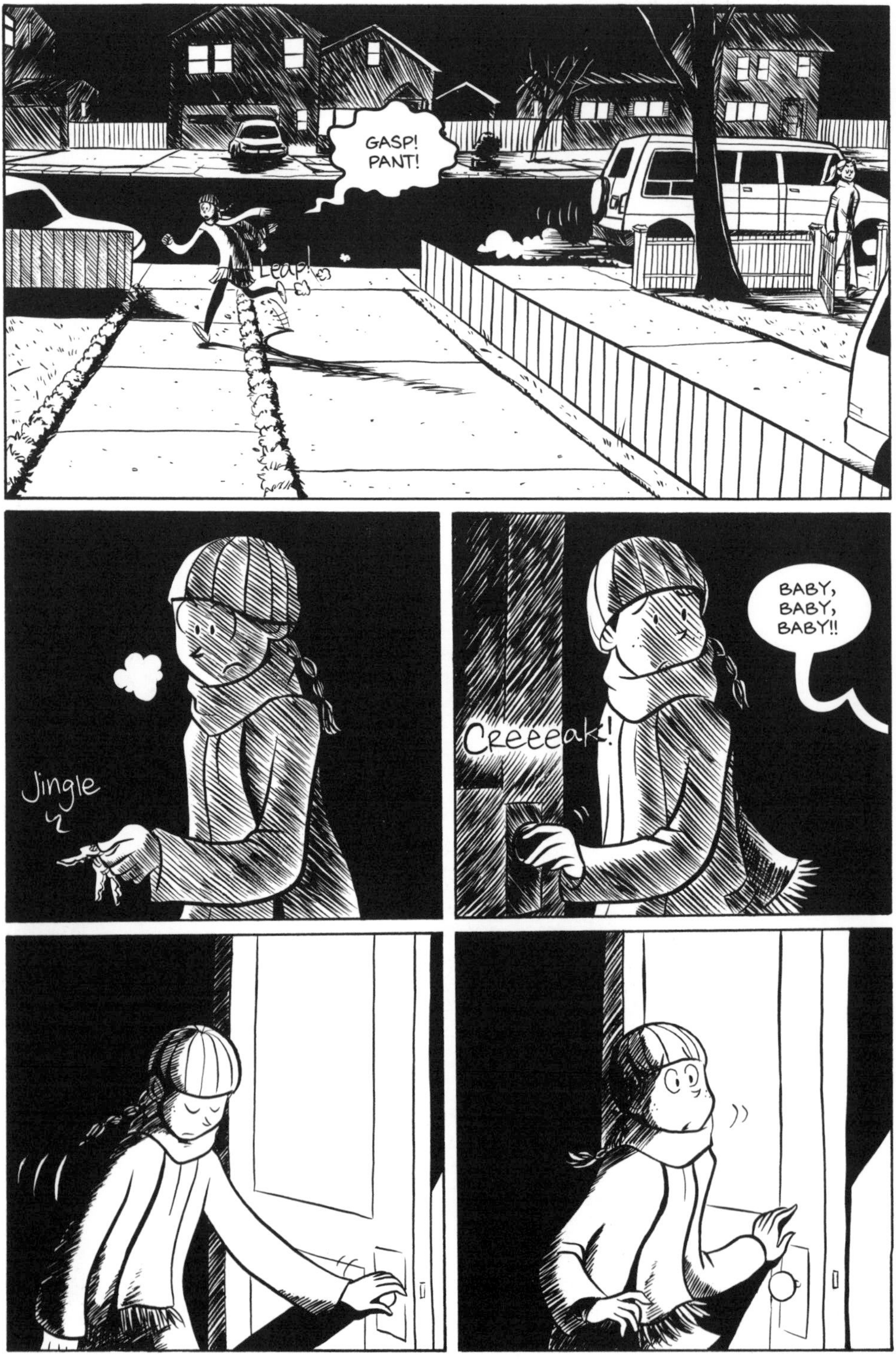
GASP! PANT!
Leap!
Jingle
Creeeak!
BABY, BABY, BABY!!

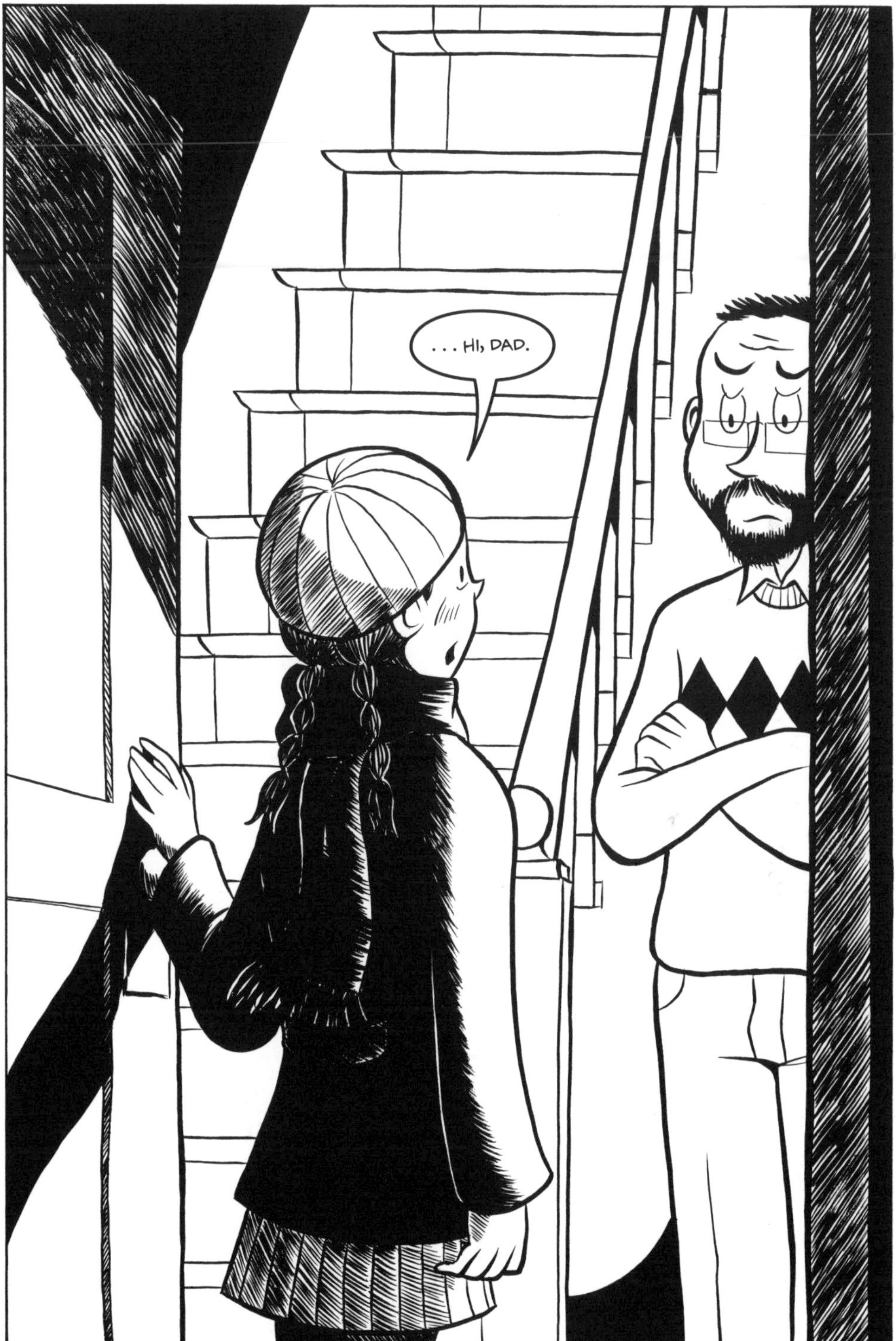
. . . HI, DAD.

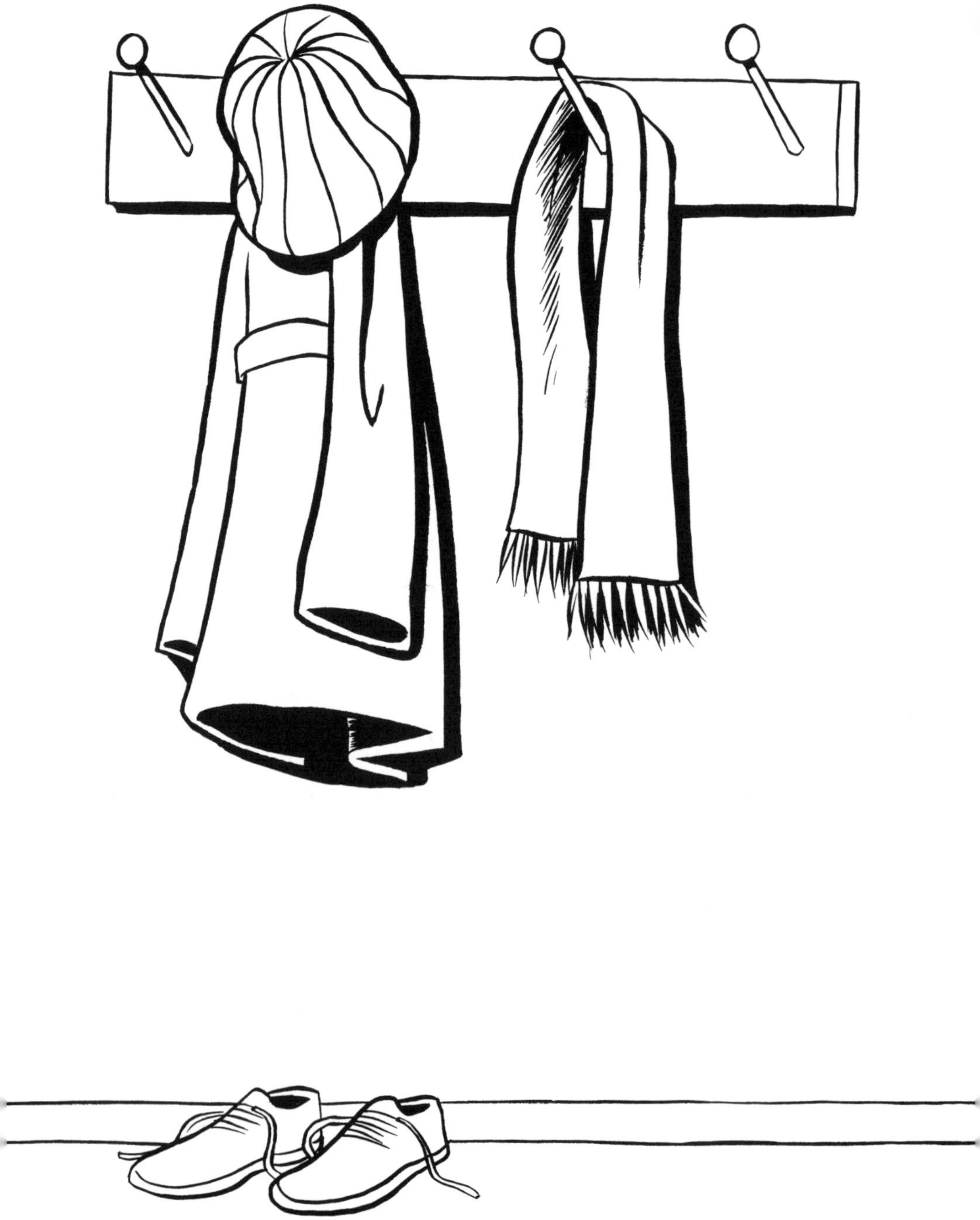

Chapter 10

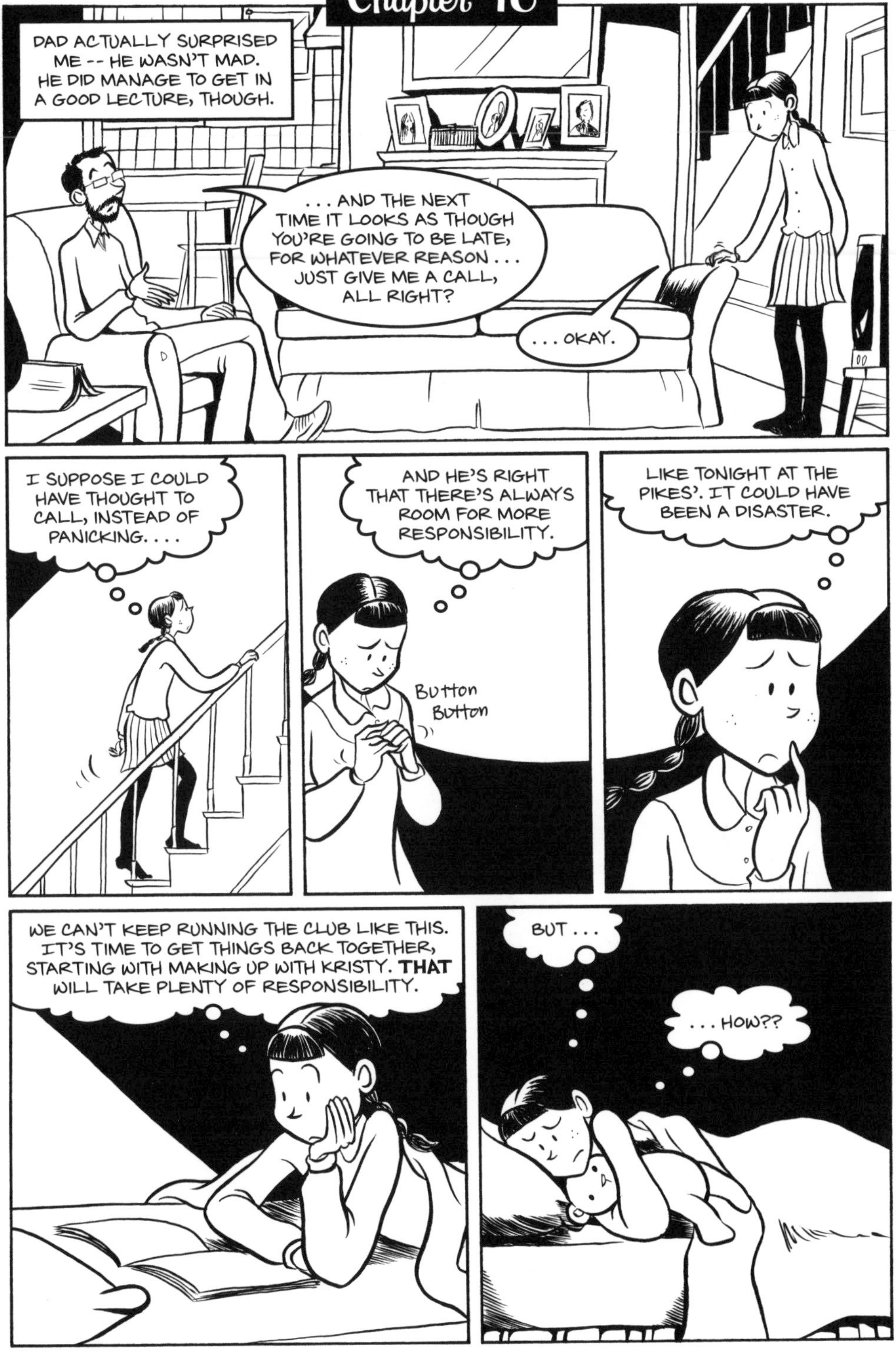

DAD ACTUALLY SURPRISED ME -- HE WASN'T MAD. HE DID MANAGE TO GET IN A GOOD LECTURE, THOUGH.
. . . AND THE NEXT TIME IT LOOKS AS THOUGH YOU'RE GOING TO BE LATE, FOR WHATEVER REASON . . . JUST GIVE ME A CALL, ALL RIGHT?
. . . OKAY.
I SUPPOSE I COULD HAVE THOUGHT TO CALL, INSTEAD OF PANICKING. . . .
AND HE'S RIGHT THAT THERE'S ALWAYS ROOM FOR MORE RESPONSIBILITY.
Button Button
LIKE TONIGHT AT THE PIKES'. IT COULD HAVE BEEN A DISASTER.
WE CAN'T KEEP RUNNING THE CLUB LIKE THIS. IT'S TIME TO GET THINGS BACK TOGETHER, STARTING WITH MAKING UP WITH KRISTY. THAT WILL TAKE PLENTY OF RESPONSIBILITY.
BUT . . .
. . . HOW??

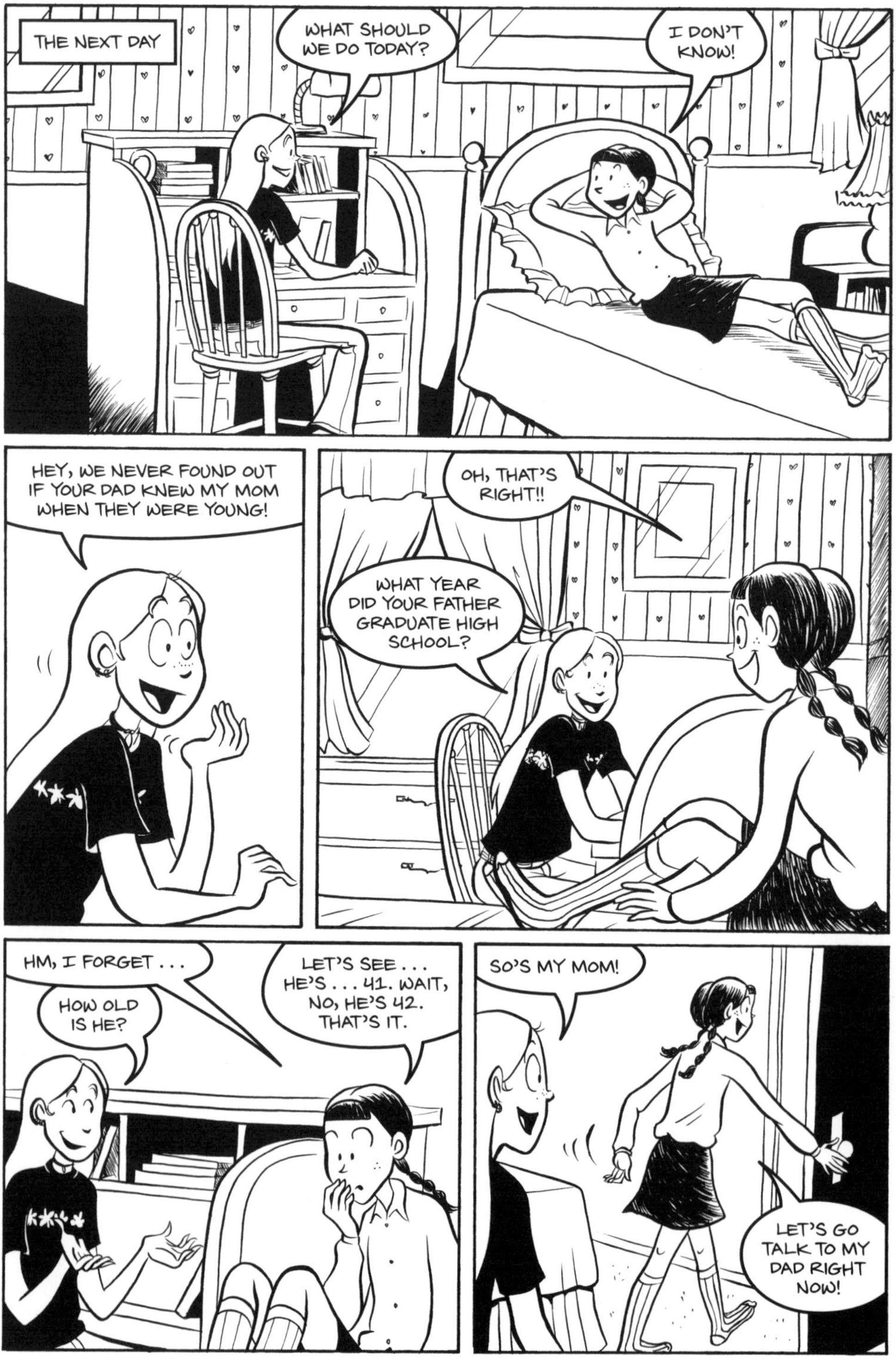
THE NEXT DAY
WHAT SHOULD WE DO TODAY?
I DON'T KNOW!
HEY, WE NEVER FOUND OUT IF YOUR DAD KNEW MY MOM WHEN THEY WERE YOUNG!
OH, THAT'S RIGHT!!
WHAT YEAR DID YOUR FATHER GRADUATE HIGH SCHOOL?
HM, I FORGET . . .
HOW OLD IS HE?
LET'S SEE . . . HE'S . . . 41. WAIT, NO, HE'S 42. THAT'S IT.
SO'S MY MOM!
LET'S GO TALK TO MY DAD RIGHT NOW!

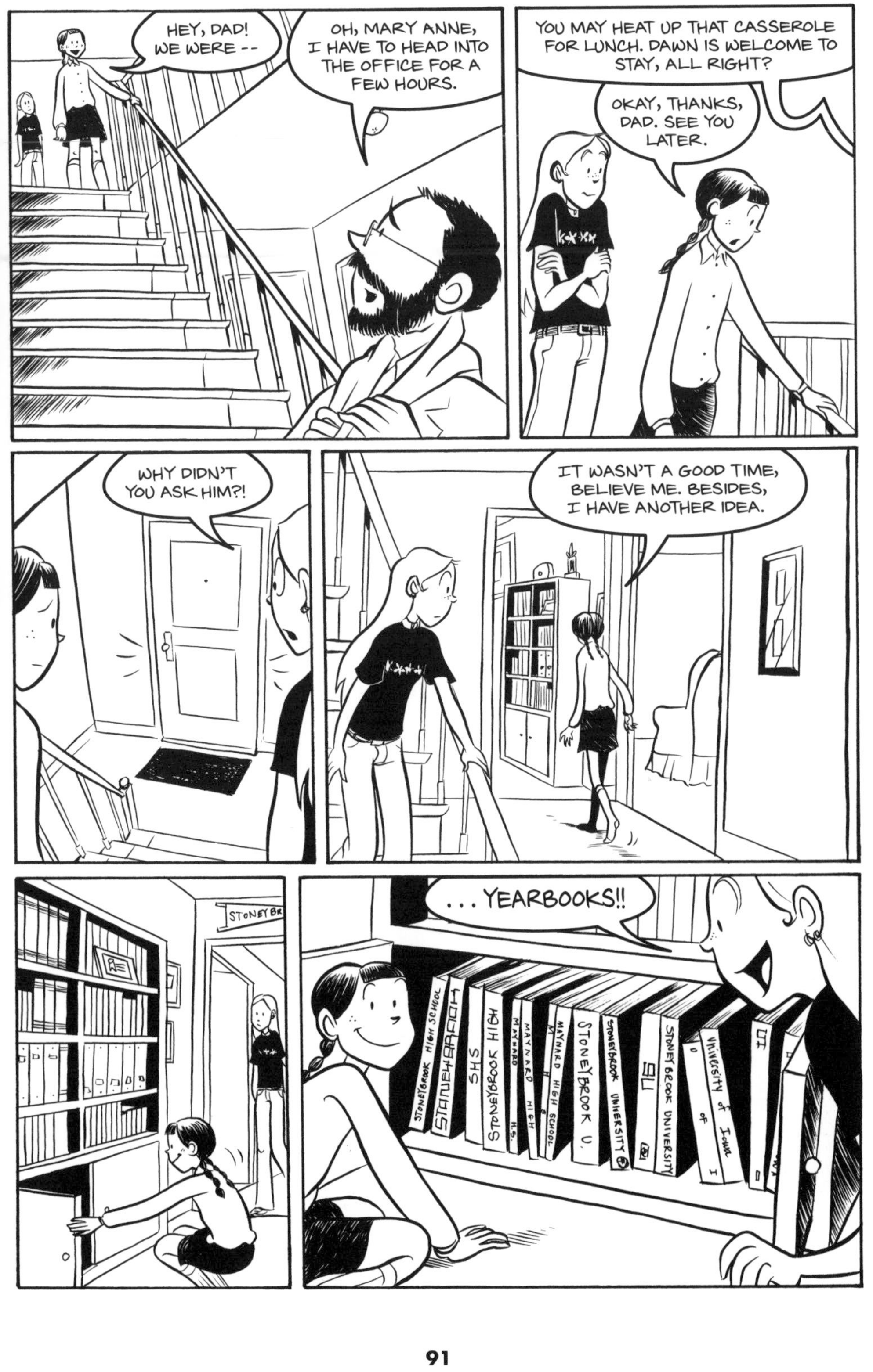
HEY, DAD! WE WERE --
OH, MARY ANNE, I HAVE TO HEAD INTO THE OFFICE FOR A FEW HOURS.
YOU MAY HEAT UP THAT CASSEROLE FOR LUNCH. DAWN IS WELCOME TO STAY, ALL RIGHT?
OKAY, THANKS, DAD. SEE YOU LATER.
WHY DIDN'T YOU ASK HIM?!
IT WASN'T A GOOD TIME, BELIEVE ME. BESIDES, I HAVE ANOTHER IDEA.
STONEYBR
. . . YEARBOOKS!!
STONEYBROOK HIGH SCHOOL
STONEYBROOK
SHS
STONEYBROOK HIGH
MAYNARD H.S.
MAYNARD HIGH
MAYNARD HIGH SCHOOL
STONEYBROOK U.
STONEYBROOK UNIVERSITY
SU
STONEYBROOK UNIVERSITY
University of Iowa

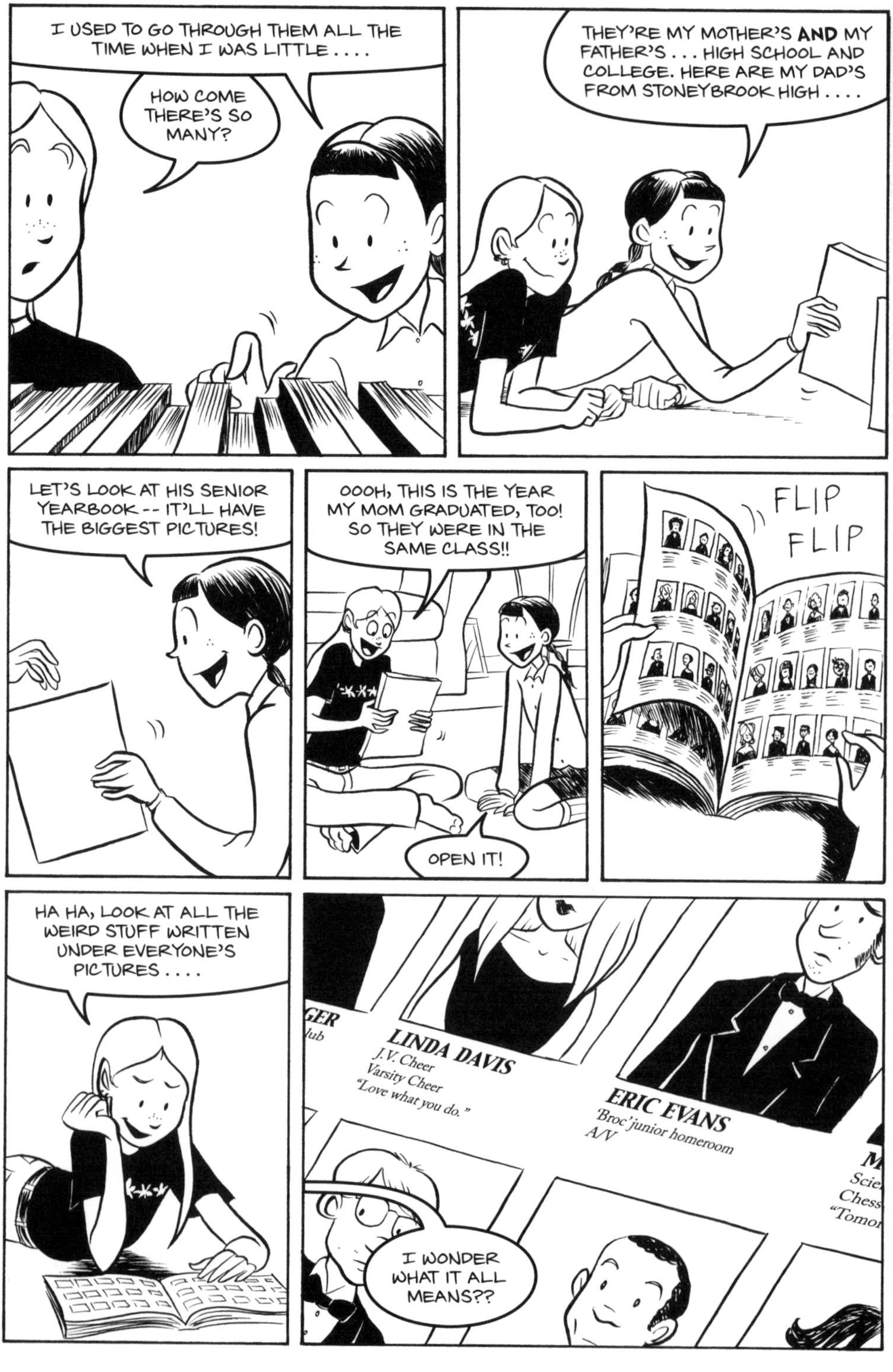
I USED TO GO THROUGH THEM ALL THE TIME WHEN I WAS LITTLE . . . .
HOW COME THERE'S SO MANY?
THEY'RE MY MOTHER'S **AND** MY FATHER'S . . . HIGH SCHOOL AND COLLEGE. HERE ARE MY DAD'S FROM STONEYBROOK HIGH . . . .
LET'S LOOK AT HIS SENIOR YEARBOOK -- IT'LL HAVE THE BIGGEST PICTURES!
OOOH, THIS IS THE YEAR MY MOM GRADUATED, TOO! SO THEY WERE IN THE SAME CLASS!!
OPEN IT!
FLIP FLIP
HA HA, LOOK AT ALL THE WEIRD STUFF WRITTEN UNDER EVERYONE'S PICTURES . . . .
LINDA DAVIS
J.V. Cheer
Varsity Cheer
"Love what you do."
ERIC EVANS
'Broc' junior homeroom
A/V
I WONDER WHAT IT ALL MEANS??

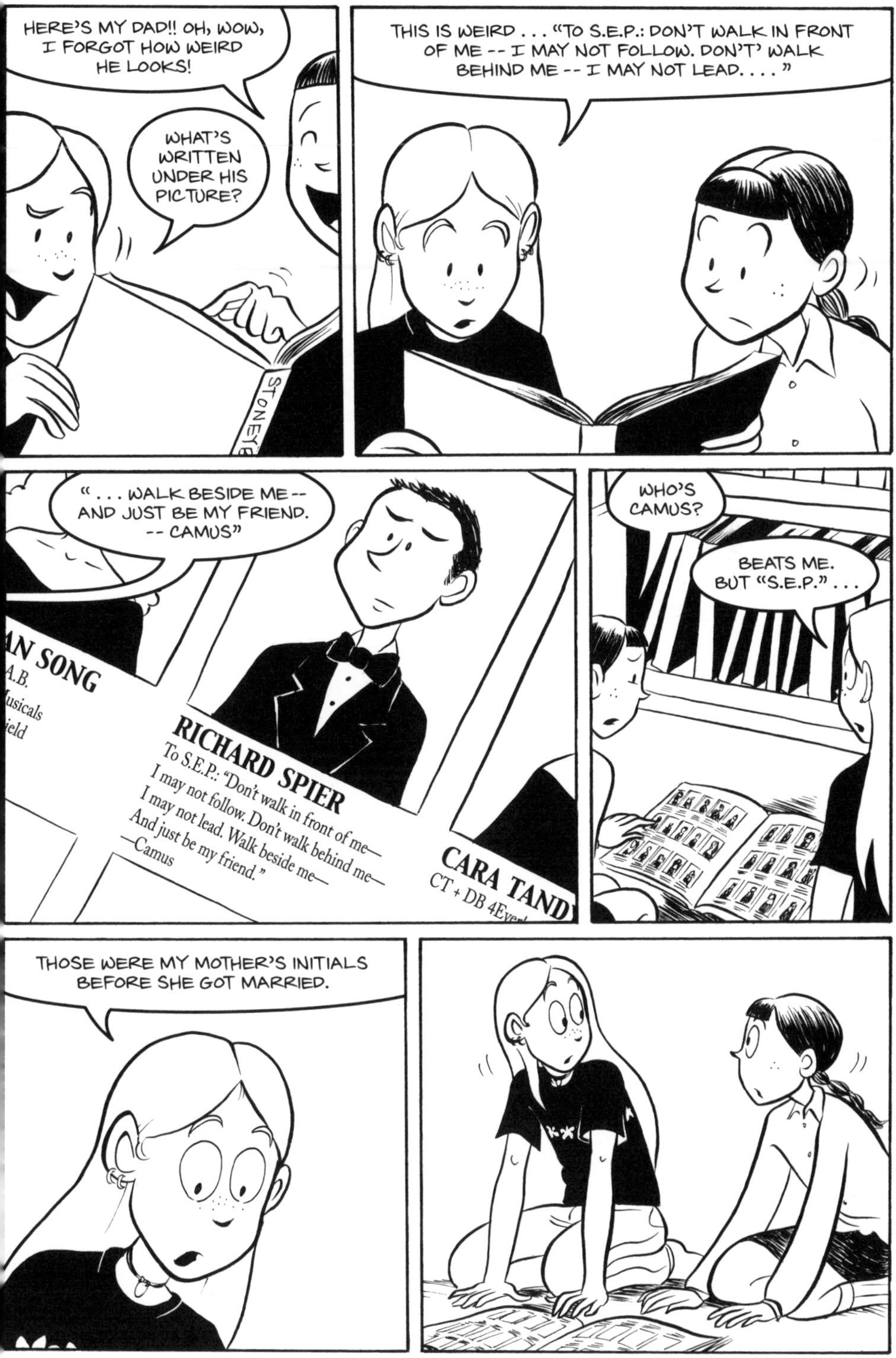
HERE'S MY DAD!! OH, WOW, I FORGOT HOW WEIRD HE LOOKS!
WHAT'S WRITTEN UNDER HIS PICTURE?
STONEY
THIS IS WEIRD . . . "TO S.E.P.: DON'T WALK IN FRONT OF ME -- I MAY NOT FOLLOW. DON'T' WALK BEHIND ME -- I MAY NOT LEAD. . . . "
" . . . WALK BESIDE ME -- AND JUST BE MY FRIEND. -- CAMUS"
AN SONG
A.B.
usicals
ield
RICHARD SPIER
To S.E.P.: "Don't walk in front of me—
I may not follow. Don't walk behind me—
I may not lead. Walk beside me—
And just be my friend."
—Camus
CARA TAND
CT + DB 4Ever
WHO'S CAMUS?
BEATS ME. BUT "S.E.P." . . .
THOSE WERE MY MOTHER'S INITIALS BEFORE SHE GOT MARRIED.

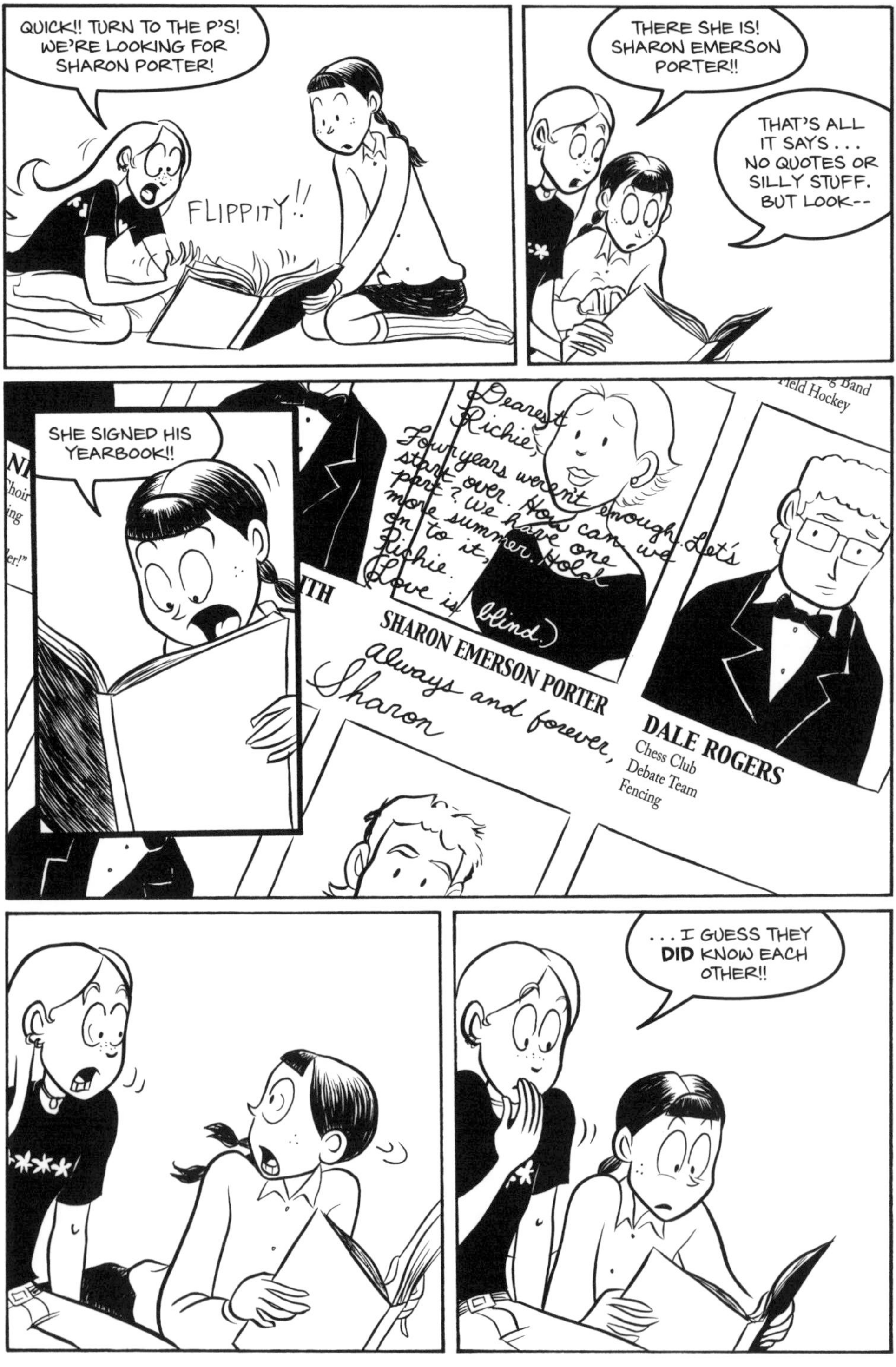

QUICK!! TURN TO THE P'S! WE'RE LOOKING FOR SHARON PORTER!
FLIPPITY!!
THERE SHE IS! SHARON EMERSON PORTER!!
THAT'S ALL IT SAYS . . . NO QUOTES OR SILLY STUFF. BUT LOOK--
SHE SIGNED HIS YEARBOOK!!
Field Hockey
Dearest Richie,
Four years weren't enough. Let's start over. How can we part? We have one more summer. Hold on to it, Richie.
Love is blind.)
SHARON EMERSON PORTER
Always and forever, Sharon
DALE ROGERS
Chess Club
Debate Team
Fencing
. . . I GUESS THEY DID KNOW EACH OTHER!!

Chapter 11

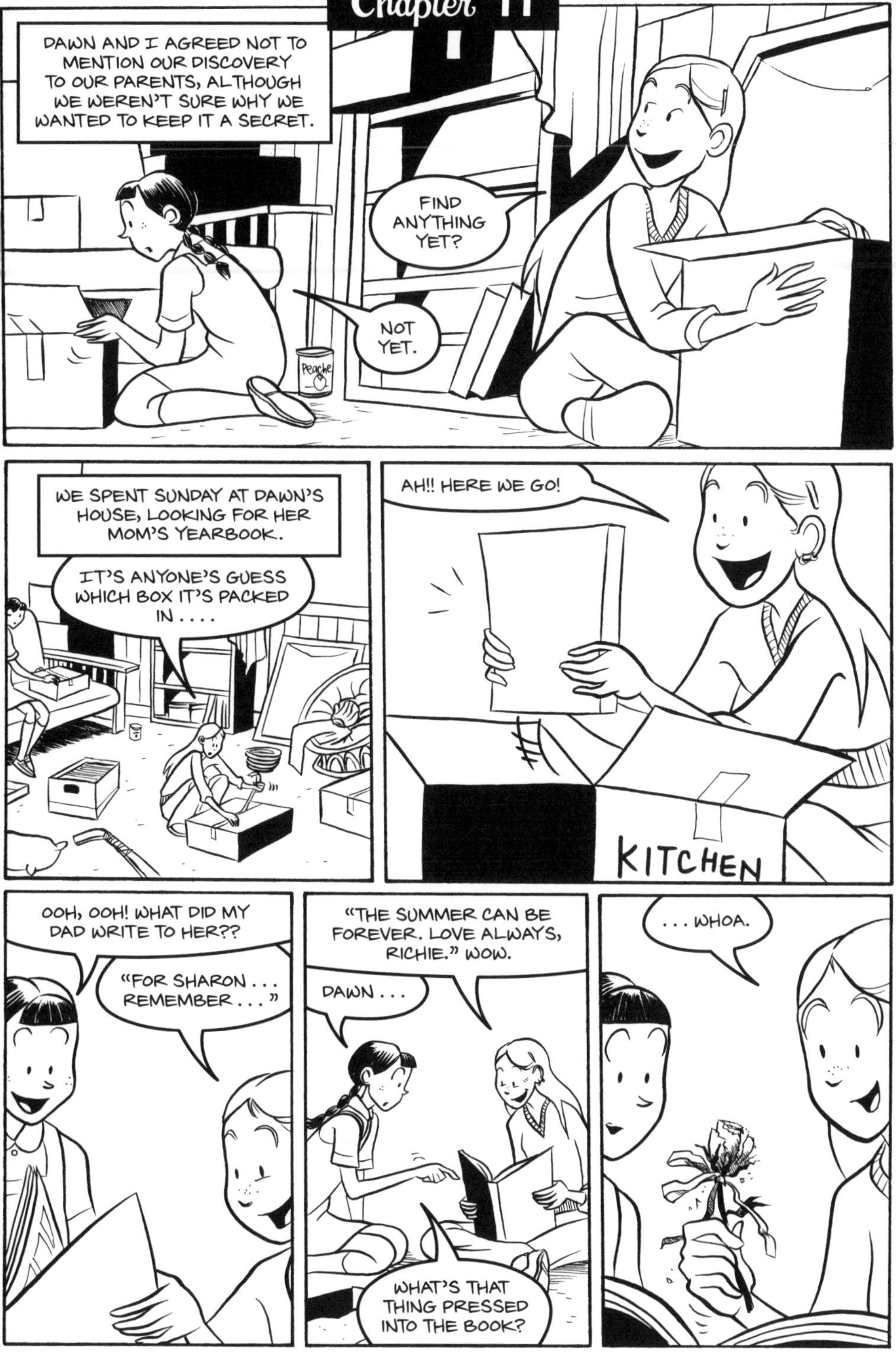
DAWN AND I AGREED NOT TO MENTION OUR DISCOVERY TO OUR PARENTS, ALTHOUGH WE WEREN'T SURE WHY WE WANTED TO KEEP IT A SECRET.
FIND ANYTHING YET?
NOT YET.
Peache
WE SPENT SUNDAY AT DAWN'S HOUSE, LOOKING FOR HER MOM'S YEARBOOK.
IT'S ANYONE'S GUESS WHICH BOX IT'S PACKED IN . . . .
AH!! HERE WE GO!
KITCHEN
OOH, OOH! WHAT DID MY DAD WRITE TO HER??
"FOR SHARON . . . REMEMBER . . ."
"THE SUMMER CAN BE FOREVER. LOVE ALWAYS, RICHIE." WOW.
DAWN . . .
WHAT'S THAT THING PRESSED INTO THE BOOK?
. . . WHOA.

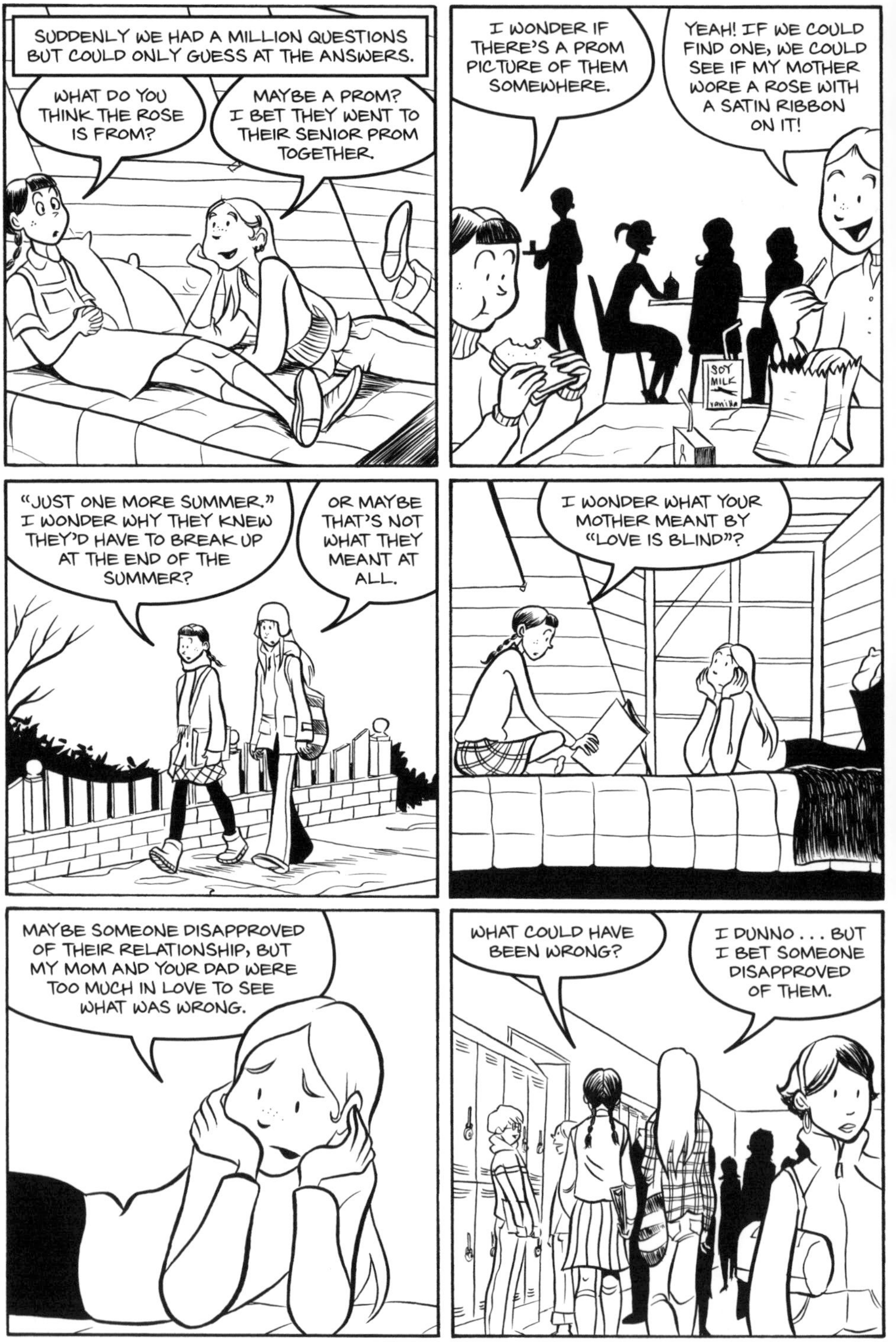
SUDDENLY WE HAD A MILLION QUESTIONS BUT COULD ONLY GUESS AT THE ANSWERS.
WHAT DO YOU THINK THE ROSE IS FROM?
MAYBE A PROM? I BET THEY WENT TO THEIR SENIOR PROM TOGETHER.
I WONDER IF THERE'S A PROM PICTURE OF THEM SOMEWHERE.
YEAH! IF WE COULD FIND ONE, WE COULD SEE IF MY MOTHER WORE A ROSE WITH A SATIN RIBBON ON IT!
SOY MILK
vanilla
"JUST ONE MORE SUMMER." I WONDER WHY THEY KNEW THEY'D HAVE TO BREAK UP AT THE END OF THE SUMMER?
OR MAYBE THAT'S NOT WHAT THEY MEANT AT ALL.
I WONDER WHAT YOUR MOTHER MEANT BY "LOVE IS BLIND"?
MAYBE SOMEONE DISAPPROVED OF THEIR RELATIONSHIP, BUT MY MOM AND YOUR DAD WERE TOO MUCH IN LOVE TO SEE WHAT WAS WRONG.
WHAT COULD HAVE BEEN WRONG?
I DUNNO . . . BUT I BET SOMEONE DISAPPROVED OF THEM.

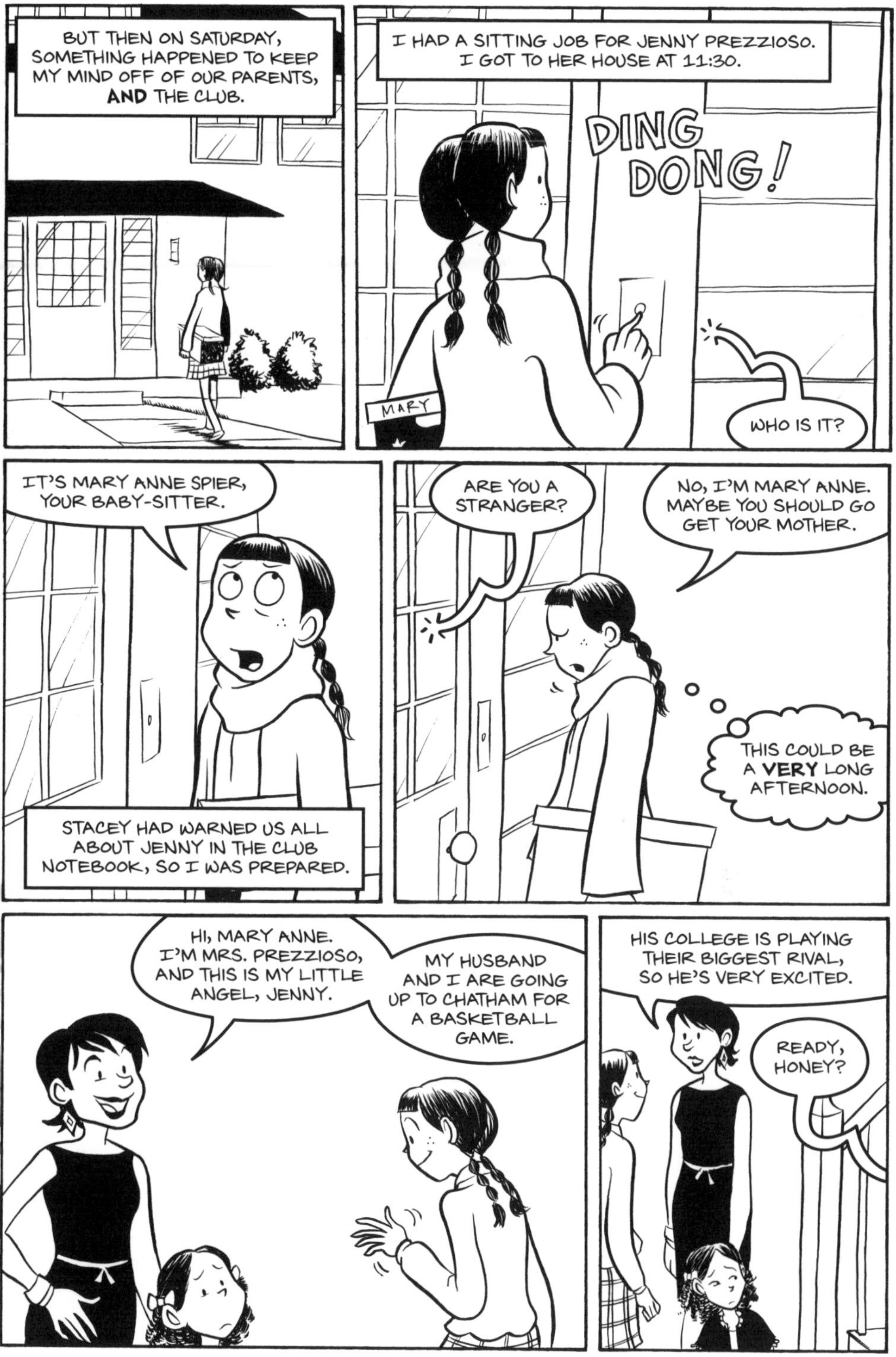
BUT THEN ON SATURDAY, SOMETHING HAPPENED TO KEEP MY MIND OFF OF OUR PARENTS, **AND** THE CLUB.
I HAD A SITTING JOB FOR JENNY PREZZIOSO. I GOT TO HER HOUSE AT 11:30.
DING DONG!
MARY
WHO IS IT?
IT'S MARY ANNE SPIER, YOUR BABY-SITTER.
STACEY HAD WARNED US ALL ABOUT JENNY IN THE CLUB NOTEBOOK, SO I WAS PREPARED.
ARE YOU A STRANGER?
NO, I'M MARY ANNE. MAYBE YOU SHOULD GO GET YOUR MOTHER.
THIS COULD BE A **VERY** LONG AFTERNOON.
HI, MARY ANNE. I'M MRS. PREZZIOSO, AND THIS IS MY LITTLE ANGEL, JENNY.
MY HUSBAND AND I ARE GOING UP TO CHATHAM FOR A BASKETBALL GAME.
HIS COLLEGE IS PLAYING THEIR BIGGEST RIVAL, SO HE'S VERY EXCITED.
READY, HONEY?

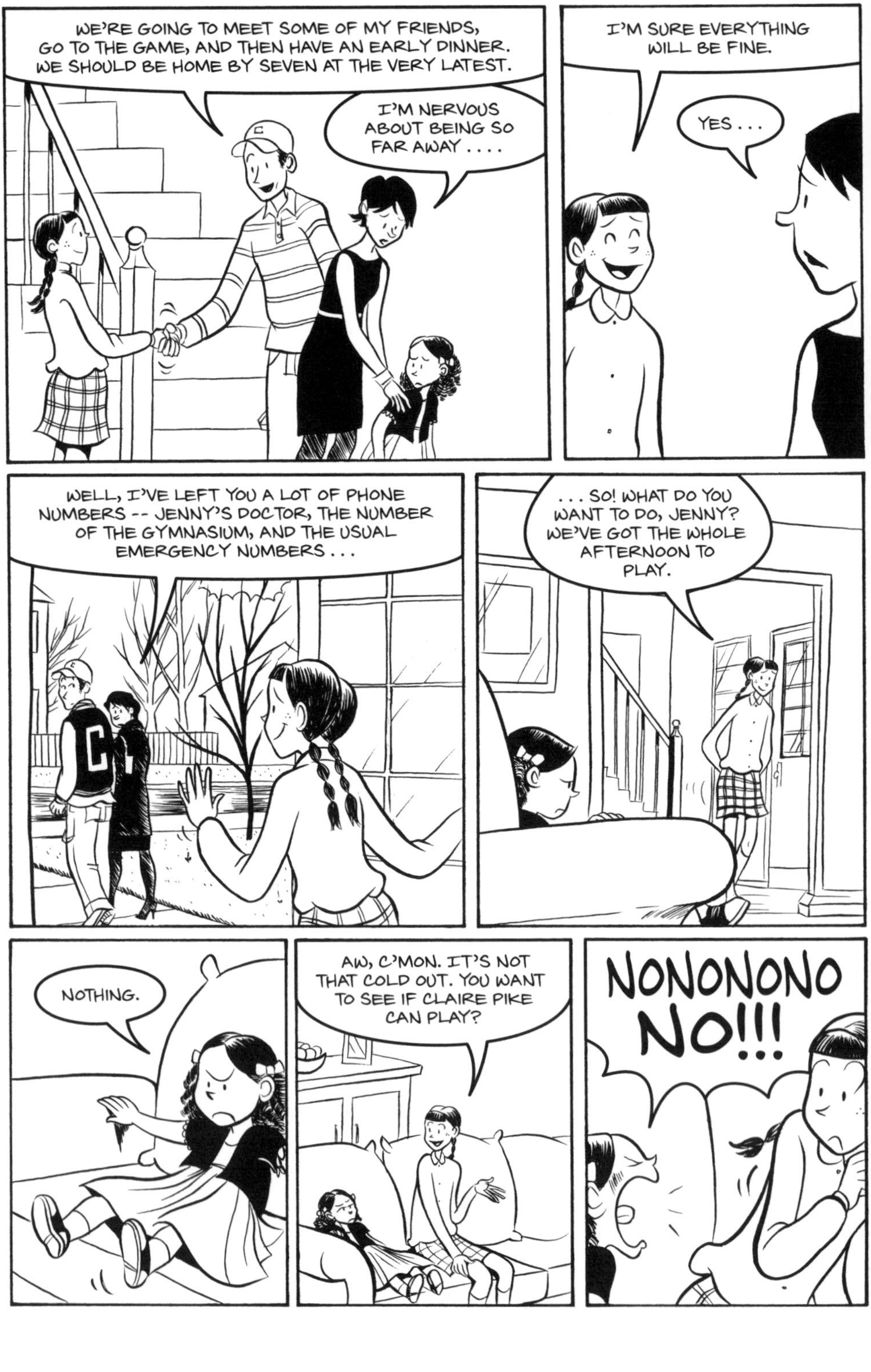
WE'RE GOING TO MEET SOME OF MY FRIENDS, GO TO THE GAME, AND THEN HAVE AN EARLY DINNER. WE SHOULD BE HOME BY SEVEN AT THE VERY LATEST.
I'M NERVOUS ABOUT BEING SO FAR AWAY . . . .
I'M SURE EVERYTHING WILL BE FINE.
YES . . .
WELL, I'VE LEFT YOU A LOT OF PHONE NUMBERS -- JENNY'S DOCTOR, THE NUMBER OF THE GYMNASIUM, AND THE USUAL EMERGENCY NUMBERS . . .
. . . SO! WHAT DO YOU WANT TO DO, JENNY? WE'VE GOT THE WHOLE AFTERNOON TO PLAY.
NOTHING.
AW, C'MON. IT'S NOT THAT COLD OUT. YOU WANT TO SEE IF CLAIRE PIKE CAN PLAY?
NONONONO NO!!!

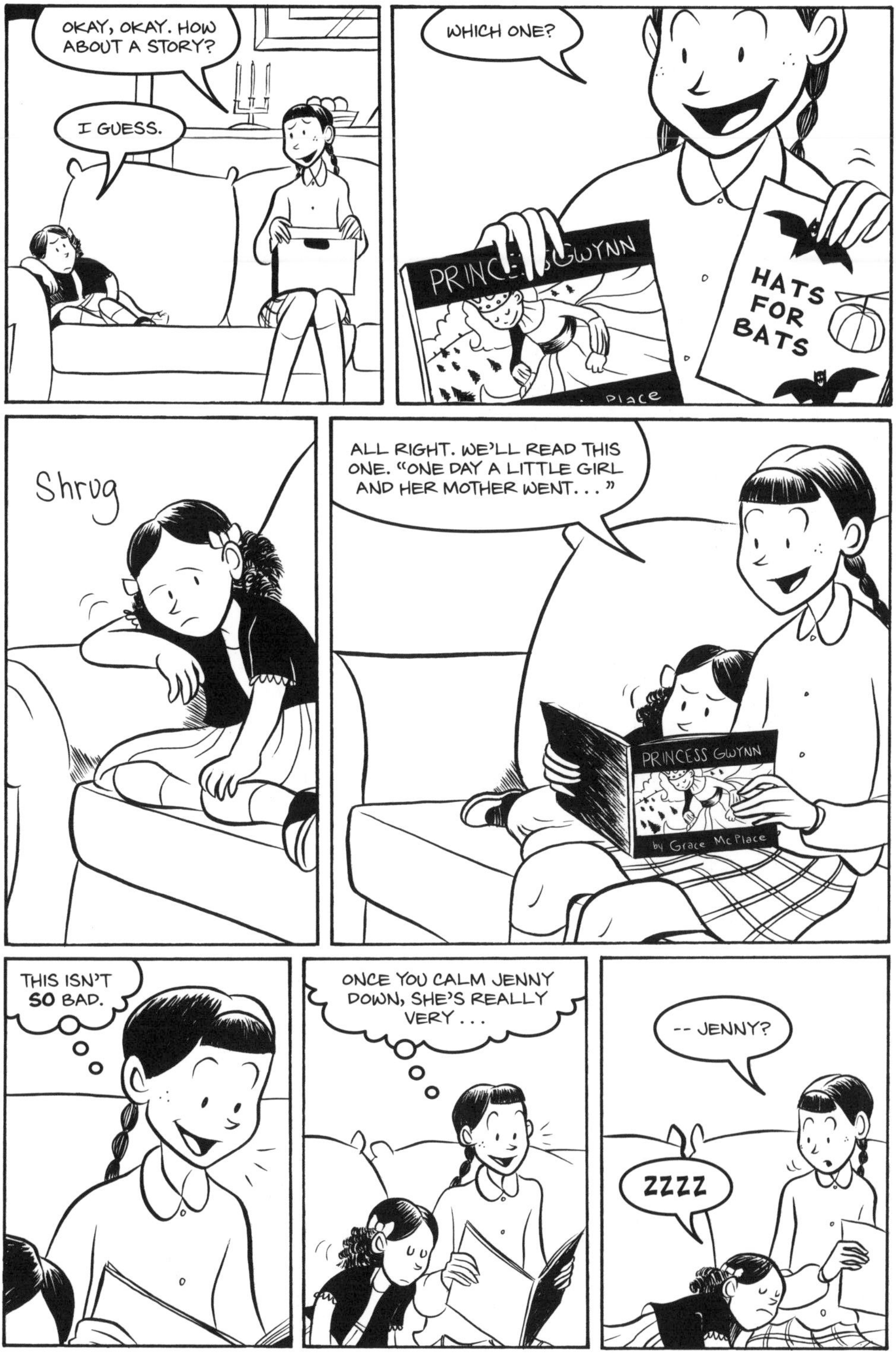
OKAY, OKAY. HOW ABOUT A STORY?
I GUESS.
WHICH ONE?
PRINCESS GWYNN
HATS FOR BATS
Shrug
ALL RIGHT. WE'LL READ THIS ONE. "ONE DAY A LITTLE GIRL AND HER MOTHER WENT . . ."
PRINCESS GWYNN
by Grace McPlace
THIS ISN'T **SO** BAD.
ONCE YOU CALM JENNY DOWN, SHE'S REALLY VERY . . .
-- JENNY?
ZZZZ

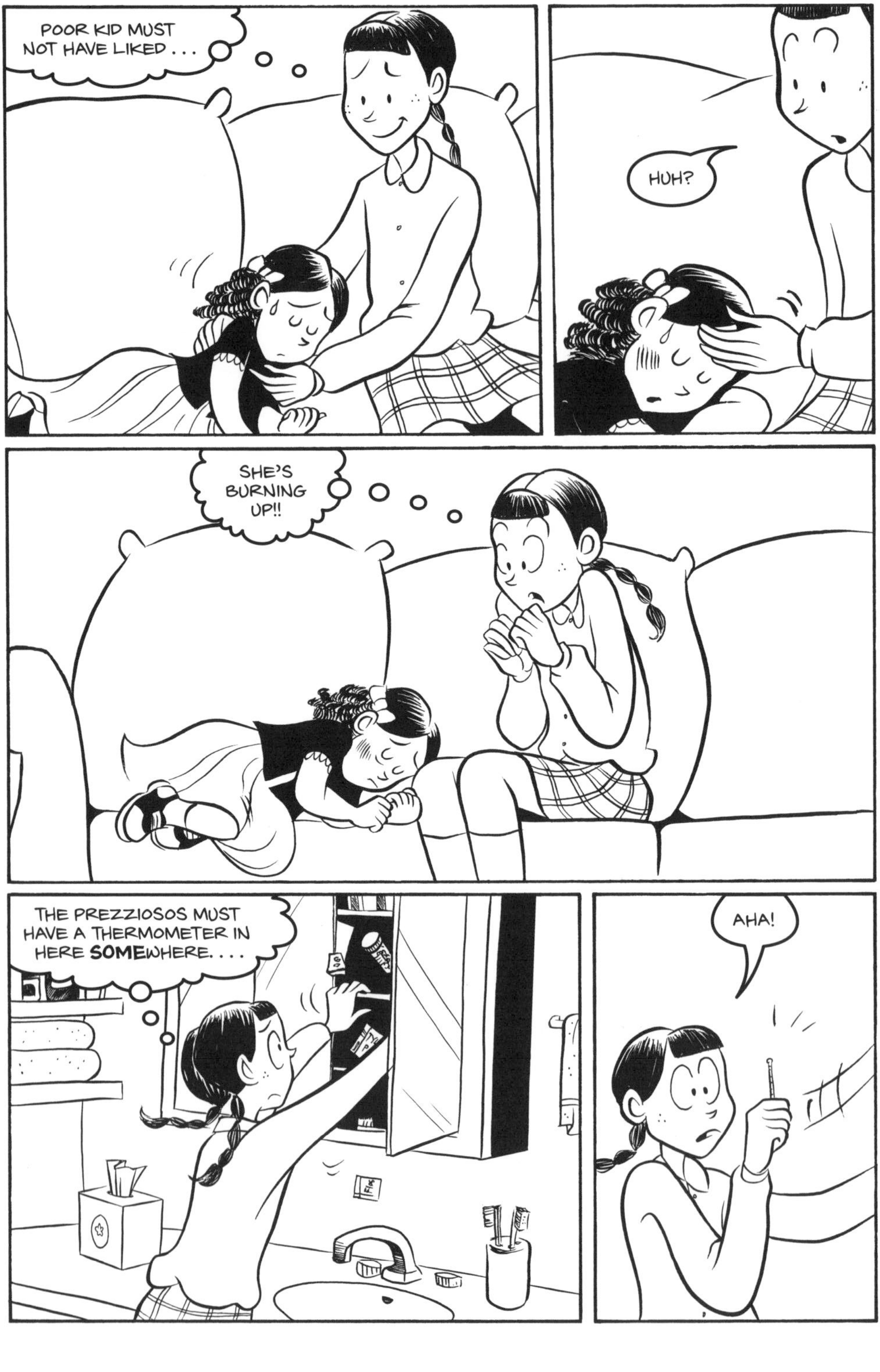
POOR KID MUST NOT HAVE LIKED . . .
HUH?
SHE'S BURNING UP!!
THE PREZZIOSOS MUST HAVE A THERMOMETER IN HERE **SOME**WHERE. . . .
AHA!

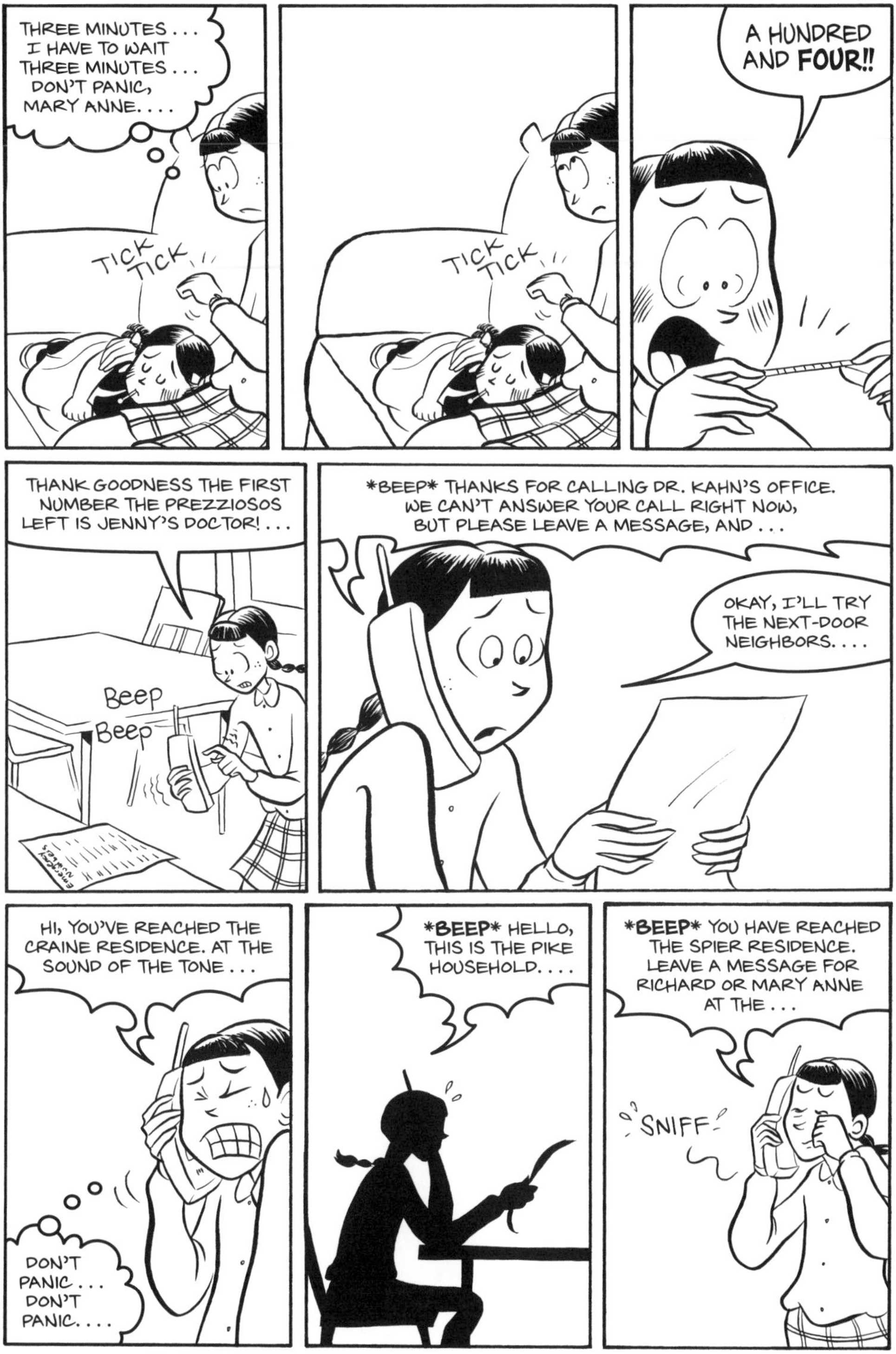
THREE MINUTES . . . I HAVE TO WAIT THREE MINUTES . . . DON'T PANIC, MARY ANNE. . . .
TICK TICK
TICK TICK
A HUNDRED AND **FOUR!!**
THANK GOODNESS THE FIRST NUMBER THE PREZZIOSOS LEFT IS JENNY'S DOCTOR! . . .
Beep Beep
BEEP THANKS FOR CALLING DR. KAHN'S OFFICE. WE CAN'T ANSWER YOUR CALL RIGHT NOW, BUT PLEASE LEAVE A MESSAGE, AND . . .
OKAY, I'LL TRY THE NEXT-DOOR NEIGHBORS. . . .
HI, YOU'VE REACHED THE CRAINE RESIDENCE. AT THE SOUND OF THE TONE . . .
DON'T PANIC . . . DON'T PANIC. . . .
BEEP HELLO, THIS IS THE PIKE HOUSEHOLD. . . .
BEEP YOU HAVE REACHED THE SPIER RESIDENCE. LEAVE A MESSAGE FOR RICHARD OR MARY ANNE AT THE . . .
SNIFF

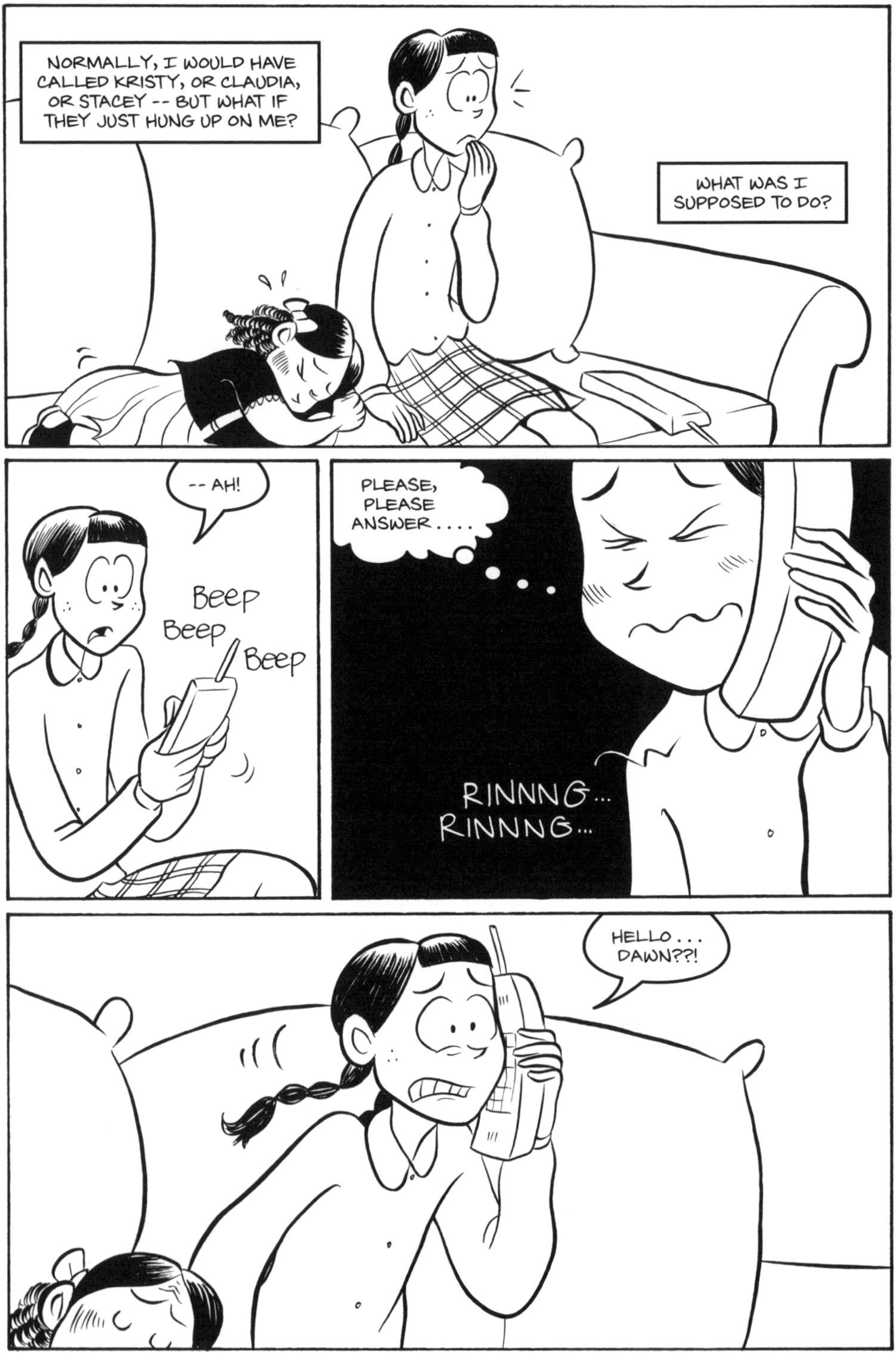
NORMALLY, I WOULD HAVE CALLED KRISTY, OR CLAUDIA, OR STACEY -- BUT WHAT IF THEY JUST HUNG UP ON ME?
WHAT WAS I SUPPOSED TO DO?
-- AH!
Beep
Beep
Beep
PLEASE, PLEASE ANSWER....
RINNNG...
RINNNG...
HELLO... DAWN??!

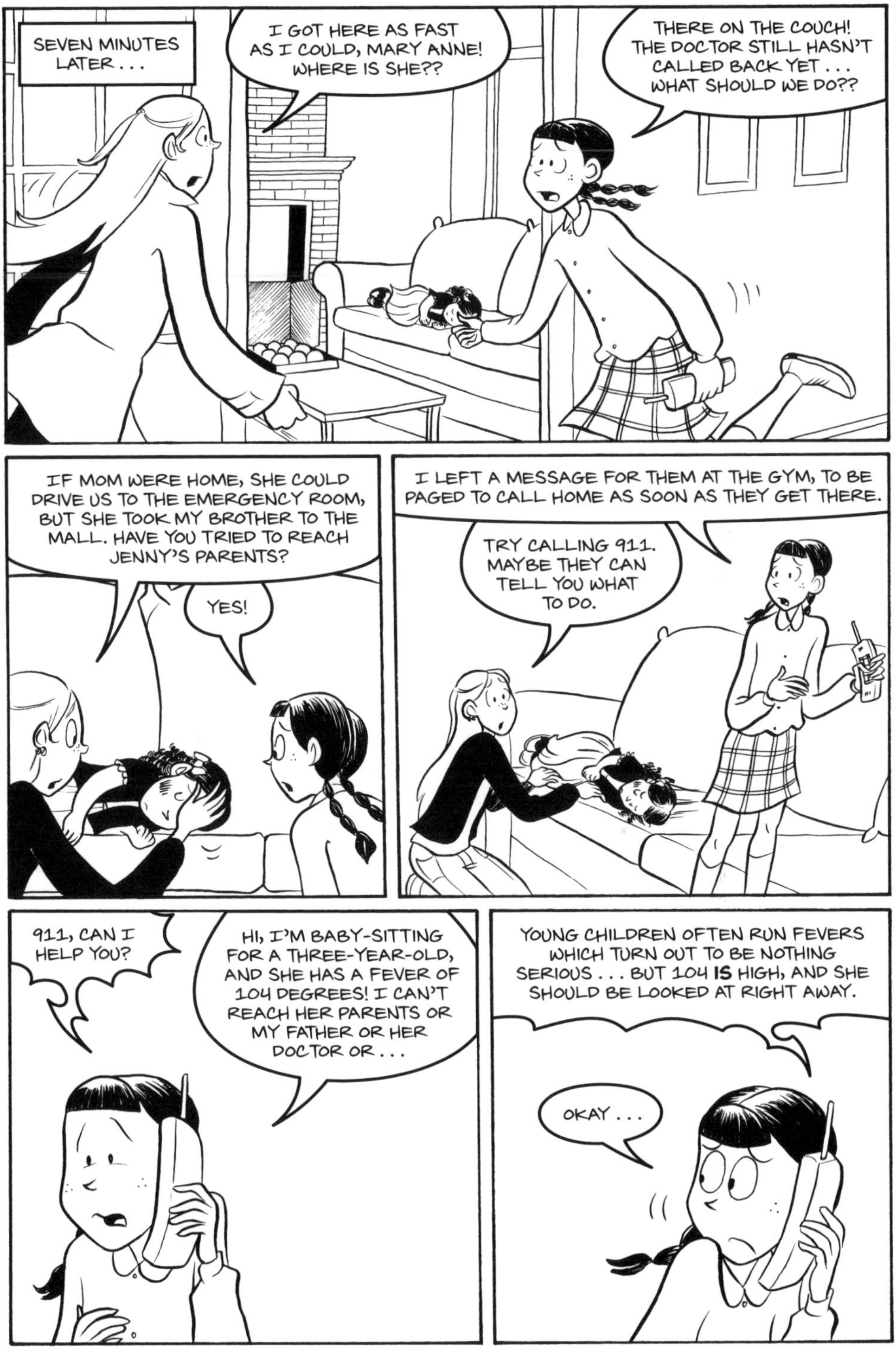
SEVEN MINUTES LATER . . .
I GOT HERE AS FAST AS I COULD, MARY ANNE! WHERE IS SHE??
THERE ON THE COUCH! THE DOCTOR STILL HASN'T CALLED BACK YET . . . WHAT SHOULD WE DO??
IF MOM WERE HOME, SHE COULD DRIVE US TO THE EMERGENCY ROOM, BUT SHE TOOK MY BROTHER TO THE MALL. HAVE YOU TRIED TO REACH JENNY'S PARENTS?
YES!
I LEFT A MESSAGE FOR THEM AT THE GYM, TO BE PAGED TO CALL HOME AS SOON AS THEY GET THERE.
TRY CALLING 911. MAYBE THEY CAN TELL YOU WHAT TO DO.
911, CAN I HELP YOU?
HI, I'M BABY-SITTING FOR A THREE-YEAR-OLD, AND SHE HAS A FEVER OF 104 DEGREES! I CAN'T REACH HER PARENTS OR MY FATHER OR HER DOCTOR OR . . .
YOUNG CHILDREN OFTEN RUN FEVERS WHICH TURN OUT TO BE NOTHING SERIOUS . . . BUT 104 **IS** HIGH, AND SHE SHOULD BE LOOKED AT RIGHT AWAY.
OKAY . . .

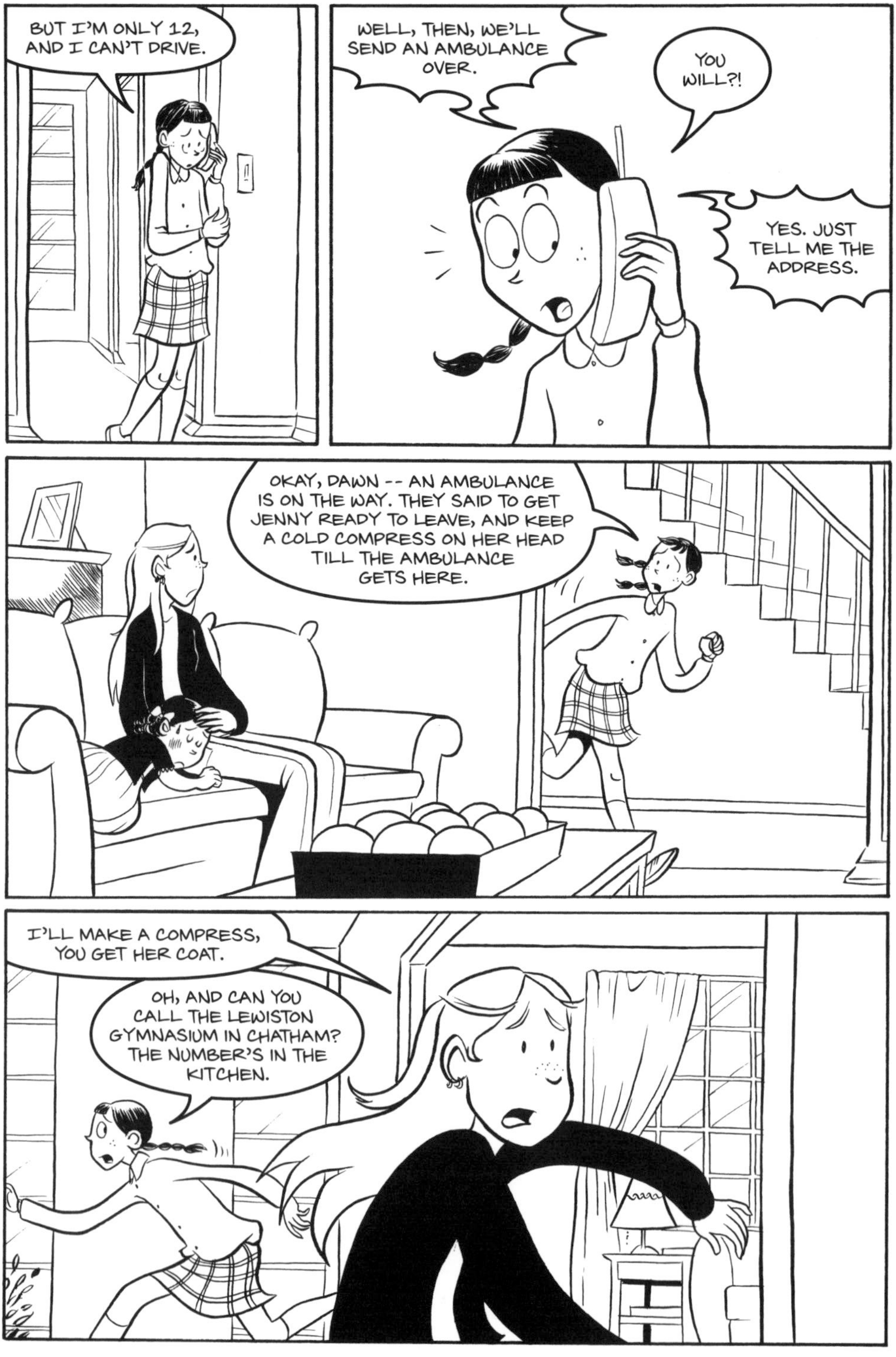
BUT I'M ONLY 12, AND I CAN'T DRIVE.
WELL, THEN, WE'LL SEND AN AMBULANCE OVER.
YOU WILL?!
YES. JUST TELL ME THE ADDRESS.
OKAY, DAWN -- AN AMBULANCE IS ON THE WAY. THEY SAID TO GET JENNY READY TO LEAVE, AND KEEP A COLD COMPRESS ON HER HEAD TILL THE AMBULANCE GETS HERE.
I'LL MAKE A COMPRESS, YOU GET HER COAT.
OH, AND CAN YOU CALL THE LEWISTON GYMNASIUM IN CHATHAM? THE NUMBER'S IN THE KITCHEN.

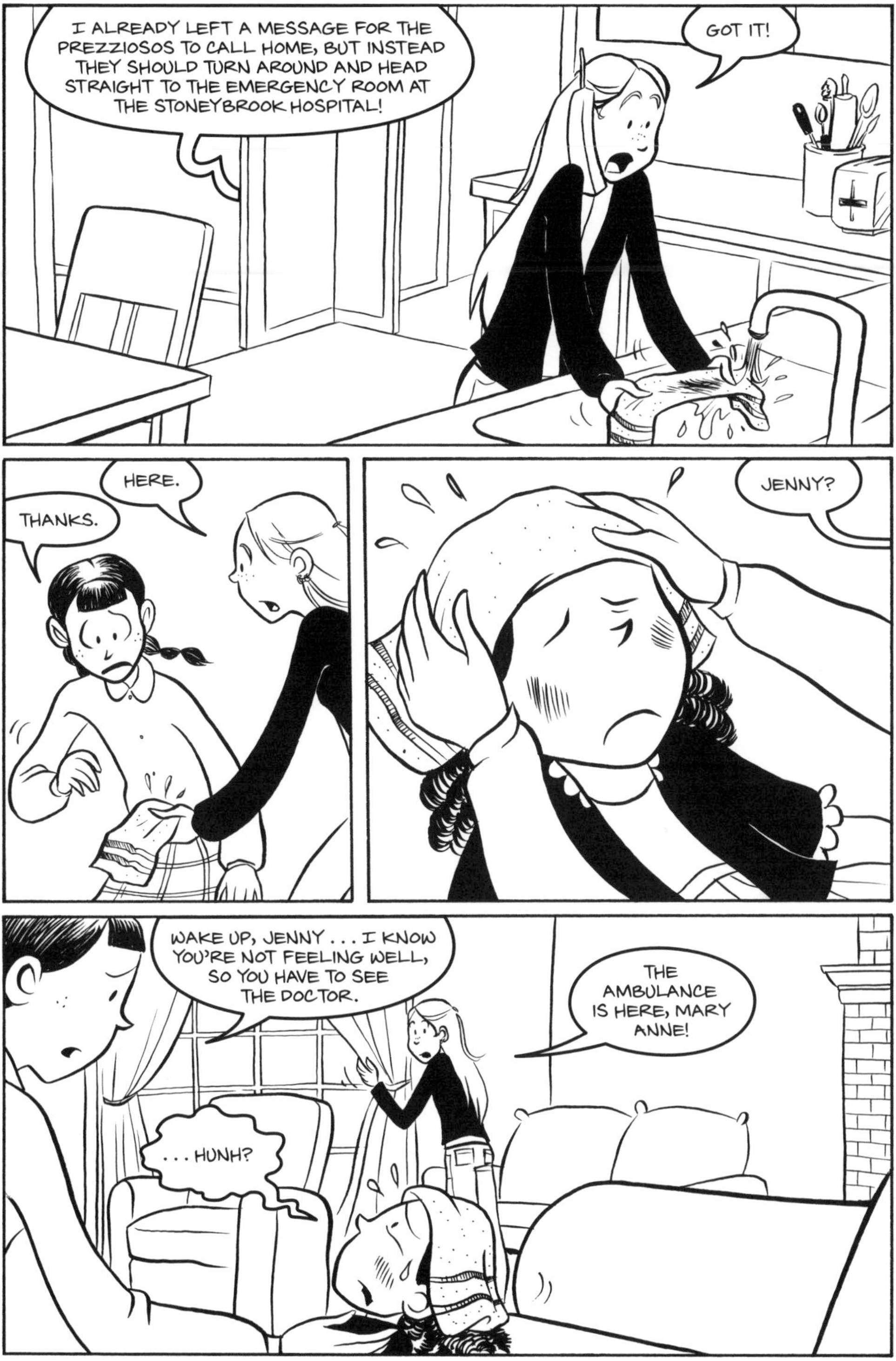
I ALREADY LEFT A MESSAGE FOR THE PREZZIOSOS TO CALL HOME, BUT INSTEAD THEY SHOULD TURN AROUND AND HEAD STRAIGHT TO THE EMERGENCY ROOM AT THE STONEYBROOK HOSPITAL!
GOT IT!
HERE.
THANKS.
JENNY?
WAKE UP, JENNY . . . I KNOW YOU'RE NOT FEELING WELL, SO YOU HAVE TO SEE THE DOCTOR.
THE AMBULANCE IS HERE, MARY ANNE!
. . . HUNH?

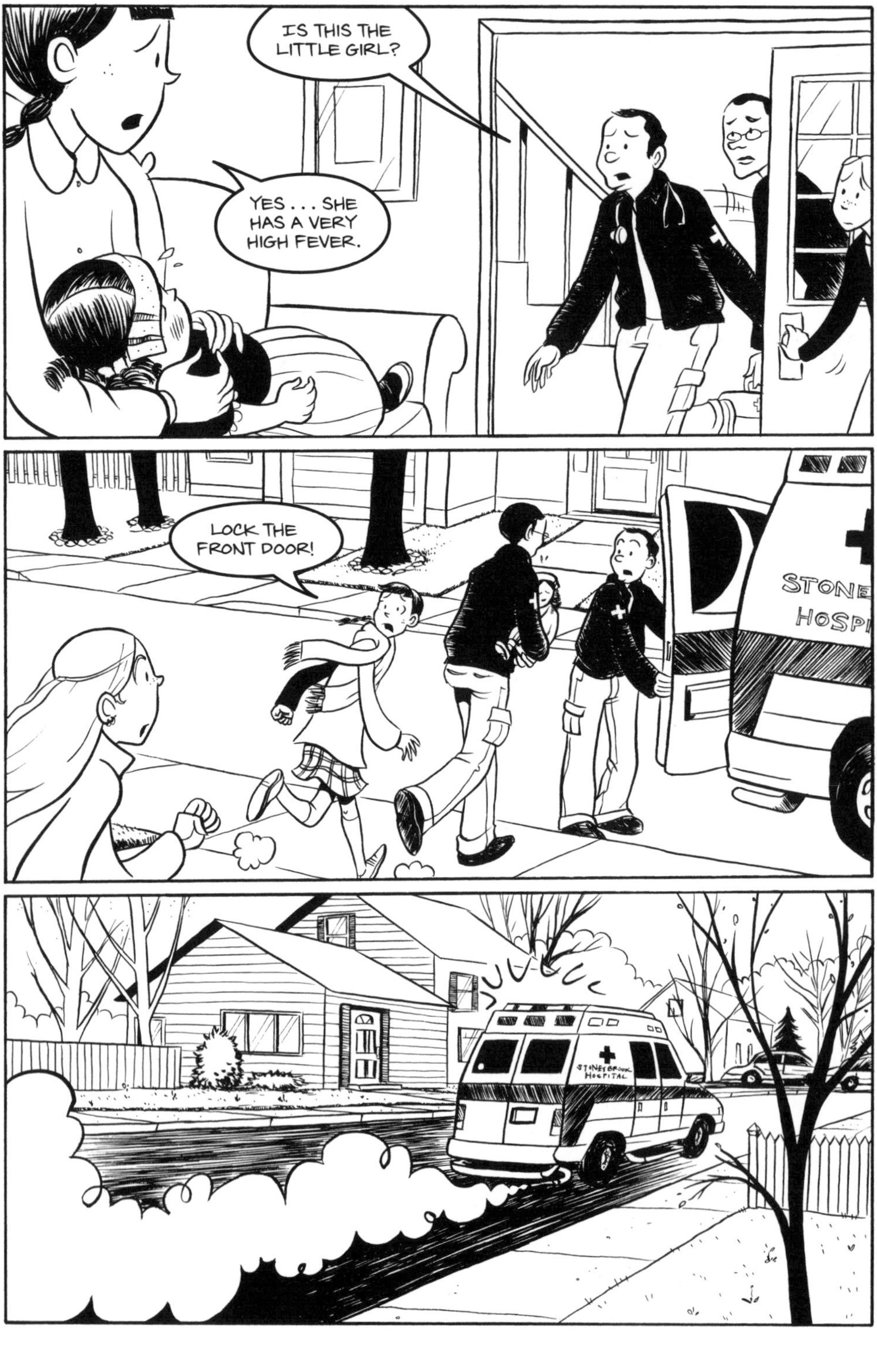
IS THIS THE LITTLE GIRL?
YES . . . SHE HAS A VERY HIGH FEVER.
LOCK THE FRONT DOOR!
STONE
HOSPI
STONEYBROOK HOSPITAL

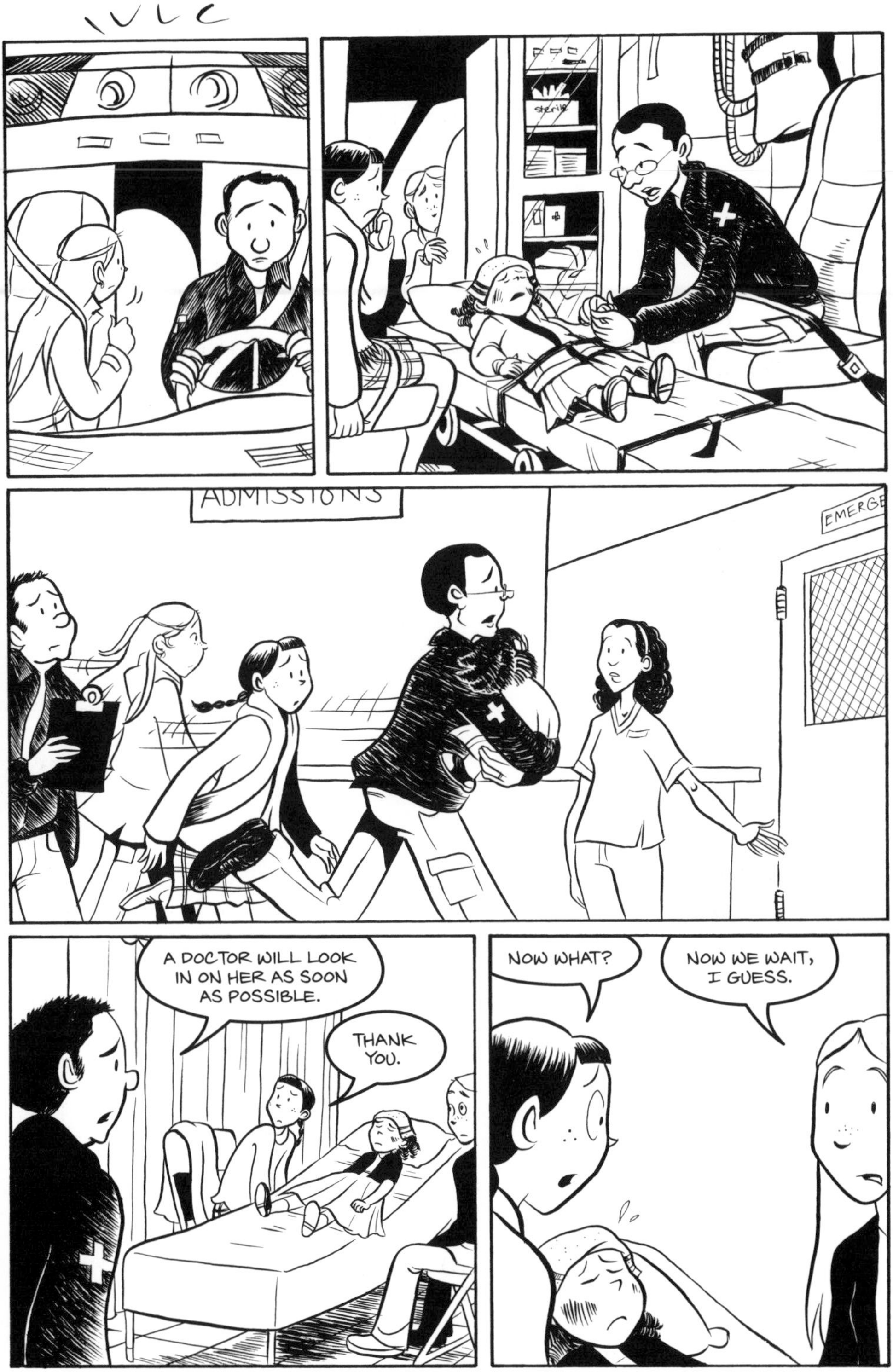
sterile
ADMISSIONS
EMERGE
A DOCTOR WILL LOOK IN ON HER AS SOON AS POSSIBLE.
THANK YOU.
NOW WHAT?
NOW WE WAIT, I GUESS.

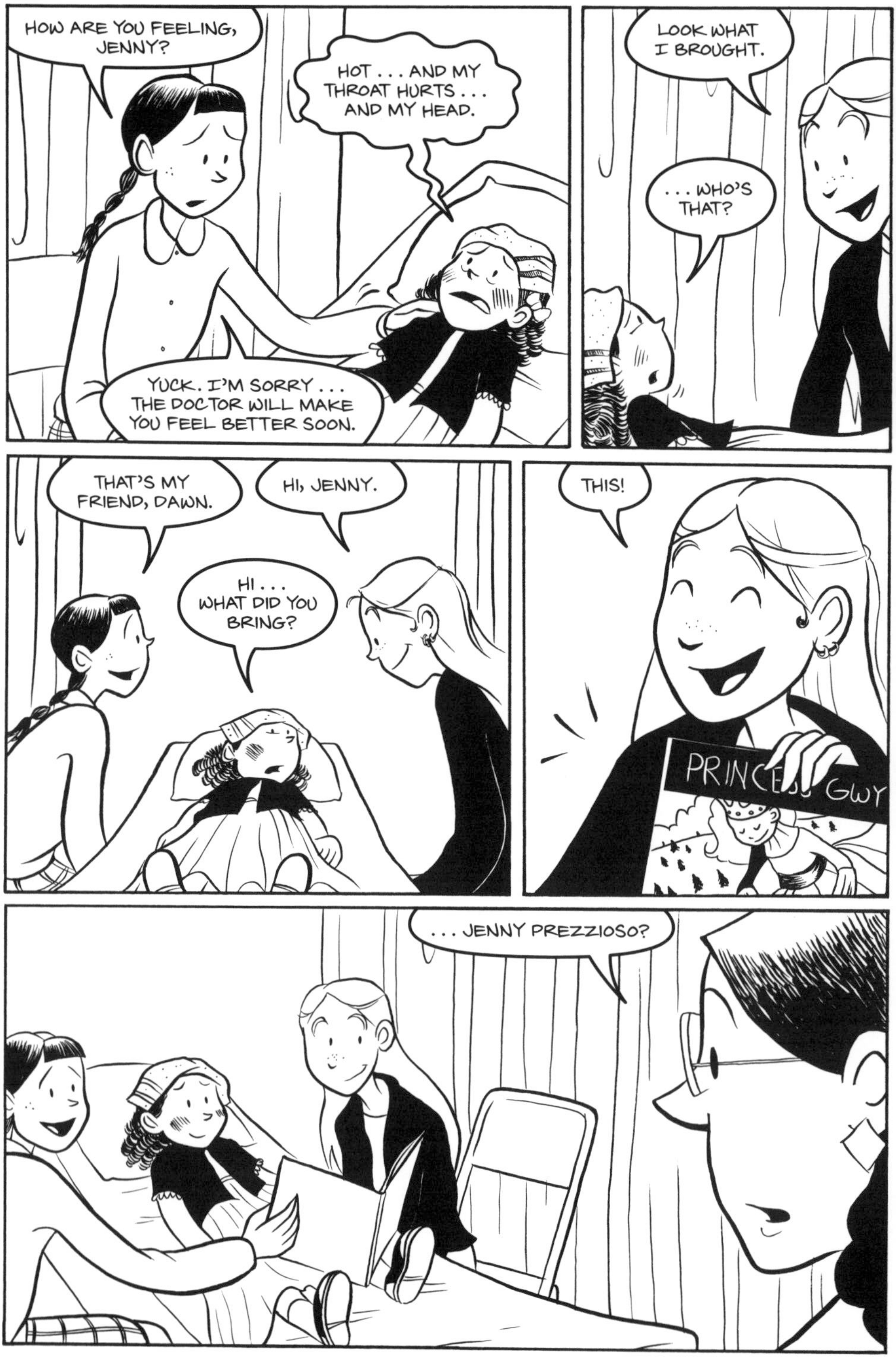
HOW ARE YOU FEELING, JENNY?
HOT . . . AND MY THROAT HURTS . . . AND MY HEAD.
YUCK. I'M SORRY . . . THE DOCTOR WILL MAKE YOU FEEL BETTER SOON.
LOOK WHAT I BROUGHT.
. . . WHO'S THAT?
THAT'S MY FRIEND, DAWN.
HI, JENNY.
HI . . . WHAT DID YOU BRING?
THIS!
PRINCESS GWY
. . . JENNY PREZZIOSO?

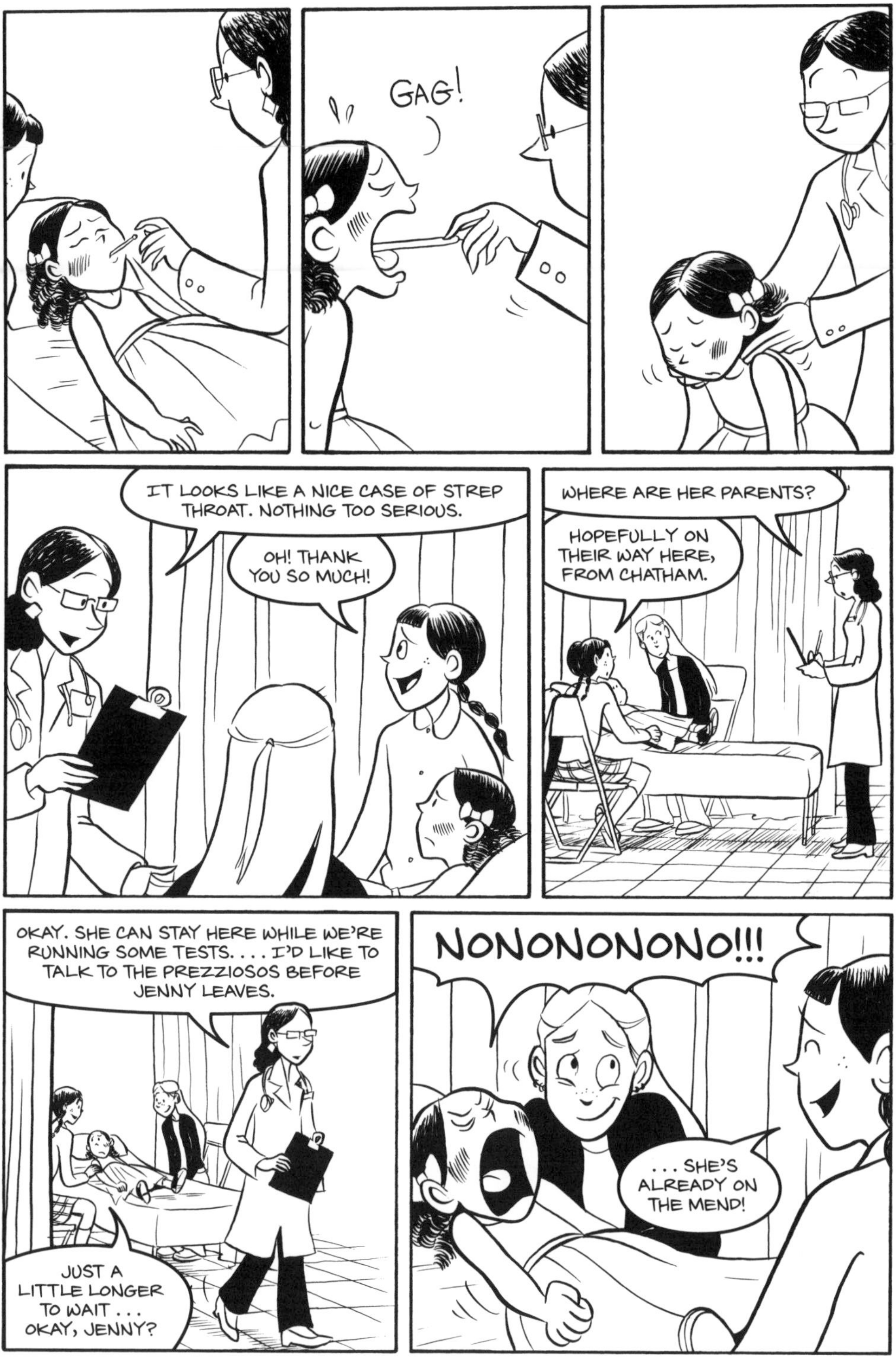
GAG!
IT LOOKS LIKE A NICE CASE OF STREP THROAT. NOTHING TOO SERIOUS.
OH! THANK YOU SO MUCH!
WHERE ARE HER PARENTS?
HOPEFULLY ON THEIR WAY HERE, FROM CHATHAM.
OKAY. SHE CAN STAY HERE WHILE WE'RE RUNNING SOME TESTS. . . . I'D LIKE TO TALK TO THE PREZZIOSOS BEFORE JENNY LEAVES.
JUST A LITTLE LONGER TO WAIT . . . OKAY, JENNY?
NONONONONO!!!
. . . SHE'S ALREADY ON THE MEND!

Chapter 12

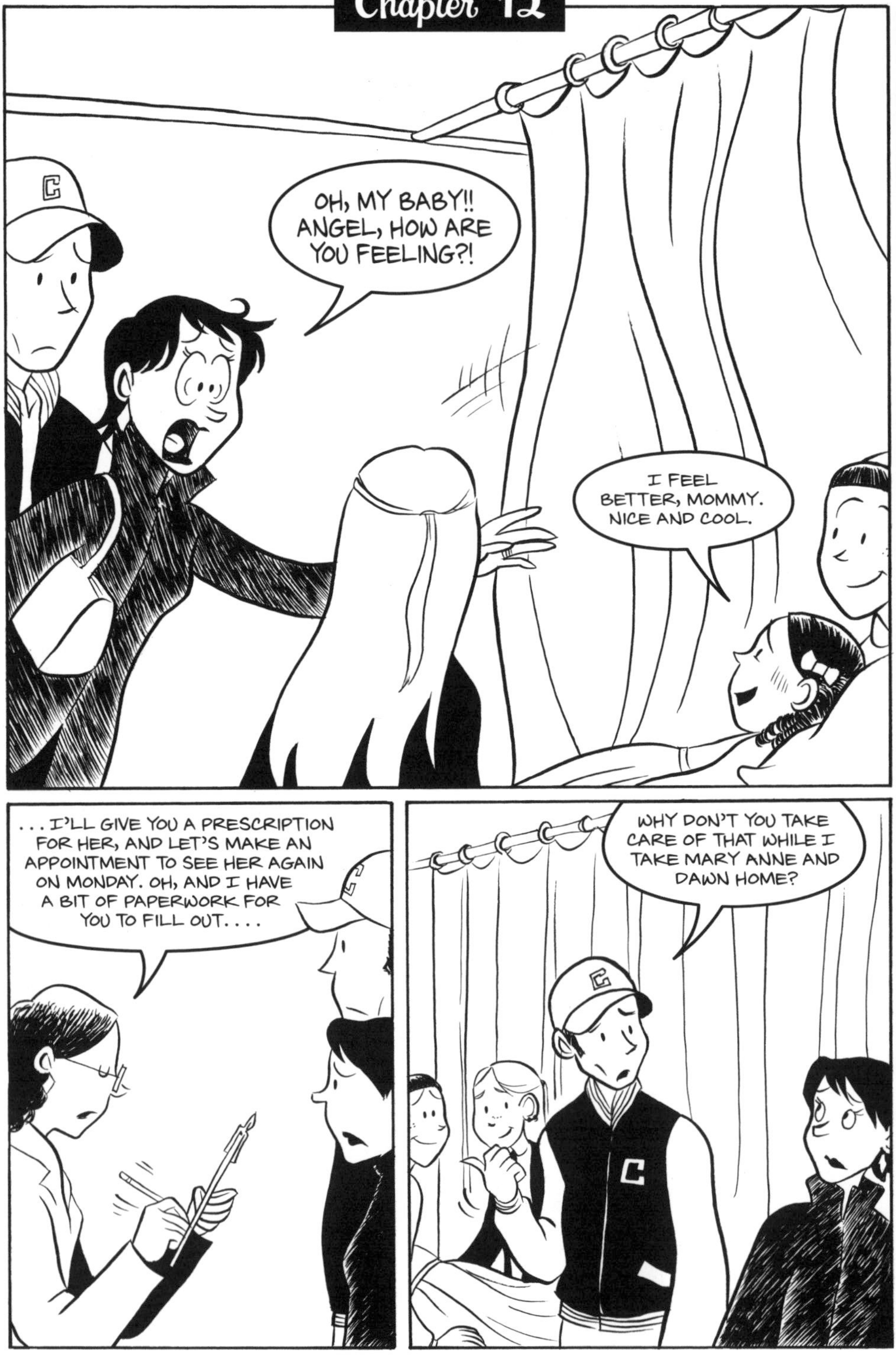

OH, MY BABY!! ANGEL, HOW ARE YOU FEELING?!
I FEEL BETTER, MOMMY. NICE AND COOL.
. . . I'LL GIVE YOU A PRESCRIPTION FOR HER, AND LET'S MAKE AN APPOINTMENT TO SEE HER AGAIN ON MONDAY. OH, AND I HAVE A BIT OF PAPERWORK FOR YOU TO FILL OUT. . . .
WHY DON'T YOU TAKE CARE OF THAT WHILE I TAKE MARY ANNE AND DAWN HOME?

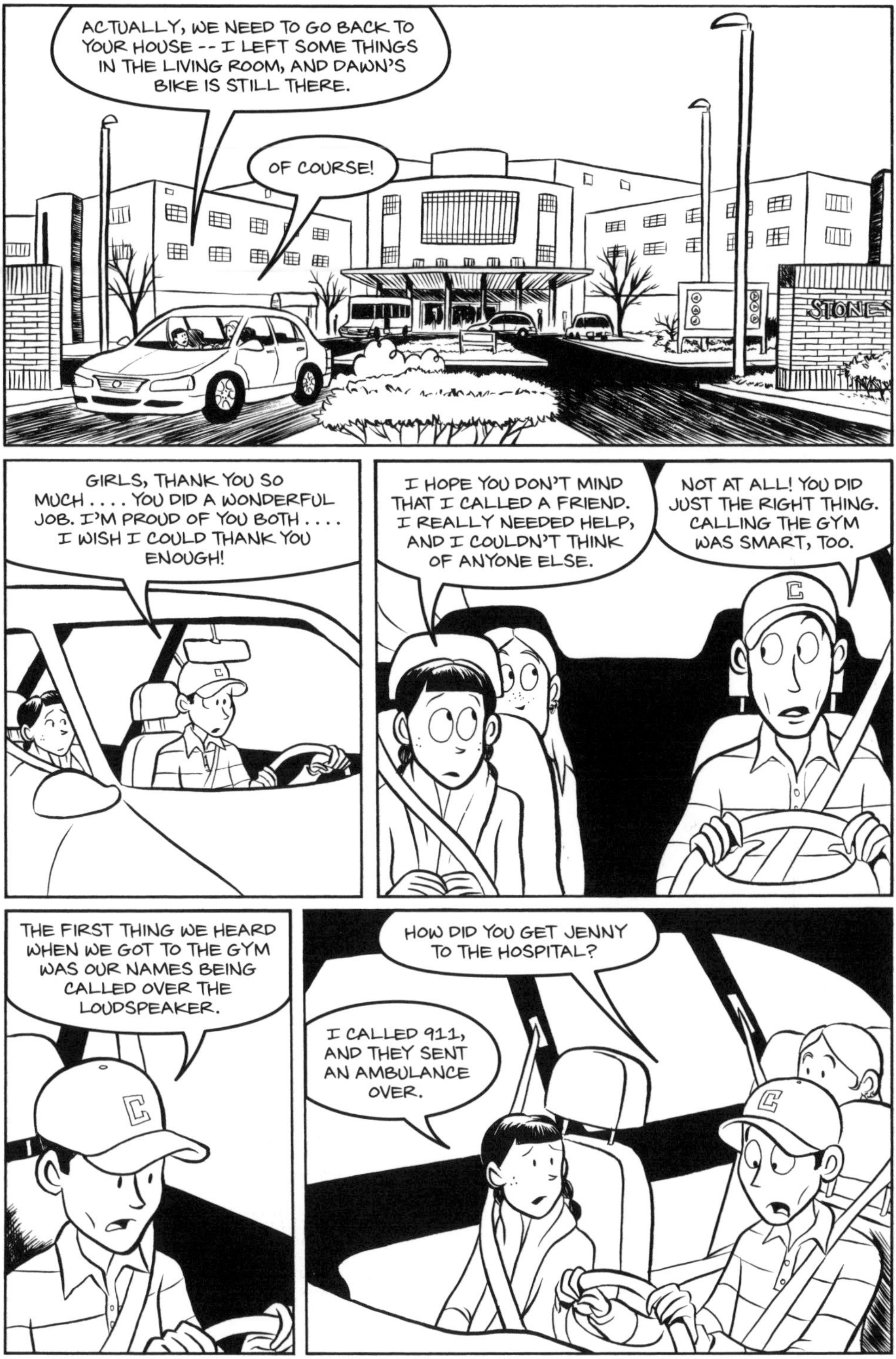
ACTUALLY, WE NEED TO GO BACK TO YOUR HOUSE -- I LEFT SOME THINGS IN THE LIVING ROOM, AND DAWN'S BIKE IS STILL THERE.
OF COURSE!
GIRLS, THANK YOU SO MUCH . . . . YOU DID A WONDERFUL JOB. I'M PROUD OF YOU BOTH . . . . I WISH I COULD THANK YOU ENOUGH!
I HOPE YOU DON'T MIND THAT I CALLED A FRIEND. I REALLY NEEDED HELP, AND I COULDN'T THINK OF ANYONE ELSE.
NOT AT ALL! YOU DID JUST THE RIGHT THING. CALLING THE GYM WAS SMART, TOO.
THE FIRST THING WE HEARD WHEN WE GOT TO THE GYM WAS OUR NAMES BEING CALLED OVER THE LOUDSPEAKER.
HOW DID YOU GET JENNY TO THE HOSPITAL?
I CALLED 911, AND THEY SENT AN AMBULANCE OVER.

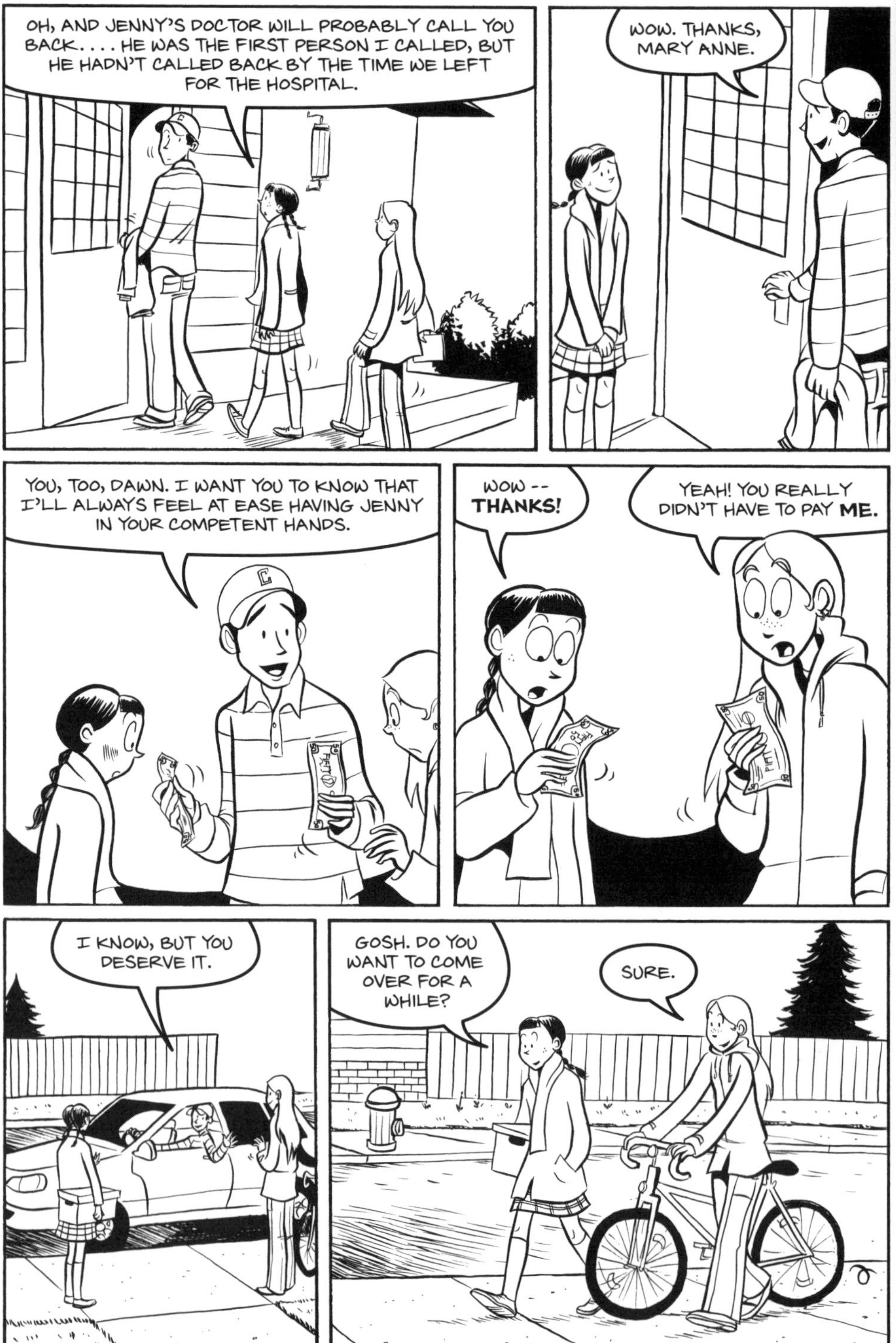

OH, AND JENNY'S DOCTOR WILL PROBABLY CALL YOU BACK. . . . HE WAS THE FIRST PERSON I CALLED, BUT HE HADN'T CALLED BACK BY THE TIME WE LEFT FOR THE HOSPITAL.
WOW. THANKS, MARY ANNE.
YOU, TOO, DAWN. I WANT YOU TO KNOW THAT I'LL ALWAYS FEEL AT EASE HAVING JENNY IN YOUR COMPETENT HANDS.
WOW -- **THANKS!**
YEAH! YOU REALLY DIDN'T HAVE TO PAY **ME.**
I KNOW, BUT YOU DESERVE IT.
GOSH. DO YOU WANT TO COME OVER FOR A WHILE?
SURE.

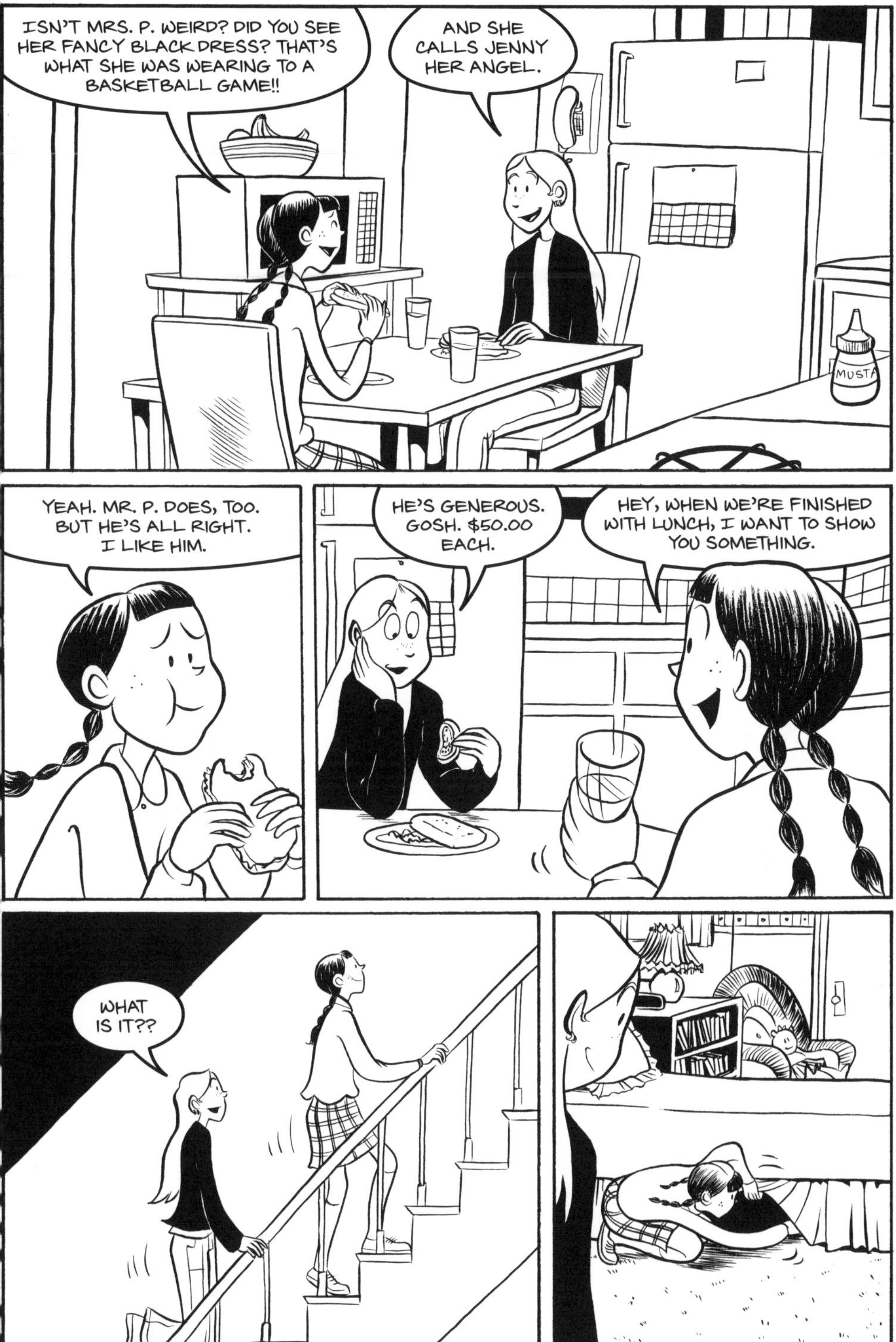
ISN'T MRS. P. WEIRD? DID YOU SEE HER FANCY BLACK DRESS? THAT'S WHAT SHE WAS WEARING TO A BASKETBALL GAME!!
AND SHE CALLS JENNY HER ANGEL.
MUSTA
YEAH. MR. P. DOES, TOO. BUT HE'S ALL RIGHT. I LIKE HIM.
HE'S GENEROUS. GOSH. $50.00 EACH.
HEY, WHEN WE'RE FINISHED WITH LUNCH, I WANT TO SHOW YOU SOMETHING.
WHAT IS IT??

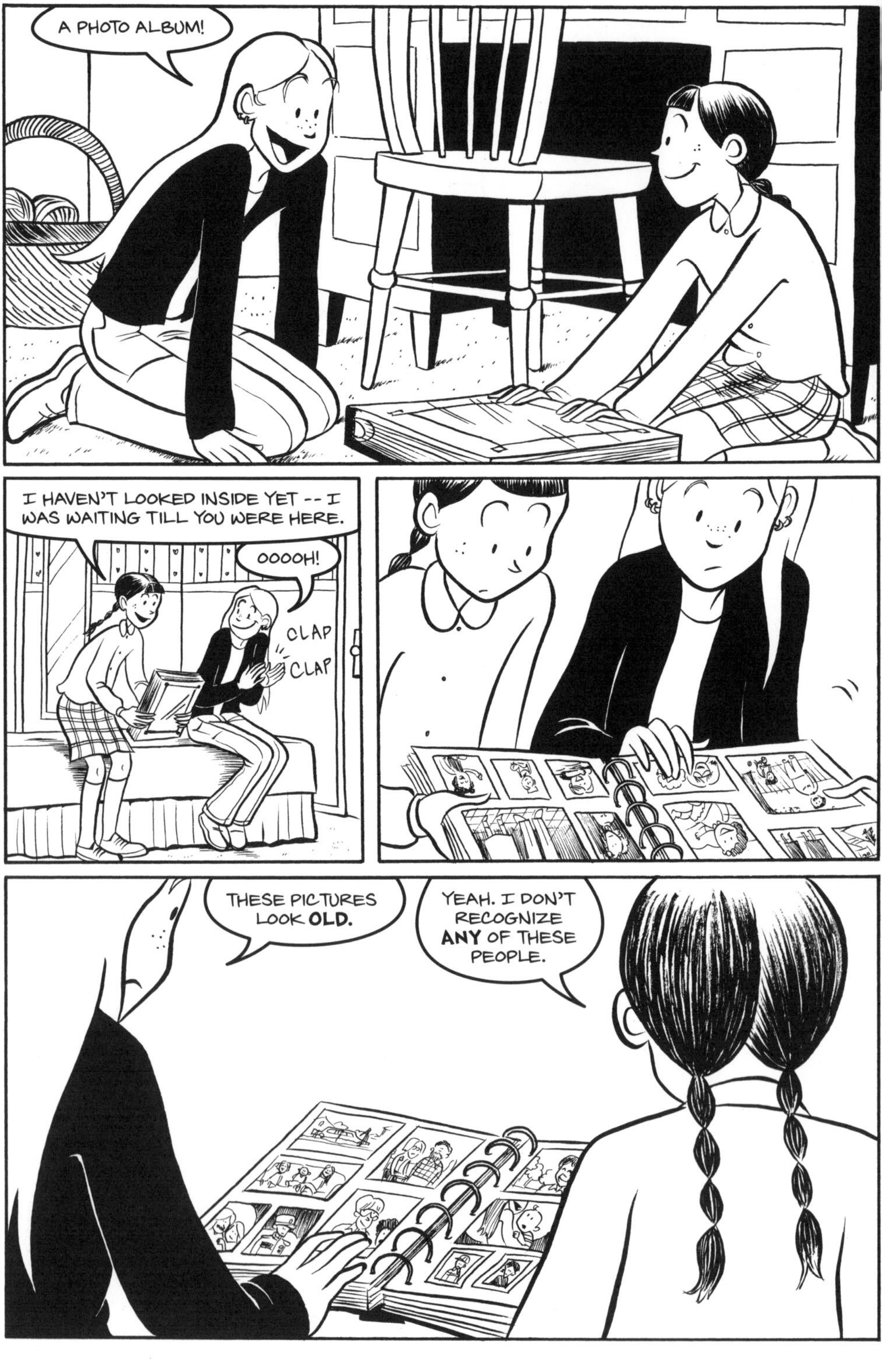
A PHOTO ALBUM!
I HAVEN'T LOOKED INSIDE YET -- I WAS WAITING TILL YOU WERE HERE.
OOOOH!
CLAP
CLAP
THESE PICTURES LOOK **OLD.**
YEAH. I DON'T RECOGNIZE **ANY** OF THESE PEOPLE.

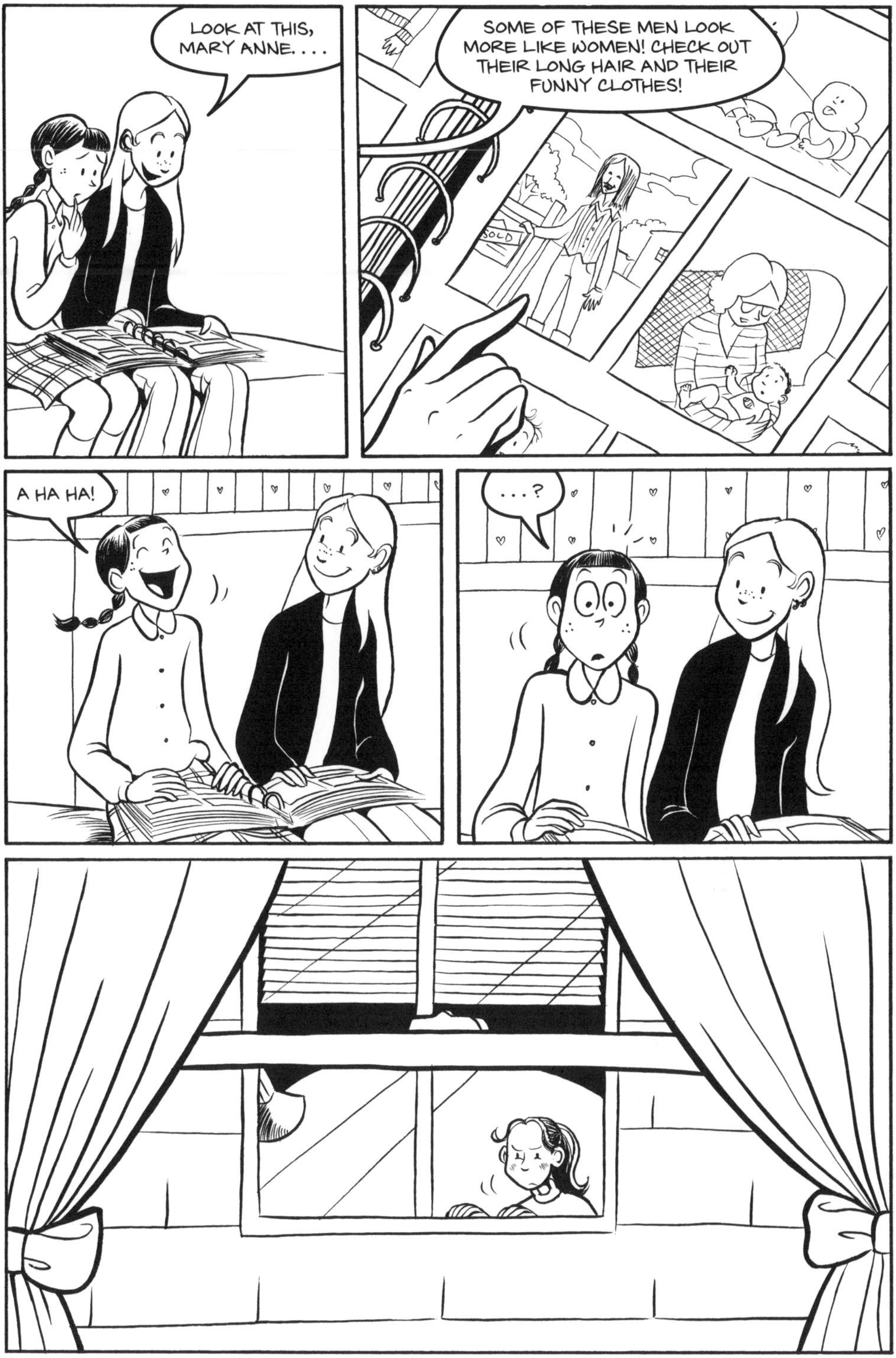
LOOK AT THIS, MARY ANNE. . . .
SOME OF THESE MEN LOOK MORE LIKE WOMEN! CHECK OUT THEIR LONG HAIR AND THEIR FUNNY CLOTHES!
SOLD
A HA HA!
. . . ?

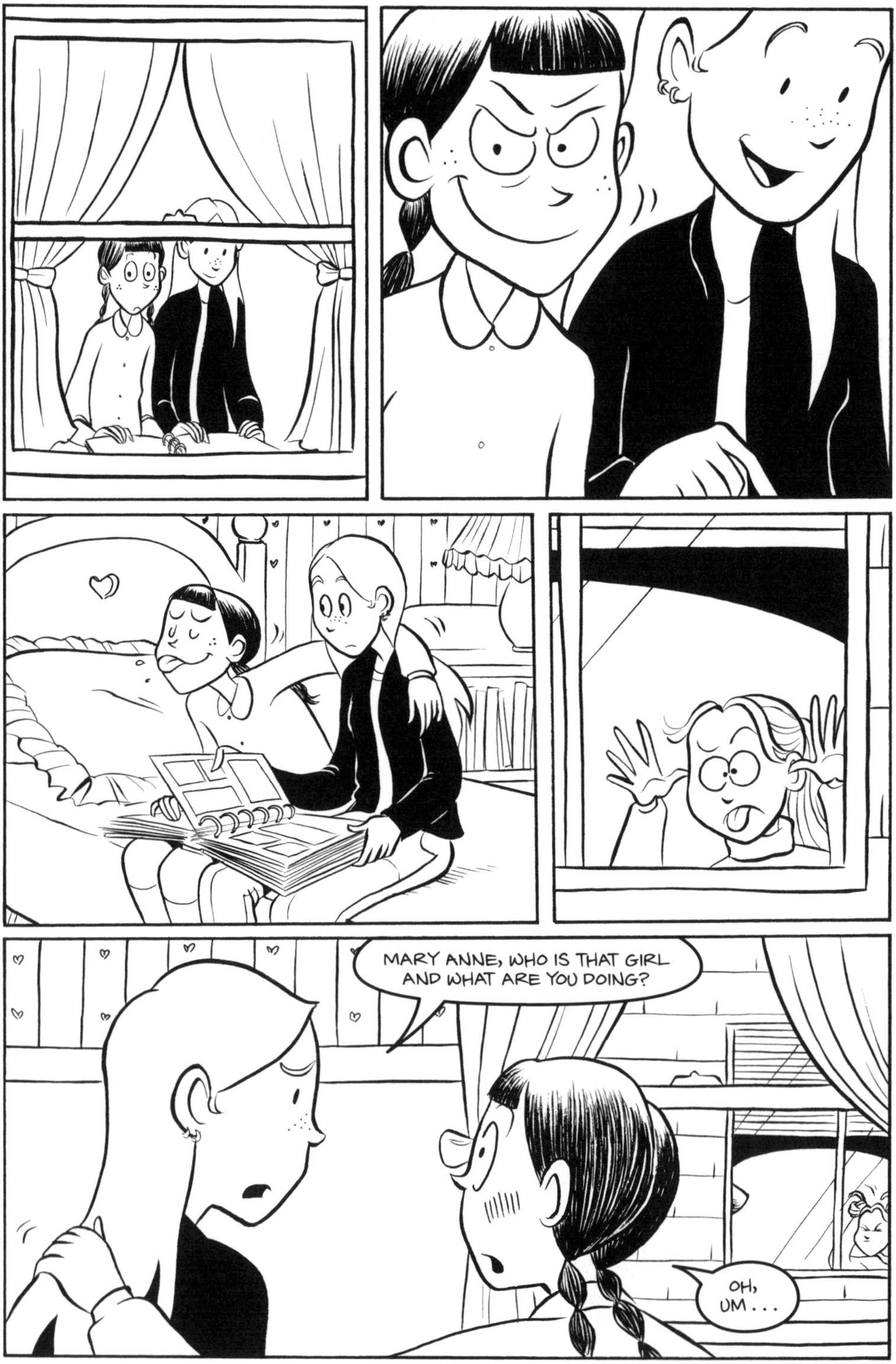
MARY ANNE, WHO IS THAT GIRL AND WHAT ARE YOU DOING?
OH, UM . . .

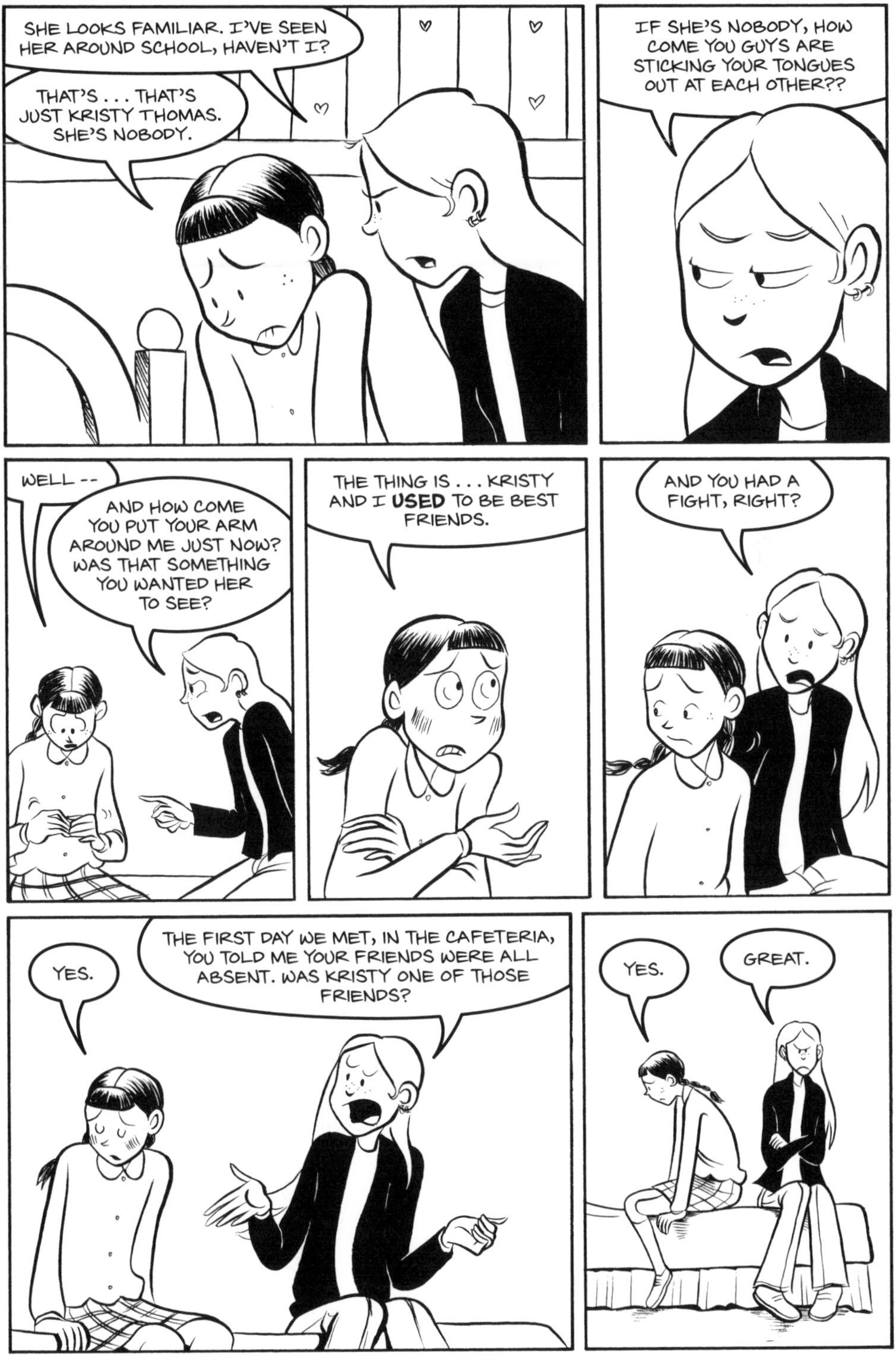
SHE LOOKS FAMILIAR. I'VE SEEN HER AROUND SCHOOL, HAVEN'T I?
THAT'S . . . THAT'S JUST KRISTY THOMAS. SHE'S NOBODY.
IF SHE'S NOBODY, HOW COME YOU GUYS ARE STICKING YOUR TONGUES OUT AT EACH OTHER??
WELL --
AND HOW COME YOU PUT YOUR ARM AROUND ME JUST NOW? WAS THAT SOMETHING YOU WANTED HER TO SEE?
THE THING IS . . . KRISTY AND I USED TO BE BEST FRIENDS.
AND YOU HAD A FIGHT, RIGHT?
YES.
THE FIRST DAY WE MET, IN THE CAFETERIA, YOU TOLD ME YOUR FRIENDS WERE ALL ABSENT. WAS KRISTY ONE OF THOSE FRIENDS?
YES.
GREAT.

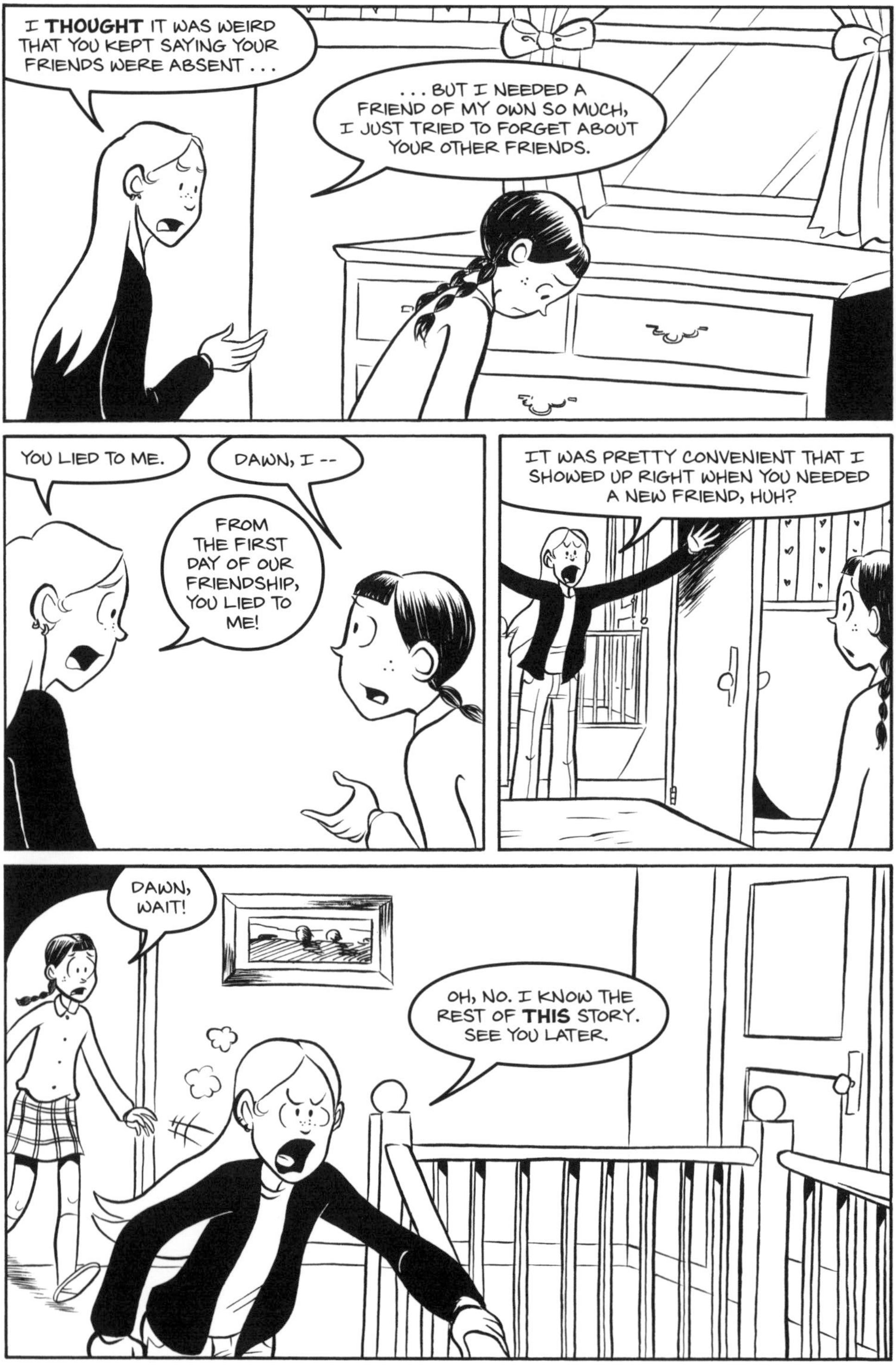
I **THOUGHT** IT WAS WEIRD THAT YOU KEPT SAYING YOUR FRIENDS WERE ABSENT . . .
. . . BUT I NEEDED A FRIEND OF MY OWN SO MUCH, I JUST TRIED TO FORGET ABOUT YOUR OTHER FRIENDS.
YOU LIED TO ME.
DAWN, I --
FROM THE FIRST DAY OF OUR FRIENDSHIP, YOU LIED TO ME!
IT WAS PRETTY CONVENIENT THAT I SHOWED UP RIGHT WHEN YOU NEEDED A NEW FRIEND, HUH?
DAWN, WAIT!
OH, NO. I KNOW THE REST OF **THIS** STORY. SEE YOU LATER.

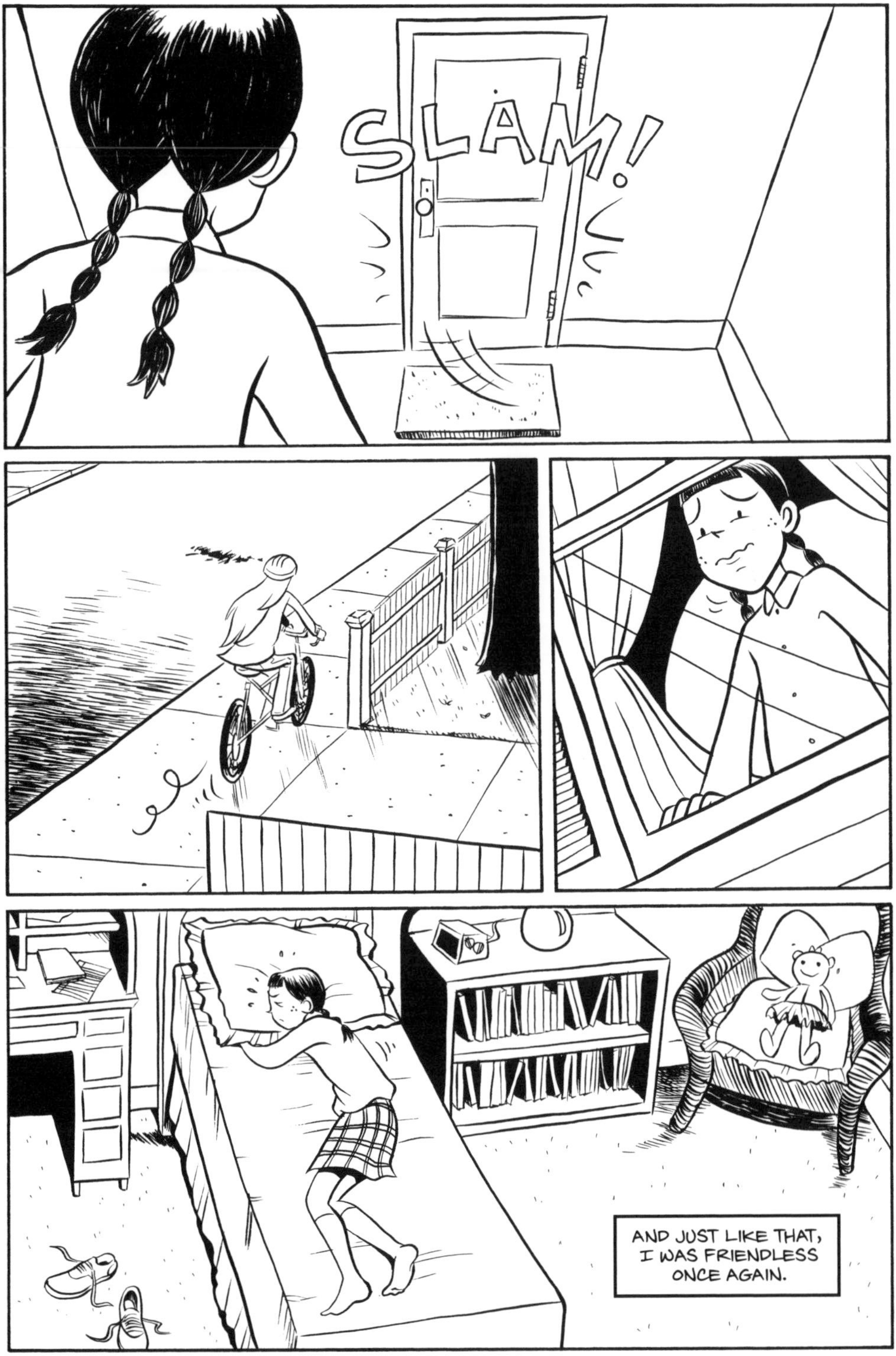
SLAM!
AND JUST LIKE THAT, I WAS FRIENDLESS ONCE AGAIN.

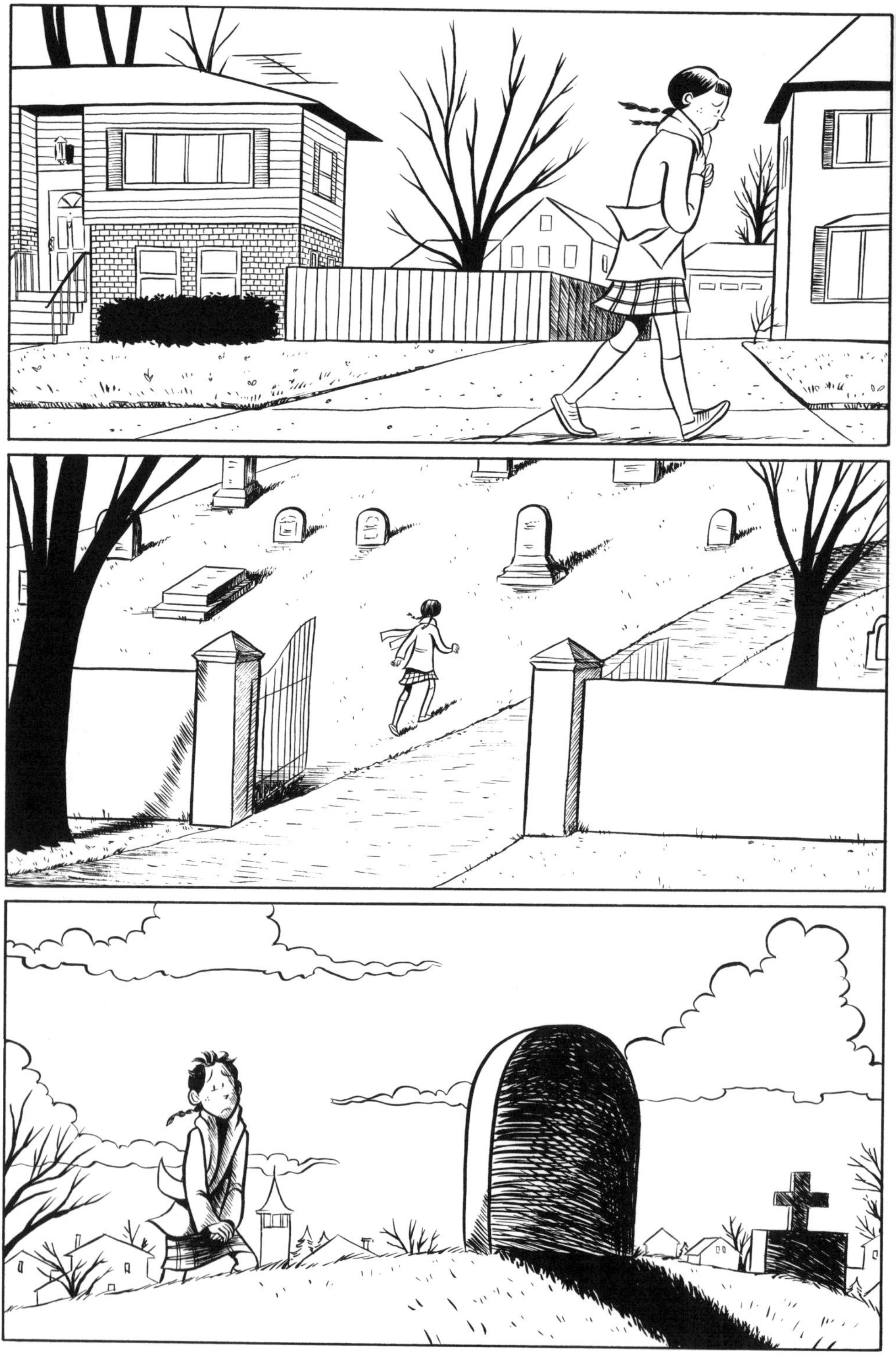

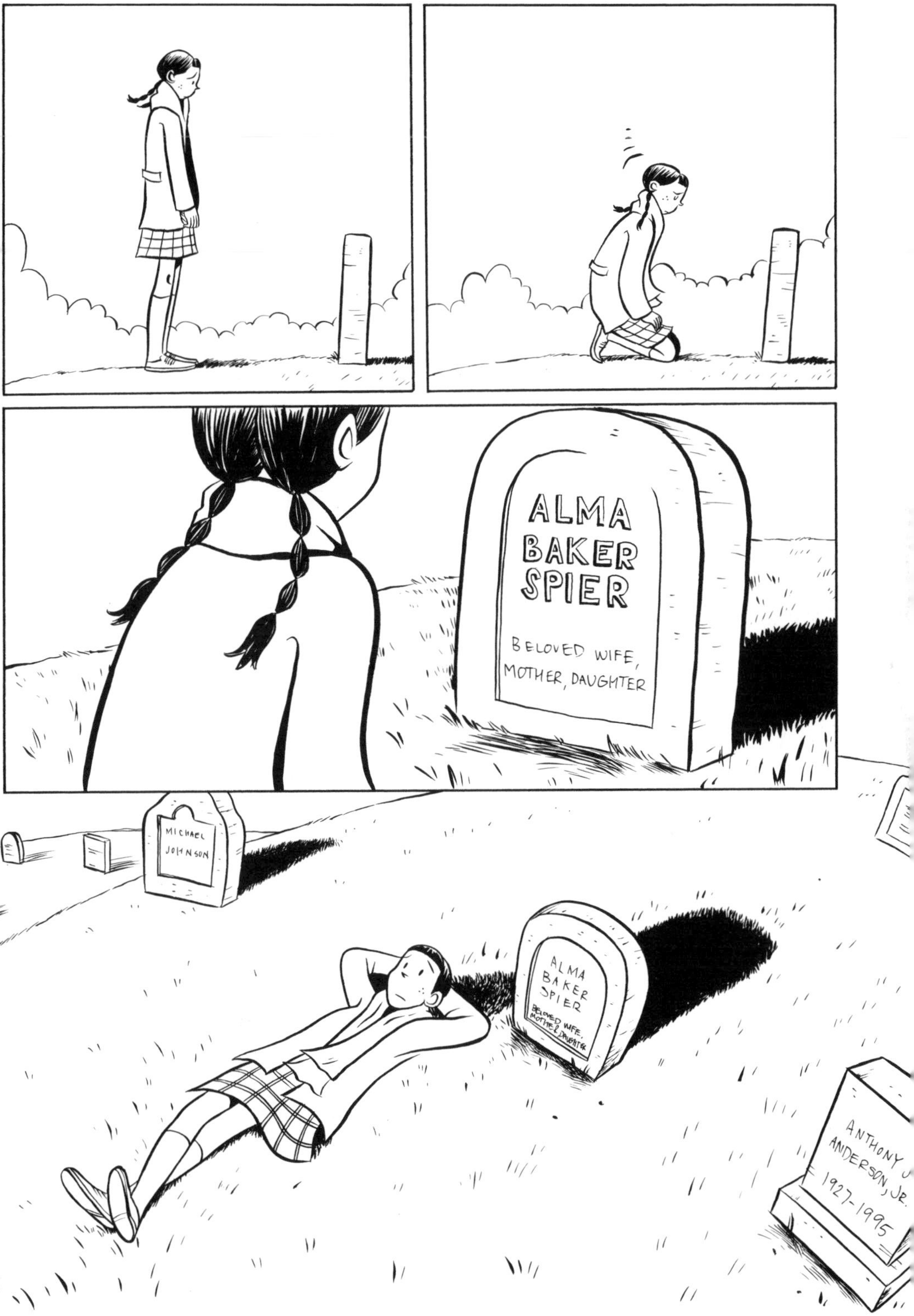
ALMA
BAKER
SPIER
BELOVED WIFE,
MOTHER, DAUGHTER
MICHAEL
JOHNSON
ALMA
BAKER
SPIER
BELOVED WIFE,
MOTHER, DAUGHTER
ANTHONY
ANDERSON, JR.
1927-1995

Chapter 13

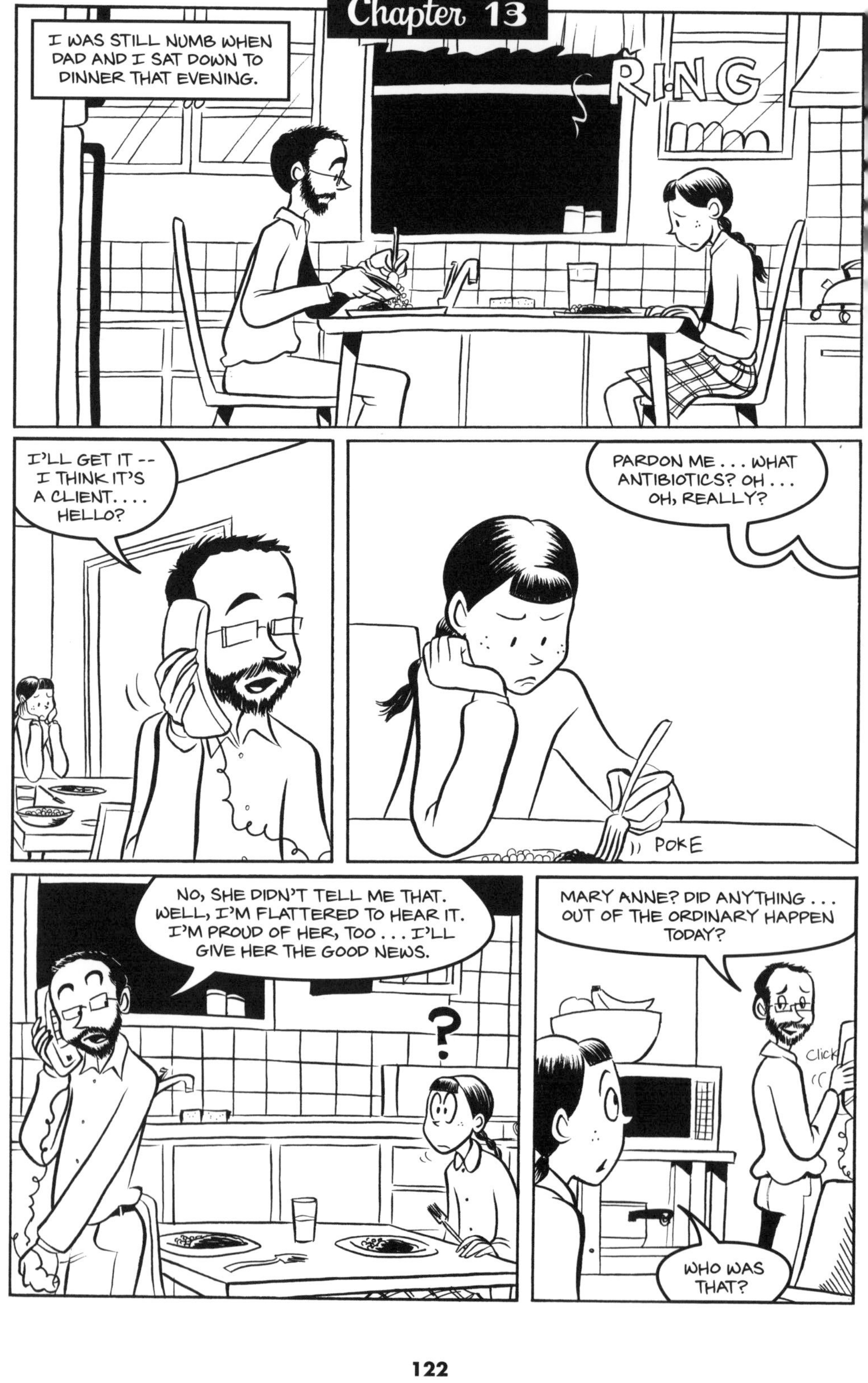
I WAS STILL NUMB WHEN DAD AND I SAT DOWN TO DINNER THAT EVENING.
RING
I'LL GET IT -- I THINK IT'S A CLIENT. . . . HELLO?
PARDON ME . . . WHAT ANTIBIOTICS? OH . . . OH, REALLY?
POKE
NO, SHE DIDN'T TELL ME THAT. WELL, I'M FLATTERED TO HEAR IT. I'M PROUD OF HER, TOO . . . I'LL GIVE HER THE GOOD NEWS.
?
MARY ANNE? DID ANYTHING . . . OUT OF THE ORDINARY HAPPEN TODAY?
Click
WHO WAS THAT?

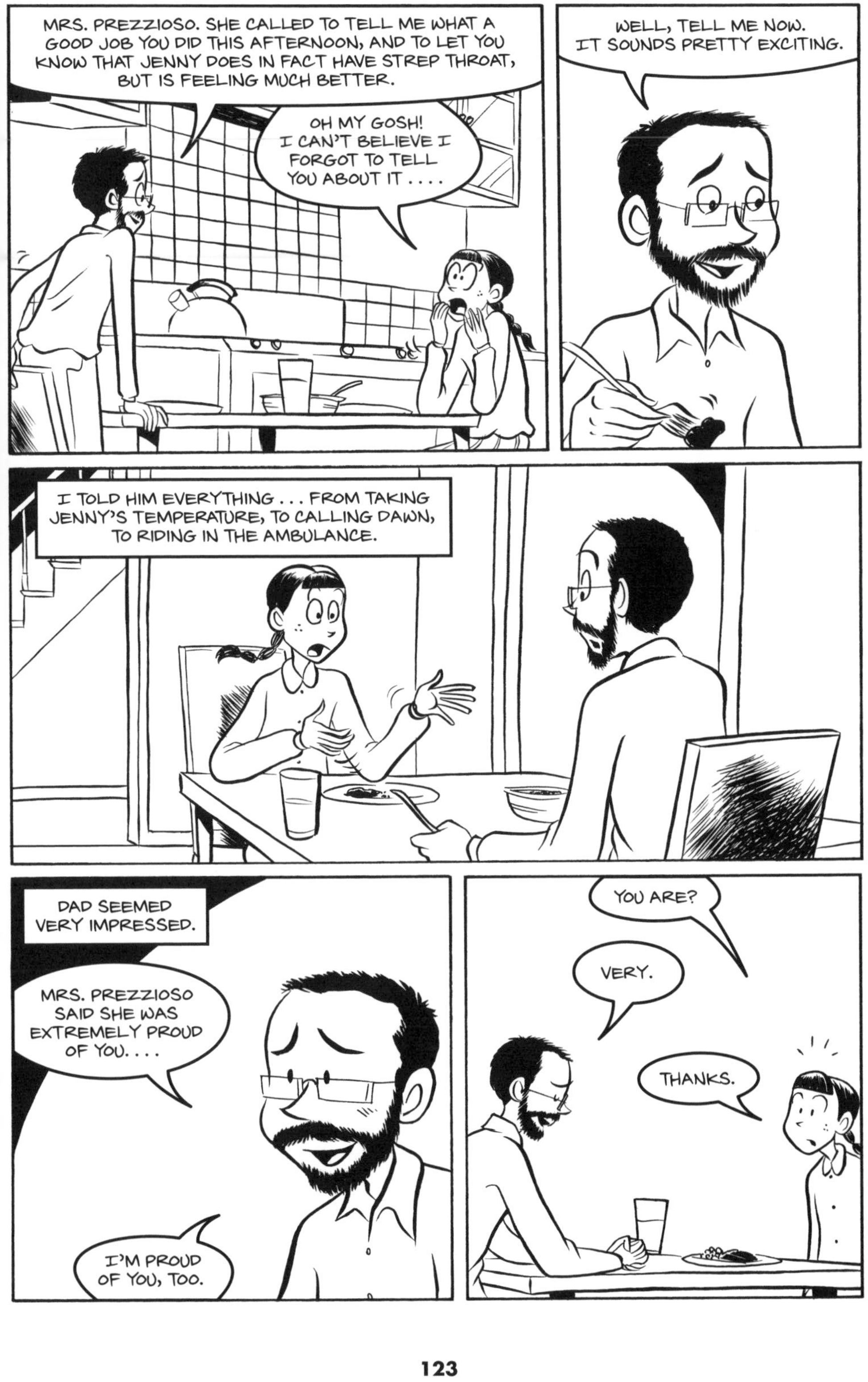
MRS. PREZZIOSO. SHE CALLED TO TELL ME WHAT A GOOD JOB YOU DID THIS AFTERNOON, AND TO LET YOU KNOW THAT JENNY DOES IN FACT HAVE STREP THROAT, BUT IS FEELING MUCH BETTER.
OH MY GOSH! I CAN'T BELIEVE I FORGOT TO TELL YOU ABOUT IT . . . .
WELL, TELL ME NOW. IT SOUNDS PRETTY EXCITING.
I TOLD HIM EVERYTHING . . . FROM TAKING JENNY'S TEMPERATURE, TO CALLING DAWN, TO RIDING IN THE AMBULANCE.
DAD SEEMED VERY IMPRESSED.
MRS. PREZZIOSO SAID SHE WAS EXTREMELY PROUD OF YOU. . . .
I'M PROUD OF YOU, TOO.
YOU ARE?
VERY.
THANKS.

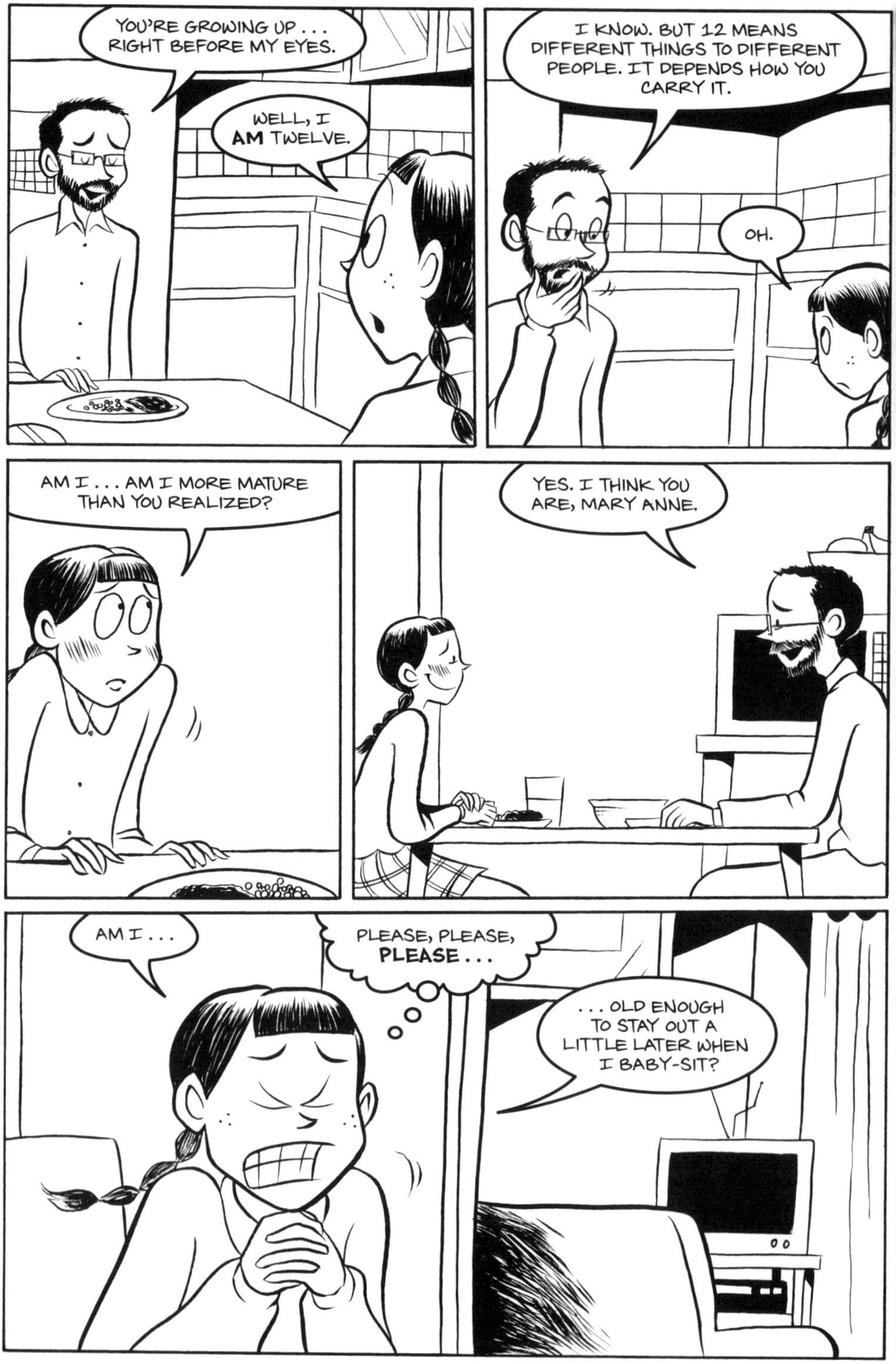
YOU'RE GROWING UP . . . RIGHT BEFORE MY EYES.
WELL, I **AM** TWELVE.
I KNOW. BUT 12 MEANS DIFFERENT THINGS TO DIFFERENT PEOPLE. IT DEPENDS HOW YOU CARRY IT.
OH.
AM I . . . AM I MORE MATURE THAN YOU REALIZED?
YES. I THINK YOU ARE, MARY ANNE.
AM I . . .
PLEASE, PLEASE, **PLEASE** . . .
. . . OLD ENOUGH TO STAY OUT A LITTLE LATER WHEN I BABY-SIT?

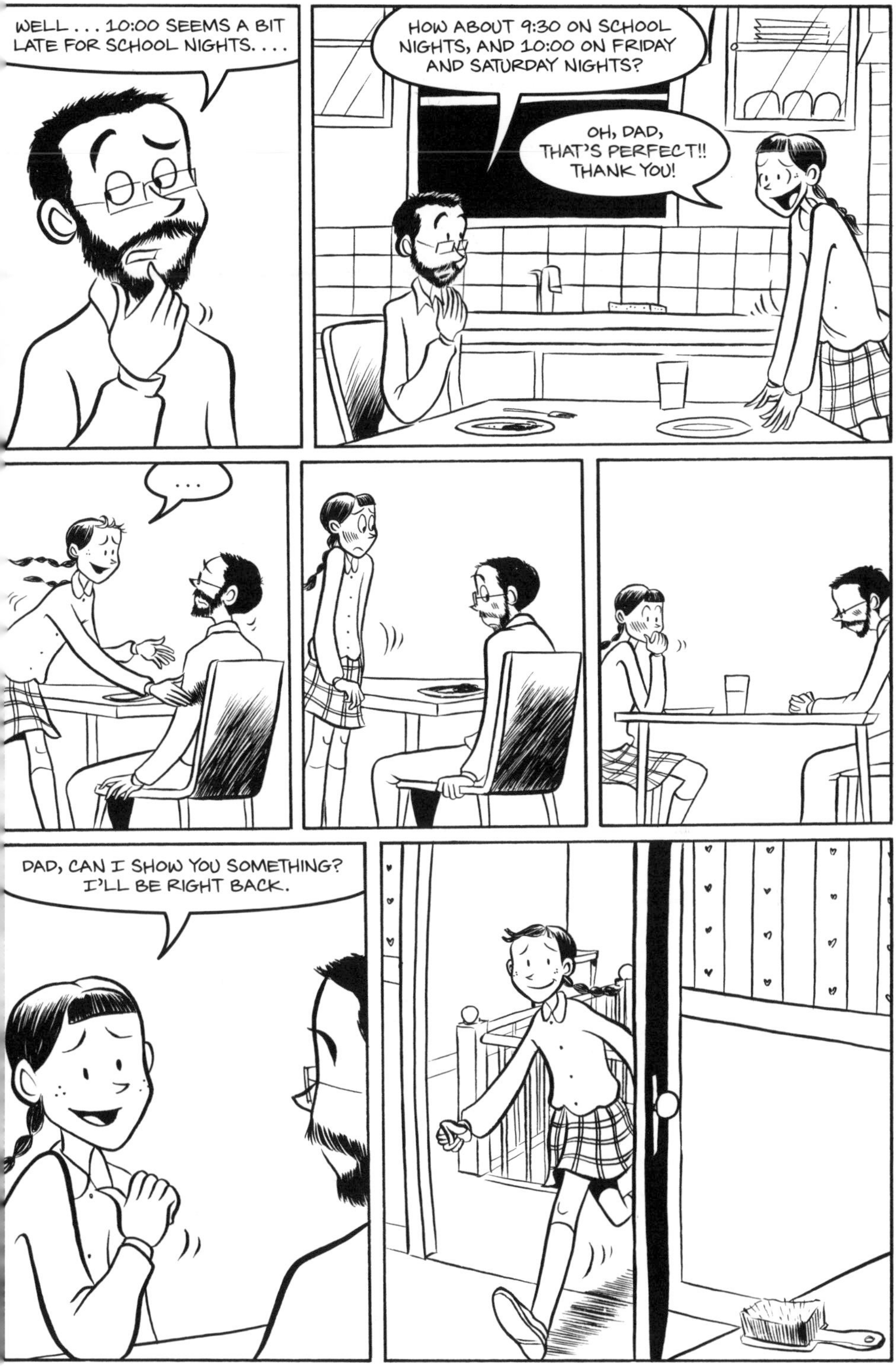
WELL . . . 10:00 SEEMS A BIT LATE FOR SCHOOL NIGHTS. . . .
HOW ABOUT 9:30 ON SCHOOL NIGHTS, AND 10:00 ON FRIDAY AND SATURDAY NIGHTS?
OH, DAD, THAT'S PERFECT!! THANK YOU!
. . .
DAD, CAN I SHOW YOU SOMETHING? I'LL BE RIGHT BACK.

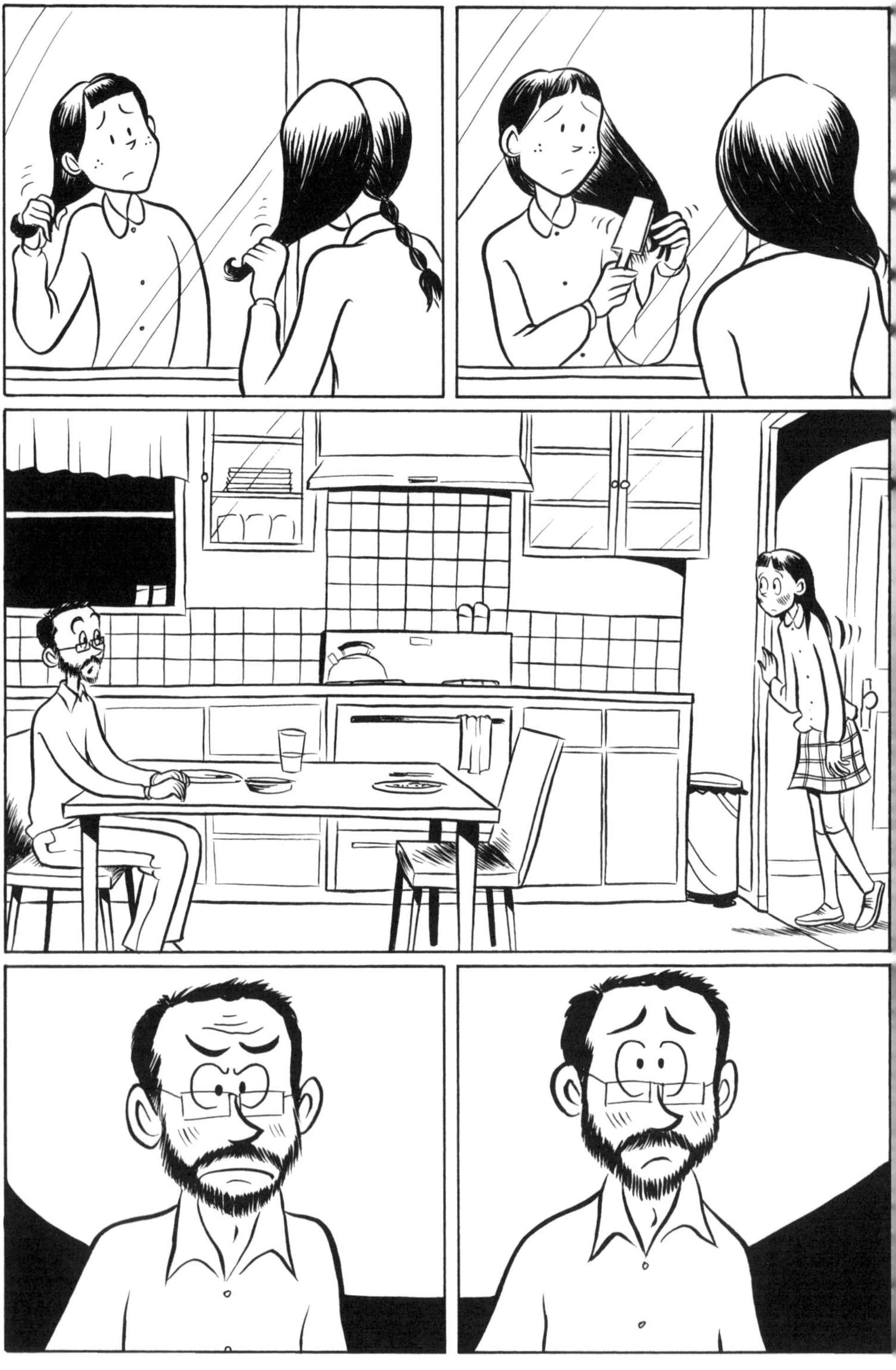

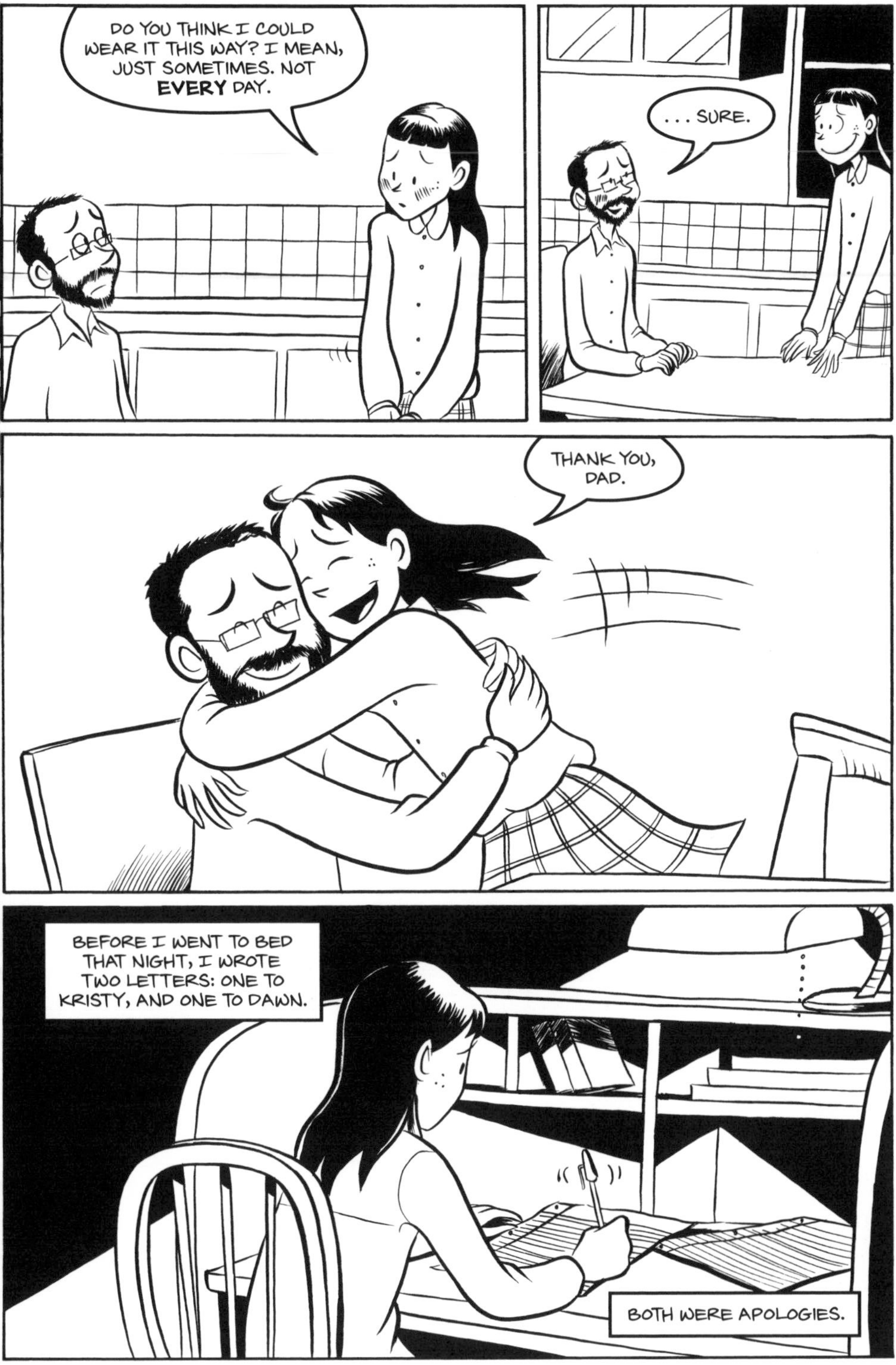
DO YOU THINK I COULD WEAR IT THIS WAY? I MEAN, JUST SOMETIMES. NOT **EVERY** DAY.
. . . SURE.
THANK YOU, DAD.
BEFORE I WENT TO BED THAT NIGHT, I WROTE TWO LETTERS: ONE TO KRISTY, AND ONE TO DAWN.
BOTH WERE APOLOGIES.

Sunday, February 8

The members of the Baby-sitters Club have been enemies for almost a month now. I can't believe it. Claudia, Kristy, and Mary Anne—I hope you all read what I'm writing, because I think our fight is dumb, and you should know that. I thought you guys were my friends, but I guess not.

I'm writing this because tomorrow the four of us have to help out at Jamie Newton's birthday party, and I think it's going to be a disaster. I hope you read this before then because I think we should be prepared for the worst.

P.S. If anybody wants to make up, I'm ready.

Stacey

Chapter 14

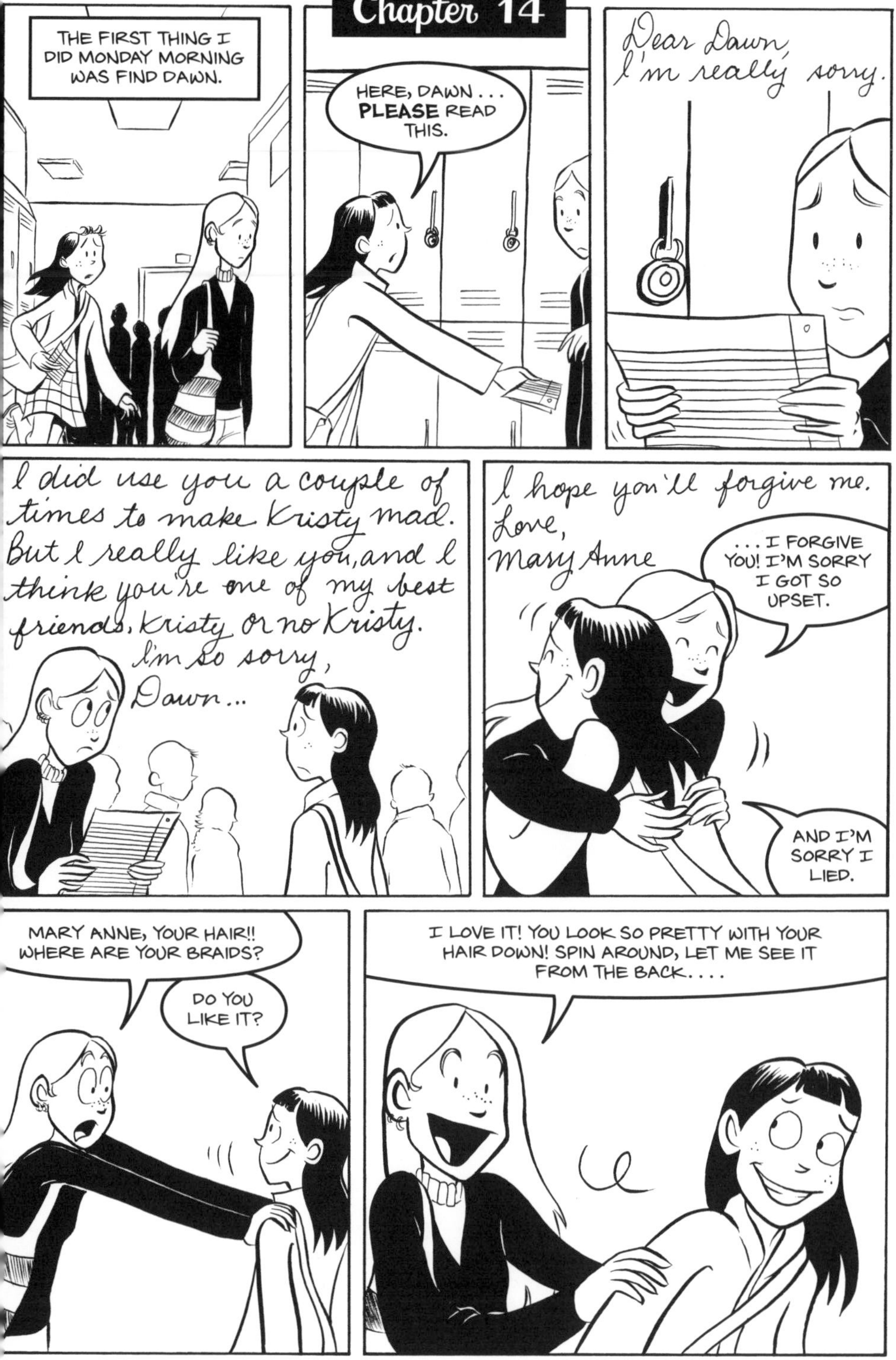

THE FIRST THING I DID MONDAY MORNING WAS FIND DAWN.
HERE, DAWN . . . **PLEASE** READ THIS.
Dear Dawn, I'm really sorry.
I did use you a couple of times to make Kristy mad. But I really like you, and I think you're ~~one~~ one of my best friends, Kristy or no Kristy. I'm so sorry, Dawn...
I hope you'll forgive me. Love, Mary Anne
. . . I FORGIVE YOU! I'M SORRY I GOT SO UPSET.
AND I'M SORRY I LIED.
MARY ANNE, YOUR HAIR!! WHERE ARE YOUR BRAIDS?
DO YOU LIKE IT?
I LOVE IT! YOU LOOK SO PRETTY WITH YOUR HAIR DOWN! SPIN AROUND, LET ME SEE IT FROM THE BACK. . . .

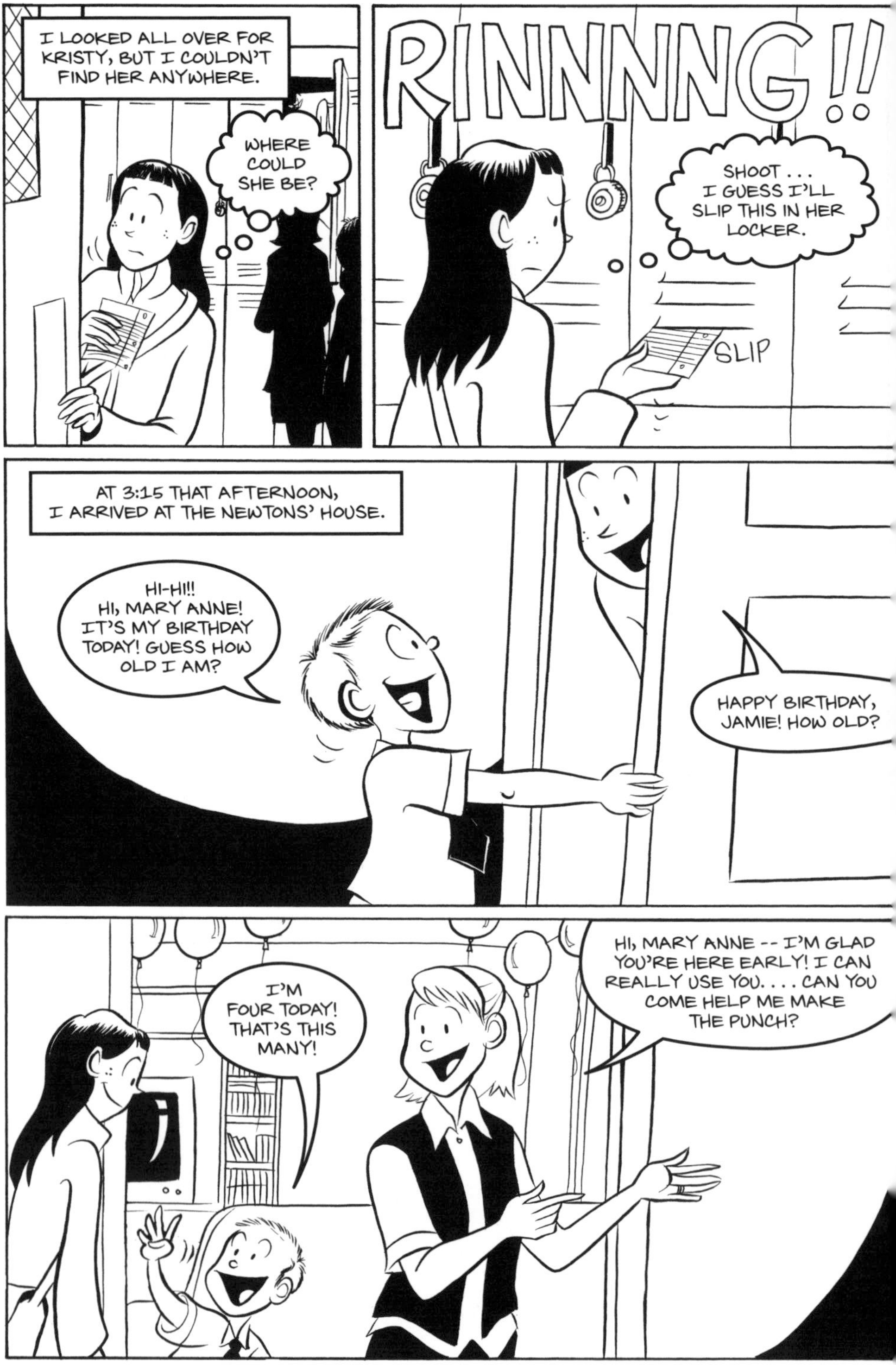

I LOOKED ALL OVER FOR KRISTY, BUT I COULDN'T FIND HER ANYWHERE.
WHERE COULD SHE BE?
RINNNNG!!
SHOOT . . . I GUESS I'LL SLIP THIS IN HER LOCKER.
SLIP
AT 3:15 THAT AFTERNOON, I ARRIVED AT THE NEWTONS' HOUSE.
HI-HI!! HI, MARY ANNE! IT'S MY BIRTHDAY TODAY! GUESS HOW OLD I AM?
HAPPY BIRTHDAY, JAMIE! HOW OLD?
I'M FOUR TODAY! THAT'S THIS MANY!
HI, MARY ANNE -- I'M GLAD YOU'RE HERE EARLY! I CAN REALLY USE YOU. . . . CAN YOU COME HELP ME MAKE THE PUNCH?

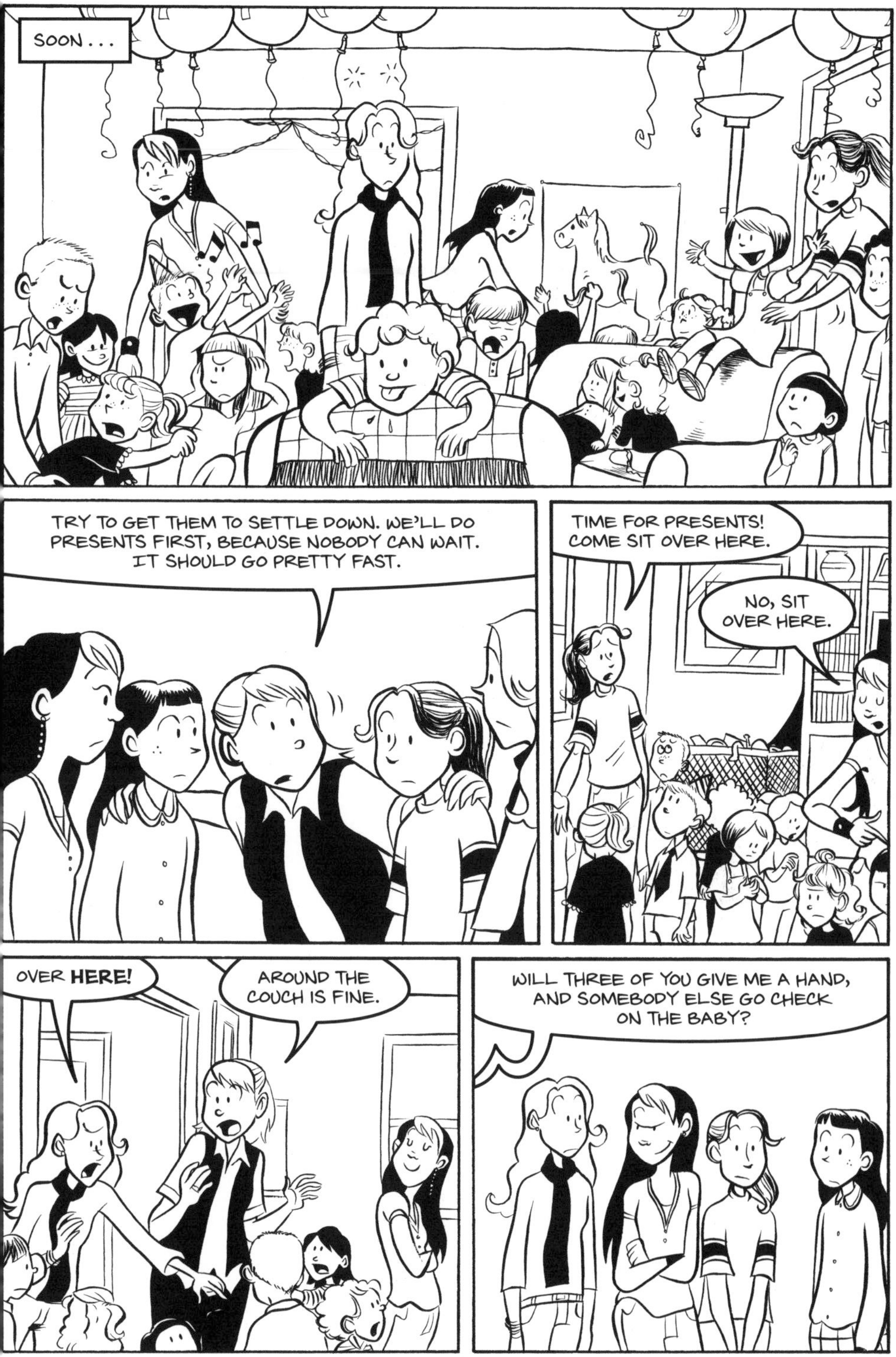
SOON . . .
TRY TO GET THEM TO SETTLE DOWN. WE'LL DO PRESENTS FIRST, BECAUSE NOBODY CAN WAIT. IT SHOULD GO PRETTY FAST.
TIME FOR PRESENTS! COME SIT OVER HERE.
NO, SIT OVER HERE.
OVER **HERE!**
AROUND THE COUCH IS FINE.
WILL THREE OF YOU GIVE ME A HAND, AND SOMEBODY ELSE GO CHECK ON THE BABY?

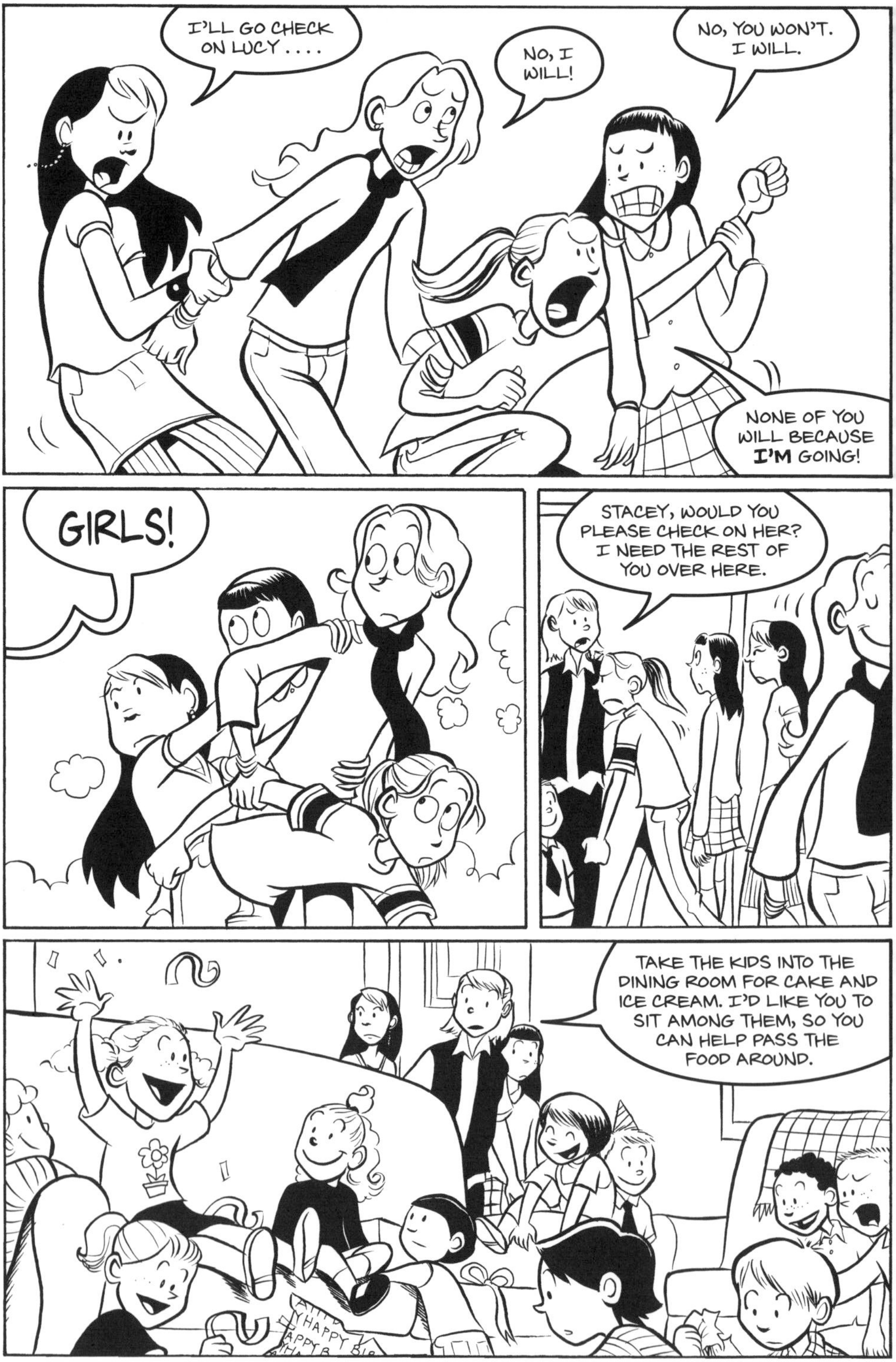
I'LL GO CHECK ON LUCY . . . .
NO, I WILL!
NO, YOU WON'T. I WILL.
NONE OF YOU WILL BECAUSE **I'M** GOING!
GIRLS!
STACEY, WOULD YOU PLEASE CHECK ON HER? I NEED THE REST OF YOU OVER HERE.
TAKE THE KIDS INTO THE DINING ROOM FOR CAKE AND ICE CREAM. I'D LIKE YOU TO SIT AMONG THEM, SO YOU CAN HELP PASS THE FOOD AROUND.

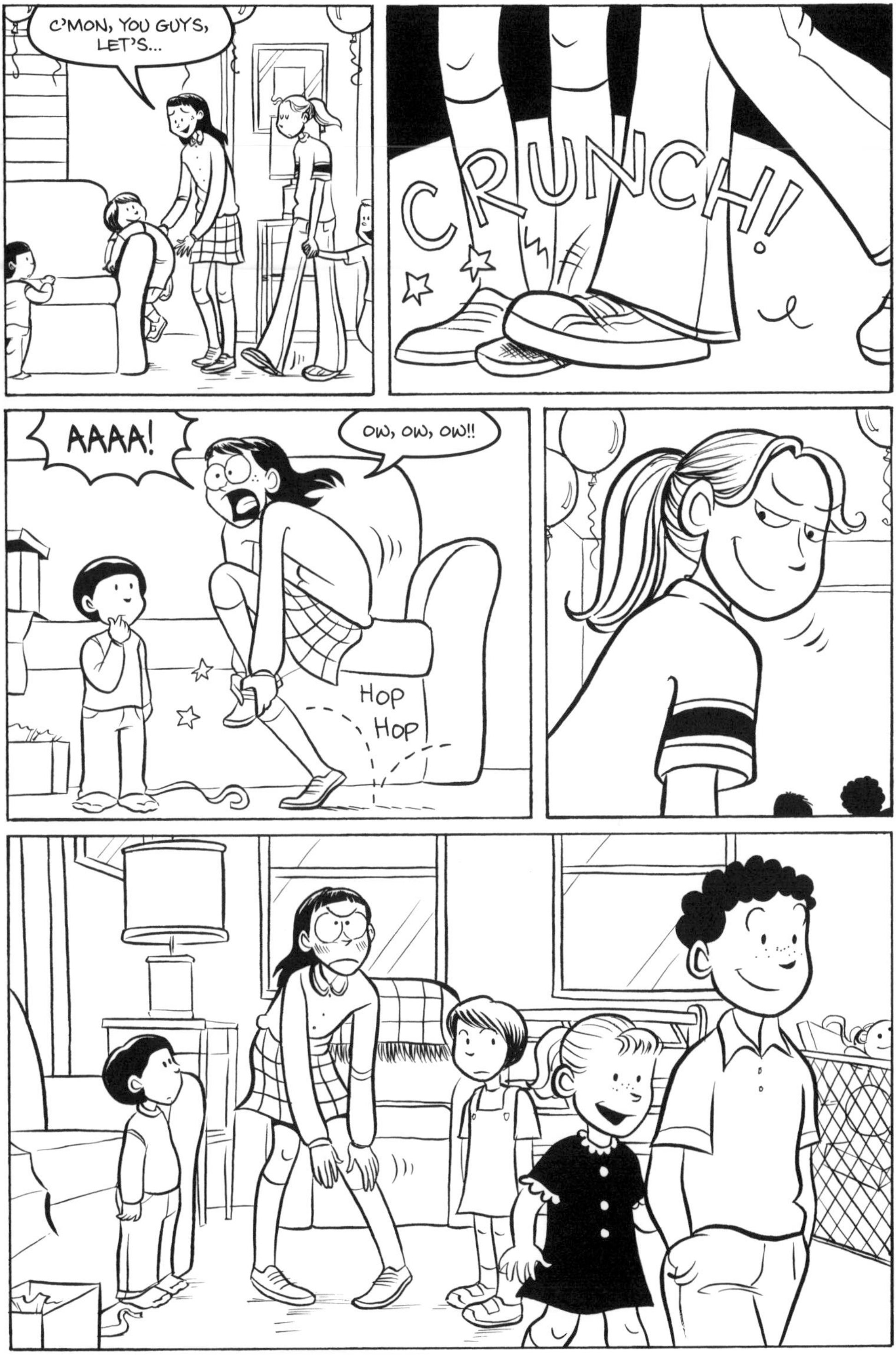
C'MON, YOU GUYS, LET'S...
CRUNCH!
AAAA!
OW, OW, OW!!
Hop
Hop

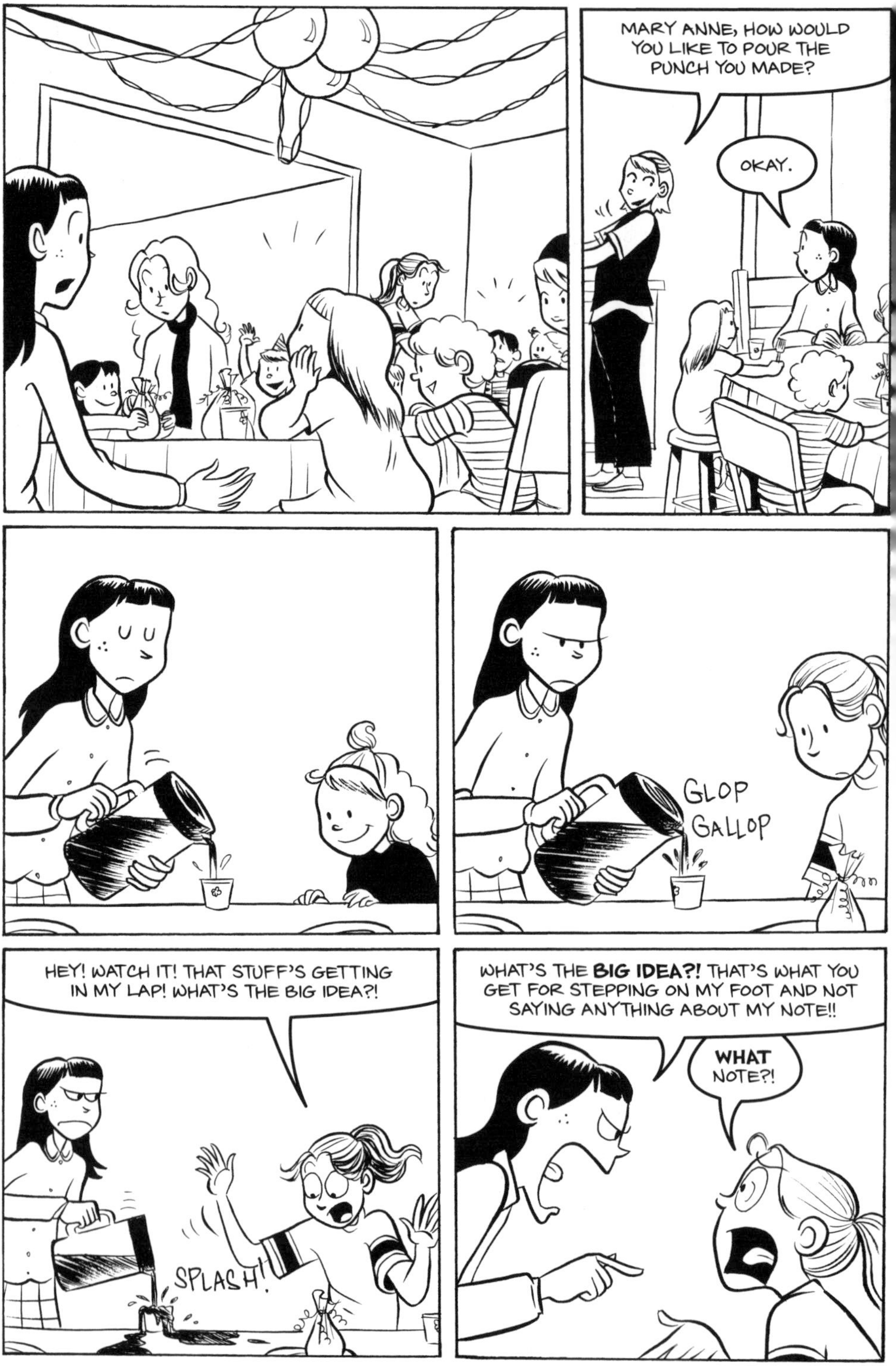
MARY ANNE, HOW WOULD YOU LIKE TO POUR THE PUNCH YOU MADE?
OKAY.
GLOP
GALLOP
HEY! WATCH IT! THAT STUFF'S GETTING IN MY LAP! WHAT'S THE BIG IDEA?!
SPLASH!
WHAT'S THE **BIG IDEA?!** THAT'S WHAT YOU GET FOR STEPPING ON MY FOOT AND NOT SAYING ANYTHING ABOUT MY NOTE!!
WHAT NOTE?!

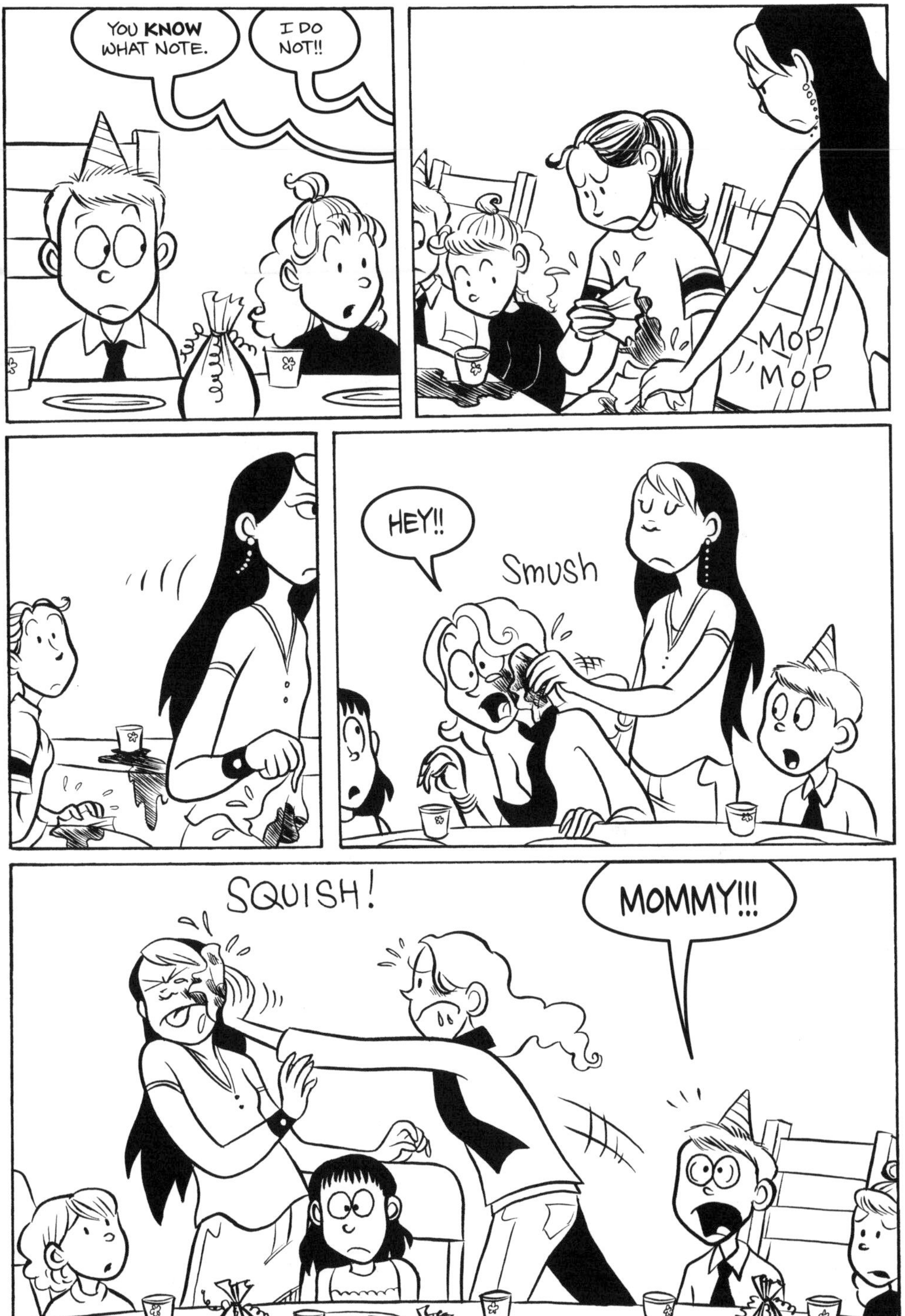
YOU **KNOW** WHAT NOTE.
I DO NOT!!
MOP MOP
HEY!!
Smush
SQUISH!
MOMMY!!!

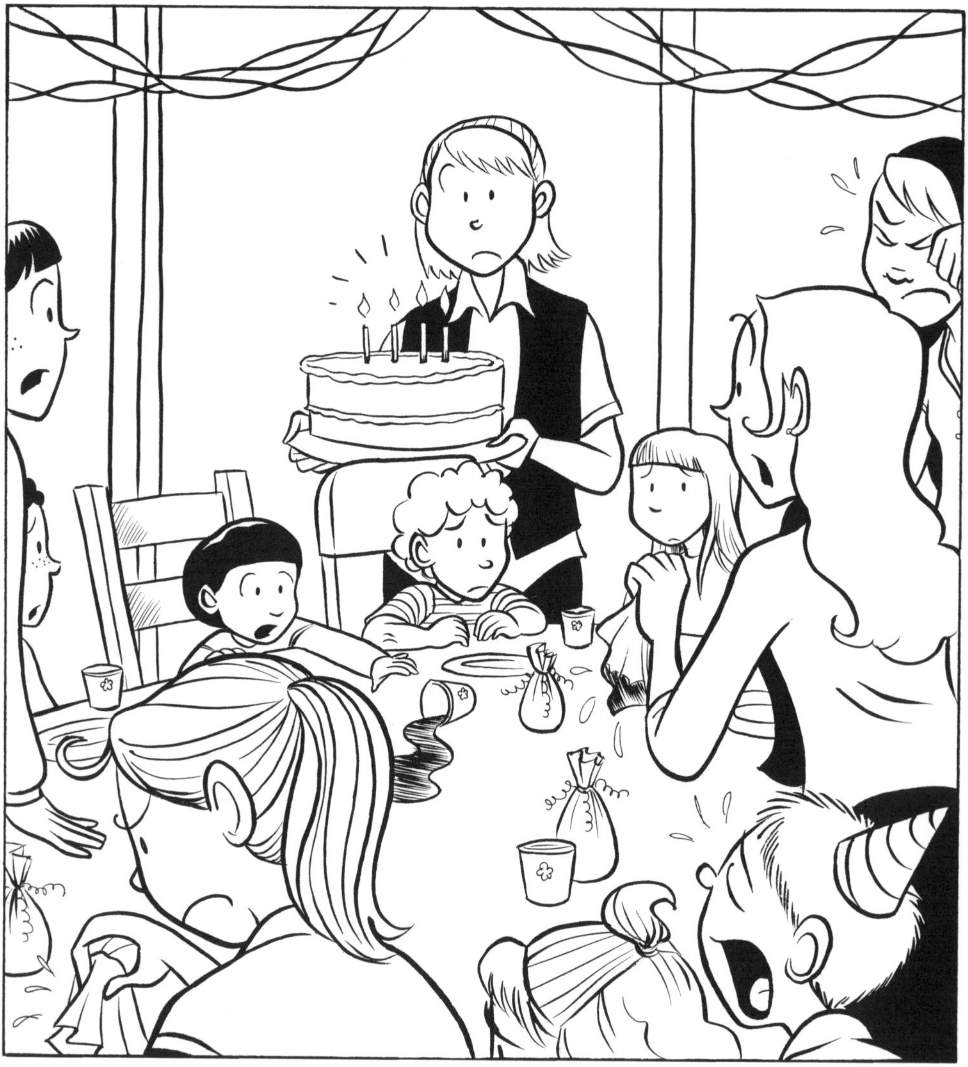

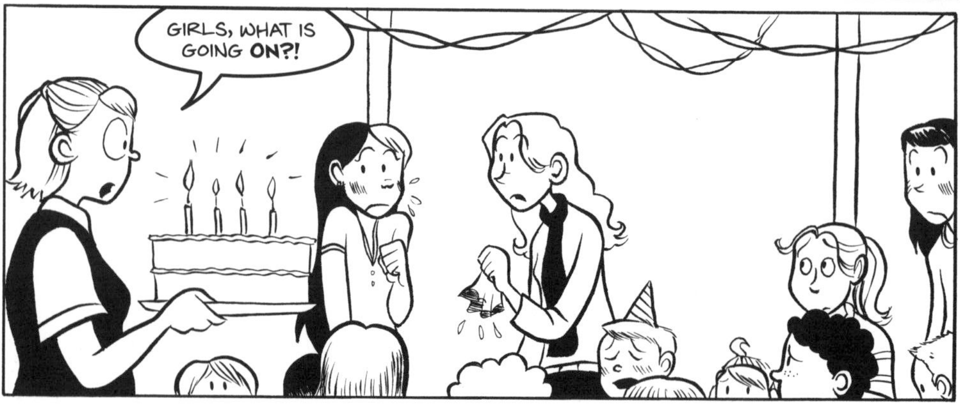
GIRLS, WHAT IS GOING **ON?!**

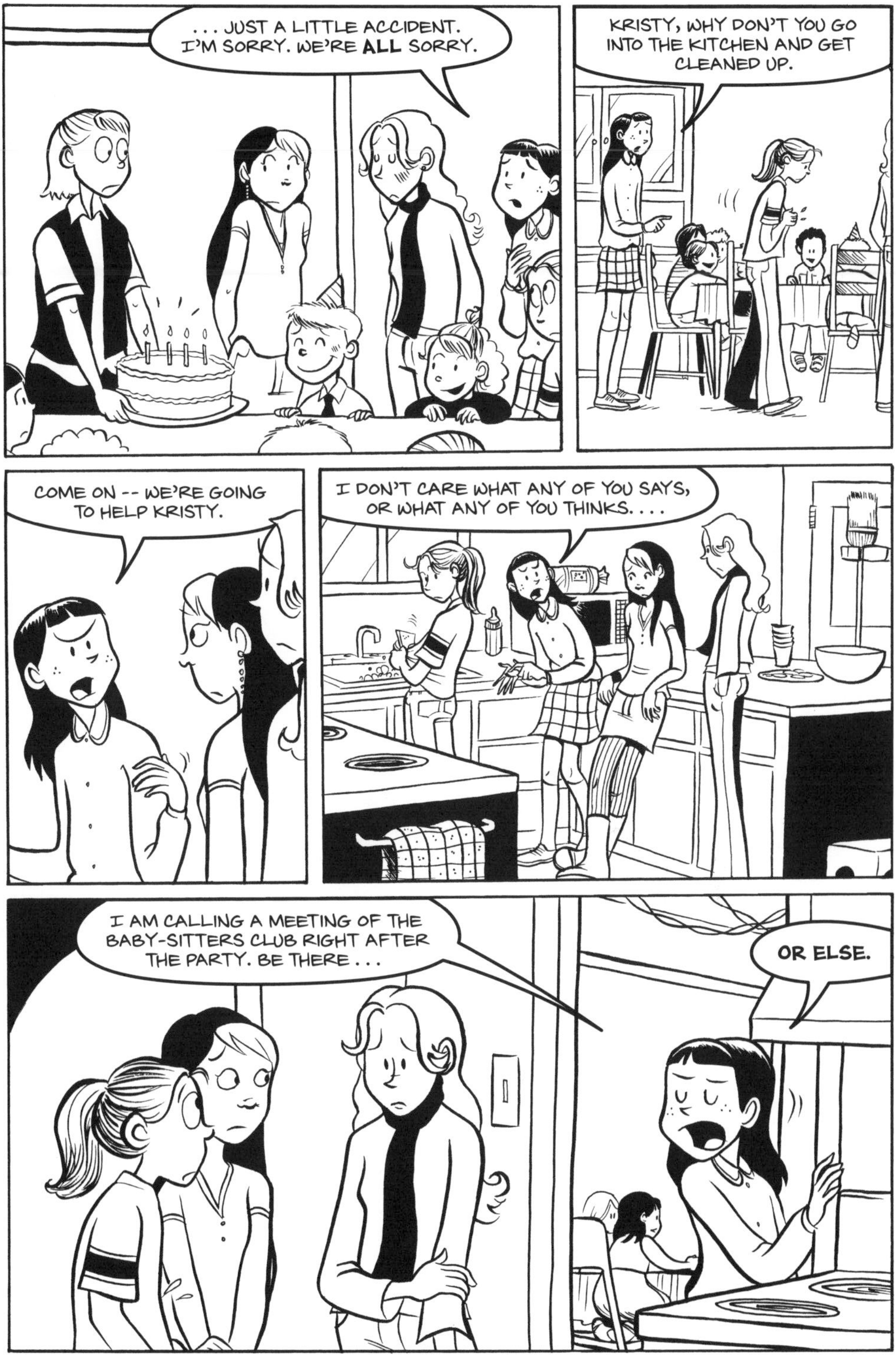

. . . JUST A LITTLE ACCIDENT. I'M SORRY. WE'RE **ALL** SORRY.
KRISTY, WHY DON'T YOU GO INTO THE KITCHEN AND GET CLEANED UP.
COME ON -- WE'RE GOING TO HELP KRISTY.
I DON'T CARE WHAT ANY OF YOU SAYS, OR WHAT ANY OF YOU THINKS. . . .
I AM CALLING A MEETING OF THE BABY-SITTERS CLUB RIGHT AFTER THE PARTY. BE THERE . . .
OR ELSE.

Chapter 15

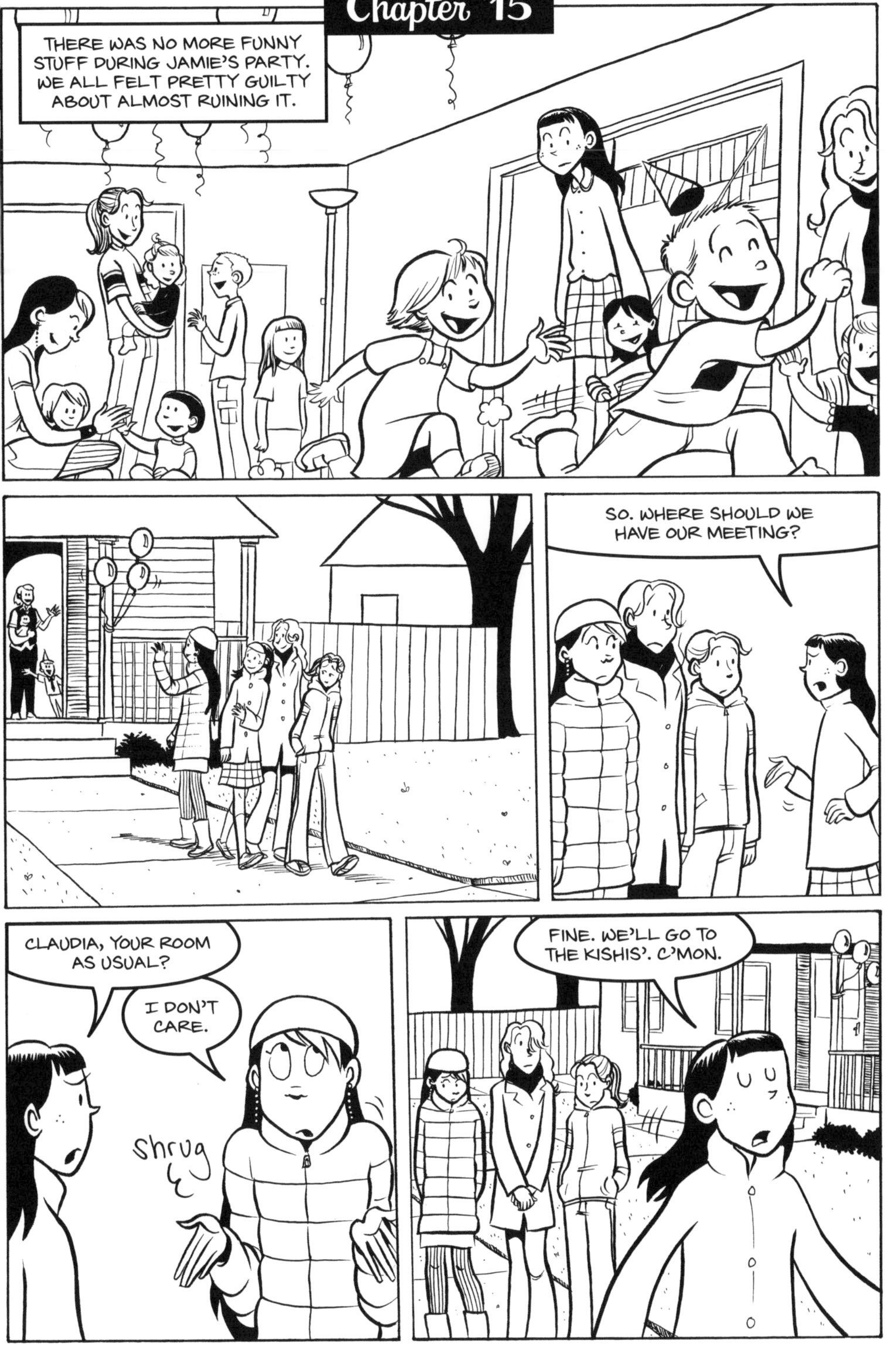
THERE WAS NO MORE FUNNY STUFF DURING JAMIE'S PARTY. WE ALL FELT PRETTY GUILTY ABOUT ALMOST RUINING IT.
SO. WHERE SHOULD WE HAVE OUR MEETING?
CLAUDIA, YOUR ROOM AS USUAL?
I DON'T CARE.
shrug
FINE. WE'LL GO TO THE KISHIS'. C'MON.

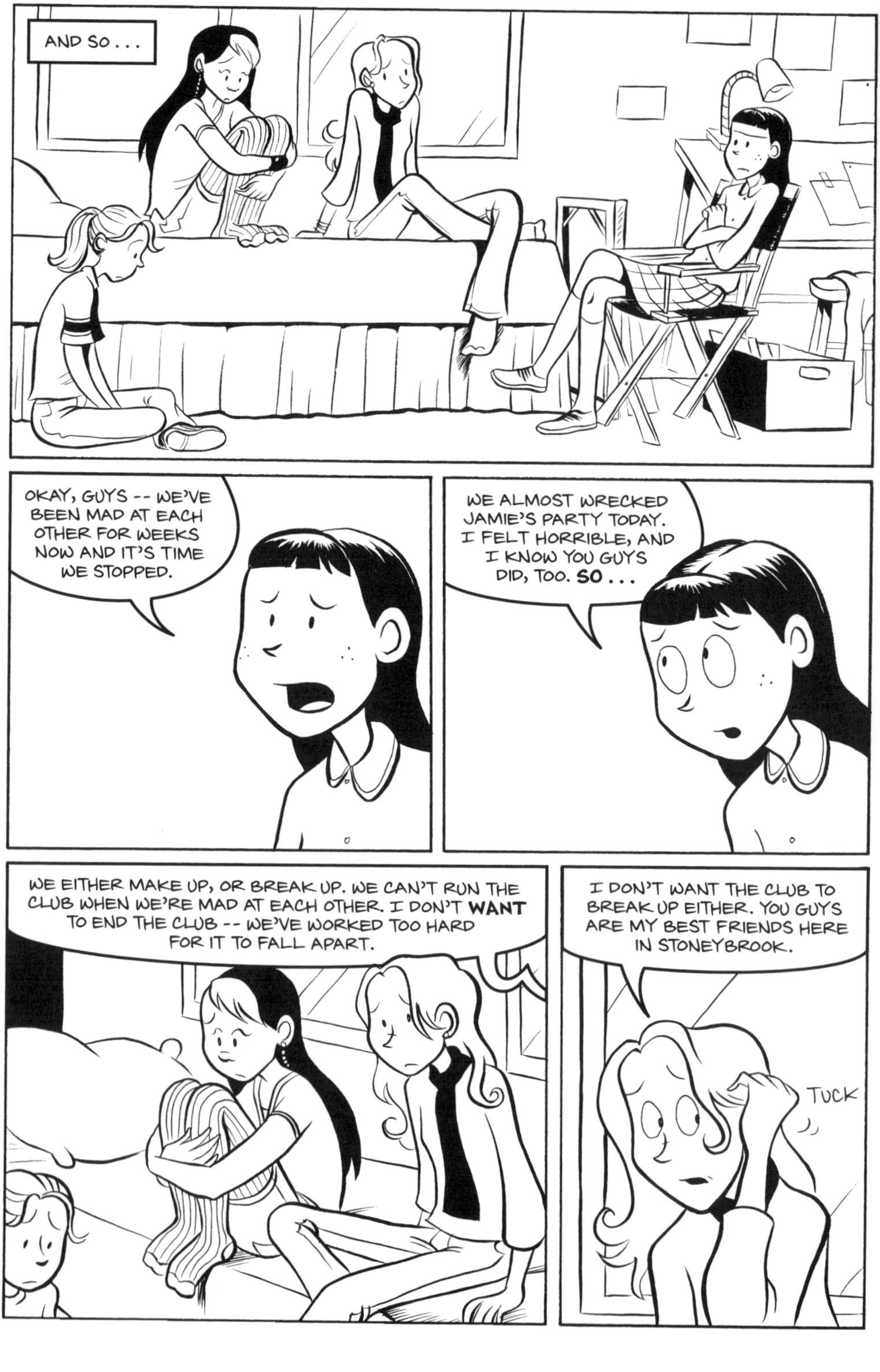
AND SO . . .
OKAY, GUYS -- WE'VE BEEN MAD AT EACH OTHER FOR WEEKS NOW AND IT'S TIME WE STOPPED.
WE ALMOST WRECKED JAMIE'S PARTY TODAY. I FELT HORRIBLE, AND I KNOW YOU GUYS DID, TOO. SO . . .
WE EITHER MAKE UP, OR BREAK UP. WE CAN'T RUN THE CLUB WHEN WE'RE MAD AT EACH OTHER. I DON'T WANT TO END THE CLUB -- WE'VE WORKED TOO HARD FOR IT TO FALL APART.
I DON'T WANT THE CLUB TO BREAK UP EITHER. YOU GUYS ARE MY BEST FRIENDS HERE IN STONEYBROOK.
TUCK

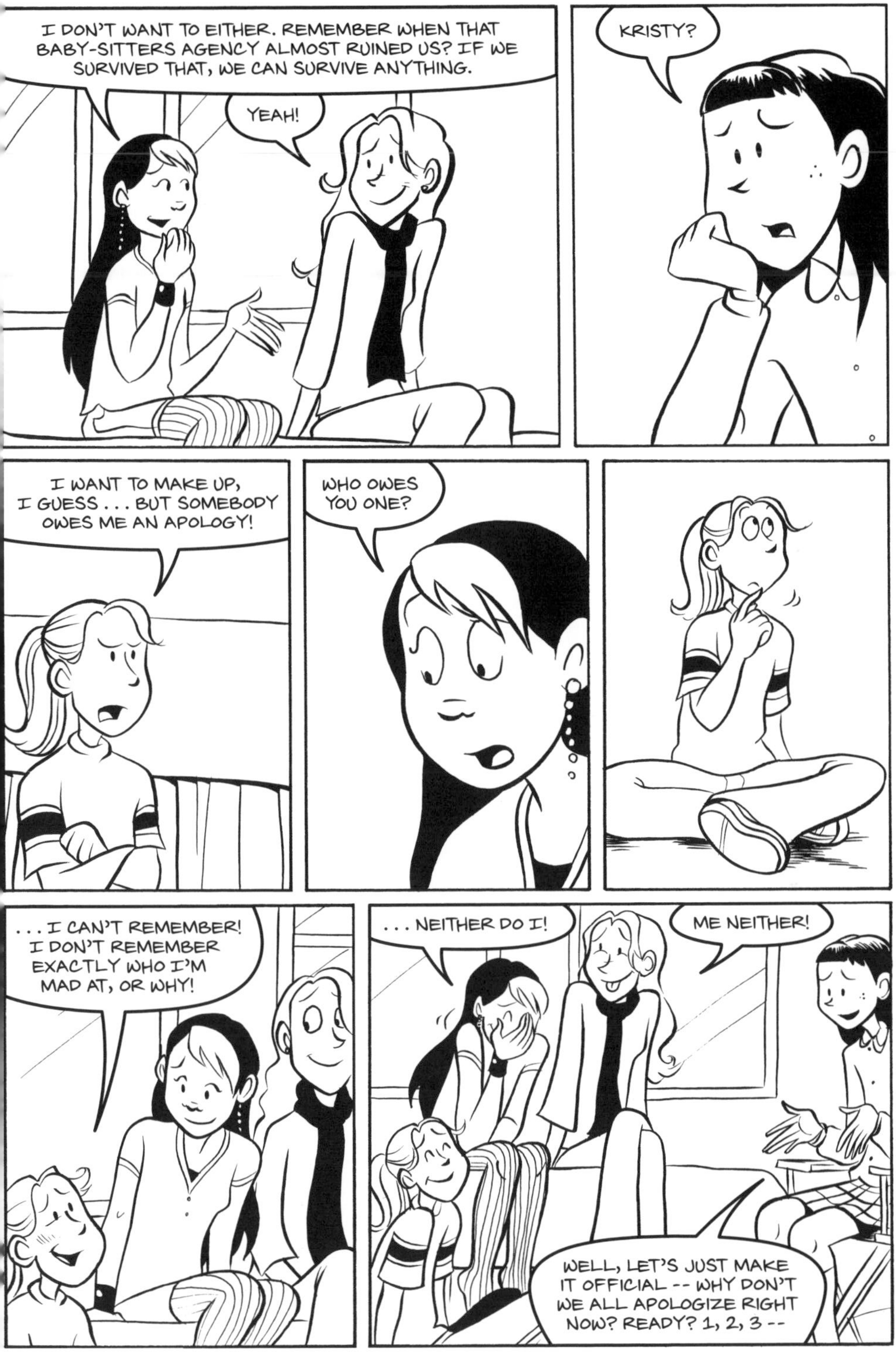
I DON'T WANT TO EITHER. REMEMBER WHEN THAT BABY-SITTERS AGENCY ALMOST RUINED US? IF WE SURVIVED THAT, WE CAN SURVIVE ANYTHING.
YEAH!
KRISTY?
I WANT TO MAKE UP, I GUESS . . . BUT SOMEBODY OWES ME AN APOLOGY!
WHO OWES YOU ONE?
. . . I CAN'T REMEMBER! I DON'T REMEMBER EXACTLY WHO I'M MAD AT, OR WHY!
. . . NEITHER DO I!
ME NEITHER!
WELL, LET'S JUST MAKE IT OFFICIAL -- WHY DON'T WE ALL APOLOGIZE RIGHT NOW? READY? 1, 2, 3 --

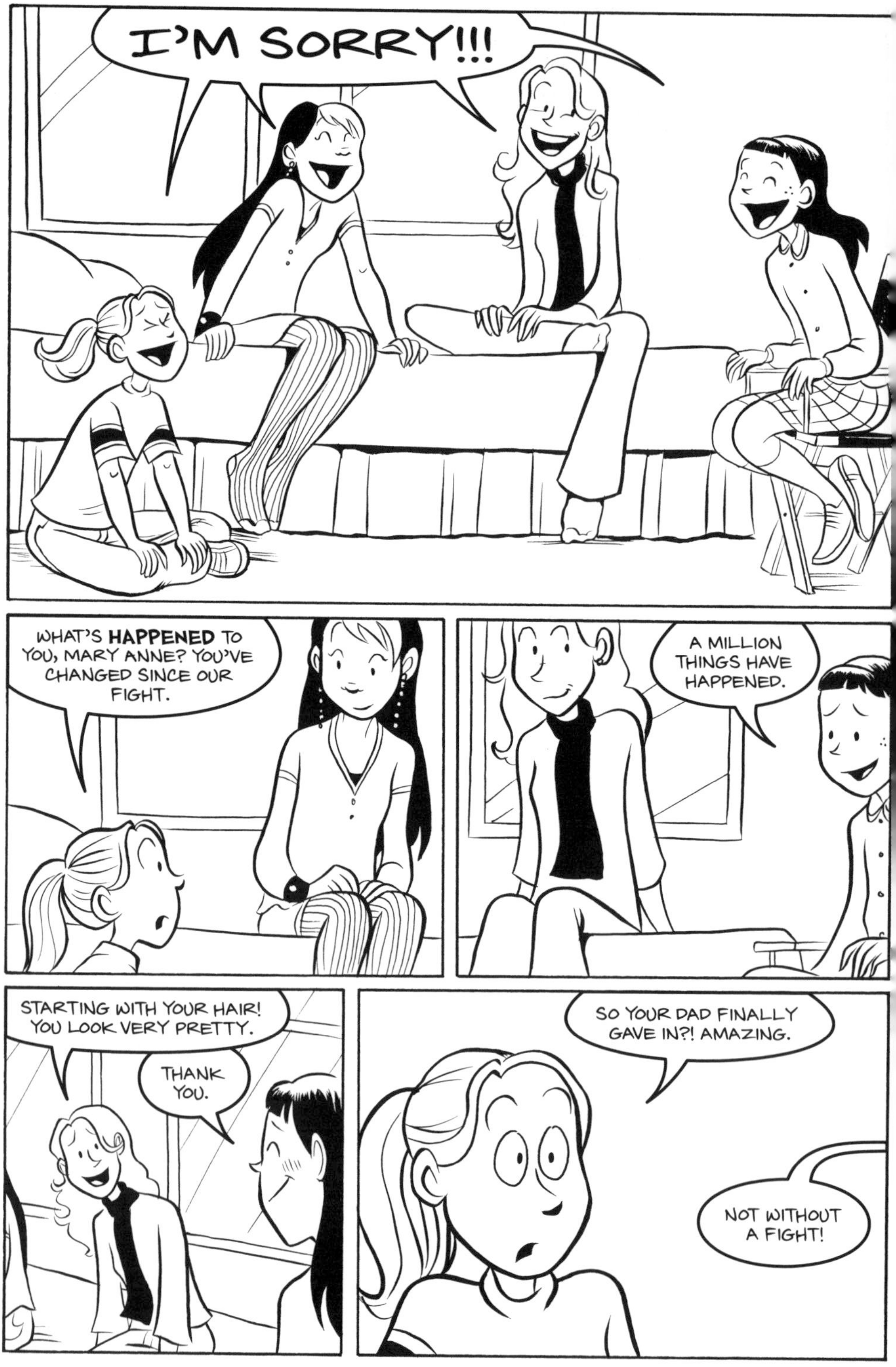
I'M SORRY!!!
WHAT'S **HAPPENED** TO YOU, MARY ANNE? YOU'VE CHANGED SINCE OUR FIGHT.
A MILLION THINGS HAVE HAPPENED.
STARTING WITH YOUR HAIR! YOU LOOK VERY PRETTY.
THANK YOU.
SO YOUR DAD FINALLY GAVE IN?! AMAZING.
NOT WITHOUT A FIGHT!

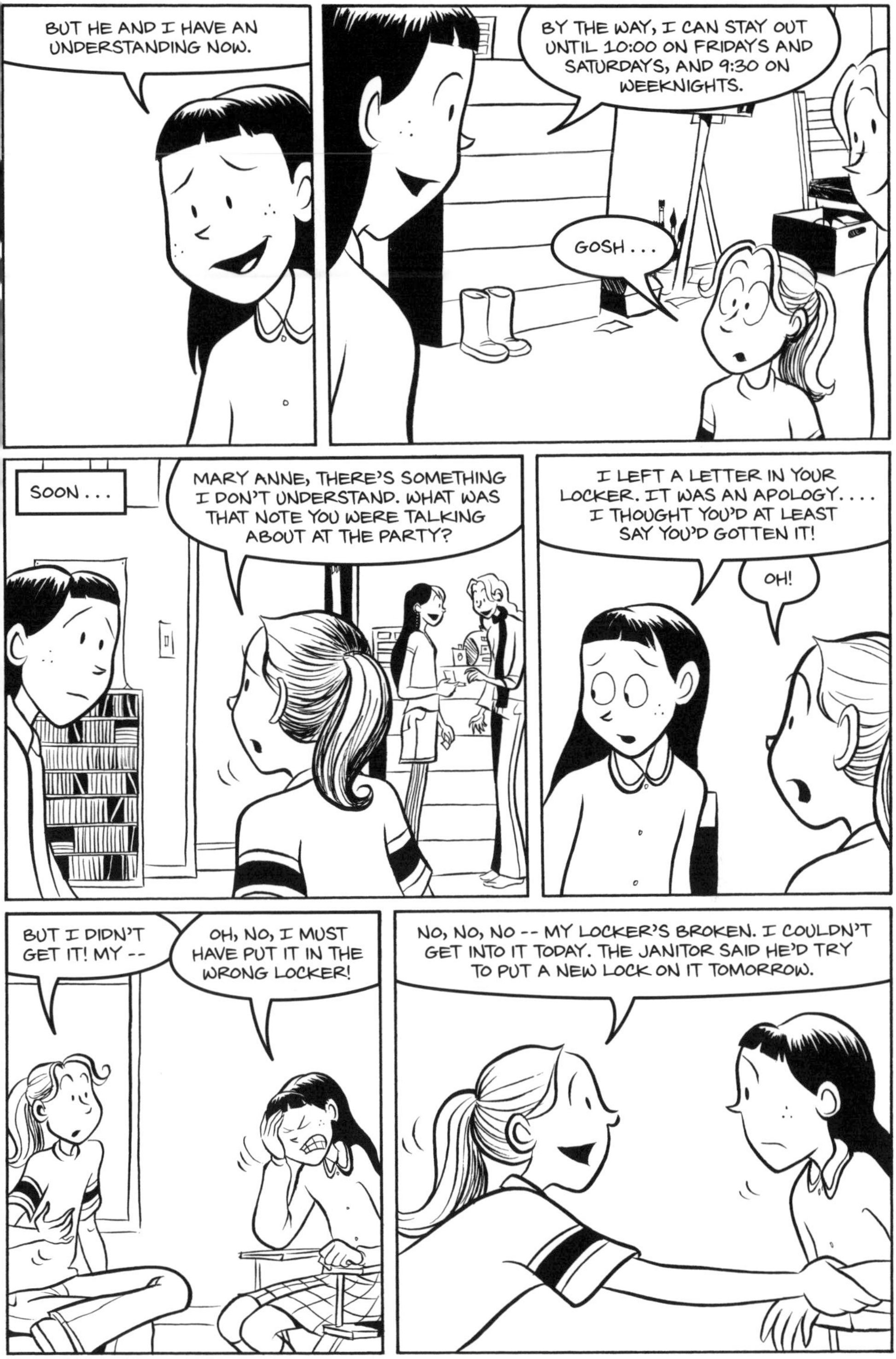
BUT HE AND I HAVE AN UNDERSTANDING NOW.
BY THE WAY, I CAN STAY OUT UNTIL 10:00 ON FRIDAYS AND SATURDAYS, AND 9:30 ON WEEKNIGHTS.
GOSH . . .
SOON . . .
MARY ANNE, THERE'S SOMETHING I DON'T UNDERSTAND. WHAT WAS THAT NOTE YOU WERE TALKING ABOUT AT THE PARTY?
I LEFT A LETTER IN YOUR LOCKER. IT WAS AN APOLOGY. . . . I THOUGHT YOU'D AT LEAST SAY YOU'D GOTTEN IT!
OH!
BUT I DIDN'T GET IT! MY --
OH, NO, I MUST HAVE PUT IT IN THE WRONG LOCKER!
NO, NO, NO -- MY LOCKER'S BROKEN. I COULDN'T GET INTO IT TODAY. THE JANITOR SAID HE'D TRY TO PUT A NEW LOCK ON IT TOMORROW.

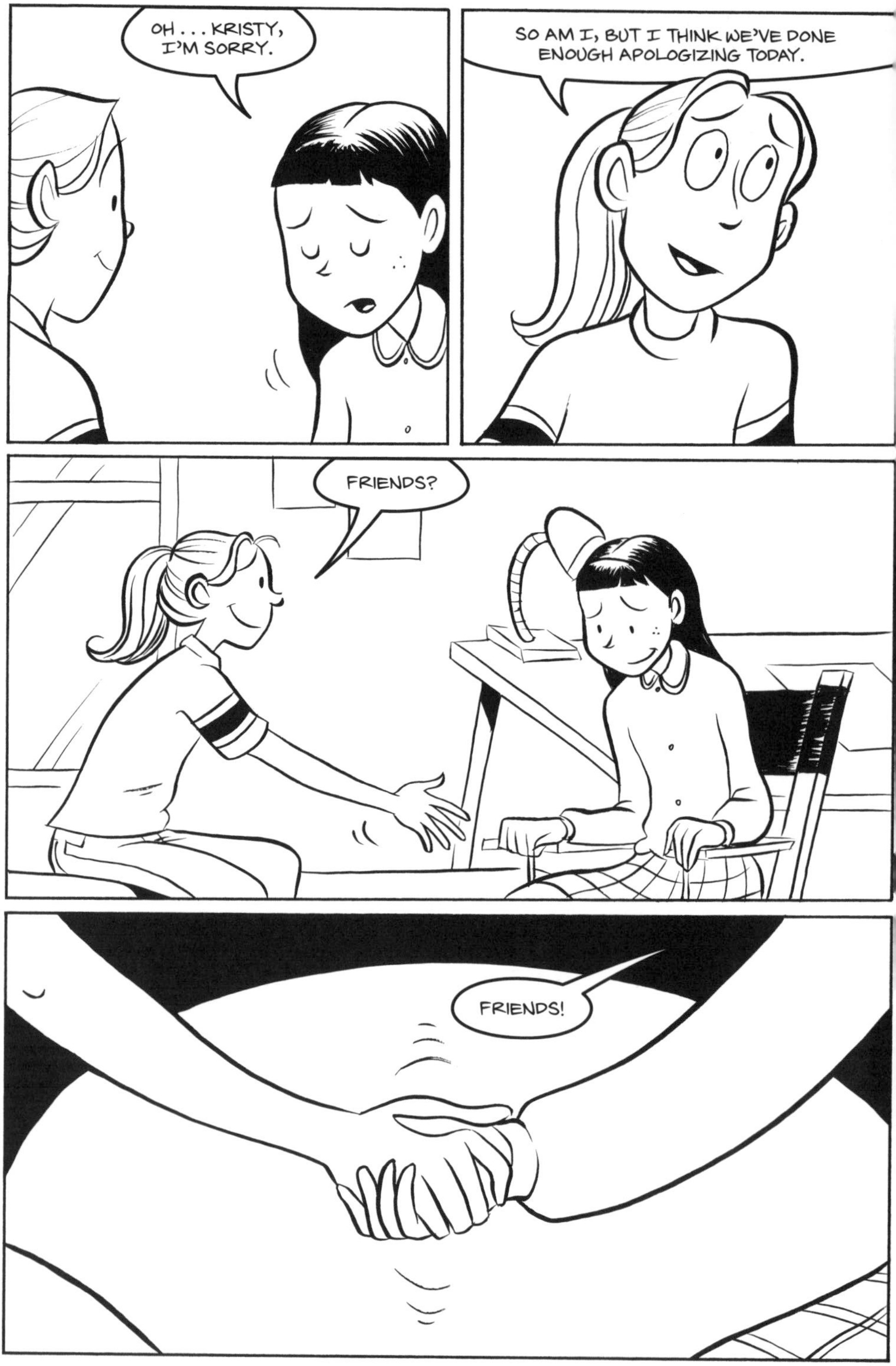
OH . . . KRISTY, I'M SORRY.
SO AM I, BUT I THINK WE'VE DONE ENOUGH APOLOGIZING TODAY.
FRIENDS?
FRIENDS!

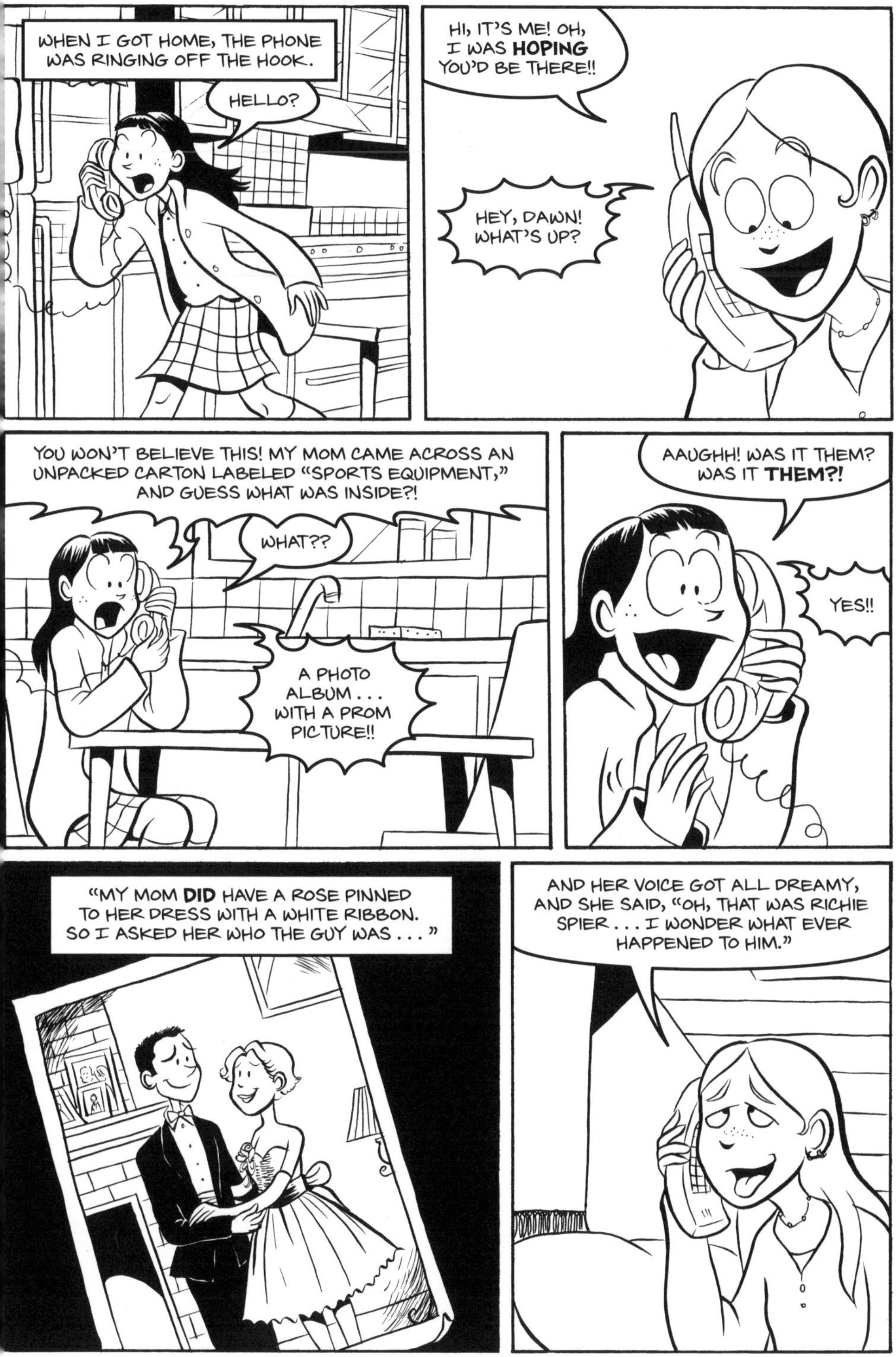
WHEN I GOT HOME, THE PHONE WAS RINGING OFF THE HOOK.
HELLO?
HI, IT'S ME! OH, I WAS **HOPING** YOU'D BE THERE!!
HEY, DAWN! WHAT'S UP?
YOU WON'T BELIEVE THIS! MY MOM CAME ACROSS AN UNPACKED CARTON LABELED "SPORTS EQUIPMENT," AND GUESS WHAT WAS INSIDE?!
WHAT??
A PHOTO ALBUM . . . WITH A PROM PICTURE!!
AAUGHH! WAS IT THEM? WAS IT **THEM?!**
YES!!
"MY MOM **DID** HAVE A ROSE PINNED TO HER DRESS WITH A WHITE RIBBON. SO I ASKED HER WHO THE GUY WAS . . . "
AND HER VOICE GOT ALL DREAMY, AND SHE SAID, "OH, THAT WAS RICHIE SPIER . . . I WONDER WHAT EVER HAPPENED TO HIM."

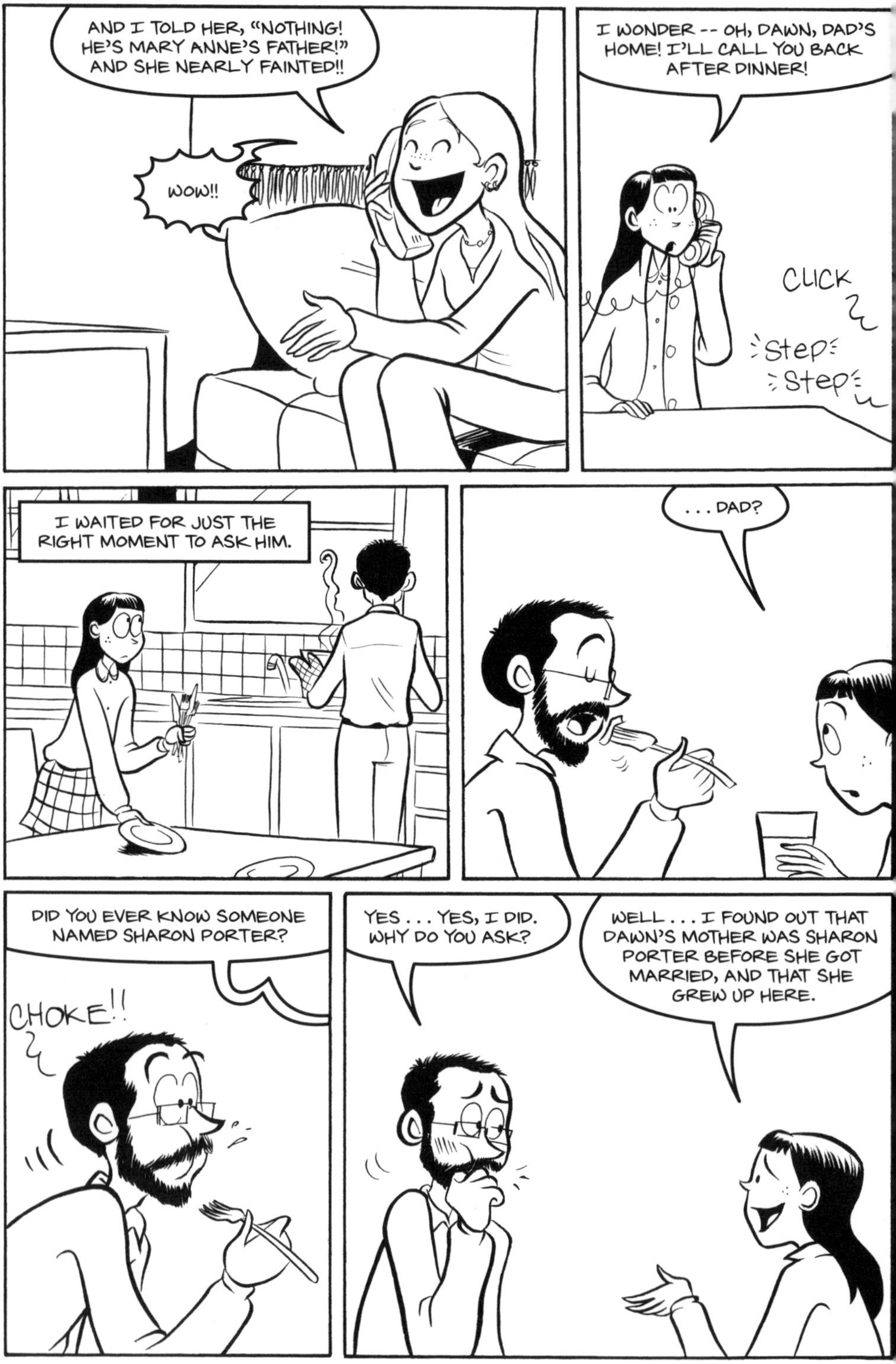
AND I TOLD HER, "NOTHING! HE'S MARY ANNE'S FATHER!" AND SHE NEARLY FAINTED!!
WOW!!
I WONDER -- OH, DAWN, DAD'S HOME! I'LL CALL YOU BACK AFTER DINNER!
CLICK
Step
Step
I WAITED FOR JUST THE RIGHT MOMENT TO ASK HIM.
. . . DAD?
DID YOU EVER KNOW SOMEONE NAMED SHARON PORTER?
CHOKE!!
YES . . . YES, I DID. WHY DO YOU ASK?
WELL . . . I FOUND OUT THAT DAWN'S MOTHER WAS SHARON PORTER BEFORE SHE GOT MARRIED, AND THAT SHE GREW UP HERE.

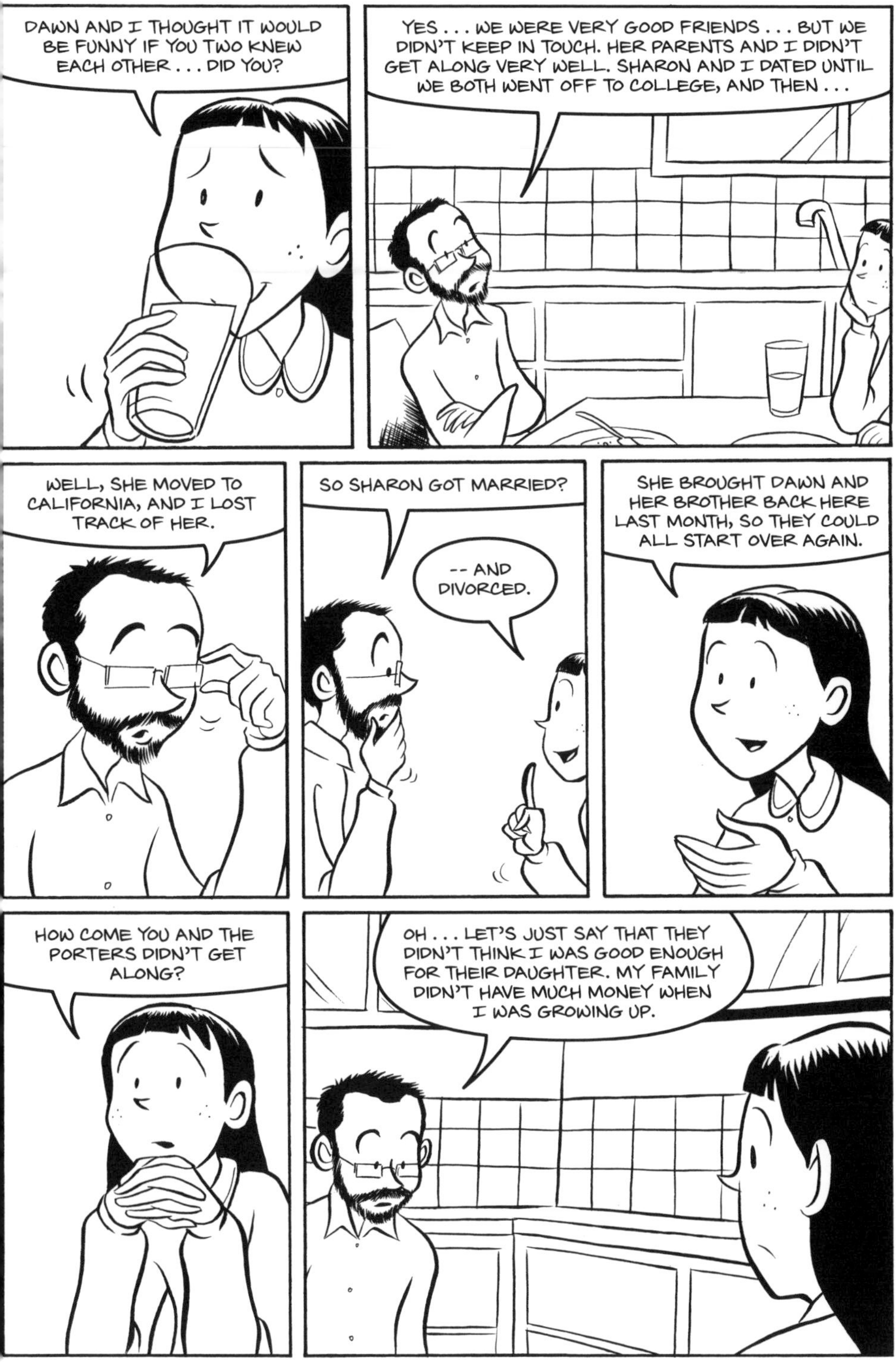
DAWN AND I THOUGHT IT WOULD BE FUNNY IF YOU TWO KNEW EACH OTHER . . . DID YOU?
YES . . . WE WERE VERY GOOD FRIENDS . . . BUT WE DIDN'T KEEP IN TOUCH. HER PARENTS AND I DIDN'T GET ALONG VERY WELL. SHARON AND I DATED UNTIL WE BOTH WENT OFF TO COLLEGE, AND THEN . . .
WELL, SHE MOVED TO CALIFORNIA, AND I LOST TRACK OF HER.
SO SHARON GOT MARRIED?
-- AND DIVORCED.
SHE BROUGHT DAWN AND HER BROTHER BACK HERE LAST MONTH, SO THEY COULD ALL START OVER AGAIN.
HOW COME YOU AND THE PORTERS DIDN'T GET ALONG?
OH . . . LET'S JUST SAY THAT THEY DIDN'T THINK I WAS GOOD ENOUGH FOR THEIR DAUGHTER. MY FAMILY DIDN'T HAVE MUCH MONEY WHEN I WAS GROWING UP.

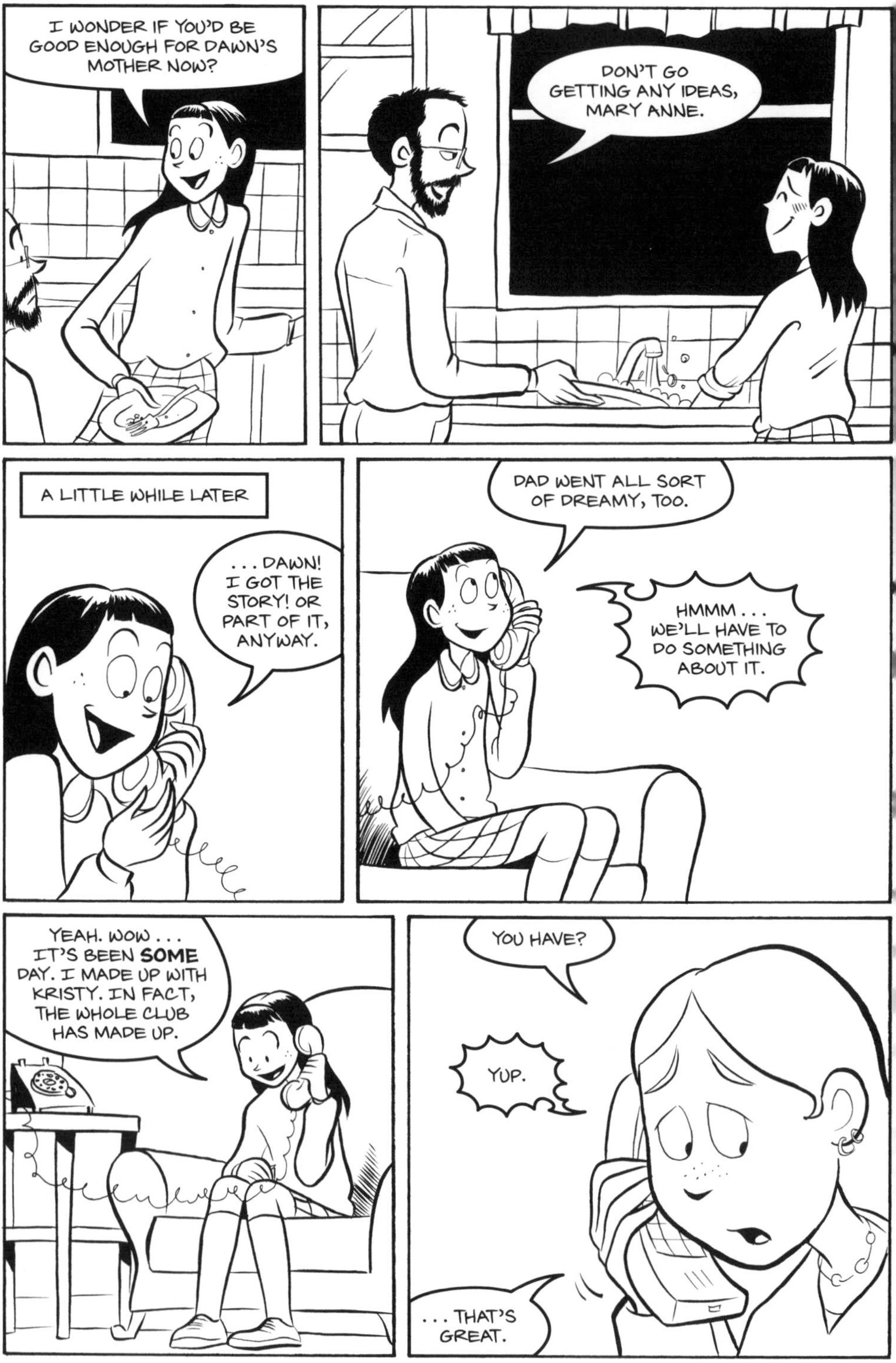
I WONDER IF YOU'D BE GOOD ENOUGH FOR DAWN'S MOTHER NOW?
DON'T GO GETTING ANY IDEAS, MARY ANNE.
A LITTLE WHILE LATER
. . . DAWN! I GOT THE STORY! OR PART OF IT, ANYWAY.
DAD WENT ALL SORT OF DREAMY, TOO.
HMMM . . . WE'LL HAVE TO DO SOMETHING ABOUT IT.
YEAH. WOW . . . IT'S BEEN **SOME** DAY. I MADE UP WITH KRISTY. IN FACT, THE WHOLE CLUB HAS MADE UP.
YOU HAVE?
YUP.
. . . THAT'S GREAT.

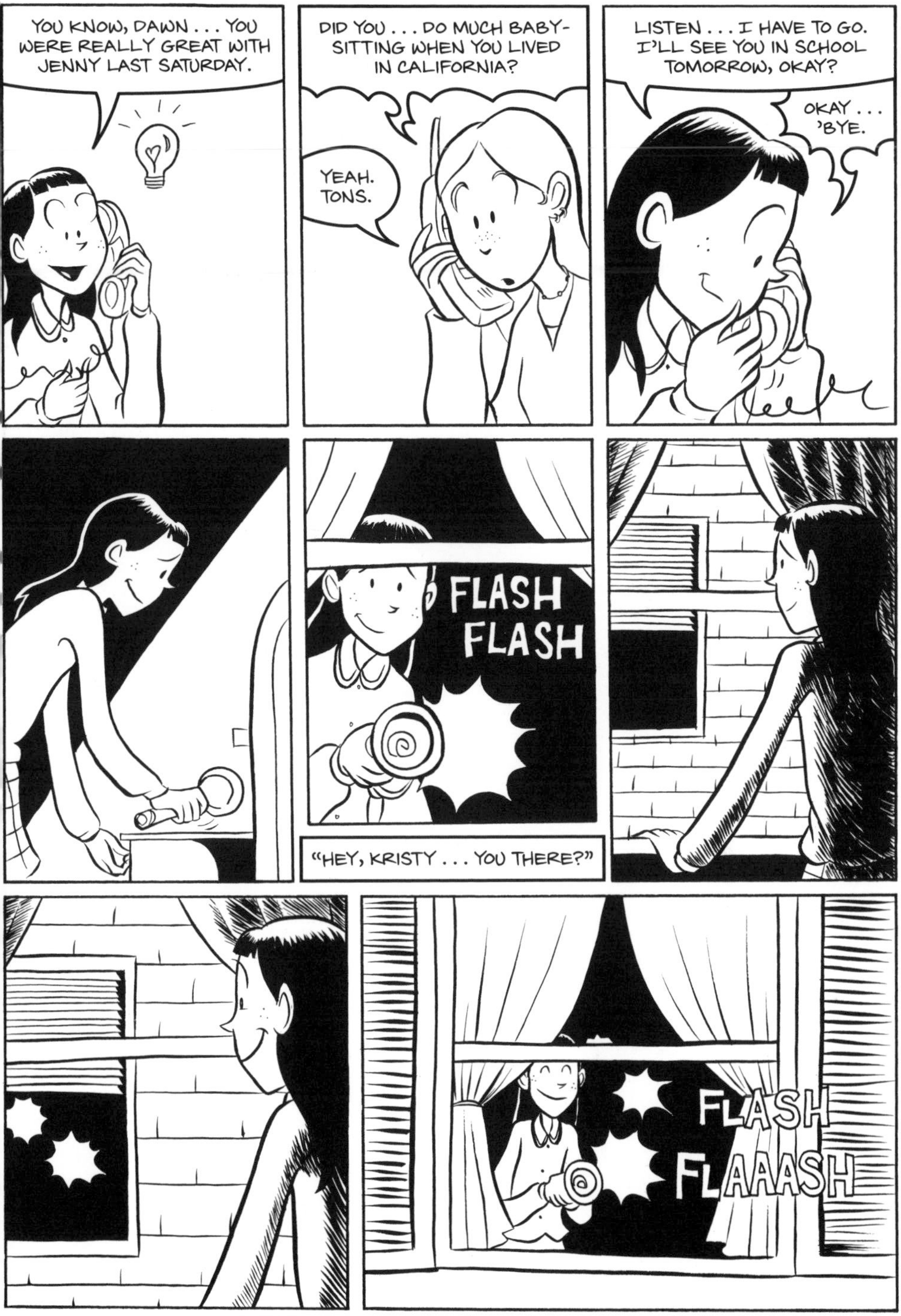

YOU KNOW, DAWN . . . YOU WERE REALLY GREAT WITH JENNY LAST SATURDAY.
DID YOU . . . DO MUCH BABY-SITTING WHEN YOU LIVED IN CALIFORNIA?
YEAH. TONS.
LISTEN . . . I HAVE TO GO. I'LL SEE YOU IN SCHOOL TOMORROW, OKAY?
OKAY . . . 'BYE.
FLASH FLASH
"HEY, KRISTY . . . YOU THERE?"
FLASH FLAAASH
"YEAH . . . WHAT'S UP?"
"I'VE GOT AN IDEA I WANT TO DISCUSS WITH YOU!"

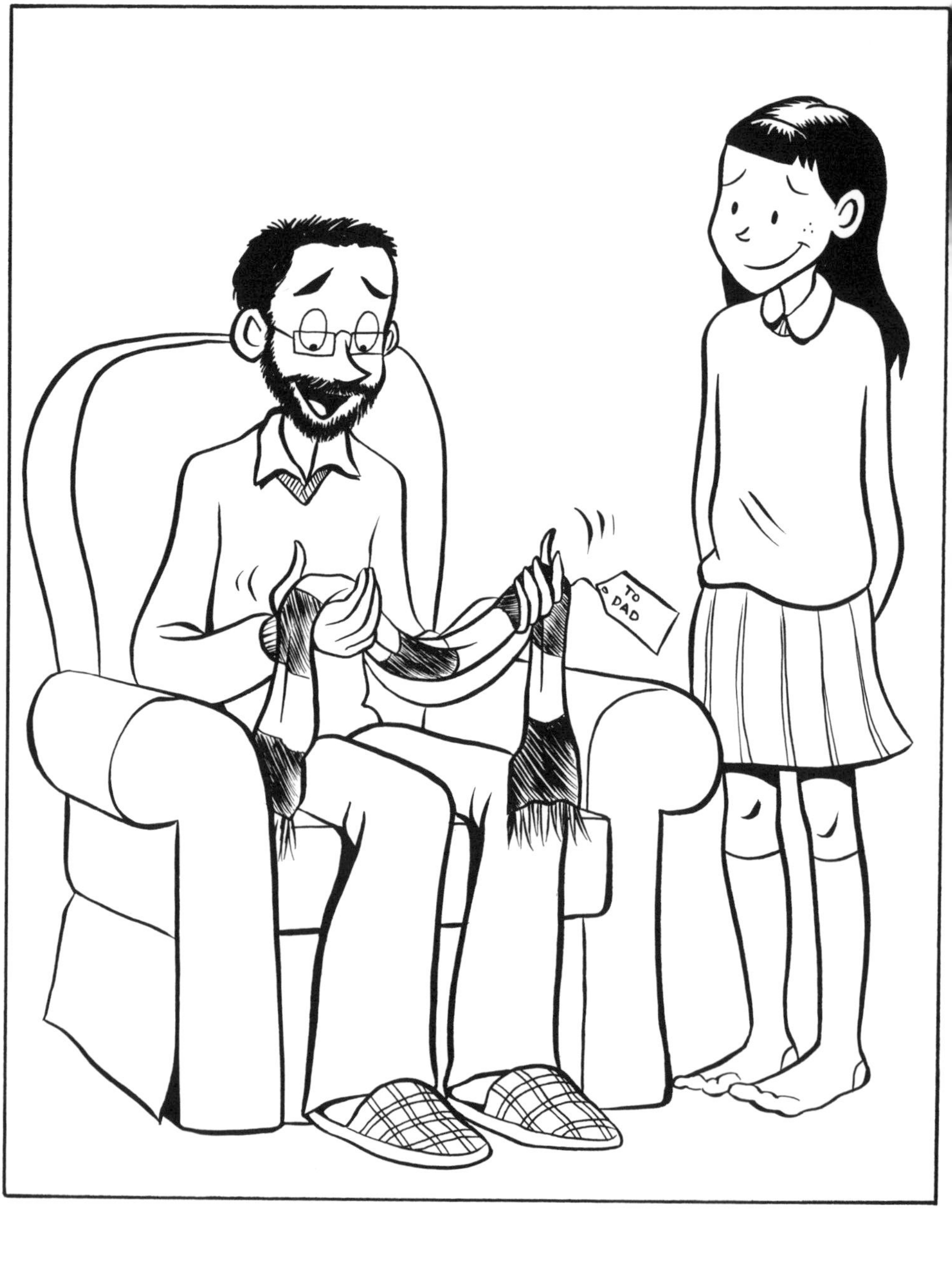
TO DAD

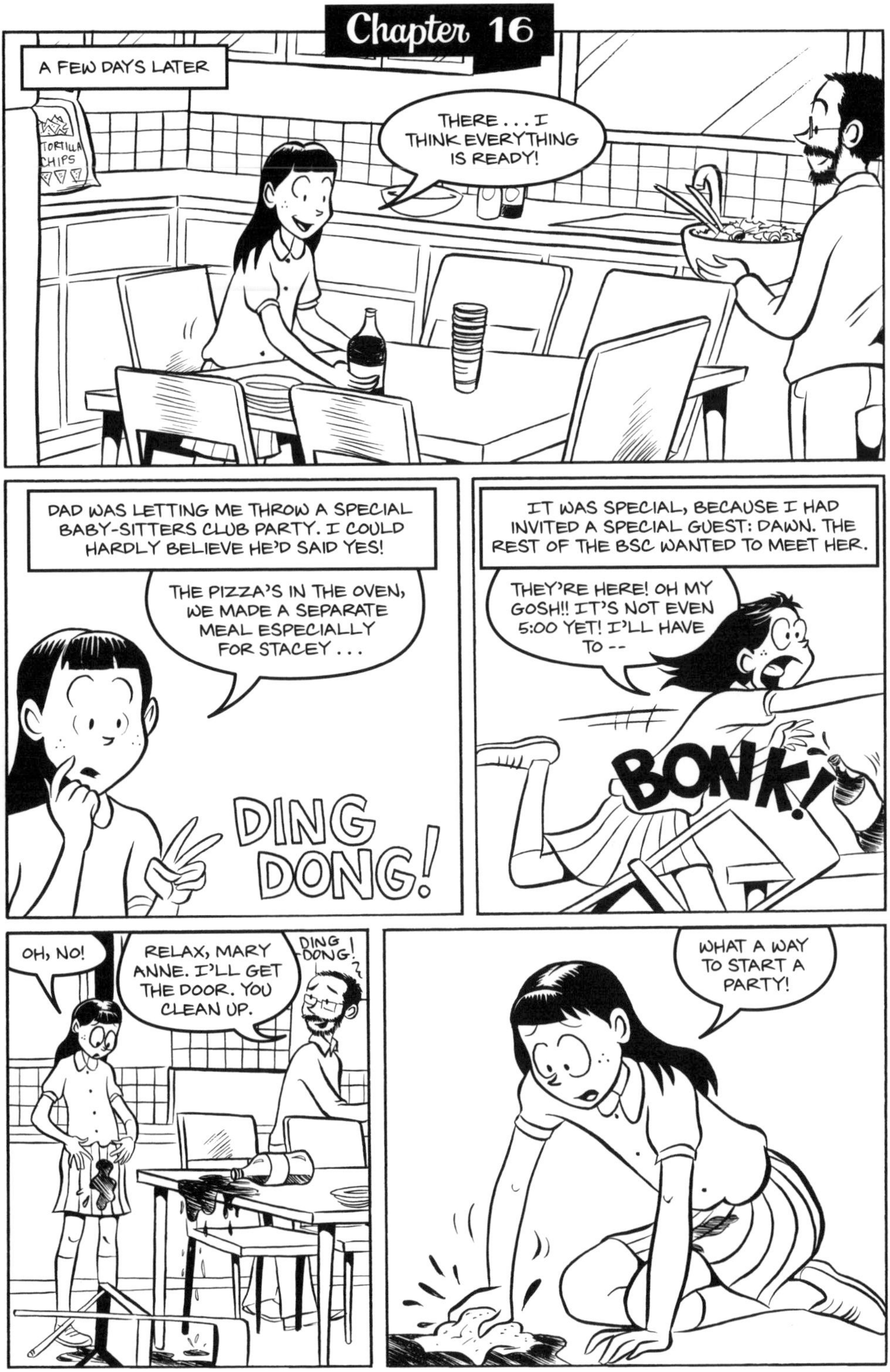
Chapter 16
A FEW DAYS LATER
TORTILLA CHIPS
THERE . . . I THINK EVERYTHING IS READY!
DAD WAS LETTING ME THROW A SPECIAL BABY-SITTERS CLUB PARTY. I COULD HARDLY BELIEVE HE'D SAID YES!
THE PIZZA'S IN THE OVEN, WE MADE A SEPARATE MEAL ESPECIALLY FOR STACEY . . .
DING DONG!
IT WAS SPECIAL, BECAUSE I HAD INVITED A SPECIAL GUEST: DAWN. THE REST OF THE BSC WANTED TO MEET HER.
THEY'RE HERE! OH MY GOSH!! IT'S NOT EVEN 5:00 YET! I'LL HAVE TO --
BONK!
OH, NO!
RELAX, MARY ANNE. I'LL GET THE DOOR. YOU CLEAN UP.
DING DONG!
WHAT A WAY TO START A PARTY!

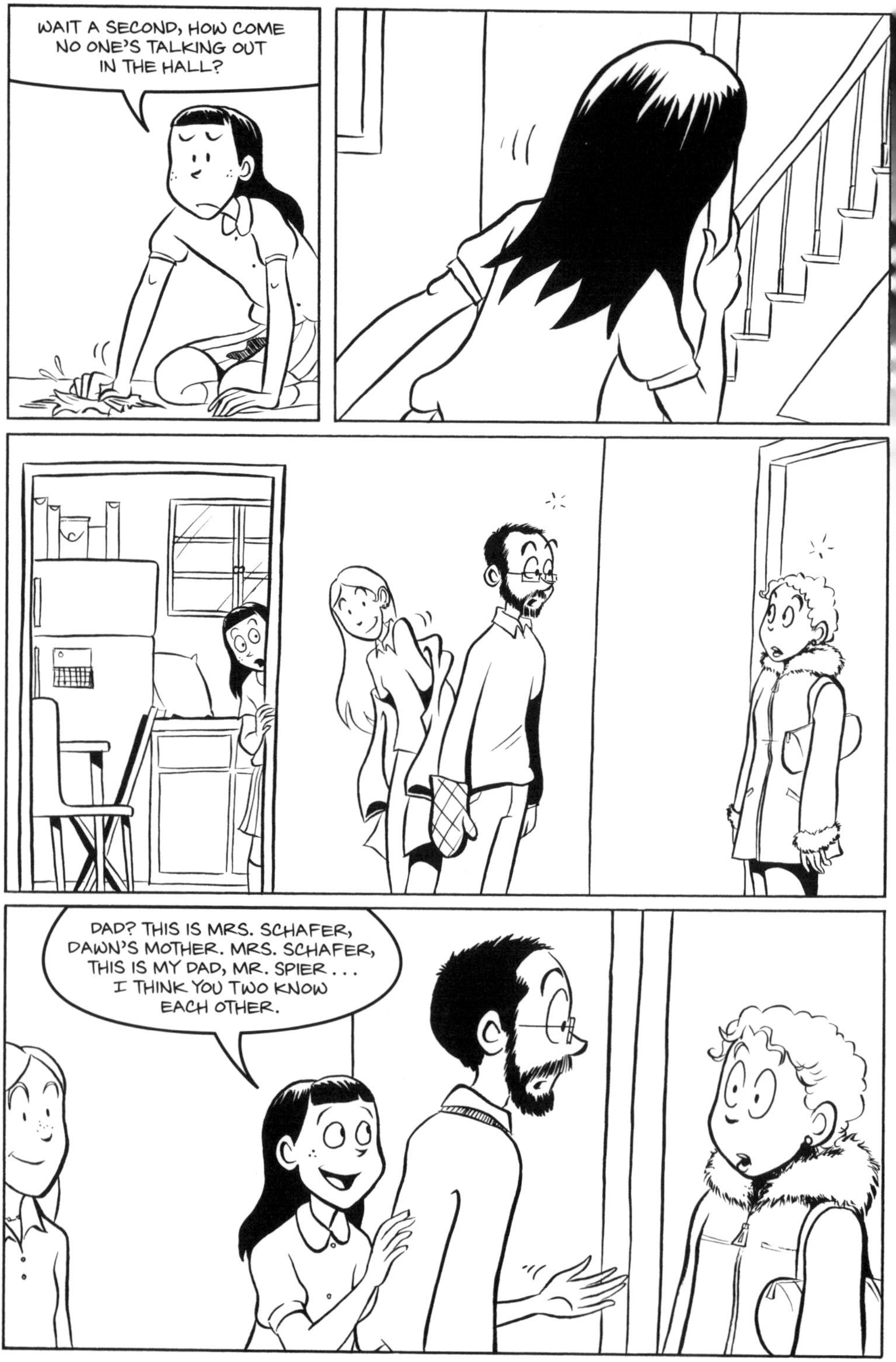
WAIT A SECOND, HOW COME NO ONE'S TALKING OUT IN THE HALL?
DAD? THIS IS MRS. SCHAFER, DAWN'S MOTHER. MRS. SCHAFER, THIS IS MY DAD, MR. SPIER . . . I THINK YOU TWO KNOW EACH OTHER.

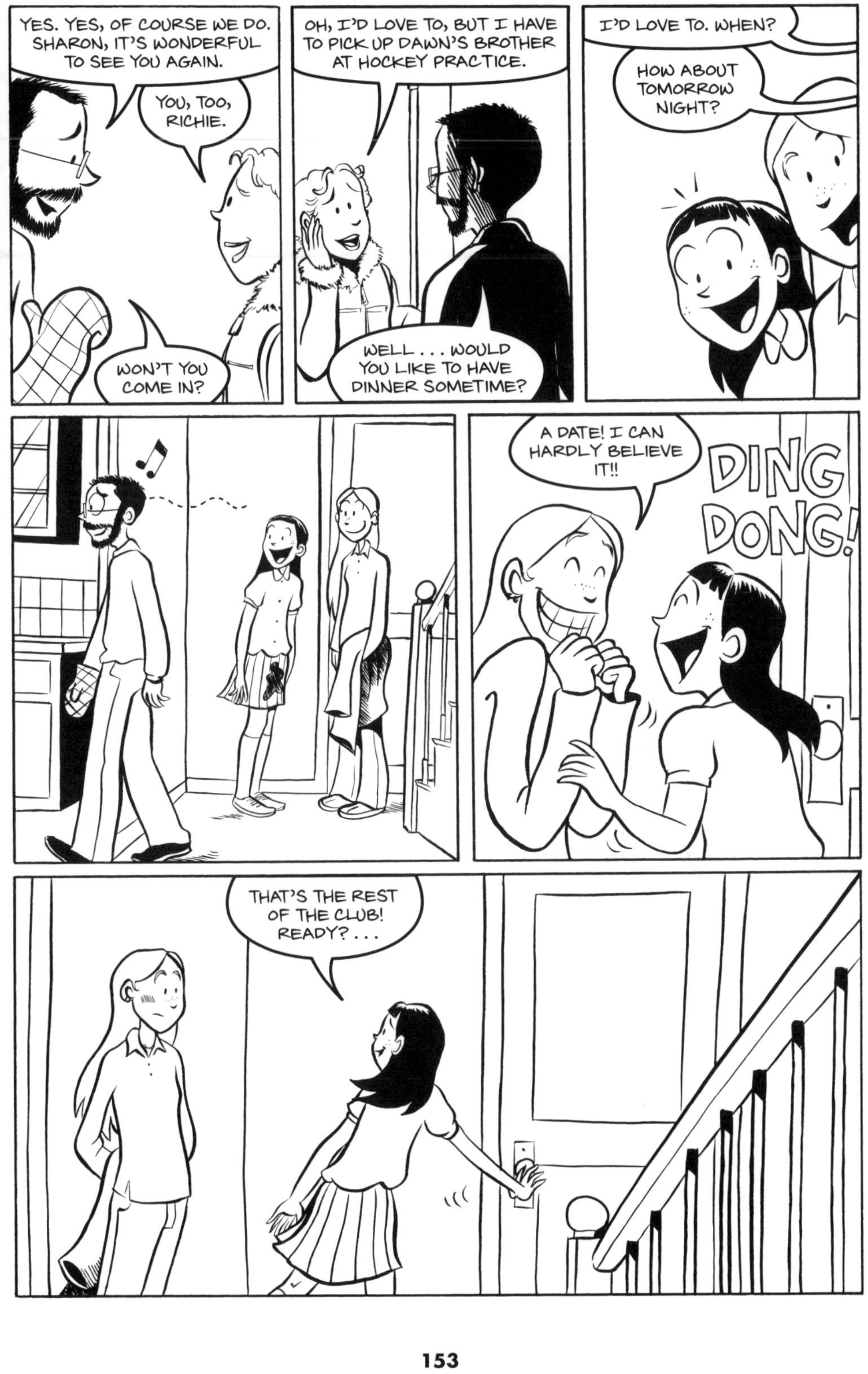
YES. YES, OF COURSE WE DO. SHARON, IT'S WONDERFUL TO SEE YOU AGAIN.
YOU, TOO, RICHIE.
WON'T YOU COME IN?
OH, I'D LOVE TO, BUT I HAVE TO PICK UP DAWN'S BROTHER AT HOCKEY PRACTICE.
WELL . . . WOULD YOU LIKE TO HAVE DINNER SOMETIME?
I'D LOVE TO. WHEN?
HOW ABOUT TOMORROW NIGHT?
A DATE! I CAN HARDLY BELIEVE IT!!
DING DONG!
THAT'S THE REST OF THE CLUB! READY? . . .

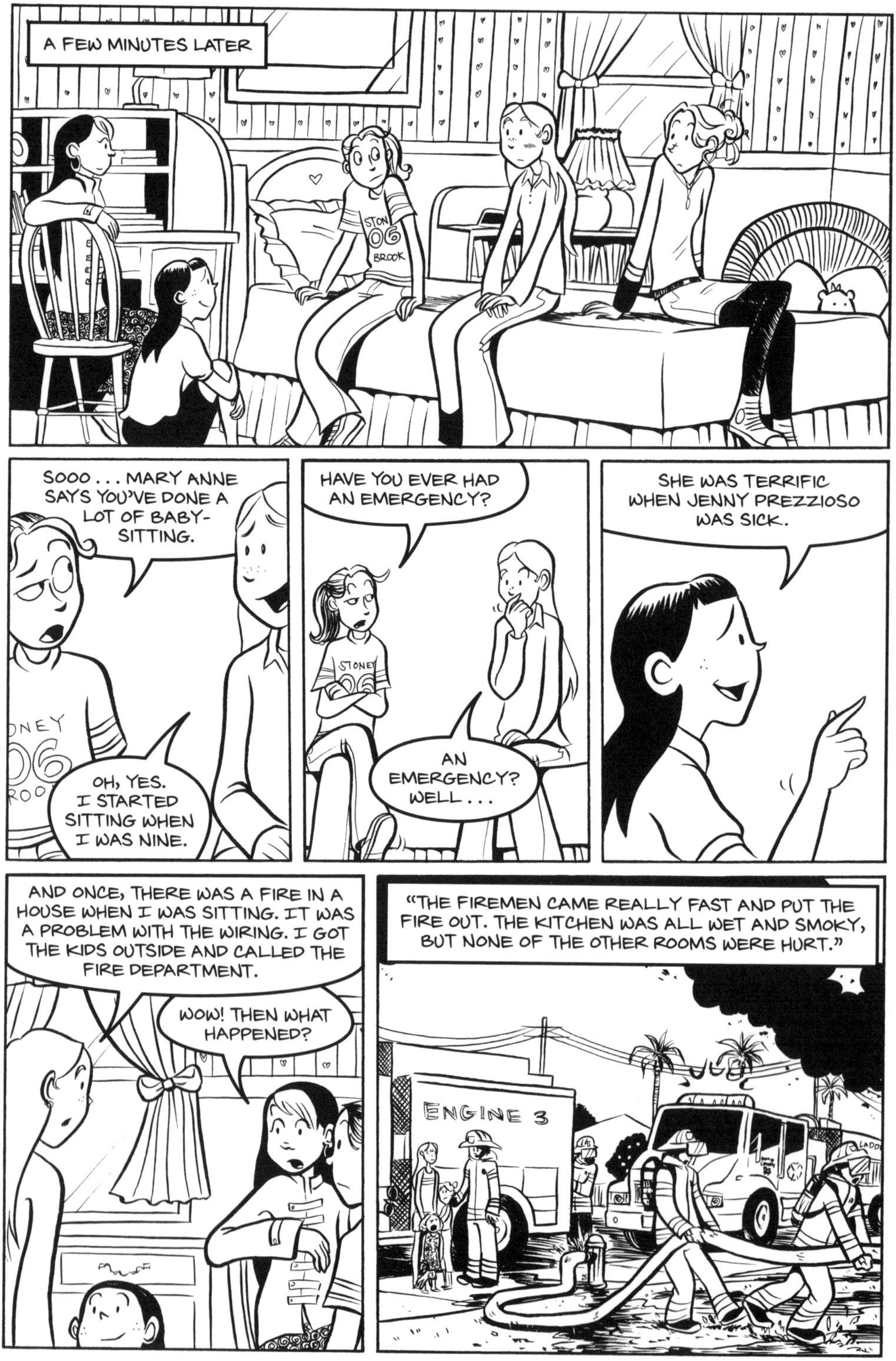
A FEW MINUTES LATER
STON 06 BROOK
SOOO . . . MARY ANNE SAYS YOU'VE DONE A LOT OF BABY-SITTING.
OH, YES. I STARTED SITTING WHEN I WAS NINE.
HAVE YOU EVER HAD AN EMERGENCY?
AN EMERGENCY? WELL . . .
SHE WAS TERRIFIC WHEN JENNY PREZZIOSO WAS SICK.
AND ONCE, THERE WAS A FIRE IN A HOUSE WHEN I WAS SITTING. IT WAS A PROBLEM WITH THE WIRING. I GOT THE KIDS OUTSIDE AND CALLED THE FIRE DEPARTMENT.
WOW! THEN WHAT HAPPENED?
"THE FIREMEN CAME REALLY FAST AND PUT THE FIRE OUT. THE KITCHEN WAS ALL WET AND SMOKY, BUT NONE OF THE OTHER ROOMS WERE HURT."
ENGINE 3

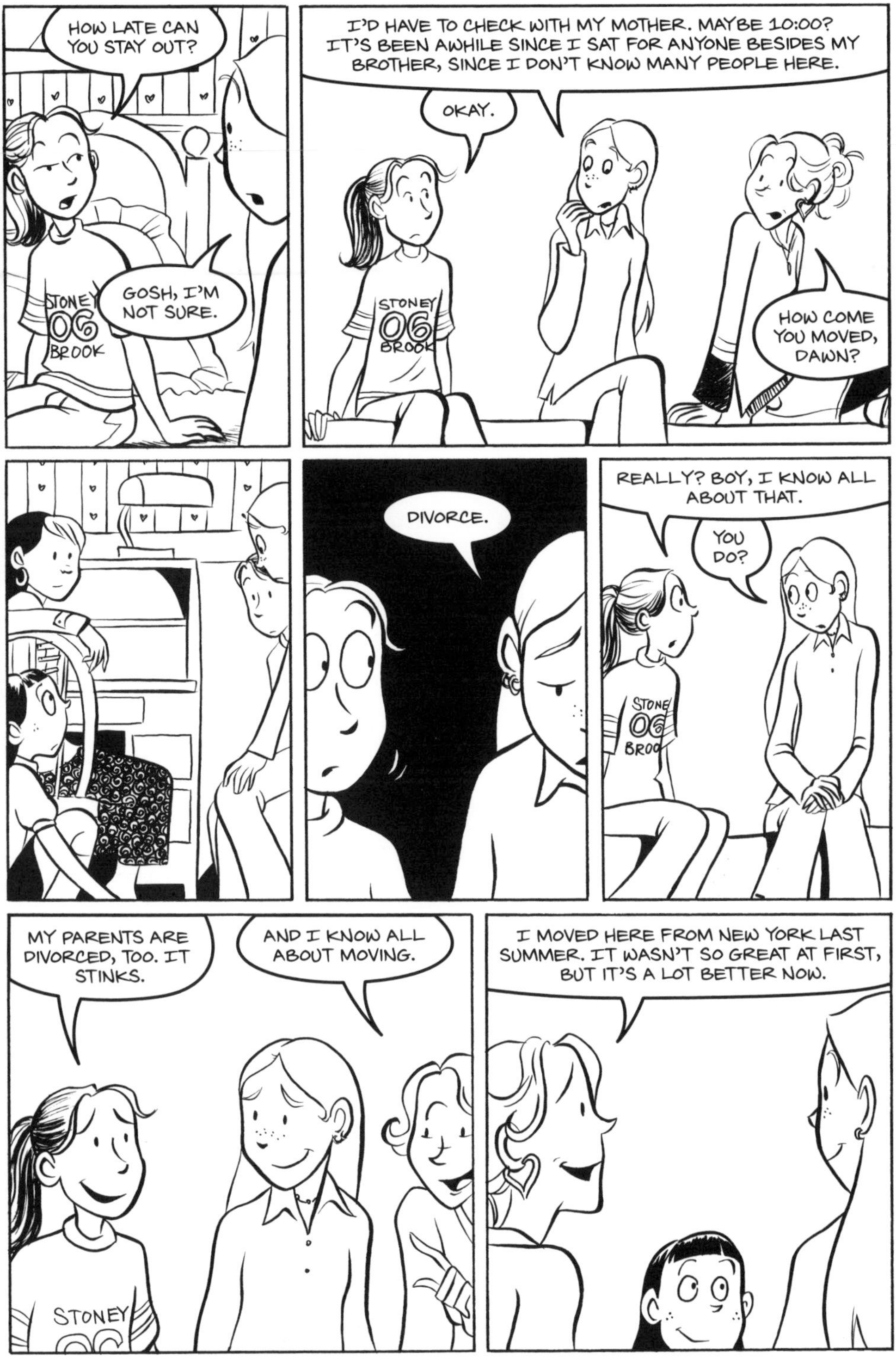

HOW LATE CAN YOU STAY OUT?
GOSH, I'M NOT SURE.
STONEY 06 BROOK
I'D HAVE TO CHECK WITH MY MOTHER. MAYBE 10:00? IT'S BEEN AWHILE SINCE I SAT FOR ANYONE BESIDES MY BROTHER, SINCE I DON'T KNOW MANY PEOPLE HERE.
OKAY.
HOW COME YOU MOVED, DAWN?
DIVORCE.
REALLY? BOY, I KNOW ALL ABOUT THAT.
YOU DO?
MY PARENTS ARE DIVORCED, TOO. IT STINKS.
AND I KNOW ALL ABOUT MOVING.
I MOVED HERE FROM NEW YORK LAST SUMMER. IT WASN'T SO GREAT AT FIRST, BUT IT'S A LOT BETTER NOW.

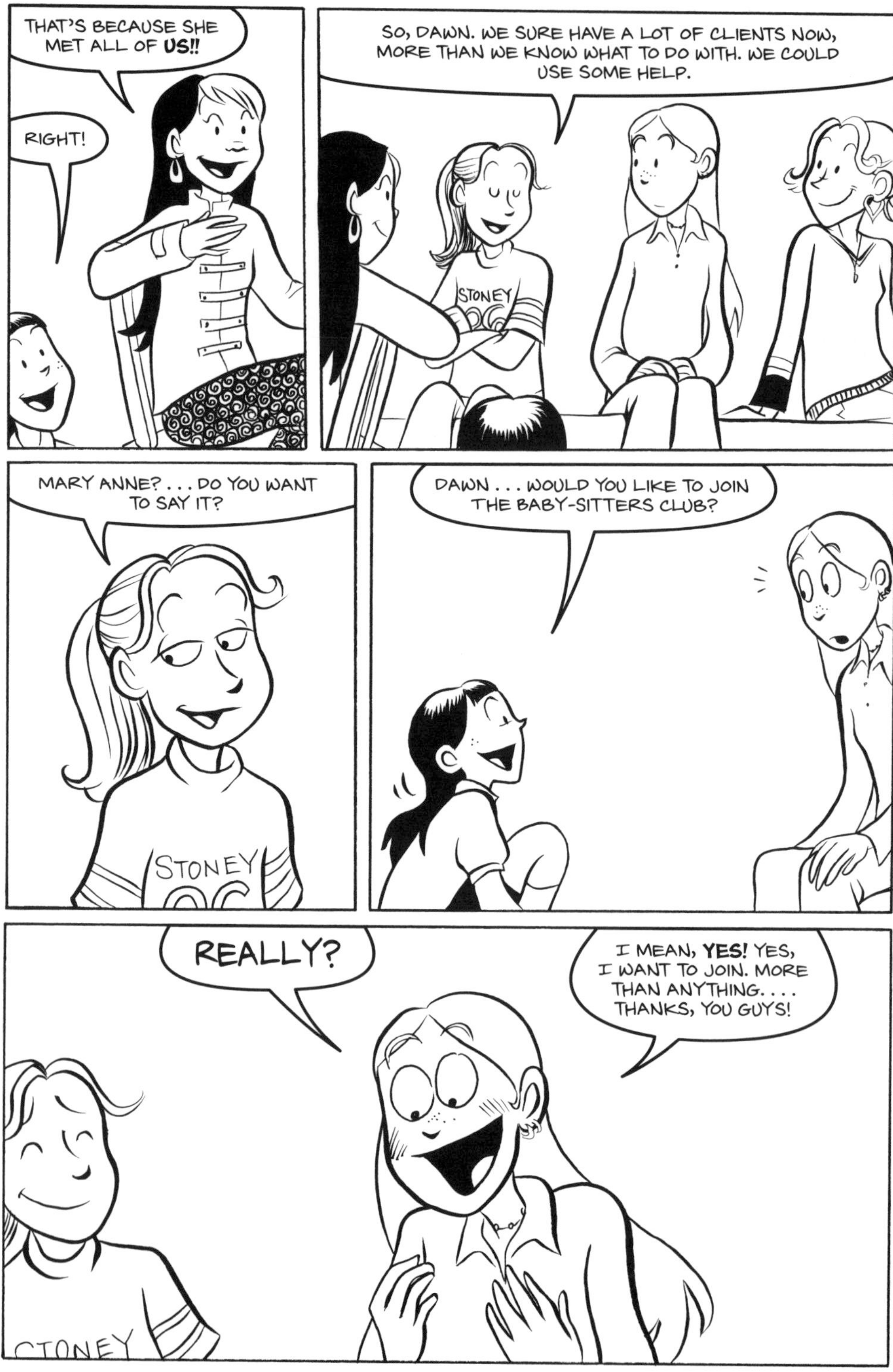
THAT'S BECAUSE SHE MET ALL OF **US!!**
RIGHT!
SO, DAWN. WE SURE HAVE A LOT OF CLIENTS NOW, MORE THAN WE KNOW WHAT TO DO WITH. WE COULD USE SOME HELP.
STONEY
MARY ANNE? . . . DO YOU WANT TO SAY IT?
STONEY
DAWN . . . WOULD YOU LIKE TO JOIN THE BABY-SITTERS CLUB?
REALLY?
I MEAN, **YES!** YES, I WANT TO JOIN. MORE THAN ANYTHING. . . . THANKS, YOU GUYS!

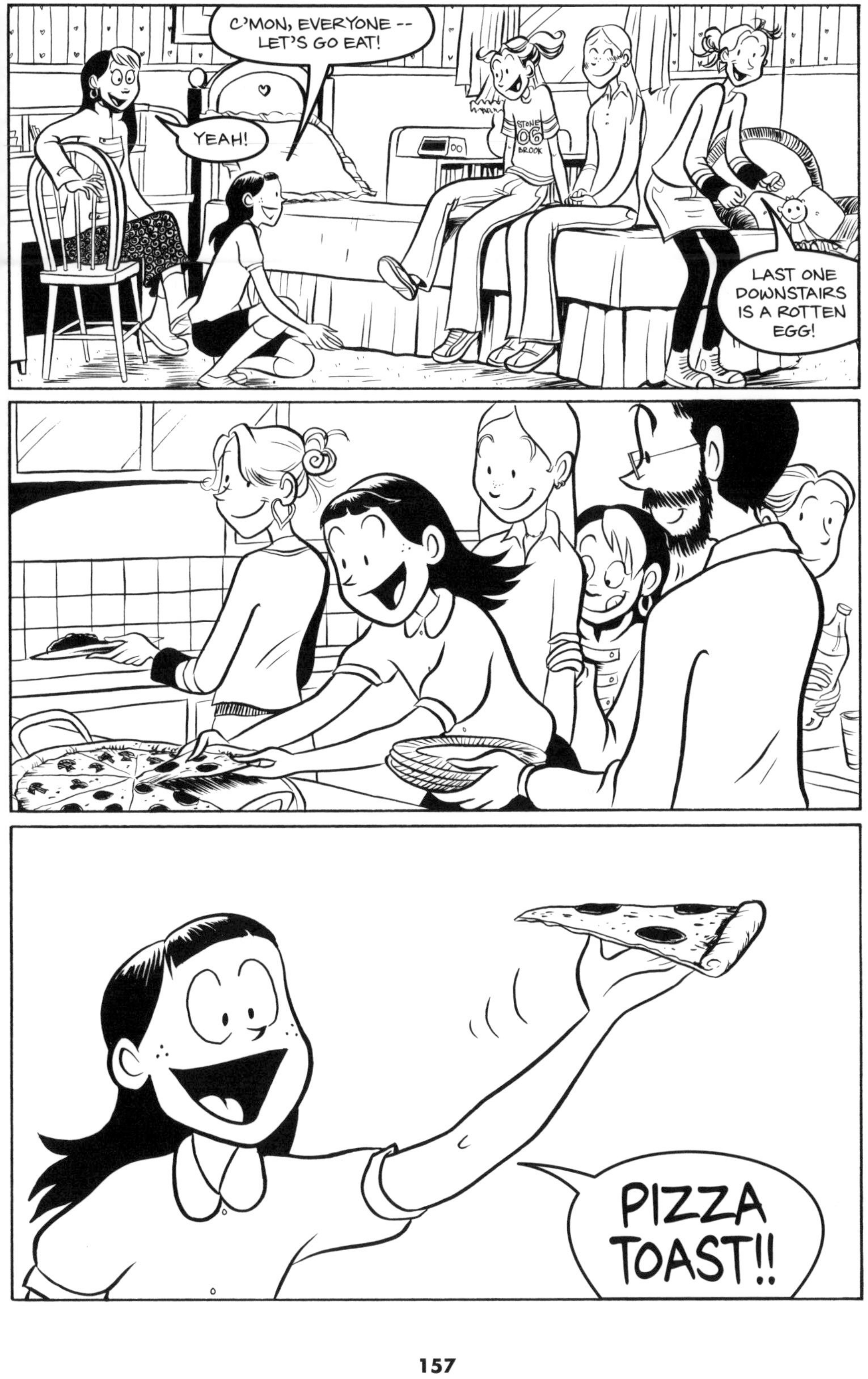
C'MON, EVERYONE -- LET'S GO EAT!
YEAH!
STONE 06 BROOK
LAST ONE DOWNSTAIRS IS A ROTTEN EGG!
PIZZA TOAST!!

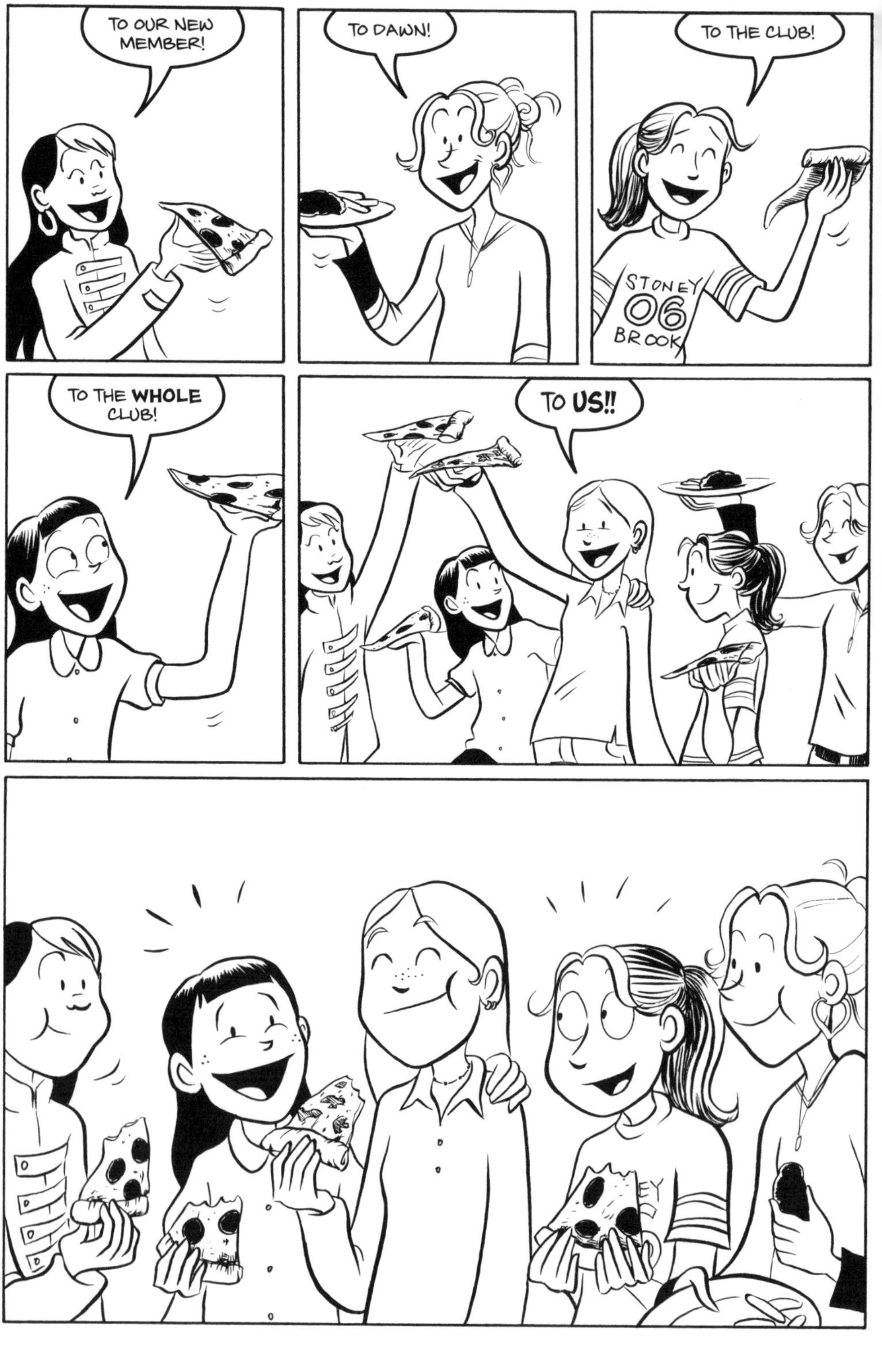
TO OUR NEW MEMBER!
TO DAWN!
TO THE CLUB!
STONEY 06 BROOK
TO THE **WHOLE** CLUB!
TO **US!!**

Ann M. Martin's

The Baby-sitters Club is one of the most popular series in the history of publishing, with more than 175 million books in print. She is also the author of the acclaimed novels *Belle Teal, A Corner of the Universe* (a Newbery Honor Book), *Here Today*, and *A Dog's Life*. She lives in New York.

Raina Telgemeier

grew up in San Francisco, then moved to New York City, where she earned an illustration degree at the School of Visual Arts. She is the creator of *Smile*, a #1 *New York Times* bestselling graphic memoir based on her childhood. It won a Will Eisner Award for Best Publication for Teens, received a Boston Globe–Horn Book Honor, and has appeared on many state reading lists. She is also the creator of *Drama*, a #1 *New York Times* bestseller, recipient of a Stonewall Book Award Honor, and one of YALSA's Top Ten Great Graphic Novels for Teens. Raina also adapted and illustrated The Baby-sitters Club graphic novels, which were selected for YALSA's Great Graphic Novels for Teens list and *Booklist's* Top 10 Graphic Novels for Youth list.

Raina lives in Astoria, New York, with her husband and fellow cartoonist, Dave Roman. To learn more about Raina, visit her online at www.goRaina.com.